STORM BORN

AMY BRAUN

Hadrian swung his sword at Mortis in an effort to wound his leg. The Mistral leader kicked it down and pinned his arm. Hadrian tried to rise again, but soon a boot was on his throat, and he was trapped.

As I watched with horror, I felt the energy around me– from the struggle Vitae and Zephys were enduring against Ferno and Turve, to the crumpled forms of Declan and Piper, to the restrained control of Mortis, to the fragile tether with Hadrian.

I could feel it all now, and I knew the only way to help my Guardians was to unleash it.

While I centered myself and prepared to grab the energy swirling around me, I heard Mortis's voice carry over the sounds of battle.

"Impatient and inferior. Just as Sonus was. I always knew you would take after him. You are not even half the Guardian he was." Mortis pressed harder on Hadrian's neck. "At least he could keep his charges alive."

I felt the weather and the air sweeping over me, and the rough energy coating my tether. I gripped them both, and then I let go.

I screamed and felt my body rip apart. The pressure in my body erupted like a volcano, fierce and merciless. A huge gale crested behind me. The energy was everywhere, snared by the power I was wielding. The pain was unrelenting, but the feeling of complete control and undiluted power was even stronger. And far more welcome. I felt that if I pushed hard enough, I could take it all.

Winds the speed of rockets detonated toward the Guardians. I saw them look at me, shock widening their eyes. A tiny pulse beat at my brain, as if telling me not to do anything to the Guardians dressed in shades of blue. It was like I was supposed to recognize them. But I couldn't remember why.

It was probably better that way. The Guardians were not my friends. They were my keepers. They would lock me away as soon as they could. They had told me as much. I did not want to be controlled. I did not want to be stopped.

I would take what I could for as long as I could.

Cover Design: Deranged Doctor Design

ISBN: 978-0-9938758-6-1

For my loved ones and Mother Nature, who will hopefully never send minions like this down on us.

PRAISE FOR AMY BRAUN

DEMON'S DAUGHTER

"I'd say the Cursed series is going to be one to watch for any urban fantasy fan." – Ivana, One Book Two

DARK DIVINITY

"The twists and turns of both storylines were both interesting and unpredictable. I especially enjoyed the fact that Braun never sacrifices emotional development to the rip-roaring pace." Christina Ochs, author of *The Desolate Empire* series

CRIMSON SKY

"One word to describe this book: "In-freaking-credible"!! I admit I don't give out many 5 stars, but this one is it. It is a "one-sit" wonder. I started reading after work and didn't put it down until the very end." – Nell, One Book Two

"One thing is for certain this author keeps reader's hearts thumping with explosive scenes and heart wrenching endings." – T's Blogging

"There are so many twists in Crimson Sky, you will be hooked immediately. Though this is an excellent stand-alone book; I see a great start to an action packed series. I would highly recommend this to any reader, regardless of genre preference." – Boundless Book Reviews

PATH OF THE HORSEMAN

"This woman is officially an auto-buy author for me!" – The Bookish Crypt

"Courage is being scared to death but saddling up anyway." – John Wayne

"Cheer up, the worst is yet to come." – Philander Johnson

CHAPTER 1

"They're almost here," my father said.

I watched the heavy storm front dragging over the violently churning ocean. It towered over the houses and shelters, a menacing wall of pitch black cloud. The darkness beyond it seemed endless, like the horizon was being swallowed up by a black hole.

So much for this summer's tan, I thought to myself.

Spastic light cracked past the windows of the house. The flashes weren't lightning, though the rain was falling heavily onto the roof of our house. Gusts of wind pummeled the streets, pushing the palm trees so hard I was certain they would bend in half.

We'd proofed it as much as we could for the Centennial, but it wouldn't be enough. Even though we knew this was the year, that history and technology had given us the tools and warning we needed, it hadn't made a difference.

Nothing could have prepared us for the Centennial Storm, or the *things* that came with it.

The flashes of light increased in frequency. With them came a low, rumbling sound from overhead. It sounded like thunder, but wasn't. It didn't crack in a loud burst and grumble back to the clouds. No, this went the *opposite* way. The thunder started in a low menacing growl, then became louder and louder until it was a roar that sent a shudder through the entire house.

My vision still had white spots from the light flashes. My father grimaced as he slammed the last of the iron hatches shut and locked the window closed. The thick metal looked like it belonged on a bank vault, but it didn't reassure me like it should have.

We hadn't won the Lottery, so we weren't to be evacuated underground, and there was nowhere we could run. The Centennial didn't just hit our unlucky little state of Florida.

The Centennial hit the entire *world*.

I suppose we should have been a little more grateful to the Storm Protection Union for making sure we had supplies and a thoroughly reinforced house, but honestly, I would have rather been underground with the rich and powerful, and the lucky Lottery winners. They might be trapped under five hundred feet of earth, but at least they were safe. All the rest of us could do at this point was ride it out and hope for the best.

The "thunder" that had made our house violently shudder before was now shaking it. Photo frames collapsed and shattered on the floor. Chairs skidded and toppled. Sofa legs and tables squeaked as they scraped over the floorboards. Something over our heads ripped. I clutched my father's arm and looked up. Pieces of the ceiling were being torn away; exposing meager joists, crumbling drywall, cracked plaster, and fragments of a tumultuous grey sky.

My father grabbed my hand and dragged me to the storm-shelter in the basement. My mother and little brother were already inside, waiting for us. James was ten, and he wasn't strong enough to reinforce the house. Especially not with his asthma. I was twenty-one and used to lifting heavy things around at my job– whoever said being a waitress was for the weak had clearly never done the work before– so I took Mom's place to help Dad.

We were supposed to be done ten minutes ago, but with Dad's back problems and my stupid curiosity with the Centennial, we stayed up here longer than we should have.

I swore it would be the last time I ever stopped and stared at a hurricane with dread fascination.

Dad reached the basement door and knelt down to pry it open. The veins in his neck bulged and his face was tight with pain. I wanted to help him, but it was a set of dual metal doors with two thick iron door pulls acting as handles, both of which were only big enough for one set of hands to grip. All I could do was wait, shoving my trembling hands through my hair and try not to have a complete meltdown.

I couldn't hear anything over the raging storm. Looking around, I could see more furniture bouncing across the floor. The tremors from the thunder rippled up my legs, sinking into my bones. My entire body felt like it was caught in an electric shock, though there was no pain.

I guess I should have been grateful. The worst injury I'd ever had was a sprained ankle, and I intended to make sure that the worst thing I ever endured.

Dad finally heaved the door open, the metal groaning heavily. I peered down, seeing the wide terrified eyes of James and my mother. He was crying; his little arms wrapped around her so tight he was all but strangling her. My mother held him close, gripping his inhaler like it was a sword. Her eyes, bright and blue like mine, were bulging from her head with fear.

I knelt down and was about to climb into the basement when I looked at my father.

Beads of sweat sheened across the line of reddish-grey hair on his forehead. His eyes were pinched shut with pain, his hands clamped over his shoulders. He must have pulled something–

The front door groaned and swung open, smashing into the wall so hard it left a dent. Beyond it, I could see the hammering rain, the ocean water flooding the streets, tumbling garbage cans and mailboxes...

And the flash of white light that streaked down from the clouds.

My heart clenched in my chest.

We were in the center of it. They were here.

Another gust of wind screamed through the door, pushing a gale of water into the front entrance. My father and I staggered back. The water snapped around our feet and poured into the basement. My mom and James both screamed. Salt water continued to flow inside. In seconds, it covered our ankles.

My Dad's eyes flicked to the door, then locked with mine.

"Get inside, Ava!"

I hesitated, thinking about the way he was holding his shoulders, the pain he was trying– and failing– to hide. He was going to close the door, but with his back issues and pulled muscles, he wouldn't be able to do it fast enough, if he could at all. The basement would flood, and we would all drown.

"I'll get the front door!" I shouted at him.

"No!" he yelled back immediately. "Don't even think about it–"

"I'm not hurt!" I roared back. "I can close the door and open the basement door again. Just hide!"

My Dad didn't want to leave me, but he knew I was right. He was too hurt to do close both doors. I wasn't exactly Xena, Warrior Princess, but I had enough strength to close the front door, get into the shelter, and close it behind me.

Salty ocean water whipped around my calves. It funneled into the basement where James and Mom were screaming for us to get inside. I grabbed my father's arm and started pushing him down. He tried to fight me, tried to protest, but he grimaced when I touched his shoulder. I made sure he was able to hold the ladder, then grabbed the heavy metal door and pulled it shut. The door was watertight, so there was no chance they would drown. The water had been high, but not high enough to cause them real distress.

The water around *me*, on the other hand… Different story and a *severely* different stress level.

My eyes stung from the sea salt as the water splashed across my face. I stood up, my arms and legs now soaked and my clothes clinging to my skin. I splashed through the water and raced for the door. Well, not exactly raced. More like dragged. The torrent of ocean water crashed against me, trying to push me back into the house. I made it to the door, but had to cling to the frame to keep my balance. I gripped the edges of the heavy iron and started to pull. The metal resisted me, unwilling to move against the heavy flow of water.

A flash of light slashed through my vision. My traitorous eyes followed it.

Bits of shingle and roofing spiraled through the air like flakes of deadly ash. The trunks of palm trees splintered as they snapped in half, their big leaves ripped from their crowns. Flooded cars were carried through the flow of water barreling down the street. Trash and debris followed it. If anyone was crazy enough to still be outside, I couldn't see them, couldn't hear them scream.

But I wasn't really looking at the destruction. I was looking at the center of the street, directly across from me. The way the water broke apart around the figure standing in it, as if it were Moses beginning to part the Red Sea.

I was frozen with shock. I saw it. I was *looking at one.* I could barely believe it, but I knew it was true.

A Stormkind.

Its body was made of water, shafts of pale blue light outlining its skeleton. The water shimmered over the light like water over stone, rippling and calm.

For a second, that's exactly what it was— calm. It just stood there. Maybe it was looking around, though I didn't know how it would have done so. It had no nose or mouth. Two almond-shaped eyes glowed from its face like halogen headlights. It was a disturbing, alien thing.

Nobody knew what the Stormkind really were or where they had come from, because nobody that encountered one had gotten close enough to study them, let alone stop to have a chat with one.

That single second ended, and I remembered why.

The Stormkind lifted its arms. The water around it crested in a tidal wave. The Stormkind twisted and pushed its hands toward the houses across the street. The tidal wave mimicked its movements and slammed into the houses, obliterating them like they'd been made of matchsticks.

I clamped my hand over my mouth to stifle my scream, thinking about my neighbors that lived in those houses. The Wilsons with their unbearably loud truck. Mrs. Tucker with her yappy dog. The Cortez's with their newborn baby.

None of them had won the Lottery. All of them could be dead now.

The Stormkind bent its arm over its head in an awkward wave. A huge gust of wind crested over the street, pushing the debris and snapping more palm trees. It also pushed the water closer to the Stormkind.

That was when I saw the body.

I couldn't really see who it was. I recognized them as being male, but that was it. They flailed and thrashed as their head bobbed up and down in the water. I wanted to help, but I was frozen at the door. I couldn't have moved even if I wanted to.

And I wasn't sure I did. As terrifying as all this was, I had to admit that I was amazed. Everyone who had seen a Stormkind before today was now dead. Photographs of them were rare and accused of being fakes. But I knew what I was seeing was real. It couldn't be anything but genuine. Morbid curiosity had dug its hooks into me, and I didn't know how to let go.

The man drifted to the Stormkind. He tumbled out of the wave and rolled onto the concrete. The Stormkind reacted with quick, violent grace. It grabbed the man's shoulders– my heart lurched when I recognized Mr. Cortez– and lifted him like he was a rag doll.

Then the icy blue light in its body drifted up, out of its face, and slid into Mr. Cortez's screaming mouth. The light obscured their faces, but I saw the illumination in the Stormkind intensify. Mr. Cortez's legs kicked and jerked helplessly.

Then they stopped. The light drew back from the Stormkind's face.

Mr. Cortez was limp and grey.

The Stormkind dropped my neighbor's lifeless body and scurried around the street, pushing the winds and gathering more water. It shoved the waves aside, each one battering more homes to splinters. One of the waves crashed onto my street, sending a barrage of ocean water right into my face.

I coughed it out and spat the salt from my mouth. Served me right for standing and gawking at the alien controlling the hurricane on my street.

I backed up and gripped the iron door. While I'd been gawking, the water flooding into my house reached my thighs. I panicked when I thought about how it could have drowned my family, but threw the thought aside when I remembered they were safe in the basement, locked behind a watertight door.

A door I had no chance of opening now that it was smothered in a layer of heavy water.

My heart thundered with panic. I didn't have a way to protect myself. Even if I could close the front door– and another minute of pushing and cursing told me I couldn't– I had no protection in the house. The roof was coming apart. The first level was totally flooded. If I weren't hurled through the air from the wind, I would drown in the flood.

I shoved my hands through my hair again, gripping the red strands by the roots as if it would help me think.

But I couldn't even do that. I was too damn scared. My heart was on a rampage, punching at my ribcage while my brain screamed at me to *think think think!*

There were procedures for this kind of thing. When the Storm Protection Union realized this would be the year of the next Centennial, they made the government pass laws that forced schools to teach us how to handle natural disasters. Dust storms, floods, tornadoes, hurricanes, blizzards, anything and everything. It was like being in the Spetsnaz, but without being trained how to kill.

Yet try as hard as I did– and I was two seconds away from giving myself an aneurysm due to the pressure I was putting on my brain as I scoured it for memories– I couldn't remember anything. The information just wouldn't come.

My best bet now was to find an SPU station. They were everywhere, especially in the oh-so-weather-lucky state of Florida. They had the best facilities for anyone who didn't win the Lottery and couldn't afford to modify their house. If I could find them, I could ride it out. I would be safe.

The nearest SPU station was... *Oh, God, look at the tide...* Park Vista, my old high school! Five blocks away.

Might as well have been on the goddamn moon.

But I could get there. I *would* get there. I mean, how hard could it be? I liked to surf, and I was the best swimmer at my school.

I was also clinging to adrenaline, fear, and hopeless dreams, but I didn't have time to focus on rationality.

I took a deep breath, gathered the remnants of my courage and sanity, and left my house.

The hurricane winds knocked me over. I yelped when I hit the rising water, but was able to at least turn around.

Okay. Not a great start. But at least I wasn't upside down.

I dragged my arms through the current, turning my head to check on the Stormkind. It must have had its back to me because the houses across from me were still being destroyed. It ran back and forth, swinging its arms wildly, water and wind battering the wood to splinters. It drew the ocean water forward, then hurled it aside. Was it looking for other people to...You know what? I didn't actually want to know. Swimming faster. That's the secret I wanted to uncover right now.

My arms strained as I punched them into the water. It fought me the whole way, but I kicked and pushed myself. I moved through the water slowly, but I was making progress. I was almost at the end of the block, and while the ocean water and heavy rain was absolutely *freezing* me– warm, Florida seawater, this was not– I concentrated on the SPU station. They would have everything: strong walls, warm blankets, dry clothes, hot chocolate–

The current I was in abruptly crested. Salt water pooled in my throat and surrounded me. My body was lifted, out of control. I felt myself being pushed, but I didn't know where I was going. Up and down were perceptions. My eyes burned as I tried to look through the murky grey water. My mouth was closed, but I could taste the salt water I'd stupidly swallowed scorching through my throat. The violent churns of the ocean pummeled my ears, becoming nightmarish. My heart was beating way too fast.

I had no idea where I was, or what was in the water with me. I was trapped, helpless to do anything if a submerged mailbox or car hit me. Oh God, why did I do this? What the hell was I thinking? Where was I, what was around me, where was the surface, I needed to breathe, *I can't breathe–*

The tidal wave punched into my back. I flipped end over end until my spine crashed into slick, unforgiving concrete. I hacked and vomited water, dragging air into my parched lungs. I was shaking, though I didn't register the cold.

What I did register were the walls of water around me, cocooning me in the single open space on the street.

Horror filled my aching body. Mr. Cortez's corpse was no longer in this space.

But I wasn't alone.

I flipped over, a scream hitching in my throat.

The Stormkind towered over me like some ancient ocean god, its glowing white eyes searing my own retinas. Water cascaded around its featureless body, making the beacons of light in its skeleton shiver.

It reached for me, and I raised my arm uselessly, opening my mouth to scream–

A flash of light seared my vision. It concealed a dark shape that crashed into the ground inches from my feet. I shrieked and scuttled back. My heart couldn't take much more of this. If I didn't pass out, I might become one of the only twenty-one year olds to die of a heart attack.

The light between me and the Stormkind faded. In its place stood a man.

Not a Stormkind, but legitimate man. He was tall and broad, his hair the same silver as the long-sword in his hand. He was as drenched as I was, rainwater running across the black leather and steel plating of his armor. On the metal plate covering his back was some kind of insignia– a series of jagged waves sliced in half by an upturned sword.

I could barely comprehend what just happened, who this man was, and why he looked like he was on his way to some kind of Renaissance Fair for Badasses. But I did know that the Stormkind didn't attack him.

It moved *away* from him.

Whoever this man was, the Stormkind was terrified of him.

"You have devoured already, Wild One," the man said, his voice deep and raspy, like gravel mixing with smoke. "This one is not yours."

The man turned on his heel and looked at me. My heart skipped another beat.

He was in his late forties, and alarmingly handsome. The shockingly silver hair was tied at the back of his neck, displaying a hawkish face of sharp angles. His skin was paler than my own, and he didn't have so much as a single blemish or age-worn scar. The man looked perfect, in a harsh way.

Except for his eyes.

They were so dark they appeared black to me, twin voids that threatened to suck the life from me if I stared into them for too long. I saw nothing in them, no emotion that I could recognize. This man chilled me worse than any part of the storm I was trapped in.

When he spoke again, I felt my heart freeze.

"This one is mine."

I must have heard him wrong. He couldn't have meant me. I was nobody. A waitress struggling to pay her way through college. I didn't have any big connections and had never gotten so much as a parking ticket.

But this man didn't see me that way. He eyed me like I was prey.

A panicked breath strained out of my chest and I flipped around, desperate to get to my feet. The man grabbed my ankle and pulled. I landed hard on my stomach. He pulled me across the concrete. My fingers scrabbled and skidded over the road, burning and slipping away from traction I didn't have.

He let go of my ankle and grabbed my hair instead. I yelped at the sharp pain as he pulled me back to meet his eyes.

They weren't just dark. They *were* black, so deep I couldn't even see his pupils.

I wanted to beg, fight, do anything to make him let me go. But I knew I was mercilessly trapped.

Helpless.

His inky eyes traced my body, scrutinizing instead of leering.

"You are not ideal," he growled. "But I am short on time. You will have to do."

I didn't know what he meant, didn't even know how to start asking, when he reached for his belt and took out a dagger with a light in the crystal blade.

I didn't have time to admire the weapon's beauty before the man stabbed it into my chest.

I screamed at the pain, but it wasn't just because I'd been stabbed. I only felt that initial sharp, burning punch for a single second.

After that, I felt everything else.

Agony whipped through my body in a blistering wave. A sharp, hammering sensation pounded through my chest, spilling into my veins like a violent flood. My insides thrashed viciously, as though they were being electrocuted. Hot and cold needles stabbed into my bones and skull. It felt as if my insides were charred, broken into pieces that would never be whole again.

I couldn't see past the white spots snapping through my vision. I couldn't hear anything but my screams. I had never wanted to die before.

Now it was the only thought on my mind.

Just when I was certain the splinters of torture had finished destroying my very being, something dislodged from my chest, a weight lifted from my heart.

I had no more breath to scream. My body had lost all tension. Then there was nothing at all.

CHAPTER 2

Alarms. There were too many damn alarms. Wailing sirens that just wouldn't stop. I wanted to go back to sleep. My waterbed must have been punctured by something as I slept, because I was soaked–

Wait. I didn't have a waterbed, and the alarms I heard were *sirens*.

Police cars. Ambulances. Fire trucks. God knows what else. I recognized every sound.

I was still alive.

And I hurt *everywhere*.

The first thing I did was open my eyes. Who knew that something so simple and common would feel like peeling back a layer of raw skin?

Light stabbed into my vulnerable eyes and sent a fresh pulse into my throbbing head. Apparently a construction crew had taken up residence in my skull while I was unconscious.

I closed my eyes, then opened them again slowly. It still hurt, but after a couple seconds, I was able to keep them open.

The sky over my head was crystal, perfect blue. Not a cloud could be seen in it. The SPU told us this happened after the Centennial Storm, that once it was over, the skies were wide and open. Peace always came after calamity, they said.

I felt as if I were lying on a grassy hilltop to see the sky without obstruction. But I didn't feel grass at my back. Whatever I was lying on was wet and hard.

I had to be on the road still.

A memory threatened to push past the delirium in my head. I pushed it right back.

Sitting up was embarrassingly difficult. Somewhere during my ordeal, my bones had turned into metal. The muscles in my back and hips stretched like strained bruises. I grimaced and rubbed them, only to find the feeling had spread to my arms as well. I turned my head to look down the road–

There were no houses, and I wasn't on the road.

Twisting around, despite the tension in my body, I realized I wasn't even on the ground. I was on the top of a building.

I scrambled to my feet, my head spinning from vertigo. I staggered drunkenly, quickly shutting my eyes and evening out my breathing. I opened my eyes slowly, relieved that the world was no longer spinning. I turned and saw the rooftop door behind me. At least this building was intact. I could probably use that door to get off the roof.

But how the hell did I get up here?

The memories threatened again, phantom pain shuddering through my chest and slithering to the tips of my toes. I closed my eyes and breathed in a shaky whisper, murmuring to forget. This wasn't the time. Don't think about it. Not now. Not yet. Focus on the bigger problem– finding out where exactly I was.

Lantana wasn't Florida's biggest city, so I just needed to peer over the ledge and see where I was. I could only imagine the damage, but I would probably still be able to find my house. I knew the city pretty well.

Taking slow, steady steps, I walked to the edge of the roof, in the direction of those still blaring sirens. I was amazed at how quickly they'd responded. Policemen, paramedics, and firefighters all received training courses from the SPU when they confirmed the Centennial would hit us this year, and the Army provided specialized vehicles to each state in an effort to expand its aid, but getting them out of storage was supposed to take a few days, depending on the level of debris.

Then again, maybe the rumors were wrong. Maybe it wasn't so bad. Maybe...

I jerked to a stop at the roof's ledge. My legs turned to water and I buckled. A gasp hitched in my throat as I collapsed back onto the concrete. My heart pounded as I scrambled to the edge of the building.

In school, they showed us photos of the damage from the last Centennial Storm. A way of preparing us for the devastation we could be facing.

Seeing photographs was one thing. Seeing it from a bird's eye view was... I couldn't even comprehend it.

Nothing remained standing. *Nothing.* Every single house was flattened into piles of crushed bricks, shattered stone, and splintered wood. Windows from apartment buildings and businesses were shattered, leaving dark, gaping holes in their wake. Palm trees lay across the streets in crumpled heaps. Flattened beneath them were telephone lines and power poles, their wires wrapped haphazardly around overturned cars and trucks like pythons squeezing around their prey. It was like a rain of giant fists had pounded into the city, hammering without mercy until only shambles remained.

Complete devastation spanned as far as I could see, all the way to the horizon and the ocean beyond. The water was calm and placid now, but I saw upturned boats and remnants of the docks bobbing helplessly in the water.

Ocean water sloshed over the roads. Emergency vehicles struggled to drive through it. The black SPU SUVs were parked wherever the damage was at its worst, whether it was beside the houses that had meshed together during their collapse, the lower levels of flooded apartments, or the shopping districts with caved-in boutiques. Dozens of red lights flashes below me, their sirens wailing together into one unending cry.

The sirens were loud, but not loud enough to conceal all the screams.

Hundreds, *thousands* of people waded through the streets, weaving awkwardly around the debris. They huddled on piles of broken housing, waving their arms and begging for help. Groups of desperate families tossed refuse aside to find their lost and loved, dozens of names shouted into an incoherent echo.

Some survivors were pulled from the wreckage. Their screams of fear and relief were almost as loud as the sirens.

My eyes traced over the chaos, searching for my house. All I could think about were my parents and brother, trapped and terrified in the storm shelter. What if the house had been demolished in the hurricane? Their exit would be covered by debris. Would Dad's cell phone be able to get reception underground so he could call for help? Every shelter was supposed to have an emergency alarm installed to alert the SPU, but the power had to be out. How would they get help? How many inhalers did Mom have for James? What if the floor caved in? Our house was old and needed renovations. It might not have been able to withstand that kind of destruction.

My family could be trapped. They could be dead.

Tension knotted around my heart like a noose. It was painful to breathe. I shoved my hands through my hair and gripped it tight. Tears pricked my eyes. The city below me blurred. I didn't know where I was. This landscape had been replaced by something strange, something unfamiliar and horrible.

A sob wrenched up my throat as I tried to get my bearings. A steady, cool wind brushed my drenched clothes. The wind began to push the water inland again.

I closed my eyes and breathed in short, jagged pants, but I managed to stop hyperventilating.

I had to get home.

Okay, I had a goal. First things first: get off the roof.

Easy enough.

I turned and ran toward the access door. My legs felt like wooden planks encased in iron, so I didn't run very far. Jogging wasn't an improvement. I settled with a brisk walk.

Better than nothing.

I pulled the access door open and peered inside. There wasn't a lot of light, so I fumbled along the edges of the wall until my hands circled the cold railing. My footsteps echoed as I stomped down the corridor. The roof access led to the emergency staircase, so I followed it all the way to the bottom.

I was huffing and puffing the whole way down, my legs burning with every step I took. God, wasn't it supposed to be easier going *down* stairs instead of up them?

Oh well. At least I would get my exercise in for the day. I had been complaining that I wanted a better beach body this summer, but this wasn't exactly the workout I'd had in mind.

Maybe, if it were still stocked somewhere, I would let fantasies of a beach body slide and find some ice cream.

I jerked to a stop on the staircase. Phantom pain drifted through me. A blistering, agonizing cold wrapped itself around my limbs, smothering them with ice.

I squeezed my eyes shut and breathed through the memory.

Not here, not here, don't think about it, Ava. Don't think, don't think...

I cracked my eyes open and continued my descent.

Light streaked through the open door and rippled through the water flooding the exit of the apartment building. I slipped into the cool, salty water that covered my knees. I tried not to think about how heavy my clothes were on my body or what was in the water.

I wanted to shower, but this wasn't the kind of water I wanted to use.

Nudging through the door, I entered a world of chaos.

Spinning lights, blaring sirens, terrified screams, crashing rubble, and cool water coalesced into the worst kind of symphony. I thought I was disoriented when I was staring down from the roof, but now I wasn't so sure. Nothing was familiar, and I knew Lantana like the back of my hand. I'd never left the town, never had a reason to. Working at the restaurant meant a lot of tourists asking where they could find certain shops or hotels or clubs, so I committed myself to knowing where all of them were.

Now I couldn't even tell what the building across from me had been when it was still intact. I spun in a circle, trying to orient myself. Honestly, I felt like an alien. Maybe I'd been picked up by one of those brutal winds and thrown into another planet.

No. That's not what happened to you. What happened was–

I shut it out. I had to. I couldn't face it. Couldn't break down here. I needed to get home. Then I could have a meltdown.

One foot in front of the other. That's what I had to do. That's what I *would* do. Nothing more, nothing less.

My gut pulled me to the left, so to the left I went. Salt water splashed against my thighs and stomach. I spotted volunteers everywhere, authorities and civil workers and rescuers combining forces with the black-clad SPU officers to drag whoever they could from stone and wood wreckage. Some of the people they found were screaming and holding their hands up to the blaring sun. Some were disoriented and bleeding. Some weren't moving at all.

Ambulances were loaded up and sped toward SPU hospitals. Dozens of them had been set up underground for when the general hospitals and medi-centers in Florida were destroyed. I dreaded to think how packed they must be now, and how difficult and terrifying it would be for the survivors to be lowered into the ground after suffering injuries that crippled or nearly killed them. My stomach churned at the thought of all those helpless bedridden people, unable to escape when the worst of the Centennial hit.

Hearing so many anguished cries broke my heart. I wanted to do something, but I would just get in the way. I didn't know CPR, stood barely over five feet tall, tripped over my own feet more often than not, and didn't know the first thing about search-and-rescue. The last thing I needed was to get yelled at because I moved something the wrong way and hurt someone. Right now, my priority was getting home. Once that was over, I could focus on helping others.

Floating in the water on my right was half of a snapped wooden sign. I grabbed it and held it up. The board was missing both its ends, but I read the letters –EAFOOD BA– perfectly.

I recognized the sign for The Seafood Bar, a place my best friend would take me to for special occasions.

The Seafood Bar was in West Palm. At least a thirty minute drive from where I lived.

How the hell had I gotten into another city?

Images flashed across my mind. Water circling my legs. Drowning in a current. The hard, cold road. The Stormkind–

The sign slipped from my fingers and splashed into the water. Dizziness swam through my head again. I closed my eyes and breathed through it. I couldn't think about how I'd gotten so far away. The hundreds of questions and barely restrained trauma were eating at my brain, but I wouldn't let myself be devoured.

Not yet, anyway.

Gathering the last of my composure, I started walking again. Lantana was south of West Palm, so that's the direction I went. It would probably take close to four hours to walk home, but I would make it.

I forgot my ordeal as I looked around, witnessing rescues and hearing shouts for help. After an hour of walking, the water on the street grew shallower. My sneakers squished against the concrete, plastic rubbing against my skin above my ankle socks.

So I was going to get blisters *and* soggy feet. Great.

Still, I kept walking. I wanted to ask someone from the SPU for a ride home, but there was no way I would bother them when they were working so hard to rescue people who actually needed help. I was just lost.

But so were thousands... maybe millions of other people.

When I found Olive Avenue, I knew I would make it home. From here it was just a straight walk down the highway to Lantana. From there, I'd orient myself.

The further I went, the more shelters I noticed. They weren't much– military grade tents propped up and guarded by police and SPU volunteers. Emergency vehicles led the homeless and injured to seek food and medical help.

The smell of cooking food drifted over the air, and my stomach growled violently. I winced and pressed my hand over my middle. I had no idea what time it was, but hours must have passed since my last meal. I needed to find something to eat, and soon.

I looked at the dozens of dark green tents lining the highway, amazed and grateful that a tent city had been set up so quickly. I mean, the storm only happened yesterday. Tent cities like this took a while to set up, didn't they?

I guess it didn't really matter. People were getting help, and that was the important thing. The SPU was very good at corralling volunteers and organizing aid. Climatologists and meteorologists had predicted that this would be the year of the Centennial almost a decade ago, and the SPU had been training ever since. Everyone knew the gravity of the situation, and had prepared as best as they could.

My eyes skittered forward, and I knew that all the preparation hadn't been enough.

By the front entrance of the tent city was a series massive wooden boards. Every inch of them was covered in papers and photographs. The Missing Boards.

Survivors huddled in front of the boards, stapling new photographs or sketches of loved ones to the wood, or holding each other for comfort. Quiet sobs and unending tears streaked their faces. My heart ached, and I wondered if I should stop at the boards. If I looked through all those photos, would I see my family's smiling faces with the ominous words "MISSING" stamped over their heads? Would I see *my* face? If I'd woken up this far from home, who was to say that my parents hadn't? That James hadn't gotten lost, too?

Just because the Centennial was over and the skies ahead were clear, didn't mean that the dangers had passed.

I steeled myself and kept marching. I told myself that my family wasn't on those boards. They'd made it into the basement and probably wouldn't have been able to get out yet.

Oh, God, I hoped Dad remembered to punch the panic button for the SPU. I knew they had enough food and supplies to last them for three months, but I didn't want them to be trapped underground for so long.

When we learned about the Centennial, the government made it mandatory that every building have an accessible storm shelter. They worked with the SPU to have emergency alarms installed. Once the panic button was pressed, it would send a satellite signal to the nearest emergency or SPU station. Unfortunately, since *millions* of people would be pressing those buttons and the number of volunteers and civil workers was so small, a waiting list was formed. The date and time the panic buttons were pressed was recorded underground with the wealthy and the Lottery winners. Whoever pressed the button first would be helped first. Rescue workers then had to go down the list. It would take days, weeks, possibly months before everyone was rescued from their basements and shelters. For those who had faulty wiring with their panic buttons would wait the longest, until the largest, final search begun and the state could be searched grid by grid.

Dad was an electrician, so I wasn't worried about the wiring. Mom was a nurse, so she would know what to do about waste and would ensure that James would have enough inhalers. But how long would it take for them to be rescued? I didn't know if Mom pressed the panic button when she took James into the basement, or if Dad had done it when I told him to go inside.

Did they think I was dead? Were they okay? Had the floorboards been able to support the weight of the water rushing into the house? What if–

"Ava!"

I jumped near out of my skin when I heard my name. I spun around and looked at the truck cruising down the highway. I had been so lost in thought that I hadn't even heard the damn thing.

I shuffled to the side of the road and peered in the back of the truck, which was packed with survivors. A slim brown hand waved desperately at me from the back.

Tears pricked my eyes when I saw my best friend, Piper.

She shouted for the driver to stop. When he did, she leaped out of the back and ran for me. We collided, and the tears spilled over.

"Oh my God," my voice shook as I crushed her into a hug. "Thank God you're okay!"

"You too," she cried.

She sniffled against my shoulder before pulling back and looking at me.

Piper was gorgeous. No, gorgeous is the wrong word. Ethereal is better. Even soaked and dirty like I was, she looked like a goddess with flawless, bronze skin, velvet black hair, big sepia eyes, a wide smile, perfect body, and mile long legs. Piper had three different modeling contracts and was working on becoming a spokeswoman for a new make-up brand. She was as wealthy as she was beautiful, living with her investor parents in one of the million dollar houses on Ocean Boulevard. She had academic, volunteer, and basketball scholarships that would pay for almost all of her tuition to the University of Florida. Piper was the kind of girl that made pale, skinny redheads like me feel self-conscious and insecure.

Instead, I loved Piper. She was the sister I never had, and she never made me feel bad about myself.

"I didn't even know you were in West Palm," she said.

"I wasn't," I blurted.

Piper's eyes widened. Did she look nervous? "What do you mean?"

Before I could explain what happened, or ask why she was in West Palm herself, another voice interrupted us.

"Either get in the truck or get out of the way!"

My eyes moved over Piper's shoulder to the guy who'd growled at us. My heart sank, and I cursed my luck. I'd been so happy and relieved to see Piper that I didn't think I would also cross paths with the boy I hated.

Declan Garner was a walking stereotype. I honestly think he went out of his way to be just like the bullying jocks that are often exaggerated in movies. He was the star quarterback at our college, a self-proclaimed beer pong champion, and an absolute jerk. So of course, he was also ridiculously handsome.

With thick muscles, well-styled dark blond hair, calculating brown eyes, and a cold smile, Declan seemed disarming and friendly at first. Dozens of girls at our school had crushes on him.

But underneath the charm and lies he spewed, he was a thug. When no one was looking, he would grab the quiet kids or the loners and trick them into thinking they belonged, only to humiliate them later. Whether through embarrassing pranks or pointed fingers, Declan made sure everyone knew he was above them. His favorite thing to do was start fights after school when he knew none of the teachers would be able to do anything. The only injury I would ever see on Declan was bruised knuckles.

Rumors circled that he was having a difficult time at home, that his low grades, struggling athletic career, and alienation from his parents was going to get him kicked out of his house, but I wasn't about to ask him if things were okay. It might make him tear my head off.

"Make up your mind, Ginger!" he shouted at me.

Piper threw him an angry glare, but didn't say anything. We had both seen how volatile his temper could be on the football field. Even though he was quarterback, he would go out of his way to mow down anyone in his path. I'd seen him stomp on more than one unfortunate team member because he couldn't be bothered to go around them when they fell.

Piper slid her hand into mine and led me toward the truck. "The driver is one of my agent's cousins. Everybody in here is going back to Lantana," she informed. "I'll tell him to drop you off at your house."

"Thanks," I muttered.

While Piper went to talk to the driver, I climbed in the back of the truck and sat as far from Declan as I could. There were five other people packed in the truck bed and all of them were squished together on one side. I huddled in the corner, wishing Declan weren't so big, and wondering what I could bribe Piper with so I didn't have to sit next to him.

"Can't believe you made it," Declan grumbled, eyeing me. "Never pegged you as a survivor."

I looked at my hands and rubbed them together. The sun was out and high in the azure sky, but I couldn't get warm.

"You always seemed like the type that would be the first to go," he went on. "You must have been close to an SPU station. No way you would have been able to defend yourself."

I knew what he was doing. He needed to assert his caveman status by bragging about how he saved himself and a bunch of other people. He wanted to act like the Centennial hadn't probably made him pee his pants. Picking on me and provoking me was a good way of doing it.

Didn't help that he was right. I hadn't saved myself. I hadn't really saved anybody. I was caught in the flood, shoved onto concrete, faced with a Stormkind, and then–

I wrapped my hands around my stomach and hunched over.

"Jesus, Ginger, you better not puke," he warned.

"Leave her alone, Declan."

I looked at Piper like she was my lifeline. Guess that was appropriate, since she was making sure I got home.

She pulled herself into the truck bed and glared at Mr. Jackass Jock. An old flare of jealously filled my stomach. Piper was always so composed and confident and strong. She thought I was joking whenever I told her that she could run for president and win.

I always told her that with a straight face.

"Whatever," growled Declan. He stretched out against the side of the truck as it started moving along the highway. He draped his arm over the top, causing his fingers to brush against my shoulder. His feet pushed against the two people across from him. They didn't meet his eyes and huddled closer together.

"You okay?" Piper asked me quietly.

I realized my hands were still on my stomach, as if I really did look ready to hurl.

"I just…" My chest was tight when I breathed. "I can't believe it. All that happened…"

"Yeah," she whispered, shuffling closer to me. "They did so much to prepare us, but it wasn't enough. Nowhere near enough."

We sat in silence for what was only a few minutes, but it felt like an eternity. Even Declan kept his mouth shut. Looked like miracles could still happen, after all.

"Where were you?" I asked tentatively, desperate for something to talk about. I wanted to know, and it wasn't the appropriate time to ask her what her plans for the weekend were.

"I had a photo shoot on the beach," complained Piper. She scoffed and shook her head. "Stupid hotshot photographer wouldn't reschedule. He said it *had* to be today and we wouldn't stay on the beach for long." Her shoulders tensed beside mine. "I saw the whole thing forming so fast, I didn't think I was going to make it. I don't even remember how I got into the city. I got tangled in a wave and passed out." Piper's eyes went dark with what I imagined were harrowing memories. Then she looked at me and smiled. "At least I managed to get my clothes back on. Could you imagine me running around looking for help in a bikini?"

"I can."

We both scowled at Declan. He didn't notice; his eyes were glued on Piper's chest. She folded her arms over her breasts, her long blue tank top covering her curves. His eyes went to her cut off shorts and bare legs instead.

"Stop looking at me," she warned.

"Can't help it." Declan lifted his eyes slowly and grinned. "You've always looked like an Egyptian goddess."

I guess the look he gave her was what could have been called "bedroom eyes," but I wouldn't know. No one had ever looked at me with anything resembling interest. I was passed over because I was shy and not well endowed. At times like this, it was a blessing. Other times, it just made me feel lonely.

Piper narrowed her eyes. "I'm Puerto Rican."

His grin widened and he shrugged a shoulder. "Same difference."

Wow. Guess he wasn't as smart as I thought.

Ignoring him, Piper turned her eyes back to me. "What about you? Why were you in West Palm? You should have texted me."

Chills wracked my body again. I dragged my knees closer to my chest. I barely noticed the truck stopping. We must have arrived at someone's house. One of the men across from us scrambled to his feet and began exiting the truck bed.

"I wasn't in West Palm," I muttered quietly.

"What?"

I could feel my heart shuddering through my chest. I tightened my grip on my arms and breathed steadily.

"I was at home. In Lantana." Pressure built behind my ribcage, and words began to spill from my lips. "Dad and I were barricading the house. He hurt himself and the front door slammed open. The house started flooding, so I told him to get into the basement with Mom and James, and I..." My eyes stung. "I couldn't get back in the basement so I went outside–"

Piper gasped. "Oh, God, Ava..."

Declan snorted.

My eyes began to burn. "I was trying to get to Park Vista to the SPU station, but I got caught in the flood, and... and..." I whirled to face my best friend. Her eyes were as wide and horrified as mine must have been.

"I saw one, Piper."

She stared at me, not sure what I meant, and seemingly afraid to ask.

"I saw a Stormkind."

Piper's eyes bulged, her pretty mouth becoming a shocked "O."

"Bullshit you did," growled Declan. The truck had stopped again, more survivors getting out. "Nobody's ever seen them. All that historical account crap they make us read in school? None of it proves anything. *Actual* scientists have proved that the Centennial is just a freak occurrence."

"What about those photographs and films they show us? The ones that soldiers from the war recorded when they saw them land on the battlefield in the middle of a storm?"

I remembered what she was talking about, the grainy black and white images of WWI soldiers shooting and running across the battlefield, a flash of light smashing into the earth.

A figure rising from the dirt, scrambling left and right and chasing the already terrified soldiers, hurling winds, ice, water, and dirt at the men. The massive storms that made the Great War even more grueling.

There were critics who accused the videos and films of being hoaxes, tricks of the light and illusions created by the sheer terror from that war, but other historians spent their whole lives digging into history and finding old journals or ancient sketches that detailed accounts of great storms happening every hundred years. The most reliable evidence came from the WWI accounts, when millions and millions of men and women had been writing about the atrocious things they'd seen. Finding fifty thousand accounts that mentioned strange beings falling from earth and controlling the weather was hard to ignore.

It was up for debate whether or not the SPU believed the historians and their feverent displays of evidence. But after a collective of meteorologists looked up records of the massive storms and theorized what would happen if another storm like the Centennial happened in our lifetime, they formed the Storm Protection Union and began to prepare. The years had changed, but the paranoia remained the same.

Though some people just wouldn't bend to the possibility of the supernatural.

"Right," Declan scoffed. "Because you can really rely on the story of a terrified fifteen year old soldier in World War One. They won't have massive PSTD or delusions or anything."

Something snapped in me. I whirled and shouted at Declan, forgetting that he was twice my size and liked to break things.

"I saw it! I saw it, and then–"

Piper's hands gripped my arms. "Ava, calm down. It's okay."

My best friend tugged me away from Declan and wrapped her arms around me. One of us was shaking, but I couldn't tell who it was. I wouldn't have admitted it any more than she would have.

Declan narrowed his eyes and glowered, but I was too rattled to say anything else. All I could do was see a skeleton of light surrounded by a featureless, liquid face, its very presence reminding me of how small and simple I was, how easy it had absorbed the life of my neighbor, and then the man, the man with the dagger, and the pain—

The truck jolted to a stop. Piper and I bounced in the truck bed. I blinked rapidly, remembering where I was, and where I was headed.

Home. I was finally going home.

I pinched my eyes shut and forced out another breath. I really did not like these panic attacks.

The truck started again, and Piper's arms were still tight around me. She was whispering something in my ear, but my brain refused to process her voice into coherent words.

For whatever reason, when I opened my eyes, they went straight to Declan.

I don't know what I expected when I looked at him. Maybe the usual disdain and indifference.

I didn't anticipate the confusion. Or the unease. Declan was looking at me like I was an animal he wasn't sure I should approach.

He looked at me like I was dangerous.

The expression was gone so quickly from his face that I was sure I'd imagined it. I must have. Declan wouldn't be afraid of a nobody like me. I was just another player on his field, ready for him to stomp on.

The truck pulled to a new stop and he looked over the side.

"Well, this is my stop, ladies. One of the docs said I took a good hit to the head and need to get it checked out." He rolled his eyes, and I suppressed the urge to tell him there was no need to check his head— there was nothing decent inside of it. He looked at Piper. "Hottie, I hope I'll see you around. Ginger..." Declan's eyes flicked up and down my body, lingering too long on my skinny legs and insubstantial chest. "Well, I won't be looking for you."

Declan sneered at us and leaped over the side of the truck.

"God, he's such an asshole," Piper grumbled. She released me from her hold. "Are you sure you're okay, Ava?"

I hesitated for a split second, only one more memory threatening to resurface. I turned to my best friend and smiled weakly. "Yeah. I'm good. It's just... It was just scary, you know?"

Piper's face twisted into a grimace, and she *still* looked beautiful. Not fair.

"Scary's not the word I would use," she remarked. "Pant-shittingly terrifying is better."

I gaped dramatically. "You swore! You *never* swear!"

She held up a delicate finger. "First of all, *you're* the one that never swears aloud, and second," she lowered her hand, unease filling her eyes, "you have to admit it fits the situation."

No argument there. I couldn't imagine what she went through. I mean, blacking out in the middle of a hurricane? She was lucky to be alive. I wanted to tell her about... the other part of my little adventure, but Piper was going to have her own nightmares now.

Besides, I didn't want to think about my last conscious moments in the hurricane. I wasn't ready. Right now, I just needed to get home.

"Yeah, I guess it does." I tried to smile, but it felt wrong on my face.

We sat in silence until the truck pulled to another stop. I stayed in the truck bed, wanting to look over the side, but too scared of what I would see.

"Ava," prompted Piper. "We're here."

"I know," I said. "Just... give me a second."

She nodded and said nothing. I closed my eyes and sent out a silent prayer to any deity that was listening.

Please, please, please, let my family be okay. Please don't take them away from me. I can't be alone. I won't know what to do. Please let them be safe. That's not too much to ask, is it?

Knowing there was no point in delaying any longer, I opened my eyes and dragged myself to my knees. Piper let down the truck bed then turned and turned to face me. Her eyes dropped to my chest and she frowned.

"Where did you get that?"

Bewildered, I looked down to the spot over my heart where her eyes were locked.

Peeking out from the top of my tank top was a white, circular scar with jagged edges. Exactly the kind that would have been left if I'd been stabbed.

Panic welled in my chest again. I clenched my fists and my jaw, willing the memory away.

"Ask me later, okay?" I whispered.

Piper nodded slowly. Her hand rubbed over her own heart, as if guarding it. She looked like she wanted to say something, but chose not to. Silence was what we both needed.

Piper opened her arms and wrapped me in a hug. We both needed that, too.

"I'll come see you as soon as I can, okay?"

I nodded and hugged her tight. I didn't know what happened to her parents, and I couldn't help her without knowing what happened to my own family. We had no idea what kind of state we would be in when we saw each other again. If we'd both be whole, or broken.

"Be safe, Piper."

We let each other go and I slipped out of the truck bed onto my old street. I think the truck drove away, but I didn't notice. All I could see was my house.

Or what *used* to be my house.

My eyes noticed irrelevant things, like how the ruins of my house were bunched together like a flat pyramid. Shingles were everywhere, slipping through cracks of the caved in walls. Tattered, snapped furniture was piled on the waterlogged grass behind warped metal appliances. The garage was completely flattened into the driveway. I couldn't see Mom or Dad's cars, and had no idea where the mailbox was.

I walked forward in a daze, my aching, soggy feet dragging heavily through the grass. I went toward the furniture, touching it and stupidly wondering why it was outside on the lawn. It wasn't supposed to be here. It was supposed to be inside–

"Ava?"

I turned around and looked at the people standing in the middle of the road. I hadn't looked back when Piper dropped me off. I went straight for my house, thinking that's where my parents and little brother were. I didn't think to look back, where they were standing now.

My eyes took in all of them. My Dad's wide, shocked eyes as he held my little brother's hand. My mother's joyous tears as she ran for me.

Fresh tears slipped past my own eyes. I choked on a sob and ran for my family.

Mom met me in a crushing hug. I shuddered and cried into her chest, like I was a lost baby. She soothed me like I was one.

"Oh, thank God, Ava, thank God, thank God."

Hearing the fear in her voice only made me cry harder. When I felt my Dad and brother wrap their arms around me, I was almost screaming.

It was eternity before they pulled away. I didn't want to let go. I was still a shaking, crying mess.

Mom cupped my face in her hands and looked in my eyes. "Where have you been? We were looking for you everywhere."

Speaking past my tears and the released pressure in my chest was harder than I thought it would be.

"I couldn't get the door closed," I sobbed out. "I tried, but I couldn't so I tried to get to my school because I didn't want to drown, and I... I..."

I couldn't tell them about the Stormkind the way I had with Piper. I'd gotten too upset to know if she believed me or not. With my family, I was just too relieved they were alive to care. I would tell them later.

Just as I would tell them about that other part. I would have to tell them eventually. If Piper had seen the scar on my chest, there was a chance my family would too.

"When I woke up, I was in Palm Beach. I got a ride with Piper."

"Did you stay with her?" my Dad asked.

Confused, I turned to look at him, but a crying baby caught my attention. I looked past him to where a young mother stood, holding her child. She was talking frantically to SPU soldiers. All across the road, my neighbors were standing together, moving debris and talking to authorities. They were *everywhere*, packed on the road like homeless sardines.

That's what we were now. Fish out of water.

My eyes went back to the crying baby. To the woman that held her.

To the patch of street they were standing on.

Where Mr. Cortez had died. Drained of his life force by the Stormkind. I saw its skeleton glow bright in my mind. Watched it glow brighter as it stood over me, reached for me.

Saw a shadow and a pair of cruel eyes.

Felt a sharp punch in my chest before the world exploded into agony.

"Ava? Ava, sweetie, what's wrong?"

I barely heard my mother. Hardly felt James touch my hand. The memory was clouding my mind. It hurt to breathe.

"Sit down, honey, sit down."

I couldn't make myself move. Dad had to help me. He knelt next to me with his arm around my shoulders. Steadying me. The ground felt wet. Everything was drenched. I felt like my very soul was soaked.

"It's okay, Ava. You're safe now."

It was what I needed to hear. It was true.

It didn't keep me from shaking.

I stared blankly ahead, unaware that I was still holding James' hand until I noticed the white papers in his hand. Relieved to have something to focus on, I nodded to them.

"What are those?"

James frowned, then turned the papers over.

My smiling face stared back at me, printed on a piece of white paper. The girl in the photo seemed like a stranger now. I barely recognized her.

Blocky, capitalized text glared over my photograph. MISSING.

I looked at my Mom, confused and a little hurt. "You were going to declare me missing? After a few hours?"

Mom froze. Then her jaw began to droop, her eyes bulging. James had a similar expression on his little round face.

"Ava," my Dad said. "You haven't been gone for a few hours."

I looked at him, alarmed by the confused, scared look in his eyes. A look I'd never seen my father wear.

I understood why when he said, "You've been gone for a week."

CHAPTER 3

Before the Centennial, I liked routine. There was comfort in the familiar. I woke up, had breakfast, showered, went to school, went to work, came home, went to bed. That's all I ever did, and while I complained about it, I secretly craved it. I knew exactly where I was and what I had to do.

Having a week of my life disappear threw all of that out of whack, and even though three weeks had now passed since the Centennial, I was struggling to catch up.

To the dismay of every student, all schools and colleges would resume in September. Temporary structures would be built until the real schools could be solidified. The road and streets were still— mostly— intact, so once the rubble and debris could be safely moved, sorted and recycled in the landfills, reconstruction would begin on the original spots. Park Vista would be in the same plot it always had been, like it had never been gone at all.

At least, until the next Centennial.

The federal government enforced mandatory volunteer laws to help rebuild the country. For the next three months, every able-bodied man, woman, and child over thirteen was required to help their city. The kind of work they did depended on what they were capable of. The government provided the SPU with a list of medical and employment records— which caused no small amount of outrage from basically everyone— to determine what skills people had. Carpenters and engineers would build houses, though the amount of work they did was dependent on their physical limitations. Nurses worked round the clock in makeshift hospitals. Athletes became messengers. Seniors without serious memory problems or senility watched over young children. Technicians and electricians worked to get power back up. Business executives oversaw everything from construction sites to food distribution, labor and rations became the new currency.

Even people like me who worked the leftover jobs– retail workers, clerks, baristas, and waitresses– went back to our regular jobs. Granted, there were a few changes. Retail workers were required to take sewing courses. Fabrics would be sewn by hand and traded until we could rebuild the country and begin imports again, since the post offices were still shut down and there were no longer airports to allow planes to land safely.

In a way, waitresses had it easy. Sure, we didn't get tips anymore, but we were at least able to pretend we weren't back in the Stone Age. Large tents were set up for restaurants and cafés. Barbecues were placed outside along with the canned food brought up from the underground. The cooks were challenged to make food with whatever was left from the stores, and we basically turned into soup kitchens. Or barbecue kitchens, since my restaurant didn't serve soup.

Rescue and construction workers could lumber in and ask for something from the limited menu, and they would eat free. Obviously we got freeloaders, but my boss, Mikey, was a big Hawaiian guy who had no problem tossing out anyone who wasn't volunteering nearby. Or who didn't have any beer to trade.

All of this was primitive, but necessary. I was told that the military had used Morse code for the first week to communicate with the SPU. The radios were getting back into working order, but they were only short range. The wealthy and important were still working underground with the Lottery winners to communicate with other countries to assess the global damage and determine how to offer aid. The entire planet was a mess. The most we could do right now was work at piecing ourselves back together, and hoping we could return the States to what they had been before dozens of storms had ravaged it.

Florida had been one of the states hit worst in the Centennial and was still soaked in water from high tides and light rainstorms, but it was by no means the only area affected by monster storms. Typhoons and tsunamis ravaged California. Dust storms spiraled through Arizona and Nevada. Tornados obliterated Kansas and Nebraska. Floods had half of Mississippi submerged. There were even blizzards in North Dakota and Michigan.

Blizzards. In freaking *July*. Anyone who thought that this was something natural was either really stubborn or really stupid. There was nothing natural about the Centennial, no matter what the SPU and their professional climatologists and meteorologists claimed. The only thing I believed from them was the guarantee that there would be no more repercussions from the Centennial. Whatever force was behind it was gone now.

True enough, there hadn't been a cloud in the sky for two weeks.

No– three weeks. Three. Because I'd been missing for one.

"Order up, Ava!"

Crap. I lowered my hand from my chest, alarmed that I'd been touching my scar. The panic attacks had stopped, but I'd been having nightmares almost every single night. Well, not really nightmares. More like blurring flashes through my mind, and a scorching pain in my chest when I woke up. I told myself it was just my memories screwing around with me, that the rigid white scar over my heart couldn't hurt me now because it was healed over.

Lying to myself wasn't as comforting as it should have been.

I scurried through the tent, weaving through the mostly empty tables to the second flap. I was happy the construction workers two blocks down were close friends of Mikey's and loved his cooking. It meant that the Papaya

Cantina was getting first dibs on rebuilding. Right now, it was nothing more than a skeletal wooden frame draped with a thick blue tarp, but Mikey made the most of it. Ten mismatched and scuffed tables and foldout chairs were propped in the center. At the far left corner was a counter top for the hot food, served on paper plates. In the far right was the trading box, where customers could leave donations of supplies for payment and tips. Money stopped meaning anything. At least for now. I imagined the wealthy bankers and celebrities still underground were going crazy without their fancy cars and overpriced clothes.

I stopped at the counter and peeled back the second flap of the tent. Beyond it, Mikey stood at the barbecue, flipping mouth-watering burgers with metal spatula. The framework was bare of a tarp, so the smoke flowed freely and there was no real risk of fire. His wife Maci worked behind him, pulling freshly cooked potatoes from the stone fire pit. I tilted forward, breathing in the smell of heaven.

Now *these* were freshly cooked French fries.

"Smells great, Mikey," I remarked, grabbing a paper plate and a freshly cut hamburger bun from the table at my side.

"Yup," the robust Hawaiian said with a cheery smile. "And it's not for you, Ava, so don't sneak the fries."

I pouted. "We've only got one customer right now."

"*Right now*, are the key words, darling. We're gonna get a rush soon. Ryan's crew will be coming in soon."

"So you're telling me I need to take my break now?" I smirked, piling small packets of salt, pepper, ketchup, relish, and mustard on the plate before giving it to Maci.

"Nice try, honey," she replied. She was a plump, friendly woman with sparkling eyes. "You've already had your break."

"Not that you did anything," spat a voice to my left.

I frowned at the other waitress, a tall, doe-eyed blonde named Carrie. She got the best tips and trades, mostly because her shirt was too tight around her ample chest, the edges rolling up to reveal a toned stomach, and her shorts were so small I could honesty see the edges of her butt cheeks hanging out of the denim. Carrie complained they were the only clothes she had left.

I called bullcrap on that.

"All you did was stare at the door and rub your chest." Carrie's eyes flicked down. She grinned maliciously. "Rubbing them won't make them grow, honey."

My cheeks flared with embarrassment, but Carrie just flicked her bleached blonde hair over her shoulder and sauntered out into the restaurant.

"Ignore her, Ava," muttered Mikey. "You know that if it were up to us, you'd be our only waitress."

I nodded grimly, going back to the table and piling on processed cheese and pickles. Those were the only other condiments we had, since fresh food hadn't been found yet. A year prior to the Centennial, farmers and factories had been required to provide a portion of their output to SPU mandated warehouses that would freeze, dry, and dehydrate the food so it could be rationed. The food was placed in highly secured bunkers underground with locations known only to the government and top SPU personnel. Anyone withholding portions of food would be fined and even threatened with jail time once the Centennial was over. There had been protests, lawsuits, job losses, and even small riots, but the SPU refused to abandon their protocols. They assured us that this food would be necessary, since the Centennial would bring all food production to a brutal, screeching halt.

My diner was almost closed down because of those mandates, but I couldn't really fault them now. All that food was divvied up and sent to restaurants that had filled out the required forms to be turned into non-profit retailers. Requests were granted based on location, food and safety regulations, and the amount of profit earned by customers.

We were lucky, so we didn't complain.

Before the Centennial, the Papaya Cantina had been fully staffed. Now there were only four of us. Mikey was right about the construction guys. We were swamped during the rushes and no matter what I thought about Carrie's use of her figure, there was no denying that she brought in more business.

"Here," Maci said. She plucked the plate from my hand and finished loading it with fries. Mikey put the burger on the bun, closed it, and let Maci hand it back to me. "Take this out to your table. I'll fix you up a plate of fries. Once you wipe down the tables, you can have another five minutes, okay?"

I smiled. "Thanks, Maci."

I carried the plate out of the kitchen and into the restaurant to where our one customer was sitting in my section. He was one of the doctors at a first aid station by one of the construction sites, and he looked half awake. I was actually happy to drop off his food, and told him he didn't have to trade anything. He was already working his butt off to treat the wounded, one of whom had been Piper's dad, who suffered a broken leg in the Centennial.

After I dropped off his food, I started wiping down the tables. Carrie was somewhere in the back, probably doing her nails or cutting off more of her shorts or something, so it was just me and the doctor. I was debating going back to talk to him about the scar on my chest, if only to ask why it healed so quickly, when the front flap of the tent was pulled open, and Adonis walked in.

Okay, so he wasn't exactly Adonis– more like Adonis' dark cousin– but he was so damn gorgeous that I actually froze.

He was tall and muscular without being blocky. He stood like a warrior, his perfect blue eyes tracing over the tables like he thought they might attack. Thick black hair brushed the shoulders of his rugged leather motorcycle jacket. High cheekbones and sharp lips gave him a regal appearance. He looked like a prince trying to disguise himself as a biker.

I gotta say– the look suited him.

Mystery Man's eyes stopped their assessment and locked on me. My heart skipped a beat once, then again when he gently smiled. The smile didn't reach his eyes, but damn, was it ever sexy.

"May I sit?" he asked.

Oh God, his voice… could he get any hotter? His voice was deep and smooth, like velvet and chocolate and all things pleasurable.

I started nodding, and the motion seemed to help me get my cool back. "Yeah, yes, of course, anywhere you like."

Mystery Man dipped his head politely and walked to one of the corner tables. It was technically in Carrie's section, but she was in the back, and I was bored, and he was so *hot*, that I scurried to grab a handwritten menu off the first table I could and all but ran to him.

He sat with his back to the edge of the tent, allowing his eyes to trace over the restaurant like a hawk's. That's what he reminded me of. A predator. Dangerous and beautiful, a born heartbreaker. I mean, he was breaking my heart, and I didn't even know him.

I held the menu out to him, which he accepted with another one of those small smiles and an incline of his head. I was genuinely distraught when he lowered his eyes to the menu, because his irises weren't one shade of blue. They were bright baby blue around the pupils, while the edge near the whites was a sparkling sapphire. The kind of eyes girls like me are helpless against.

"What can I get you?" I blurted.

Mystery Man lifted his eyes. Holy crap. When did it so hot in here?

"I haven't finished reading the menu yet," he responded slyly. "Is there something you would recommend?"

Probably, but you need to give me a second to breathe.

"Well, it's not on the menu, but Mikey and Maci make this mean coconut rice stir fry. I saw them making it earlier, so there should still be some leftover." I replayed the words in my head, and backtracked immediately.

"I mean, it was made today, so it's not really leftover, they just made too much." I was talking way too fast. "The fries are really good, too. Salty but not greasy. I could eat three whole plates of them."

I really needed to stop talking.

"I see," Mystery Man remarked. He handed me back the menu. "I'll have both."

"Both?" I asked stupidly.

"The rice and the fries."

"Really? Wow, you must be hungry."

He smiled that charming smile again. "My work requires a significant amount of energy."

I tilted my head, studying him. He was very well spoken, so I didn't think he was a construction worker. Most doctors wore their scrubs, and he was too well built to be a teacher or a cook.

Plus, I didn't get that vibe from him. He was something else.

"Are you part of the SPU?"

His smile slipped a little. Almost like he was confused. Maybe I'd spoken too fast. Probably.

"The Storm Protection Union," I enunciated.

His smirk came back, a little more guarded than before. "A division of it, yes."

I wanted to ask him more, like what kind of divisions the SPU had and which one he worked for. Honestly, I just wanted to keep talking to him. Cute guys barely even looked at me. This guy was a walking fantasy, and he was actually looking in my eyes when I spoke to him, as if he was interested in what I was saying.

No way I could be this lucky.

Better to play it cool, though. Last thing I wanted to do was creep Mystery Man out.

"That's really impressive. And super brave."

He did his smirk-slight-nod thing again. It might have been automatic for him, but I thought it was super sexy. Especially with that warm look in his blue, blue eyes.

"Okay, I'll get this started for you. Can I get you something to drink? We've got filtered water and freshly squeezed orange juice if you don't mind pulp."

Mystery Man grimaced. I couldn't help but laugh. "Water it is."

His face relaxed. "Thank you, Ava."

My heart skidded again. "How do you know my name?" *And can you say it again?*

His smile widened and he dropped his eyes to my chest, jutting his chin. I looked down, and felt like an idiot.

"Name tag. Right. At least I remembered to wear it today."

This guy was making me a flustered mess, but I couldn't be mad at him. Not when his smile was so open and inviting. I turned and left before I could make an even bigger fool of myself.

After I delivered the order, which made Carrie suspicious because it wasn't often that we offered anything off menu, I hurried to the jugs of fresh water we kept under the table. I filled a glass and all but sprinted out of the kitchen to the restaurant.

Mystery Man was still sitting with his back to the corner. He was back in hawk-mode, looking left and right as if on the prowl for threats. He saw me making my way over and grinned at what was probably a goofy expression on my face.

My heart was beating a little too quickly, but I was working up the courage to at least ask his name. Even if I never saw him again, I didn't want to let him leave as just a stranger. My luck was holding so far.

Then I handed him the glass, and our fingers touched.

And I got the biggest static shock of my life. It ran up my whole arm and snapped into my heart.

"Ow," I grimaced. I pulled my hand back and shook it out. "Sorry, that was weird."

I looked at Mystery Man and went still.

He'd gone as rigid as a statue, his eyes wide and a look of shock on his face. The glass of water remained in his outstretched hand, like he didn't know he was holding it.

"Um, are you okay?"

He just stared at me, making me uncomfortable for the first time. Then he set the water glass down, and his glittering eyes sharpened like blades.

"Yes," he said coldly. "I'm fine."

I could have sworn there was a growl in his voice. It kind of scared me.

"Uh, well, your food will be here soon. Is there anything else I can get you?"

Good thing I said that all the time. Repetition might save me.

"No."

Or not.

"Okay. I'm sorry." *Though I don't know what I did.*

Having no desire to aggravate him further– he looked like the kind of guy who was familiar with fistfights– I hurried over to the doctor. He thanked me and left, so I started cleaning his table.

More customers began to trickle in, and though I hurried to get them seated and take their orders, I felt Mystery Man's eyes on me the whole time. I wanted to glance at him and see if he still had that angry look in his face, but I was too worried he did.

I shouldn't have been scared. I should have given him some kind of attitude– *Excuuuse me, I didn't know you'd be cranky from a little static, which didn't even mess up your perfect hair*– but I wasn't brave enough. If Piper had been here, I would have asked her. She wasn't afraid to give anyone a piece of her mind.

But I wasn't as strong as Piper. I wasn't as brave.

Still, I'd taken his order, and now I had to serve him. I trudged back toward the kitchen and reached for the flap–

Carrie burst through with two plates in her hands. One with rice, another with fries.

"Uh, I think that's my order," I said.

"Oh yeah? Well, the stud over there is in my section, and it doesn't look like he's very happy with you."

I glanced over my shoulder. Sure enough, Mystery Man was glaring daggers at me. He hadn't even touched his water. I winced and quickly looked away.

"That's what I thought," Carrie said snidely. "Why don't you let the big girl handle the handsome man?"

I glared, but she brushed past me without second glance. I didn't want to watch Carrie drape herself over Mystery Man, so I shuffled back into the kitchen to do menial work. Maci and Mikey noticed my mood swings, but said nothing, which I was grateful for.

It wasn't long before the construction crew rush started, and I was forced to go back into the restaurant to wait tables. I made a point of not looking in the corner where Mystery Man was, yet I felt him watch my every movement.

From the corner of my eye, I would catch his sharp, hawk gaze on me like I was the rabbit he wanted to devour. I was starting to think I should change his name from Mystery Man to Creepy Man.

Maybe Hot Creepy Man would be truer to his nature. Unfortunately, his bad attitude didn't keep him from being physically stunning.

Carrie was relentless. Her fingers brushed his arm, his shoulders, the back of his neck. She tried to shove her boobs against his cheek more than once.

Mystery Man barely paid her a second glance, often leaning away when she got uncomfortably close. He ate mechanically and without a smile, focused on me the entire time.

Whoever said that women were more complicated and temperamental than men had clearly never met this guy.

I told myself I didn't care; he would be gone soon and we would never cross paths again, so I shouldn't have been concerned that Carrie was trying to get into his pants.

Then I saw her write on a napkin, press her lips to it, and slide it next to his plate. Though he didn't look at the napkin once, Carrie considered this a victory. She put her hand on his far shoulder, then lightly dragged her nails across the expanse of his broad shoulders. Her fingers must have touched the skin at the back of his neck, because he shifted in his seat. Carrie laughed heartily and sashayed toward the kitchen. She caught my eye from across the restaurant, smiled wickedly, and winked before disappearing.

She winked at me. *Winked.* Like this was a damn game to her.

The rush was beginning to die down, so I cleaned the tables. I cleared aggressively, dumping the half-eaten food and empty paper plates into a garbage bag. I don't know why I cared. Carrie was just being Carrie. It wasn't the first time she'd done this.

But it had never happened to me.

Typical. The first guy to actually take interest me for five minutes until he got spooked by a static shock, and she throws herself at him like a pitcher throwing to a batter.

I kept telling myself it didn't matter, that I was getting upset for no reason, that this kind of high school drama had no place in the world right now. Bigger picture. That's what I should have been focusing on.

Yet I was shoving chairs back into place. I pushed garbage into a plastic, black chasm. I almost scrubbed the paint off the tables. My effort to erase the jealously and irrational anger from my heart. I finished one, moved onto the next, and slapped my hand into it too hard.

"Ow!" I barked.

Wind billowed through the back of the tent. It had steadily gotten windy over the course of the day, the walls of the tent swaying inward and outward, but this was stronger than before. A shriek came from the kitchen.

Alarmed and worried, I dropped the rag and ran to the kitchen to see what was wrong. I threw back the curtain, and a rush of heat flashed across my face. The fire from the barbecue had surged, almost two feet high. Mikey and Maci had backed up, shock and bewilderment clear on their faces. Carrie was freaking out in the corner, blubbering and shaking.

I snapped out of the shock first, turning to the table and grabbing the pitcher of water from the countertop. It was heavy, but I managed to throw all the water on the flames. They were quickly doused, replaced by smoke and a sharp sizzling sound. We all watched the barbecue like it was going to launch itself at us and seek revenge.

When nothing else happened, I slumped back against the edge of the counter. My heart was still beating at a rapid-fire pace, but I knew we were okay.

Just to confirm, I asked, "Is everyone okay? Did anyone get hurt?"

"No," Mikey replied in a shaky voice. "No, I think we're all fine."

"What happened?"

"I have no idea. One minute the barbecue is fine, then this wind blows in and it's a fucking Roman candle." He winced and looked at me." Sorry, Ava."

I shrugged. People assumed that because I never really swore myself, I had some kind of aversion to it. Not true, I just saved it for special occasions. Kind of like chocolate– too much isn't good, but in the right amounts, it was a real treat.

Maybe I was still in shock after all.

As I stood there staring at the smoking barbecue, I barely heard Mikey say they would need to tell the fire department there was no damage or Maci comforting Carrie, but I noticed the wind.

The complete lack of it.

Not even the breeze that had been building earlier could be felt. I looked up through the open framework of the roof, past the swirling grey smoke from the fire. Clouds were forming over the sky. Nothing unusual, and the clouds were harmless white puffs, but the sky had been clear this morning. I couldn't help but feel like they were an omen of something to come.

"Ava?"

I brought my head down and looked at Mikey. "Can you go outside and make sure everyone knows things are okay back here?"

I grimaced. Last I checked– not that I had meant to– Mystery Man was the only person still in the restaurant. He'd passed the two hour mark.

But Carrie was having a meltdown, and Mikey and Maci were rattled. I gathered my pride, pasted on a smile, and walked out of the kitchen. I sucked in a breath to call at Mystery Man so I wouldn't have to go near his table and see that dark, condemning look on his face.

But he was gone.

Though he had left a tip.

I walked to his table, where his food sat barely eaten. It didn't look like he'd touched the water glass at all.

In the middle of the table was a long object bundled in grey cloth. Resting on top of it was the napkin Carrie had given him, flipped over to leave a message written in a manly scrawl:

Keep it. Protect yourself.

Okay… That wasn't foreboding or anything.

Putting the note aside, I peeled back the cloth. Silver glinted into my eyes, and I stepped back.

A slender silver dagger with a navy blue hilt wrapped in black leather stared up at me. At the top of the hilt was a circular iron pommel. Printed inside it was a design– tear-shaped rain that circled a strong arm holding up a sword.

Breath tangled in my chest. I remembered the man in the hurricane, the one the Stormkind had been afraid of.

The man who stabbed me with a crystal blade.

I put my hands on the table and struggled to even my breathing. This wasn't the same knife. I knew it wasn't. This blade was iron. The one that scarred me was crystal, almost as alive as the Stormkind had been. I knew that. I *knew* it.

But I didn't know how Mystery Man had gotten it, or why he left it with an ominous message. Maybe it wasn't meant for me. Maybe he wanted to give it to Carrie.

Carrie, who he'd completely ignored.

No. This was for me, for reasons I could only guess at.

And I didn't want it. Put a blade in your hand, and you're asking for violence. Particularly if it was a dagger like this, something that was clearly pristine and valuable.

I could leave it in the trade box. I could give it to Mikey, who could trade it for a new barbecue if he couldn't get the other one fixed. I could threaten to use it on Carrie's hair the next time she tried to steal my tips.

Okay, that was a little aggressive. No reason to lower myself to her level.

Which left me with one option– buck up and take it. Technically, it was a gift, and the streets were a little more dangerous at night.

I closed the cloth bundle and tucked the dagger into the back of my belt, lifting my shirt over it so it was concealed. I would hand it over to one of the donation facilities. There were dozens of them on the way home. Someone else could use it for protection, because as far as I was concerned, I didn't need to be protected.

Did I?

***

Whenever there was a crisis, no matter how minor, it had to be reported. Records of what was lost needed to be given to the Rations and Distributions Departments, which had been set up five years ago. They took note of what was lost, what was needed, and what could be spared.

The fire department confirmed that Mikey lost the barbecue. Since the Papaya Cantina was a highly popular source of food for the construction sites nearby, he'd get a new one tomorrow. He had to fill out forms for that. Maci had to fill out one as a witness, and I had to fill out another one as the person who took action to douse the fire.

It was all as pointless as it sounded, but having some semblance of order made us believe the state was getting back on track again. For now, all we had was a crumbled brick pile that used to be a bank.

By the time the interviews and forms were done, it was dark out. Mikey and Maci offered to walk me home, but Mikey had gotten some minor burns on his hands. I knew he was hurting, so I told him to go home and relax. Besides, Carrie had walked home, so I could too.

Granted, Carrie left before the firemen arrived, claiming emotional trauma, but it was all technicalities, really.

Though I still intended to donate the dagger Mystery Man left me, I was hesitant about making my journey home longer than I needed to. I only lived about ten blocks away, but when I'd walked home on previous nights, the streets had been alive and awake.

Now they looked desolate and creepy.

Sidewalks, once bathed in yellow light, were littered with uprooted lampposts and obstacles that would have tripped me end over end if I hadn't had my flashlight. Late night shops and cafes were now crumpled shadows that surrounded me like slumbering monsters. Cold ocean water from last night's minor flood splashed around my ankle boots– the sneakers had been done for– and salted the air.

In the distance, I could hear echoing hoots and hollers, as if some kind of celebration was going on down the street.

Only there wasn't. Those shouts were from gang members.

The idea that everyone would work together, no matter who they were or where they came from, was a nice thought. And that's all it was– a thought. A wishful fantasy that we could put aside petty differences and help each other until the city was healed.

Gangs didn't think that way. They saw brokenhearted, scared, desperate people, and knew exactly how to exploit them.

You were hungry? They would get you food, by stealing it from the Ration Depots or the restaurants. You were scared? They would protect you, as long as you were willing to give up something in return– food, water, clothes, and weapons were the least appalling favors. You were lost and alone? The gangs would take you in, give you a new family, provided you show them the fiercest loyalty and could survive a brutal beating.

Not everyone did.

The gangs started operating only a week after the Centennial, long enough for them to re-gather, stake out territory, and plot their schemes. We knew they were back in action because of the graffiti and marks left on certain buildings in downtown Lantana. The police tried to shut them down when they could, but they were too short-staffed. The Missing Boards were growing larger, the rescue workers needing every hand they could take to help dig out the thousands of people still trapped in their basements. With so many citizens working to get the town back on its legs, there was only so much volunteering the rest of us could do. Like it or not– and out here, alone in the dark, I definitely did *not*– the gangs were allowed to be out in full force.

My free hand went to my back where Mystery Man's dagger was looped through my belt. I could feel the hard steel through the cloth wrap against my skin. I took a self-defense course once, but I was no Rhonda Rousey. I would be useless in a fight. I didn't even know if I had the stomach to hurt someone with a knife if they attacked me. Maybe I could threaten them, but I seriously doubted I would intimidate anyone with my hundred and ten pound, five-foot-two frame, let alone a hardened gangster.

I quickened my pace, not wanting to gain any attention. I'd already done a great job of avoiding it, and had every intention of keeping the streak going. I was over halfway home, so I just had to–

Glass and wood shattered ahead of me. I skidded to a stop. More excited shouts filtered out of the darkness. They sounded like they were around the corner. So much for a straight shot home. Time to take a detour.

I glanced over my shoulder, and watched my luck plummet even deeper into a black hole of awfulness.

Two men were behind me in the darkness. My flashlight produced a small beam, but it was enough to be seen in the dark.

I didn't know where they materialized from or if they were following me at all, but with the way my day had been going, I was happy to assume the worst.

I made a quick left turn and hurried down the street. I looked over my shoulder to see if the shadowy guys were still walking ahead.

They weren't. They'd turned down the street and were coming after me.

My pulse sped up. The men moved with purpose, gaining distance on me. I had no what they wanted, if they wanted to rob me or worse. I wasn't going to stop and ask either.

I threw my hair over my shoulder to see how much closer they had gotten.

The answer was: very.

I had maybe twenty feet before they snatched me up. My chest was so constricted from panic that my breath was coming in jumpy bursts, like I was going to choke on it at any second.

My hand was clenched around the flashlight so hard I was sure I would crush it. I glanced left and right, wondering if there was somewhere I could hide, because there was no way I could defend myself.

The words from Mystery Man's scrawled note crept into my mind.

Keep it. Protect yourself.

Yeah. Sure. Easy enough, right? Just pull a daring defense against two full grown men. Nothing would go wrong there.

Nothing like say, getting beaten to death and left in the middle of the street to be pickpocketed before being dumped in one of the swelling graveyards for those who weren't so lucky to survive the Centennial.

My mind raced, scrambling for even the semblance of a plan. It didn't have to be a good plan. At this point, I just wanted something to keep me alive.

The worst part was that they weren't saying anything to me. No catcalls or hollers. They acted as if I hadn't seen them, when they must have known otherwise. They moved with a cold, sharp precision, similar to the way Mystery Man moved when he'd come into the restaurant.

Where are you now, Mystery Man? Why can't you be here to protect me?

The fantastical thought had barely left my mind when I heard wood beams splash and clatter onto the wet street. The men behind me cursed. I didn't stop to see if they were going to follow me, didn't even turn around to see what had caused the noise. I followed the single instinct that seemed to be spoken by Mystery Man himself.

Run.

I bolted like the Devil himself was on my heels, pumping my legs so fast and so hard I thought I would shatter something. I turned around the nearest slump of ruined houses, snapping off my flashlight and hiding from view. The sudden dark sent a spike of fear into my heart. I stood in place, shaking and waiting for my eyes to adjust to the anemic moonlight spilling over the streets. Down the street from where I'd run, I could hear the sounds of a fistfight.

Wanting to know how much time I'd bought myself, and partly curious about how a fight had broken out, I crouched and peered around the pile of ruined housing.

All I could see were shadows, but the two guys who'd followed me were fighting against a third. They were good. *Really* good.

But they weren't better than the third guy.

He ducked under a sweeping kick and snapped back to his feet, punching his fist into the kicking-man's chest. He whipped his other fist across my second follower's jaw, sending him spinning. The third man barely let his attackers touch him, moving like water. Violent, uncontrollable, powerful water.

I wondered who he was, and where he had come from.

Instinct took me over again.

Run.

Part of me wished I were brave enough to march out into the street and help my savior, but odds were that I would just distract him. Besides, if the sudden sweeping kick he gave to the man on his left was any indication, he could take care of himself.

Thanks, Mystery Guy, I thought, making the distinction between him and Mystery Man.

I turned around and fumbled through the dark, jogging blindly for a couple minutes until the sounds of the fight had faded from my ears. Only then did I turn on the flashlight, slow my pace, and think about three questions that would nag me for the rest of the night:

Who were the people following me?

Who was the man that saved me?

And how the hell did I get onto Pine Street?

CHAPTER 4

Since I made it "home" safely about thirty minutes later– I *totally* took a wrong turn near the end, thanks to my skittish nerves on seeing that fight– I thought the night wouldn't get any worse.

"Home" for my family and me was now Park Vista Community High school, the place I had tried to escape to. It was a volunteer and SPU facility that held three thousand survivors alone, not including the fifty nurses, supply distributors, and SPU guards to keep pandemonium and panic to a minimum. We all slept in sleeping bags in classrooms and hallways, since the gym had been converted into a guarded supply and medical station where hungry and moaning wounded could be secluded from the rest of us who were newly homeless.

I made it to the school as stormy clouds began to form overhead, folding over the moonlight. Nobody was looking forward to a rainstorm so soon after the Centennial, but it wasn't like we had a choice in the matter. Mom was a mess with worry, bundling me in a spare blanket and all but spoon-feeding me the stew from the cafeteria. I wasn't cold and not hungry thanks to my little adventure on the walk home, but she was being a mom, so I let her fuss over me.

After telling her, Dad, and James what happened– though I decided to skip on the details of the fight, since I didn't want them to worry and working at the restaurant gave me something to do– I looked for Piper. I had seen her a couple times at the school, but we hadn't talked much. She was worried about her dad's leg and had been snappier than I was used to. Something was going on with her, and she wouldn't tell me about it.

That also meant I couldn't tell her what was happening to me, and I needed to tell someone. I was missing a week of my life and apparently being stalked by creepy guys in the shadows. I couldn't have that. Not with the piece of memory I did have before that blank week.

The memory that wouldn't leave me alone, not even when I finally dropped onto my sleeping bag in the hallway and found sleep…

Pain. Four simple letters, one little word. It didn't even sound that threatening, really, and it certainly didn't encompass the depth of what he'd put me through.

Every hour, every minute, every second was torture. Detailed and intimate. A bone-deep anguish that stripped me down to the marrow.

I didn't know where I was. The ground was hard and unforgiving, just like every other surface I'd lain on for… however long I had been here. My body was soaked and beaten, like I'd been drowned and pummeled with an inch of my life.

For all I knew, I had been.

"Fascinating," a hoarse voice said. "She survived the torrent. I did not believe she was so strong."

"Nor did I," he said. Him. The man who did this to me. The man who stabbed me with a crystal blade in the middle of a hurricane. "She is a last resort, but she has proven far more industrious than my other targets. Let us see if she can withstand the other trials."

I opened my mouth to beg, scream, anything, but something sharp touched my chest and the torture began again.

Frigid water replaced my blood, ice wrapped around my bones like glacial fingers. Frost glued to my lungs and throat, make each breath brittle and short. My heart thudded heavily against my chilled ribs, each beat threatening to crack the bones under my skin. Tears slipped from the corners of my eyes and hardened on my skin.

"It seems we have success on the second trial," he remarked. "Truly remarkable."

The intensity of the pain dulled, but I still felt its cold burn throbbing in tune with my heart.

"What are you going to try next?" the hoarse voice asked.

"Well, since you have inquired about it so reverently, I think we shall witness how she endures the transition from frost to cinders."

The switch was so immediate I almost blacked out. My skin tightened, all moisture leeched away until my flesh cracked. The water in my veins evaporated, making my blood thin and shallow. The frost in my lungs gave way to a choking dust that turned my throat to sandpaper. My eyes were as dry as my skin, swollen and burning. I gasped for oxygen, but it tasted like ash against my inflamed tongue.

I wanted to cry, but the tears dried up behind my eyelids. I felt like I was a brittle branch, about to be snapped in half under one unforgiving boot.

"Does this appease you?" he asked.

There was a pause. They were considering me, but I couldn't see them. The men hovering above me were faceless shadows in a dark room.

"It suffices," replied the hoarse-voiced man in a bored tone.

For whatever reason, those were the words that broke me. They weren't even spoken by him, the man who'd stabbed me and took me to those places to do things to me. Things I couldn't even comprehend, because it wasn't torture by the definition I knew. It wasn't a beating or a drowning or electrocution. It was something else. Something otherworldly, and a thousand times more perverse.

And I was sufficient for it.

"Please," I begged when the pain in my throat eased enough for me to speak again. "Please... Stop."

I felt their eyes on me, judging and scrutinizing.

Condemning.

"'Please stop', she says," repeated the man with the broken voice. "As if she thinks this is something to fear. As if she forgets that pain is part of her mortal condition. As if she does not realize it is the lone universal truth—"

"Silence."

Another small word. A line that carried unquestioning authority, as universal as the pain they thought I could tolerate.

I felt him lean down by my head, his rough, callused hand scratching my forehead and moving my hair from my face.

"You are afraid," he crooned. "I understand. Humans are accustomed to fear, the same as they are accustomed to pain. But you must not fear, precious girl, because you will become more than them. You are the first. You will be the first of many."

I shivered, from the cold knot of fear in my chest or the promise of his words, I didn't know.

Then he was towering over me again the way a king towers over his starving subjects.

"There is only one more test, precious girl. And I fear it is the hardest."

He gave me no other warning. No chance to beg for anything. Not even death. There was only a split second between me and the eruption of pain that ripped through my heart.

It spread like wildfire, snapping my muscles tight against my bones. My skin twisted and tightened, like it was being pulled off by invisible hooks. My lungs ballooned, as if they contained the aftershocks of an explosion. My head spun like a tornado, trashing against the inside of my skull. Everything inside me felt like it was being vacuumed out, pulled and squeezed until I was sure the flesh would rip from my bones.

Then the churning in my stomach started, a blazing wave that twisted my belly into knots. The pressure swelled and rose, creaking my ribs until it reached my heart.

Then it plunged in, and I felt my heart explode—

Water slipped into my mouth, gagging my scream.

I snapped my eyes open and pushed myself up. Water sloshed around my wrists. The sleeping bag was completely submerged and the entire front of my body was soaked. I sat on my heels, erasing the last of the nightmare to take in the chaos around me.

The entire floor was flooded. Rainwater rushed in from the front doors in crushing waves, a torrent so strong it was taking four men per door to close them.

I got to my feet and looked for James and my parents—

"Ava!"

I whirled when I heard my little brother's strangled cry. He was standing about ten feet away from me, clutching his chest while scared tears lined his cheeks. I raced through the hallway, kicking up water and gathering him in my arms. His chest bumped rapidly against mine, his breath strained and shallow in my ear. I rubbed my hand up and down his back, whispering in his ear.

"It's okay, you're okay, just breathe kiddo, just breathe."

"You—" he gasped raggedly, "screamed."

I faltered. This was the first time I noticed the ache in my throat. I knew I had been screaming in my dream, but I had no idea I'd done the same thing in real life.

"You have your inhaler?" I asked James, backing against the wall. Around me, the survivors yelled for help, directions, and loved ones. No one was ready for or wanted to endure another catastrophe so soon after the last one.

James shifted awkwardly in my arms. He struggled to match my breathing and dig out the plastic bag that held his inhaler. I helped him open the bag and took it out, placing it against his lips. I pushed the button down and felt him jump as the medication pushed into his lungs. He'd regained his breathing, but I could still feel him shaking.

Finally, I caught sight of my Dad. He was one of the men who managed to push the front doors closed. He all but ran over to us.

"You two okay?" he asked, placing one hand on my back before taking James from me.

"Yeah," I replied, though it tasted like a lie. "What happened?"

Dad shook his head. "No idea. You started having some kind of spasm. I tried to wake you up, but I couldn't. It started to pour outside and then you just... You screamed this horrible scream, and the doors broke open..."

I heard every word he said. Watched different emotions play across his face. Strength became concern, turned to fear, and then confusion.

That was when I realized I was shaking. Crying.

Behind my father, the men pushed against the door to brace it.

Dad gently put James down and wrapped me in an embrace. I shuddered against him, needing his comfort. Dad's smell was wet and his clothes were cold, but I was able to feel past it and draw comfort from him. He reminded me of the home I'd lost, the safety I'd known.

It took longer than I wanted to admit, but eventually I calmed down and eased out of his arms. Across from us, the men cautiously stepped back from the doors. The flooding must have stopped. At least one crisis had been averted.

My father and brother didn't notice the stilled waters. They only noticed me.

"What happened, Ava? Even as a child, you slept like a stone. What changed?"

A hitch grew in my throat. My body was calm, but my nerves had been shaken violently.

All I could do was tell the truth.

"I don't know."

***

Thankfully, no one was hurt in last night's flash flood. Some of the rations were lost and everyone was soaked, but once the SPU gave the all clear, we were allowed to get back onto our soggy sleeping bags and regain our sleep.

Everyone but me, that is.

By the time I dragged my feet to work, I could barely stand on them. I was exhausted and traumatized, and lying to anyone who asked if I was okay. I managed to find some coffee in the kitchen (I can tell you right now that we *all* would have lost our minds if coffee had been lost in the Centennial), and three cups later, I was awake enough to pay attention to customer orders and make sure they were going to the right tables.

I also noticed that Mystery Man was back, and that he wasn't in Carrie's section this time. He was in mine, and it was too busy for her to steal him from me. Which meant I had to deal with him.

The dagger he left me was still wrapped in its cloth and hidden against the base of my spine. I'd meant to drop it off at a donation center– I really had– but after the stalkers last night, I couldn't bear to give it away. Until I made up my mind about where it would finally go, I decided on keeping it.

It was a busy enough night that I hadn't been able to go to his table more than a couple times to refill his water glass. I gave him the barest greeting and my weakest smile to be polite. All he did was glare at me.

Three hours later, Mystery Man was still in his corner, drinking water and scowling at me. Even worse, the caffeine was wearing off. I was starting to crash. Mental note– three cups of coffee means three times the debilitation later.

I finished cleaning my tables and went to get Mystery Man's food, now that he'd *finally* ordered. Even Carrie was starting to wonder why he'd been here for so long. I laughed to myself. A smoking hot guy was creeping Carrie out. Wonders never ceased.

"Am I amusing you?"

I jumped at the deep, rolling sound of his voice. I'd forgotten I was walking over here and looking directly at him. I wondered if this was what zombies felt like.

"Sorry, I was thinking about something else," I said. It was half true.

His intoxicating blue eyes flicked to the plates in my hand. "Clearly."

I frowned, then dropped the plates in front of him and turned around.

Mystery Man cleared his throat. I whirled and fixed him with a glare strong enough to match his own.

"This isn't what I ordered."

I took a breath to tell him too damn bad, he could just appreciate it because luxury was rare. Then I noticed I'd dropped someone else's dirty plate in front of him.

I didn't know whether to laugh, or be horrified at what I'd done.

"Crap," I said. "Crap, crap, crap."

Ducking my head so he wouldn't see the embarrassment flooding my cheeks, I scurried over to correct the mistake.

"You're quite out of sorts," he remarked. Not that he sounded concerned.

"I didn't sleep well," I mumbled, lifting the plate away.

"I can see that. There are bags under your eyes."

I narrowed said eyes. "You know, most girls would like to hear that they look pretty even if they hadn't slept more than an hour all night."

His expression mirrored mine. "I'm not most men."

Clearly. "Yeah. I got that when you left a freaking knife on my table."

I didn't say it loudly, but Mystery Man went deathly still. If I'd been more rested and in a better mood, I wouldn't have snapped at him, but I wasn't, so I did.

"And did you find cause to use it?"

"Of course not," I retorted. "Why on earth would I use a knife?"

He looked at me like I was an idiot. "To keep others from harming you. What else would you use it for?"

Patience. That's what I was supposed to use here, right? Shame I didn't have any.

"Well, let's see, I could use it as a letter opener or to cut a steak, or–"

"I left you a weapon. Not a toy."

"How flattering. Want to tell me why?"

Impossibly blue eyes bored into me for so deep and so long I was certain he was reading my mind. Or trying to. I really hoped that wasn't the case. Sexy as he was, I didn't want him to know anything about me. I didn't want him to see how scared I'd been last night when I was being followed, or how I had been afraid to sleep because I didn't want to relive that torture-dream. I didn't want him to realize that even though he was being a world-class jerk, I still hoped to know him. I missed the person I met yesterday, the man with a polite demeanor and charming half-smile. And I *definitely* didn't want him to know that attitude or no attitude, I still thought he was the most gorgeous person I'd ever seen.

"I told you," he reiterated. "It's for your protection."

"How do you know I need it? What if I'm a jiu jitsu queen with an arsenal of ninja stars on my belt?"

Mystery Man stared blankly at me. Didn't even look at my belt.

I put my hands on my hips. "I didn't ask for your protection. I don't even need it." Because those men who'd followed me last night were likely beaten messes, and they'd pursued me because I was easy prey. It was a fluke, and it wouldn't happen again. The city was too big and too broken. I was a waste of their time.

"Yes, you do," Mystery Man countered. He shook his head. "You don't even realize…"

"Realize what? I had to walk home alone last night, and I'm going to walk home alone tonight, too. You didn't help me then, and you're not going to help me now."

He tilted his head back and sighed. He closed his eyes and whispered so quietly I barely heard him.

"Primes. Why am I always stuck with the stubborn ones?"

That did it. I was tired, rattled, and sick of dealing with a guy who was clearly a jerk and not-so-clearly insane. I'd started two hours earlier than I was scheduled, so I was sure Mikey would let me slip out a little early. It was getting dark, anyway, and the rush was over.

I reached behind my back and withdrew the covered knife. I moved the dirty plate to the table behind me, then smacked the blade down in front of Mystery Man. His eyes jerked toward it.

"Here's the deal, Mystery Man. I don't know who you are, what you think you can protect me from, or why you want me to think you care. You obviously don't like me, and you're not telling me anything. I'm tired, cranky, and like millions of other people, I don't have a home. You drew the last straw, buddy. So do me a favor. Give Mikey and Maci a big tip when you finish your dinner, and leave me alone."

I turned on my heel and stalked away, wondering if I had ever done something like this before. Probably not. I wasn't the kind of girl to throw hissy fits or tantrums. The stress of the Centennial and the trauma I was keeping secret from everyone was getting to me. Even hopeless ditzes like me were allowed to have meltdowns every once in a while, right?

When I asked Mikey and Maci if I could go home, they didn't even ask me why. That put Carrie in a tizzy, and a spring in my step.

After I slipped on my denim jacket and shook my hair from its ponytail, I left through the restaurant. It was the easiest way to the street, and I would be lying if I said I didn't want to show Mystery Man that he hadn't gotten the better of me.

It might have worked too, if the weirdo had been there.

His table was empty except for a set of Swiss Army knives. Figured.

The dagger remained on the table, causing me to scowl. I almost didn't pick it up again, but remembering the gangs and my creepy stalkers from the night before made me reconsider.

Mystery Man didn't want his fancy knife back? Fine. He wasn't going to get it back.

Scooping the dagger up from the table, I changed the direction of my thoughts and decided to try and find Piper. She'd been reclusive lately, which wasn't like her at all. She needed a friend, and I needed to talk. It was a win-win situation.

So of course, my luck took another turn for the worst when I stepped outside, looked up, and saw the rainclouds forming over my head.

"Really?" I cursed them. "Really?"

There was nothing I could do about the storm that sprang up from nowhere, so I tugged my jacket closed, tucked the dagger into the back of my belt, shoved my hands in my jean pockets, and made my way home.

The street was empty, as far as I could see. These days, people bolted at the first sign of a patch of grey cloud. Understandable, but it wasn't that late out, so it shouldn't have been half as dark as it was. Despite what my pride had barked at Mystery Man, I had no desire to be out here, alone in the dark.

I hunched my shoulders and tucked my head down. Until it started to rain. Then I looked up.

The rain wasn't torrential– or even that ominous– yet. For a moment, I could feel a sense of peace with it. A natural kind of feeling that crept into my skin with every drop. I stopped in the middle of the street, craned my neck back, and closed my eyes. I let it absorb through me, a balm for whatever fear and despair had crushed into my soul. For one blissful minute, my mind was blank. There had been no Centennial Storm, no distraught family, no Stormkind or man with a crystal blade. There were no distracted friends, no heartbreaking strangers, and most importantly of all, there was no fear.

It was just me and the rain. Nothing had ever felt more natural. It was such a simple, wonderful thing, that I was able to smile at it–

"You shouldn't be standing in the rain."

I jumped at the deep voice, thinking for one second it was Mystery Man. But Mystery Man's voice had a slow, soothing rumble to it. His voice didn't remind me of an agitated grizzly.

No, only Declan's voice could do that.

He stood to my left, as wet as I was, a broad smile on his face and a glint in his eyes.

A smile and a glint that were sharp as knives.

"What are you doing here, Declan?" I asked. He never came to the Papaya Cantina, for which I was grateful.

He took a step closer to me, the smile sticking to his face like tar. "Waiting for you, of course."

Well, that was unsettling to hear. But not as unsettling as the way his eyes took in my body, the way the rain had flattened my shirt to my stomach and chest.

"You know," he purred, "You don't look like a drowned rat right now. I thought you would. In fact, you're almost pretty."

I was debating on laughing or running.

"Okay," I said. "I'm going home now."

I turned to bolt as far from him as I could. I bumped into someone's chest instead. I looked up at a sharp, angled face with a pinched mouth, dust-colored eyes, and hair the color of blood.

The look he was giving me sent a chill down my spine, and I reached back for the dagger. The crimson haired man moved lightning fast. He reached behind my back and grabbed my wrist. Crushing it in his hand, he plucked the dagger from my fist and tossed it deep into the rainstorm.

So much for protecting myself, I thought grimly.

In a flash, the man grabbed my chin and jerked my head up to his.

"Is she one of them?" Another, razor-sharp voice asked from my right. Oh, God, there were three of them. Surrounding me.

"Yes. And she has been tethered."

I didn't ask what that meant. All I could focus on was his voice. The serrated growl that had seared into my mind when he stood over me, and told me I was *sufficient*.

I grabbed his wrist to pull it away from my face, but he wouldn't let me go.

"Tethered? Are you certain?"

The new voice had been getting closer. Suddenly, new hands were on me, gripping my arms and swiveling me. The third man had a tangle of pale grey hair and navy blue eyes. He was only a little taller than me, but he was broad and his grip was like iron.

The longer he looked at me, the more he scowled.

"Whom are you tethered to?" he demanded. "Who is your Guardian?"

"What? I don't know what you're talking about!"

He growled and shook me. "You lie!" The gentle rain was now a downpour.

"You're aggravating her, Turve," the man from my dream rasped.

I was suddenly ripped away from him, thrown hard onto the cold ground. I yelped and rolled, feeling a sharp sting in my elbow. Grimacing, I sat up.

That was when I noticed the armor the two strangers wore. The black leather and silver iron plating. The hilts of swords crossing behind their backs.

My heart rate staggered, and the rain fell harder.

Turve glared at Declan. "You overstepped your bounds."

Declan, still smiling, shrugged casually. "Couldn't help it. She just makes it so easy." He peered down at me. "Give me a minute, and I'll make sure she comes with us."

"No. You won't."

Turve, Declan, and the raspy-voiced stranger looked at the person behind me. So did I.

He'd swapped the bad boy biker gear for armor almost identical to that of the strangers across from me, except that the leather was midnight blue instead of black, and the plating was a frosty azure instead of silver. The ghost-pale swords in his hands were deadly sharp, streams of water slicking the three foot length and dripping from his clenched hands.

"You asked who she is tethered to," Mystery Man growled. "Now you have your answer."

CHAPTER 5

Mystery Man didn't look away from the three people across from me. He looked like a tiger, muscles coiled and ready to spring on the nearest wild boar.

"Hadrian," Turve's friend rasped. "I never expected you to receive another charge."

"Seems you and your ilk made it necessary, Ferno," Mystery Man– Hadrian– responded venomously. "It seems Edur and Giro were foolish enough to cross paths with me." His smile chilled me to my bones. "I would not expect to see them return soon."

A sickening feeling rolled through my stomach. Memories of the two men following me, the third jumping out of nowhere and saving my life... Had that been Hadrian? Had he fought those two men, who sounded like allies of Turve and Ferno, to help me escape?

Did he kill them?

"Stand up and get behind me, Ava," he commanded, cutting through my thoughts.

I didn't really want to give in to his orders, especially since I might be walking closer to a murderer, but I also didn't want to stay on the ground and get trampled.

I planted my feet and stood up–

A gust of wind slammed into my chest, pushing me away from Hadrian. Toward the people who wanted something from me. I didn't even know what it was yet.

I landed on the road, striking my other elbow. I turned over and found Declan standing over me, that stupid, smug grin on his face.

"Like my trick, Ginger?"

Before I could ask what trick he was talking about, he swung his hand upward. A blast of wind slipped under me and pushed me off the ground. I hovered three feet in the air before he lowered his hand and dropped me.

Or tried to drop me.

A cool rush of water cushioned my fall. I followed its trail, a steady river of raindrops that led directly to Hadrian, and the sword he was using to direct them. His eyes were as dark as a stormy sea, his mouth set in a fierce line.

Declan roared in frustration and kicked me while I was still in the air. I screamed at the sudden pain and yelped again when I hit the ground. Someone shouted and swords began to clash. I turned my head and watched the raspy voiced man– Ferno– rush Hadrian with both swords. Hadrian snapped his eyes to Ferno and clashed with him straightaway. They moved with unnerving speed and grace, both blades hammering against one another with so much force I swore they would break.

Ferno swung both swords at Hadrian's neck and stomach. Hadrian moved faster, using one blade to block the slash to his neck and the other to stop the one at his middle. He pushed them both away and slammed a kick into Ferno's ribs.

Turve lunged, aiming his swords at Hadrian's throat. He deftly ducked under both and jammed his shoulder into Turve's chest. As the stocky man staggered back, Hadrian spun and slammed his elbow into Turve's head.

Ferno roared and charged for Hadrian, shoving one of his blades toward his chest. Hadrian spun again and blocked the sword, but Ferno was lost in some kind of frenzy. He hacked and slashed like he was trying to cut Hadrian in half. I watched the grim determination in Hadrian's eyes as he battled, saw the anger on Turve's face as he recovered and gripped both swords. Then he whipped his head at Declan.

"Take her!"

I saw the sudden flash in Hadrian's eyes. He heard Turve and looked at me. The split second cost him. He managed to get Ferno away from him, but Turve had another plan. He put the swords across his back and manipulated his hands, like he was cupping an invisible bowling ball. Around me, the wind picked up. Turve shoved his hands outward. The same force that had been tossing me around hit Hadrian and knocked him across the road. Ferno and Turve charged him while he was on the ground.

I didn't know what to do. I couldn't watch Hadrian die, but I couldn't fight. I didn't even have a weapon–

A fist knotted in my hair and pulled up. I yelped and grabbed a thick wrist. My heels skidded along the pavement as I was dragged against a sturdy chest.

"Looks like your Guardian isn't very good at his job, Ginger. You don't even know what you're capable of now, do you?"

"Let me go!" I shouted. I thrashed and flung my arms back, uselessly, as it turned out. If I didn't hit something inconsequential on Declan's body, I missed him all together.

"You're supposed to be like me, now. Looks like they're going to make short work of your Guardian, so why don't we see how strong they made you?"

Declan let go of my hair and shoved me forward. I staggered and whirled around, shivering when I saw the cold look on his face. I had no idea what he was talking about, let alone what was going on. I didn't have time to think about it, either. Declan shoved out his hands.

A spark of blue light and a creaking noise came from my right. Whatever Declan tried to do was suddenly blocked by a creeping wall of ice. I looked over my shoulder and saw that Hadrian was standing. Frost circled his hand and the silver sword clutched in it, encasing it in a pale blue cast. He didn't look longer than he had to, ducking under Ferno's latest strike and slicing his sword toward Turve to keep him from attacking his back.

Declan shouted with rage, the wind around us picking up. Through the icy wall, I saw his shadow push forward. A gale of wind crashed into the wall and cracked it into a million pieces. I lifted my arm and blocked the jagged icy shards as best as I could. I lowered my hand as Declan charged for me.

I didn't think about what I was doing, didn't bother to understand it. I just wanted him to get *away* from me.

I held out my hands, ready to push him back.

My whole body shivered, like I'd been plunged into a cool river. Blood felt thick and sluggish in my veins, and my arms were heavy as I held them up. I grimaced at the bizarre sensation, hoping I would have enough strength to shoo Declan away. He kept storming closer, eyes wild and violent. I stepped back and thrust out my arms.

And Declan did get pushed back. But I never touched him.

Rainwater curved before my eyes. It bent in the air, the drops becoming horizontal as they darted toward Declan like needles. They struck his chest and halted him. He grimaced and clutched his chest. In that split second while he looked like he was in pain, I glanced at my hands. Only one question came to mind:

What the hell?!

Declan shifted on his feet and I looked up at him. The smug bully I'd seen before was gone, replaced with an angry brute that didn't look pleased about a little girl landing a hit against him.

"So you do know a couple tricks." His grin was murderous, which made the situation even more terrifying, because I didn't know what he was talking about. "They won't be enough, Ginger."

He was right. They weren't.

Declan pushed out his hands again. Blasts of air hit me like fists, battering the sides of my body and crushing the air from my lungs. He held me in place with one hand, then reached out to the side. I watched him flick his wrist, spinning it into a circle.

Then I watched the debris from the building on my left pitch and spiral, rising upward and turning into a funnel.

A tornado made of shrapnel.

Declan grinned his dark grin, winked at me, and swept the tornado in my direction. The whirlwind of shattered brick and serrated metal spun in a blurring cycle, churning violently and creeping out of the ruins. My hair was thrown away from the sides of my face as it drew closer, kicking aside garbage and slicing apart the raindrops around it.

I couldn't move, trapped in whatever invisible barrier Declan had crushed around me. I couldn't ask Hadrian for help when he was fighting two warriors with swords and serious animosity toward him. I was on my own.

But what the hell was I going to do?

I scrabbled for some kind of idea– *I need to move–* tried to remember how the rainwater bent to protect me. Had I done that? I didn't know for sure, but the bad guys seemed to think I had some kind of power, so I didn't see the harm in trying something outlandish and insane.

Plus, I was desperate.

I couldn't move my hands, so I concentrated on the tornado shifting toward me. I thought about stopping it, holding it in place, turning it around, anything–

Frost snaked across the ground like a streak of lightning. It crept under the shrapnel tornado and gathered at the peak. The frost interwove with the spinning shrapnel, freezing over the pieces until the stony grey particles became frosted white.

Declan bellowed again, thrusting out his hand to push the icy whirlwind at me. He concentrated so completely on the tornado that his hold on me loosened. I staggered from the released pressure, almost losing my balance.

Strong arms circled me. A hard chest pressed to my back. I opened my mouth to scream.

"Trust me," Hadrian said in my ear.

It was all he had time to say. The tornado shot toward us like a bullet, shattering out of Declan's control. Razor sharp debris exploded outward, a scattershot mess of metal and brick that would slice and batter us.

Hadrian kept his arms around me, still holding onto his swords, then pivoted so his back was to the explosion. The temperature around me dropped. His arms froze my chest. I looked down. The blades of his pale silver swords were glowing with white, frosty light. The frost swept over the ground and encased it, crawling into the air like spider-webbed glass.

He was cocooning us in ice.

I just didn't know if he would be fast enough.

Ice crunched and groaned behind me. The debris was hitting the frosty wall. Hadrian suddenly jerked and tightened his cold arms. His arms pushed against my bruised ribs, and a hiss of pain slipped from his teeth. He was hurt.

He was pressed too close to my back for me to see his face, or the injury he'd taken. All I could do was look ahead.

Turve and Ferno were still standing and scowling. Rage filled their faces. They wanted blood, and the ice wall was weak in front of us. They could have cut us down without any problem. Hadrian's grip wasn't loosening any time soon.

But they were hesitating.

Because I'm in front of Hadrian, and they want him dead. Not me. They want me for something else.

I had no idea what that something else was, and didn't want to find out.

Shards of ice spat past us. The frosty light from the swords was getting weaker. Hadrian was shaking. He couldn't protect us for much longer.

Images of rainwater bending and shooting into Declan's chest like darts rushed through my mind. Ghostly sensations prickled my skin when I recalled the thick, watery feeling in my veins.

I was scared to ask, but I did anyway. "Do I have powers like him? Declan?"

Hadrian's breath was ragged in my ear. "Yes."

Adrenaline shot through my veins. I wasn't entirely sure I believed it, but with Hadrian hurt and that group out there ready to kill him and capture me, I would play along for now.

"Tell me what to do with them," I said.

He shuddered again. "You're not ready."

I nudged him roughly with my elbow. "Bigger picture, Hadrian! Tell me what to do!"

I didn't think he would answer me. Around us, barrages of wind shoved wreckage onto the street. Bricks became wrecking balls. Strips of rebar were spears.

Then he whispered, "Imagine the rain becoming hail. Use the energy of the storm around you."

If there was a lesson more confusing than that, I didn't want to know what kind of class it was for. So I imagined it was make-believe, that I knew what I was doing with... whatever power I had.

I closed my eyes and thought about the rain dousing us. Recalled its cool caress before Declan and his new pals showed up. Wished it were colder. Harder. That the raindrops were like chunks of broken glass, deadly and sharp.

The air outside of the shield became frigid. My skin was covered in goose bumps, and my lungs were tight. The raindrops turned white, crystallized together until they were icicles.

I narrowed my eyes and watched them fall. My heart was galloping in a body that felt too cold.

In front of me, Turve and Ferno stood helplessly against the onslaught. Their arms were raised, protecting their faces but little else. The falling ice cut lines across their forearms and backs. I heard Declan yell behind me. He must have been enduring the same thing.

Hadrian's arms finally uncoiled from me. The ice wall fell away. He stepped back and turned me around.

Rain had drenched his hair, shadows played across his face and danced in the shallow cut on his cheek. His eyes were electric, the dual blues shining like cold fire.

"Take the shrapnel out."

Hadrian turned again and showed me his back. And the jagged piece of metal sticking out of his upper left shoulder blade. I winced, my eyes trailing down his back to his scabbard. Printed into the leather was a sigil, a broadsword pointed up amongst a torrent of rain. I gasped, the hail pounding the street around me. It was almost identical to the one I'd seen on the man who stabbed me.

No, that one's different. It was a sword cutting through waves, not raindrops–

"Now, Ava!" Hadrian barked, bringing me out of the memory.

I didn't want to hurt him, but that shard couldn't stay in his back. We weren't out of the fight yet.

I gritted my teeth and put one hand on the middle of his back. The other curled around the cold metal. I shoved his spine and pulled the shrapnel at the same time. Hadrian grunted and stumbled forward, released from the shard.

"I'm sor–"

He spun around, ignored me, and shoved his swords into the ground. Frost exploded from the tip of the blades, layering the road again to block us from Turve and Ferno. Then the frost hardened to ice, and another wall sprang up. This one covered in thorny icicles that stabbed out at the two warriors.

They skidded to a stop to avoid being impaled, glaring murderously at Hadrian.

Turve scowled and sliced his blades together. Metal shrieked against metal, and a crush of wind batted into us. I slipped a little, but Hadrian kept his ground. He tightened his grip on his swords and pushed the wall closer to Turve.

I didn't see Ferno until I started looking for him. The blood-haired warrior was running to Hadrian's open side, slicing his sword against a patch of unfrosted road.

Mud kicked up with it, and went straight into Hadrian's eye.

He yelled sharply, off balance and blind. Ferno ran with both swords held out.

I spun and reached for the icicles again, wanting them to dart to Ferno as I'd done with the rain to Declan.

It worked.

The shards of hail twisted and slammed into Ferno's chest like daggers. He skidded to a stop and howled in pain. The sound cut straight to my heart, and all I could see was the blood, the oozing trickles of it spilling past Ferno's armor, made all the brighter from the melting ice coating his chest–

Wind hammered around us, as if the very air had detonated. I was thrown from Hadrian's side, landing close to the spiked wall of ice. I groaned, my entire body feeling like one cold bruise.

I rolled onto my stomach and looked back, seeing Declan.

His face was a twisted combination of malice and insanity. His fists were balled at his sides. On either side of him, the wreckage and refuse from the Centennial was pitching up in waves, tumbling through the air. Broken walls, doors, cracked furniture, more brick and metal, all of it hurtled through the street in a wild tumult.

Like another hurricane.

As terrifying as it was, that wasn't what twisted the knife of fear into my heart. It was Declan's eyes. The glow from the whites drowned out any color, turning him from a bully I knew into something inhuman.

The glow reminded me of the Stormkind that had loomed over me weeks ago.

A dark shadow slid across the ice toward me. Hadrian put one sword onto his back, gathered me in his arms and stood me up.

His hand clasped– crushed– into mine. "This way!"

He pulled me off the frost and toward the flying rubble. Toward debris that would cave in my skull if it didn't take my head clean off.

I planted my feet into the ground and dragged him to a stop. He spun on his heel, a flare of anger slicing across his face. His eyes lifted over my head, snapped left and right, then fell on me again. Hadrian gripped my arms firmly– but not painfully– and pierced me with his sturdy, glowing eyes.

"You are tethered to me, Ava. You *will* be safe."

Hadrian's voice left no room for argument. With that kind of determination, the only thing I could do was believe him. And hope for the best.

He gripped my hand and dragged me through the wind to the hurtling debris. I was scared to look over my shoulder, not wanting to know how close Ferno and Turve were. The only person I managed to see was Declan, who stood stock still with his eyes glowing white and a flurry of broken housing tumbling past him. He looked like an empty vessel that was replaced by one of the Stormkind. Deadly and unnatural.

Declan's head turned ever so slightly, and while the glow in his eyes made him look blind, I knew he was looking at us. A shattered door dislodged from the pile ahead of us. It careened in our direction, spinning end over end. It was moving too fast for us to avoid it.

Hadrian drew to a stop and snapped out his free hand. A flash of ice grew in place, quickly spreading into a thick blue shield about the size of his body. He grabbed me again and turned his back to the shield. The door slammed into the shield and shattered both. Pieces of ice and wood splinters showered around us.

Hadrian never missed a stride. He found my hand and pulled me back into the windstorm. I heard Turve and Ferno shouting behind us, but I couldn't make out what they were saying.

Hadrian slid his second sword onto the scabbard across his back and lifted me onto the pile and settled me into a hollowed out area in the rubble. Once I was tightly squeezed in the space, he crawled over the opening and braced his hands on the brick. Frost drifted from his fingertips and webbed out behind him, forming another thick shield that covered most of the exit. Hadrian wedged it into the opening, then hovered only inches above me, staring straight down but not at me.

"What's going on?" I asked shakily.

Hadrian lifted his eyes slightly, but didn't meet my gaze. "They are trying to get him under control."

"How? What's wrong with him? Why can he do what he did? Why are his eyes–"

Hadrian finally looked at me. "Ava, it is taking considerable energy to keep this shield up. Save your questions for later."

I was torn between arguing and screaming until he gave in, but I decided staying safe and alive was the best option right now.

Outside, the wind howled. Our shelter shivered. My heart kicked my ribcage, beating in time with the throbbing from my bruised ribs. I squeezed my eyes shut, breathed as steadily as I could, but calm refused to come. I was shaking as bad as the rubble around me.

Even when I saw Hadrian's shoulders relax, I still trembled. Lightning quick, he lowered himself enough to turn around. He touched the ice shield and let the frost break apart and creep backward into his arm. When his hands returned to their normal color, Hadrian peered out of the crevice. Rain and hail kept pouring from the sky.

"Stay here," Hadrian abruptly ordered without looking at me. He withdrew one of his swords and was climbing out of the hole before I could tell him there was no way I was hiding in here alone.

Grimacing at the stitching pain in my side, I scurried up after him, slowing only when I reached the top. I poked my head out, looking for a safe spot to take cover. Hadrian hadn't crawled far, so I found him first. He glared at me, then shook his head. I took that as a sign it was safe enough for me to come out, so I carefully made my way over to his side.

I had just nestled beside him when I heard the screams.

"No! Get away from me!"

Declan's voice echoed through the street, his rage echoing through the empty street. The commotion had probably scared anyone outside back indoors, so I didn't think we'd be seen yet. I hoped no one had been hurt.

Focusing on the scene up ahead, I pulled my head up and watched him shove both Ferno and Turve. Neither warrior had their blades drawn anymore, and they approached Declan like he was a feral lion. The creepy light remained in his eyes, scraps of broken homes swirling around him, pushed by the wild wind.

"It is too soon," Turve soothed, walking closer. Trying to cage him in, like Declan was an animal and not a human being. "You are not ready yet. You must be further trained–"

He stepped too close. Declan suddenly roared and shoved the warrior's shoulders. The wind carried his momentum, throwing Turve thirty feet back.

Hadrian grunted scornfully. "Amateurs," I heard him mutter.

Another uncontrollable shudder wracked through me.

Ferno sprang, jumping on Declan's back and tackling him to the ground. Ruined houses pitched up in a cresting wave before dropping straight back down. The two men thrashed and rolled on the ground, trying to throw each other off. I didn't know who had the upper hand until Ferno pinned Declan onto his stomach and slammed a punch into the back of his head. Declan went still, and the wind stopped.

The rain and hail didn't.

"Primes," spat Turve, marching back to Ferno as he pulled a length of twine from his belt and wrapped it around Declan's wrists. "Why did he have to get chosen?"

"I do not know," replied Ferno, not looking up, "but the choice was never in our hands."

"No," Turve growled. "If it were, things would have been different."

Ferno quickly finished binding Declan's wrists and stood up. Because of the sleety storm, they had to shout to each other, which was the only reason we heard them.

"They will be. All four of them are still being tested."

Turve scoffed at that. "We have only found two of them, and one of them happens to be Hadrian's charge. The other could be meant for the Precips as well."

"We will find the others. And as for Hadrian's charge... Let us be realistic, Turve. Fortune has never smiled upon Hadrian's charges."

Beside me, Hadrian stiffened. I glanced at him, but he didn't seem to notice me at all. I turned my attention back to the street and the conversation the strange warriors were having.

Both of them were looking up at the tumultuous sky.

"She is powerful, is she not?" Turve remarked.

"Truly. You should have witnessed her as she endured the trials. Quite impressive, for a human. Though she did scream for an annoyingly long time."

I started shaking again. The dream I had wasn't a dream at all.

It was a memory.

Ferno had been there, at my torture.

He thought my reaction to the crushing agony he and his boss put me through was *annoying*.

The rain and hail continued their onslaught. Hadrian ducked his head and nudged me with his elbow. I barely felt it. I didn't give him a second look. My eyes were riveted ahead to where the warriors were picking up Declan's prone form.

"Should we find her?" asked Turve.

"Not yet. We need to get out of sight before the humans see us. We'll find the other one after we bring this nuisance," he nudged Declan's bound, prone form with his boot, "back to base. Besides," I couldn't see much of Ferno's face through the heavy rain, peppering hail, and drenched snow, but I heard the smile in his voice. "She's Hadrian's problem now."

They laughed together. I shrank down until I could no longer see them. The sound was lost in the downpour. We stayed crouched there for what seemed like an eternity. Hadrian looked at me. I processed everything they said. I was still shaking.

"They have gone," he told me over the storm. "You can relax."

The magic word. The one thing I wanted to be right now. The only thing I'd dreamed about since the Centennial.

The suggestion made me snap.

I whipped my head at Hadrian. "Relax? Did you just tell me to *relax*?!"

His steely blue gaze locked on mine. "You need to stop the storm, Ava."

I gaped at him, then shoved to my knees. "How?! I'm not doing this!" I waved at the rainstorm falling around me.

The sheets of water swayed with my arms. Small pieces of hail spiraled past me. Hadrian pinched his eyebrows together impatiently, a look that said, *Really?*

It would have been funny, if I weren't having a panic attack.

My chest and ribs hurt, and I couldn't breathe. I scrambled to my feet, slipping on the wet brick and nearly collapsing. Hadrian stood up quickly, moving with a fluid grace I couldn't have managed even if I weren't having a breakdown.

"You must remain calm, Ava, and end this storm."

"*I don't know how!*" I screamed. "I don't know anything! Who were those people? What do they want with me?" I suddenly backed up from Hadrian. "What are *you* going to do to me?"

He laid down his sword and held out his hands in a placating gesture. The rain drenching him from head to toe made him look cool and beautiful, the same way a blade is beautiful before it cuts you open.

"I am your Guardian, Ava. You are tethered to me—"

"I don't know what that means!"

"It means I am bound to protect you," he snapped. "It means I am supposed to prevent you from doing *this*."

He waved his hand through the storm, but neither the rain nor hail bent with his hand. Not like it did with me.

"I am not going to hurt you," Hadrian continued, "but nor can I help you or give you the answers you seek if you do not calm down."

My heart thundered violently. My breath struggled to catch up. I pressed a hand to my chest. My eyes burned from tears streaking down my face, the traitorous drops becoming lost in the cold, hard rain.

"I can't," I panted. "I can't, oh God, what's happening to me?"

Hadrian took a patient step toward me. "Ava, listen to me. You need to release this storm. You are going to cause a flood."

A flood... like the one that surged into the school after I had my nightmare. Another occasion where I was panicked and terrified of the world around me.

Ironically, the rational part of my mind said yes. That something happened to me, probably during that week I went missing. It told me I had caused the flood at the school. It reminded me of how I used the weather around to me to stand up to Declan. It persisted to tell me I was able to create hail when Hadrian told me to. It all but yelled that I was causing this rainstorm right now.

Causing water that could be flowing back into the school again, hurting my parents or drowning my little brother, who already had trouble breathing–

Strong hands curled around my arms. I jumped and choked on my scream. My eyes registered Hadrian standing in front of me, as solid and unbreakable as a wall.

"Close your eyes, Ava."

I didn't have the answers to this seriously screwed up situation. But Hadrian did. I could listen to him until I dragged the truth from him. I closed my eyes.

"Now breathe. Slowly. Concentrate on breathing, and nothing else."

Right, I thought. *As if it's that easy.*

It is not meant to be.

I jumped when I heard his voice in my head. I blinked my eyes open. Hadrian's face was stony as ever.

"How did–"

"Close your eyes and breathe, Ava. When you are relaxed, the answers will come."

I chewed my lower lip, uncertain whether I *wanted* to believe him or not, but I closed my eyes again anyway. I'd taken some yoga classes with Piper a couple months ago– she got them free as part of one of her modeling contracts– so thinking about her helped me regulate my breathing. I thought about the air filling my lungs, cool and sweet, turning warm in my chest, and sinking to the very marrow of my bones. I kept thinking about it with every breath, erasing all thoughts and fears.

Why didn't I start thinking about yoga before? I thought dumbly. Then I remembered, *Crap. Hadrian can read my thoughts.*

A stutter escaped his lips, like it was a laugh he wasn't able to hold onto. I found I enjoyed the sound, the warmth and depth of it. I also liked the way his hands covered my arms. How gentle he was being when I had seen how dangerous he actually was.

I added it to my mantra, drawing in deep breaths, absorbing warmth from them, replaying Hadrian's rumbling chuckle and feeling the strength of his hands.

That was when I noticed the hail had disappeared, and the rain was little more than a cool mist. It lightly danced on my face, a sweet sensation that drew a smile from my lips, and made my head light as a feather.

"That wasn't so bad."

My voice was slurred. When did I get drunk?

I opened my eyes and blinked against the fogginess in my eyes. Hadrian was still holding my arms, but he was frowning.

Still...

"You're cute when you pout."

I *must* have been drunk.

He sighed. "This is the first time you've Enervated, isn't it?"

"No clue what that means, handsome, but the answer is probably yes. I think I'm gonna go home and sleep now."

I tried to pull away, but he didn't release me. "That is not a good idea."

"My choice. Not yours. No more touchy."

I plucked his fingers off my arms with methodical precision. It was way harder than it should have been, but I got them off, one by one. Smirking at his stubborn expression, I took a step back. Felt a little woozy, but that was probably because I was walking on uneven, icy ground with a haze in my head. Yet my pride was strong at the moment, so I turned around and took another step.

The world swayed the moment I planted my foot down. I felt my body crumple like a wet towel. A deep voice cursed, "Primes," strong arms circled me, and then the world went black.

CHAPTER 6

I don't very drink much or very often– I'm still a year underage, but Piper always drags me to big college parties– but when I do decide to go on that particular binge, I go all out and pay for it in the morning. Usually because I'm trying to use a vice to escape the mental trauma of a college party where the students are puking up everything they've ever eaten in their short history and throwing off clothes like confetti.

This went far beyond the worst hangover I'd ever had.

My head was a maelstrom of pounding and throbbing, and I hadn't even opened my eyes yet. My stomach was one giant knot, the ends stretched and pulled like it was in a game of tug-of-war. My chest was tight and my throat was dry. Even my skin felt prickly and uncomfortable.

Putting it simply, I felt like *shit*.

"No more drinking," I rasped out. "Ever."

"You have not had anything to drink," a deep voice said from my side.

I turned my head and opened my eyes, which was a huge mistake. My neck strained and my eyeballs felt like they'd been punched. I grimaced and flopped back onto whatever surface I'd been lying on. It was some kind of springy mattress with a fleece blanket over top.

"Ow," I complained. "Ow, ow, ow."

"The pain will dull soon enough. You need to sit up."

"I'd really rather not," I grumbled.

"Then your questions will remain unanswered."

I cracked open an eye to glare in the direction of Hadrian's voice. He was resting on his knees beside me, watching my face with a pensive expression.

Resigned, I slowly opened both eyes and pushed myself up. I moved sluggishly, dragging myself up and leaning back to find the headboard. Only there wasn't one.

I gasped at my body's sudden pitch into nothingness. Hadrian's strong hand pressed against the upper part of my back and kept me from falling off the mattress.

His hand steadied me while my head spun. "I said sit up. Not lean back."

I glared at him through narrowed eyes. "Sorry. Next time I'll have to avoid getting knocked out and just obey your commands to the letter."

Hadrian's mouth was a hard line, though I swore a glimmer of amusement passed through his eyes. "That would be a relief."

My lips curled into a scowl and I sat up, leaning away from his hand. The movement cramped my stomach. I winced and wrapped my hands around my middle, simply wishing the ache away since there was nothing else I could do about it.

"Truly, Hadrian, you earn the most troublesome charges."

I lifted my head– a little too sharply– to find the new voice, and finally taking in my surroundings.

At first, I assumed I was in a pale hallway. Then I noticed the gleaming metal bars evenly spread on the walls. I was in a prison.

Standing in the middle of the cell block on my left, dressed in the same azure and navy blue leather armor, were a man and a woman. The man had smooth, sepia skin, though his eyes were hazel with dark blue circling his pupils. His arms were folded over his well-muscled chest. His hair was a curled mess around his head, which made him look like he just rolled out of bed. The smirk on his face was charming and playful. If I hadn't seen the sword hilts crossing along his back, I wouldn't have thought he was dangerous at all.

Next to him was a gorgeous middle-aged woman. She was shorter than him, but I immediately pegged her as the more dangerous of the two. It wasn't only the way she stood, with her feet shoulder-width apart and her arms loose at her sides, like she was ready for a fight at any second. It was the look on her face. A hard tension that downturned her pretty red lips, turned her azure blue eyes to slits, and made the tightness of her short blond braid look even more severe. As I absorbed her appearance, I noticed that while the base of her uniform was similar to Hadrian's and the other guy's, there was a difference.

On the top left of her chest, angled over her heart, was a silver sigil printed into the leather. It was the sword-in-the-rain sigil I'd noticed on Hadrian's back earlier this evening.

Memories of the battle slammed back into me like a sledgehammer. My lungs felt too tight for all the air I started gasping in.

I was trapped alone in a prison with three strangers. I didn't know what happened to Declan, if those people following me were still out there, or how long I had been gone. The last time I was knocked out, a week had gone by.

I didn't know much of what was going on, but I did know that these people surrounding me were like Ferno and the man who'd stabbed and tortured me. Staying with them wasn't safe.

"Where am I?" I asked. "What's going on? Who are you people?"

"You are in an empty prison facility," informed the woman, whose voice was as cold as her beauty. "The other answers should be obvious."

"Obvious how?" I fired back. "Why are you keeping me here?"

"She is confused," Hadrian grumbled from my side.

The other man looked at him, frowning. "That in and of itself is confusing," he said. "She must know she's one of the Ice now that she's under your charge."

Hadrian turned his sharp blue gaze on me. It didn't stir the feelings I hoped it would. "Perhaps she does not. I have never seen one of them like this before. She still has a human form."

A human form? I stared at him like he was speaking Latin. "Of course I do!" I shouted. "Why wouldn't I?"

Hadrian just looked at me.

"You told us she was not the only one," the woman said, leading me to believe Hadrian informed his friends of everything that happened on the street before I woke up. "The other human that attacked you knew what he was and what he was capable of."

"She used her powers as well," Hadrian added grimly. "She must know."

"No, *she* doesn't," I snapped. "Don't talk about me like I'm not here."

The other man laughed. It was a pleasant, deep sound, richer than Hadrian's. It made him instantly more charming and likeable than the broody heartbreaker sitting beside me.

"Of course," he said in a teasing voice, "the first Stormkind you take as charge in over a century, and she happens to be a delirious handful that's still in her human skin."

I barely heard the last of his taunt. All I heard was *Stormkind*. I repeated his remark over and over in my head, piecing the words together until I was sure I had their meaning.

It still didn't make sense.

"Stormkind?" I said. "You... you think I'm a Stormkind?"

Hadrian's eyes sparked and unnerved me. "I know you are. It was you who was controlling the rain and the hail, remember? What I do not understand is how. You are still in your human shell."

"In my... because I *am* human!"

"Maybe you were before," the woman said. "But you are not anymore."

Dread clawed into my stomach and scratched its way to my heart. Dizziness filled my head again.

"I need to go home," I whispered. "I need to get back to my family."

I gathered my strength and tried to push off the mattress. Hadrian's hand clamped on my shoulder and held me in place. He wasn't hurting me, but he was stronger than I could ever hope to be.

"No," he told me. "You need to stay here. We need to understand what you are. There has never been a human with the powers of a Stormkind before. It is not safe for you to walk away."

I grimaced and shoved his arm off my shoulder. "I'm not asking for your permission. I'm telling you that I'm going home."

I swung my legs off the mattress and stood up without help. I swayed, but kept my footing. Hadrian had risen with me, but I pushed him away.

"Don't come near me," I warned.

Something that looked like hurt flashed through his eyes, gone so quickly I was sure I'd imagined it. I must have. Hadrian's disdain for me was clear. I was an enigma to him.

Heck, I was an enigma to *myself.*

I started for the door, which I could see between the shoulders of Hadrian's pals. The problem was of course getting past said pals. The man and the woman edged closer to me. The man's eyes were a little more sympathetic, but the woman was a block of ice.

"You cannot leave," she stated, in a way that made her think I had no choice. "You will stay here until we discern what you are and how you became tethered to Hadrian as a human."

The temperature in the prison block seemed to drop three degrees, even though I could feel my own anger rising hot and fierce. "You can't do that to me!" I barked. "I have a family! They'll be worried sick, and my brother has asthma–"

"Those are not my concerns," she interrupted. "Nor are they yours. Not anymore."

A knife in the chest would have hurt less than her words. Then the hot spike melted against my anger.

"Don't you dare accuse them of being unimportant. You don't know anything about me or what matters to me."

The temperature dropped again. Though my temper was focused on the woman, I could see the man behind her flicking his gaze between Hadrian and me. I don't know what kind of look was on Hadrian's face, and frankly, I didn't care. I wanted to get out of here, away from these people (if they *were* people, and not something else in human skin), and never see them again.

"I know you are not natural, in any meaning of the word. I also know you are dangerous. And it is our honor-bound duty to protect this world from that which is unnatural and dangerous."

I kind of figured she would say something like that. This woman was obviously the leader of the trio, used to being obeyed and having everything happen the way she wanted it, exactly when she wanted it.

Unfortunately for her, I was in a *really* bad mood, and I wasn't going to stand here one second longer than I had to. I'd been gathering that cold sensation in me, wondering about how I could use it against her and the guys. I thought about freezing this whole prison block, making it brittle and slippery for when they inevitably chased me. I thought about the coldest wind I could imagine, using it to replace the hot anger swirling inside of me. Then I shoved out my hands and pushed.

A cynical part of me didn't expect it to work, and it didn't exactly go as planned. I mean, I hadn't anticipated the sharp tingle in my hands as they turned white and frosted. But the rush of cold that left my fingers was unmistakable. I couldn't see the gust of wind, but the two warriors were definitely pushed back by something when I shoved out my hands.

They staggered on the slick floor, which was made extra slippery by the layer of ice forming under their boots. I looked down, my jaw dropping when I saw the frost was coming from my feet and covering my legs. I could feel the cold, sense that it was there, but it didn't bother me, even if I was just wearing capris, my t-shirt, and denim jacket.

A firm hand clasped my arm. I jumped and found its owner– a very angry looking Hadrian.

"That is enough, Ava."

I scowled, the remnants of my temper exploding to ashes. I grabbed his wrist, feeling the heat of his bare skin…

The heat rolling through his pulse, warm and pleasurable, an energy like the light of the sun that slipped through my flesh and made itself at home.

I'd never experienced anything like this before. Whatever I felt under his skin was euphoric, strong, consuming, and beautiful. I felt like I could take on the world with his power. It filled in all the empty pieces of my life, made me whole. I hadn't known how empty I had been until I saw the power laying beneath him. Under nothing more than a fragile layer of flesh. Tantalizingly close, and agonizingly far away.

Letting that hot, wonderful energy drug me, I started clawing at his wrist. He jerked his arm, trying to push me free, but I didn't let go. I heard him shouting– at me or the others, I had no idea–but I couldn't make out the words. I had no care for them.

He fought me, but didn't make a move to strike me. I didn't know why. I still didn't care. Everything around me was getting cold, so cold, I just needed the warmth he had under his skin.

He kept twisting, shouting, and I needed him to stop. I clamped one hand over the back of his neck and pinched my nails hard into his wrist.

I broke the skin, but didn't feel the sweet euphoria I was expecting. I pinched harder, feeling hot blood but not that mysterious, bright heat I wanted.

He shouted my name again, and this time I looked up into his face.

That was when I saw it. There, behind his eyes, a shimmer of light and *life*. The heat I wanted, that I could feel through his skin and in his blood, but couldn't attain. I watched his lips mouth my name and other words I couldn't decipher, and found the secret to his energy.

I couldn't rip it from him. But I could drink it.

His breath misted in front of me, hot air mixing with cold. I dug my nails into the back of his neck and pushed his face toward mine–

Sharp pain exploded across the back of my skull. I yelped and lost my grip on the warrior I'd been holding. I staggered, energy suddenly crashing into me like a strike of lightning. My vision spun a mile a minute, and my heart jerked erratically. I felt my ankle twist and my body fall. I was unconscious before I hit the ground.

***

Hangover round two was everything round one had been, except this time I was *freezing*.

I shivered and reached to draw the fleece blanket to my chin–

My arm jerked to a stop and rattled. I opened my eyes and looked at my arm. Which was attached to a thick stone wall by a heavy iron chain locked around my wrist. I sat up, mindless of the pain sweeping down my body, and reached for the cuff.

My other hand snapped taught. It was restrained, too.

Fear hitched in my throat. I twisted and flailed my arms out of panic, because I didn't know how to get them free. My legs weren't bound, but even if I had a lock pick, I wasn't an Olympic gymnast or full time yoga master. I couldn't use my feet to pick the locks–

Clunk.

I swiveled my head awkwardly, then turned my whole body. I lost the blanket from my shoulders, but was able to sit the way my captors wanted me to: with my hands helplessly on either side of me, and my back to the wall.

The wall of one of the solitary confinement cells.

Hadrian walked in, gracefully carrying a blanket, a pillow, a tote bag, and a folding chair. His eyes met mine briefly, no discernible emotion crossing through them. Then he set the chair against the wall and placed the other items on the bed beside me. I dragged my knees into my chest, not wanting to be anywhere near him.

"I am not going to hurt you," he said without looking at me. His voice was heavy. Sad, even.

"I don't know that," I whispered back. "You have me chained up."

Hadrian's chin dropped. "To protect us from you."

My first instinct was to ask what that meant, but I stopped short. I was getting used to these mysterious people not telling me a damn thing.

Hadrian reached into the tote bag and pulled out a couple fruit cups, two small cans of tuna, snack packs of cheese and crackers, a bag of one bite brownies, and two bottles of water.

"This was all I could find," he said. "I'm not sure if there's anything you dislike here. If there is, I apologize."

I was speechless because of his attitude. I hadn't really known how hungry I was until I'd woken up. It hadn't crossed my mind earlier since I'd been too busy having a meltdown, but now my stomach was starting to eat itself.

Hadrian pushed the food and water in front of me. The chains on my wrists wouldn't allow me to reach further than the cot, but I could move them enough to eat. The cans and plastic didn't look tampered with, so I didn't think the food was drugged.

Besides, these people probably weren't the poisoning type. Not when they could happily bludgeon or stab me.

My appetite wavered, but I resigned myself to eat and gather my strength no matter what turmoil my emotions were in. For all I knew, this could be my last meal.

At least there were brownies.

As I dug into the food with no care for order, Hadrian moved around the cell. I tried not to watch the weight of his movements as he folded up the tote bag, pushed the pillow and blanket closer to me, unfolded the chair, and sat across from me.

My eyes betrayed me and stole glances at him. He sat hunched over with his elbows on his knees. The swords on his back were gone, and his armor was replaced with a simple black t-shirt, black jeans, and boots. I would have enjoyed the way the shirt stretched along his exquisitely muscled back and shoulders, if I weren't so angry with him.

Or if I couldn't see the guilt on his face beyond the dark curtain of his hair.

Seeing him look almost defeated should have made me pity him. But it didn't. I was his prisoner. No matter what gifts he brought me or how upset he looked, I couldn't forget that.

And I sure wasn't going to be the first person to say anything. If he wasn't going to tell me what was going on, he could stew. I had brownies to distract me for at least fifteen minutes before I started screaming or clawing at the walls.

"Are you feeling well?" he asked, not looking up.

"I'm chained to a wall," I spat. "Do you really care about how I feel?"

He didn't answer for a moment. "As I said, it is to protect us from you." He sighed. "I fear I have approached this entirely wrong. I ignored the questions you asked, because I never thought for a second that..."

Hadrian trailed off and shook his head and scrubbed his face with his hands. I thought he was going to close up again, but then he looked up and met my eyes. If I'd ever wondered what Atlas felt like when he was tricked into holding up the world, I imagined his expression would have been like Hadrian's.

"I was ordered not to answer any questions of yours until Vitae arrived, but I will answer some."

I scrutinized him. "How many questions?"

"Three."

"Small number."

He smiled weakly. "But better than one or two."

I snorted and rolled my eyes. I gave myself a mental slap for letting that slow smile curl into my heart again.

"Fine. I'll ask three questions, but first you have to tell me who Vitae is. It sounds like a woman's name, but I want to make sure if I have to deal with Bitchy McBitcherson before she shows up."

Hadrian smirked. "Is this your first question?"

"No. Nice try."

He shrugged halfheartedly. "All right. Yes, Vitae is the woman you saw. I'm going to advise you not to call her Bitchy or any other variation of the word. She won't take it kindly. And since you may as well know, the man you saw is named Zephys. He is my closest friend, and as the expression goes, the biggest pain in my ass."

"He seems okay to me."

"You have not known him as long as I have."

I wanted to laugh, but then I went still, remembering something that his friend– Zephys– said. "Are you really a hundred years old?"

Hadrian shook his head. "I am older."

A cold tingle crept up my spine. When I first met him, I knew that Hadrian was older than me, but I would have pegged him for twenty-five, at most. I was going to ask the most basic question, but I stopped. If I was going to peel information out of him, I had to do it carefully. I didn't think Hadrian was stupid enough not to know what I was doing, but he was being generous for now. I had to take advantage of it.

"You look good for... however old you are."

He smiled. "That is polite for you to say, considering I do not remember how old I am."

"Wow. Guess it's a good thing you're not senile."

A little warmth crept into his face. "Not even remotely."

That last word drew up another question to my mind. "Where am I?"

The smile tilted into a frown. "Loxahatchee Road Prison. It is emptied of prisoners, and survived most of the Centennial Storm."

That made a little more sense. The government and the Storm Protection Union both agreed that prisons would be effective safe houses and shelters capable of withstanding the worst of the Centennial. However, that had meant transferring prisoners into other, already overpopulated jails. The last I heard, Loxahatchee had been emptied, but there had been no time to refurbish it for the Centennial. I wondered how Hadrian and his people were keeping it to themselves, but I didn't want to use up my last question. Maybe it wasn't the most useful one I could have asked in my situation, but I needed to know.

"Are you going to let me go home?"

Hadrian hesitated. That told me every crushing detail I needed to know. I'd eaten almost all of my food and drank one of the bottles of water, but suddenly I wasn't hungry. I sighed and pushed it to the side, figuring maybe I could eat it later. I took the pillow and hugged it to my chest. It made me look like a child, but I was cold and defeated. The pillow was the only thing I could take comfort in.

"Ava, I…" Hadrian began. He drifted off, then suddenly stood up and closed the chair. I figured he was going to leave me to wallow in confusion alone, but instead he stood off to the side. Less than twenty seconds later, Vitae walked in.

She'd changed into plain black clothes like Hadrian, but she was wearing a tight tank top that showed off her toned arms and flat stomach. Her stern eyes riveted to me, then snapped to Hadrian.

"How much have you told her?" she demanded.

"Very little," he replied, his back ramrod straight against the wall of my cell. "You did not specify what you wanted her to know. I can begin patrols with Zephys."

"No. Stay here. This concerns you as much as it does her."

Hadrian looked like he wanted to bolt. Instead, he nodded and stood in place.

Vitae walked closer to me. This time I clutched the pillow like it was a shield. The fluffiest, most pathetic shield in the world, but it was better than sitting exposed in front of her.

"Tell me true, Wild One. Do you know what you are?"

"No," I emphasized. "I don't know what you think I am. I don't know who you people are. I don't know why I did those things, or why someone else I knew could do them. I don't know what a Guardian is. I've never heard of tethering. I don't even know why your psycho friend stabbed me."

Vitae and Hadrian's expressions froze. "What psycho friend?" she asked.

Ah. Finally. I might have the upper hand. "Let me go and I'll tell you."

Something like sympathy filled Vitae's eyes. It didn't last very long. "I am beginning to understand that this is different for you. But you attacked one of my soldiers. Nearly consumed him. I cannot release you until I know you will not do so again."

My face went slack with horror. I shot a glance to Hadrian. "Are you okay?" I rushed out.

He nodded. "You didn't hurt me, Ava."

"I... But, your wrist..."

He held it up. There were some pink, half moon marks from my claws, and I had to squint to see them. He wasn't even bandaged.

"That was nothing. I have been hurt much worse. Believe me."

My mind snapped to the memory of our fight with Declan and his new freaky friends. The shrapnel in Hadrian's back that I'd been forced to pull out.

"Your back–"

"– is completely healed. Our gifts make us capable of accelerated healing. I am fine, Ava."

He smiled, but I was still shocked. My eyes went to his wrist again. I couldn't believe how casual he was about the wound I gave him. That he could even be in the same closed space as me after I ripped open his wrist and almost did that "consuming" thing Vitae mentioned. And for what?

I could scarcely remember.

Vitae took another step closer to the bed and knelt down to meet my eyes. She seemed much more relaxed now. Approachable, even. I wondered if that was because she finally believed I didn't know what was going on, or if she was trying another tactic to get information out of me.

"The answers will come, Ava. But first, you must tell us about the man you saw. We can answer your questions once we know the circumstances."

Made sense. There was no point in hunting for answers when I didn't know how they would affect me.

So I told them. I explained how I ended up in the middle of the hurricane. What I saw the Stormkind do and what it looked like. I described the man with the crystal knife that he plunged into my heart, and how I'd seen him with Ferno in a dream-induced memory. I told them how they were trying to determine something from me, evaluating the sensations of my pain, that I would be the first of many.

Vitae's face became grimmer with every word. Hadrian balled his fists at his side. He looked *furious.*

But not at me.

"Mortis," he grated out.

Vitae sighed. "So it seems."

"Who is Mortis?" I asked.

"Our enemy," she replied. "It seems you have been caught in the middle of our conflict, Ava. For that, I am truly sorry."

Vitae sounded entirely sincere. That made me alarmingly nervous.

"Who are you people? Why are the Stormkind afraid of you?"

She exhaled heavily. "For that, I fear I must tell you a very, very old story that no human has ever heard."

Vitae stood up and looked at Hadrian. He was still tense with anger, but he handed over the folding chair. Their eyes locked for a moment longer than necessary, something unspoken passing between them. Vitae unfolded the chair and sat in front of me. Hadrian folded his arms over his chest and leaned against the wall.

"Has Hadrian told you how old we are?"

"He said he doesn't remember, but I know he's older than a hundred."

Vitae's smile was small, but it lit up her face and almost made me forget the hostility she had shown me.

"Much older. We were born shortly after the first storms were created, made by the Primordials."

I stared at her, eyebrows shooting up my forehead.

"The Primordials were the elemental beings that formed with your earth. They shaped it, drew power from it. When they used their powers, they left refuse. What you know as storms. After a time, the Primordials grew bored and began to experiment with the refuse. They condensed the power of a storm into different shapes until they held. Added some of their sentience to them. Those shapes became the Stormkind."

My eyebrows rose to an almost painful degree. This was definitely a different version of the creation myth I'd grown up with.

Vitae didn't appear to notice my astonishment, and continued her story.

"But all that concentrated energy was volatile for the Stormkind. It corroded their minds and turned them mad. They needed to balance it, so they sought other energy sources. The Primordials had yet to notice, too infatuated with creating new creatures of flesh and blood. They did not realize the Stormkind were out of control until the dinosaurs were extinct."

My eyebrows couldn't go any higher up my head, but my jaw could drop pretty damn far.

"The Stormkind killed the dinosaurs?"

Vitae nodded grimly. "During that catastrophe, humans were being created. The Primordials decided these new beings needed to be guarded, so they divided their energies one last time. Half of their powers went into the Guardians, flesh and blood warriors that would share the gifts of the Stormkind, to a lesser extent, in order to protect humanity from them. We are capable of controlling certain storms for a time. Some of us can manipulate ice or water, others can manipulate wind and dust. The more powerful of us can use both. For example, Hadrian has mastered control of ice and cold, though he is incapable of creating a blizzard. We must draw our strengths from our tempest-blades."

At my confusion, she added, "The Primordials created weapons for us that were capable of holding a limited amount of power. They help energize our gifts and make it easier for us to fight. Tempest-blades can only be passed down from Guardian to Guardian, are energized by the tethers, and can never be broken."

"What's a tether?" I remembered how seriously important that seemed to be.

"Tethers are what allow us to connect with our charges– the Stormkind. While we are capable of restraining the Stormkind, every hundred years, they are released from their cages. Their hunger simply becomes too insatiable for us to control. So they break free, and fall to earth for the event you call the Centennial Storm."

Understanding hit like a painful fist. "Like a stick of dynamite."

Vitae nodded. "An adept analogy. We use our tethers to find the Stormkind we are charged with and rely on tempest-blades to overcome them. We work as fast as we can, but the Stormkind are quite dangerous the more power they absorb. We try to stop them from attacking humans and consuming them, but... We cannot always succeed. That is why some storms last as long as they do– hurricanes, floods, tornadoes– and others merely last hours instead of the full day."

"Why do they want to consume us? I don't understand what we have to offer them."

Her cool eyes met mine levelly. "Yes. You do. You experienced it when you attacked Hadrian."

I flinched at the bluntness of her statement, even though I knew that Hadrian was okay.

Then I remembered the feel of his skin, the warmth that poured through me like the sun coating a sandy beach. The strength and pleasure of it. How it was a drug I didn't know I craved, and would never be able to get enough of. I recalled the desperation that filled my heart and warped my mind until I was mutilating him, grabbing him and trying to absorb it from his mouth–

Hadrian held up his wrist again, showing me the small pink marks on his skin. "It does not hurt, Ava. Be still."

That was when I heard the chains on my wrists rattling. I was shaking.

Vitae and Hadrian waited patiently as I calmed down. It took way longer than I wanted to admit.

"What did I–" I closed my eyes and reconsidered my question. "What do they take from us?"

Vitae didn't look like she wanted to answer me. "Life force, Ava. They steal the very energy you were created with to feed themselves."

My chest knotted. Our lives were vacuumed out of our very bodies to feed creatures that were millions of years old. I could barely wrap my mind around the concept. I groaned and dropped my head into my hands.

"Now you understand why they are so rampant with destruction when it is time for the Centennial," she said softly. "We are forced to starve them for a hundred years."

That revelation left me torn. On one hand, I knew the Stormkind were literally life-devouring monsters that used their power to destroy the world I loved. On the other, I couldn't help but pity them. They were wild animals that managed to see freedom once every hundred years, if only because they became too dangerous to control.

"You said there was another part of the Primordials that separated," I said when I found my voice again. "What was it?"

"Ah," Vitae sighed. "This is where we come to the most difficult part of our predicament. Exhausting so much energy to create the Guardians made the Primordials weak. They left the humans to evolve on their own and retreated to rest in the earth. Their power now goes into helping the earth thrive. They help keep the forests green, the soil rich, the water drinkable. We all love them for that. But humans do not understand the truth the way we do. They have no idea that with every new machine, every severed tree, every toxin or oil spill, they are destroying the last energies of the Primordials. What resides in the Guardians and the Stormkind is sufficient only for us, and while we are strong, we are not immortal. We have friends and lovers and families that can be killed in combat, either by the Stormkind, or the Mistrals."

She fell into a quiet silence, as if an old memory was resurfacing and saddening her.

"We all tried to adapt to the human ways of life," Vitae said. "We understood their fascination with the unknown, the need for competition and advancement. We know they are not so different from us, as we are simply a secret, gifted version of the human race. But we cannot abide by the way they treat the earth our ancestors left us to guard." She looked in my eyes. "I would be lying if I said I was not grateful that humanity advances very slowly after each Centennial."

I swallowed the lump of nerves in my throat. I suppose I could see her perspective, if I didn't think about the millions of people that died on the last Centennial. That had been one of the strongest pieces of evidence when the SPU began to form that the Centennial was not an event to disregard lightly– death certificates and missing persons reports that all stemmed from a single day, when millions of people across the world were killed in a flurry of freak storms.

"Yet some of us– the Precips, who are established to tether to the water and ice based Stormkind– are willing to abide by them. We will guard the humans, as the Primordials have asked us to. The Mistrals, however, have no such loyalty. They despise humans for torturing and slowly killing the Primodials that gifted them with control over the wind and dust Stormkind. They have chosen to reclaim the throne left open by the Primordials by using their ultimate weapon."

"What is..." I knew the answer as soon as I asked the question.

The Guardians were amazing warriors. I had seen that from Hadrian, Ferno, and Turve. I hadn't seen Vitae or Zephys fight, but they wouldn't be carting those swords around if they didn't know how to use them.

But I remembered the way that hurricane-Stormkind looked at the man who stabbed me– Mortis. How scared it had been of the black-eyed Guardian. The entire purpose of the Guardians was to control and restrain the Stormkind. If they were able to wield them half as well as they could wield their swords...

A shiver wracked my spine. I crushed the pillow to my chest.

"How are they going to use the Stormkind?" I whispered.

"I do not know," answered Vitae. "The Precips and the Mistrals had a grave falling out two Centennials ago. We lost many of our brothers and sisters in arms, along with any communication we had to the Mistrals."

As she spoke, I noticed Hadrian out of the corner of my eye. He was no longer leaning against the wall, but standing straight up with his arms binding his chest. The depth of the anger I saw in his eyes seemed fathomless. They were navy blue pits that threatened to swallow me whole and smother me if I looked at them for too long. So I looked away.

If Vitae noticed– and I was pretty sure she had– she didn't say anything.

"Where do I fit in?" I whispered.

"I wish I knew," she told me. "The man who attacked you– Mortis– is not known for his kindness to the Stormkind. We know the destructive nature of our charges, but we also treat them with respect. The men you encountered tonight do not have that kind of consideration."

Vitae looked at me. "The blade that pierced you. It was crystal, you said?"

"Yeah, I mean, I think so. I didn't have that long to look."

She leaned closer and held her hand out toward my chest. Her eyes lifted, seeking permission. "May I?"

My first reaction was *hell no*, since I didn't know what she was going to grab, and I didn't want her feeling me up with Hadrian watching. My second thought was that of all the things I could think about, that should have been the last.

The third and final thought was that I was chained up, and there was no way I could stop her from touching my chest, let alone strangling or punching me or whatever else she intended to do.

That being said, Vitae was obviously feeling less hostile toward me, and even though Hadrian was having some kind of inner turmoil, he'd brought me pillows, blankets, and food. I was a prisoner, but they weren't hurting me. They were scared of whatever I was, and what I could do.

I lowered the pillow into my lap and nodded slowly.

Vitae's fingers curled around the collar of my shirt and gently pulled it down. I blushed a little, knowing Hadrian was watching. I tried to tell myself I didn't really care if he saw my exposed chest– I had nothing by the way of curves to display– but the most I had ever done with a boy was at one of Piper's parties last year. There was some sloppy kissing and a couple awkward gropes before I realized I needed to get the hell away from him. I don't know what I wanted from Hadrian, assuming I should have wanted anything... but it wasn't that.

Though when Vitae pulled my shirt collar down to the beginning slope of my left breast, all thoughts of Hadrian vanished.

Ever since that awful night in the hurricane, I had noticed the weird scar. I hid it from everyone, tried not to think about the skin that shouldn't have healed so quickly. It was engrained in my mind– a raised white path of skin over my heart.

The scar was still there, an ugly patch of rippling skin and bumpy spots. I looked closer, and saw that the ripples resembled the sigil of the Mistrals, and the spots looked like the teardrops from the Precips sigil. I hadn't noticed that before, because I had never seen their sigils. I just thought it was a weird scar.

Now I knew it was something so much worse.

"What– it– it didn't look like that before." My voice was shaking. "Why did it change?"

Vitae sighed and slowly released my collar. She reclined in her chair as if all her energy had been drained. "I do not know, Ava. If you were to be marked, the scar should have resembled the one you became tethered to. Instead, your scar is a combination of water and wind, and I have no understanding as to why. I am sorry."

I pulled my collar down and rubbed the scar. I hadn't even felt it change. It didn't hurt, but I didn't want it there. I wanted to scrub my skin until it was gone.

"I wish I knew how you fit into this," Vitae told me. "I do not know how it is possible for you to be human with Stormkind powers. Because of that, I do not know how to reverse it."

Hopelessness crushed in my chest. "There has to be a way though, right?"

Vitae shook her head. "If there is, Mortis is the only one who knows it. And he is not likely to share."

Tears pricked my eyes. I looked between Vitae and Hadrian for answers, for some kind of pipe dream, anything to make me believe I wouldn't have to spend the rest of my life like this– some warped hybrid with the power to create storms, who couldn't touch anyone without being afraid that she would suck them dry of their very life.

Vitae, as if reading my thoughts, stood up from her chair. "For what it is worth, I do not believe that you can harm us or anyone else unless you choose to use your powers. I will have Hadrian remove your chains momentarily. But you cannot leave this place until we know exactly what you are capable of, and what Mortis has created you for. You touched Hadrian first, which means you are tethered to him. He will show you how to contain your gifts. As you are still human, you will likely be an adept student."

"But–"

"Ava," the harsh commander I had met was back in full force. Vitae wasn't going to take no for an answer. "Mortis has been following you. It is never wise to be on his radar. Your only chance for safety remains with us. Until we have formed an effective plan to combat Mortis and keep his Stormkind from destroying the world, you have no choice but to remain in these walls."

The tears I'd been holding in my eyes betrayed me. They slipped down my cheeks and dropped from my chin. Neither Vitae nor Hadrian seemed to notice or care. She was a stone, and he was a boiling volcano.

"I shall see to it that you are fed and provided new clothing. The showers still work, so I will escort you to the baths when you need to wash yourself. I know this is unconventional and disfavored, but please remember that you are safe with us, Ava."

With that, Vitae turned and left the prison cell. Hadrian uncrossed his rigid arms and shuffled toward me. He reached into the pocket of his jeans and withdrew a small key. He knelt in front of me and looked in my eyes.

"Do not fight me, Ava."

His tone wasn't sharp or aggressive, but he didn't leave room for argument, either. We both knew I was trapped.

Hadrian unlocked me from the wall and removed the cuffs from my wrists. They were a little sore, but not chafed. Though I barely noticed the pain because of the ache in my heart. I scrambled to gather the pillow in my arms again, needing something to hold and knowing it couldn't be Hadrian.

He pulled the chains from the wall and dropped them and the cuffs into the tote bag. I saw him moving, though my eyes were fixed on the ground. I couldn't get the tears to stop. I felt him lift the blanket from the cot. He unfolded it and wrapped it around my shoulders without a word. For whatever reason, it made me cry harder.

Hadrian knelt in front of me again. I dropped my eyes to his chest, wishing the tears would stop. Then his hand lifted and reached for my face. I flinched and shuffled back. He hesitated, as though he realized I was worried about hurting him.

I thought he would do the smart thing and pull away. Instead, his fingers deftly smoothed down my cheeks, wiping the tears away. My sobs were painful in my chest.

"Hadrian, please…"

His thumbs stroked my cheeks idly, with heartbreaking gentleness. I could tell that his hands were rough and callused from centuries– millennia– of fighting, but all I could feel was the warmth in his palms and the softness of his fingertips. He kept my face in his hands until I felt I could breathe again. Then he pulled away.

"I am sorry for the way I treated you," he said. "And I am sorry for the way I will continue to treat you."

There was a pinch in my chest, a pain that spread into an ache when he stood up, gathered his things, and left me alone in the darkness of my cell.

It didn't take long for the tears to start again.

Chapter 7

The only consolation I had was that the Precips kept their word the next morning. I was fed, given new clothes that had probably belonged to Vitae, and was taken out of my cell to be trained by Hadrian.

Not that he was very chatty when he came to collect me. He met me in the hallway outside the showers and told me to follow him. That was the extent of our conversation as we walked to the outdoor gym. He was wearing yet another tight black shirt, but had swapped the jeans for black sweatpants. Both of his swords were strapped across his back, the rain-and-sword sigil of the Precips printed on the exterior of the scabbard.

I trudged behind him, keeping my eyes on the swords so I wouldn't look at any other part of his excessively toned body, above or below the waist.

I hated my hormones for the way they acted around him. After all, I was supposed to be blisteringly angry with all of the Precips, and Hadrian in particular. Instead, Zephys had cooked me pancakes for breakfast, and Vitae had offered me some of her best soaps when I showered. For beings supposedly older than the dinosaurs, they had surprisingly human tendencies.

Which of course, sprouted a thousand new questions. I couldn't stand the silence as we walked, and even though I didn't think Hadrian would answer anything I said, I was compelled to try.

"Yesterday Vitae said that you have families," I said.

Hadrian's shoulders tensed, but he didn't turn around. He walked a little quicker, but I was able to keep up.

"Do you have a family?"

He marched on. I changed tactics. "I mean, if Zephys is some kind of distant cousin and Vitae is your sister or girlfriend, or–"

"They are not. I am the only one left of my family."

That shut me up pretty quick. "Oh. I'm really sorry, Hadrian."

I winced. *Pathetic, pathetic, what are you thinking, you tell someone you're sorry when you're late for a meeting, not when they've lost their entire family–*

"Stop thinking about it, Ava."

Right. The mind-reading thing. There was something I could ask about without risking any emotional damage. *Hopefully.*

"How does the mind-reading work? Can you hear me all the time?"

"No," he replied as we reached the end of the hall. "Only when I choose to. Telepathy is part of the tether. We connect to it and it allows us to communicate with the Stormkind."

That shocked me. "They can talk?!"

"No," he answered, taking back that shock. "Their minds are simpler. The Stormkind were modeled after humans, a test for the race the Primordials wished to create. They understand a few basic emotions. Need, hunger, fear, contentment. We know how to predict their movements when we pursue them, because when they are not causing destruction, they are looking for it. They travel through the air looking for areas with a high populace before landing on earth and restarting their hunt. Their actions make them akin to what you know as zombies. They think only of the hunger and the hunt. This might make them sound frightening–"

Might? I thought.

Hadrian glanced at me and continued, "But ironically, they are much easier to read than human minds."

"Can you read anyone else?"

"No," he told me as he reached for the door. "Only you."

"Does the tether go both ways? Am I able to read your mind?"

Hadrian's shoulders bunched. He whirled around, a fierce spark bursting in his deep blue eyes.

"Do not try to read me, Ava. It will test my very, very limited patience."

Meaning yes I could, but he would make my training much more difficult, if not impossible. Any softness or favors he might offer me would be void. He could even hate me.

"I'm just trying to understand you," I said quietly. "You were all over the map yesterday. First you were angry, then you were kind, then you were angry again, then kind again, and now there's this—"

"I do not want your understanding. I am here to show you how to control your abilities as a Stormkind hybrid. It is my duty to teach you how to resist any urge you might feel to create a storm from the energy around you, so you will not lose control and seek to devour any life-force you set your sights upon."

I would have called him out and told him to stop being a jackass— among many other things— if I hadn't heard the bitter, hate-filled way he'd said Mortis's name yesterday. Sure, I was never going to be a fan of the guy who stabbed and tortured me, but I was scared of him. Hadrian didn't seem to be. He looked a second away from exploding.

I couldn't help but wonder if Mortis had something to do with the deaths in Hadrian's family.

"Look," I said. "This is day one of my training. You're not the only one who has problems. The least you could do is pretend to be nice to me again."

Hadrian's eyes ignited, but he didn't say anything. He pushed open the door leading to the gym, and held it open for me. He shot me an impatient glance. I put a little too much effort into my smile.

"See?" I remarked with an overabundance of cheer as I passed him, "That wasn't so hard, was it?"

Hadrian rolled his eyes and shook his head. My phony smile turned a little more real.

I looked ahead, grateful to be outside and away from that box. I know there aren't any good places to sleep in a prison, and the extra pillow and blankets made the cot way more comfortable, but I was a girl who lived for the outdoors. My favorite things in the world were walking to the beach, feeling the sun on my skin and the sand between my toes. I loved the smell of dewed grass in the morning and the scent in the air before a rainfall. Being trapped alone in the dark wasn't my cup of tea.

The outdoor gym was near the entrance of the prison yard, a desolate space of cracked concrete, dead grass, bent basketball hoops, overturned picnic benches, and rusty bleachers. Wrapped around the yard was a twenty-foot chicken wire fence with coiled barbed razor wire at the top. I wasn't worried about it being electrified, because the power was still out. It wasn't like anyone was going to bother with a providing power to a prison, anyway. Not when we could cook with fire and gas grills for the next little while. If the cavemen could do it, so could we.

My eyes lifted and I took in the clouds over my head. They didn't look menacing yet, but I knew how fast the weather could change. Right now, there was no trace of a blue summer sky anywhere.

"How do you tell the difference between a natural storm and one caused by the Stormkind?" I asked.

"A good question to start your lessons," replied Hadrian. I almost jumped when I heard how close he was. If he took another step, his chest would be flush with my back.

If he noticed, he didn't say anything. He stood beside me, closed his eyes, then inhaled deeply. He released his breath after a moment and looked skyward. "Do you smell that?"

"Huh?" I was a little too transfixed by the way his face relaxed, the smoothness of his skin, the way his hair brushed against the top of his spine when he tilted his head.

Heat filled my body when he turned those one-of-a-kind blue eyes on me. "Look up and take a deep breath, Ava. Smell the air."

Uh, okay...

Knowing I couldn't keep staring at him all day– though I was sure I could have if I really wanted to– I turned my face up to the clouds. I took a deep breath and inhaled.

"What am I supposed to be smelling again?" I inquired, my eyes still closed and my face still turned to the clouds.

"Close your mind from all distractions, and smell again. Tell me if you recognize it."

I didn't know where he was going with this, but I humored Hadrian and did as he asked. I recalled the yoga lessons I took with Piper and closed my mind, breathing in and holding the air in my lungs.

Then I noticed how thick and dry the air seemed to be. It wasn't like the humid summers when the air felt like it was sweating.

My nose caught the barest whiff of salt and rainwater, a smell that dried my throat a little. Those were things I wouldn't have been able to catch if I hadn't been looking for them, even if I had been human. I opened my eyes and looked at Hadrian.

He nodded. "Your senses will likely become more attuned to the earth and air around you, especially when you choose to use your powers, because Stormkind draw their energy from them. Energy is in everything, Ava. The Primordials made sure the Stormkind knew that. Every time they land on earth, they feel it more intimately than anything humans can touch. They feel the very particles in the air, the texture of the life-forces they devour."

I cringed at the last statement, but Hadrian didn't appear to notice.

"That is how the Stormkind can bend the weather into the shapes they choose," he continued. "The Primordials ensured they would see it as a tangible thing, something they were so attuned to, they could reach out, touch it, and imagine how they wanted it to be molded for their use. Do you understand?"

"Not really," I grumbled.

Hadrian's expression softened. "You will, with practice." He looked up at the sky again. "What you smelled was a Stormkind. The Wild Ones smell like whatever they are trying to create. In this case, a thunder-Stormkind. You can tell by the scents of rain and the dry feeling in your throat."

In school, we were shown old war footage of the Stormkind sprinting through various countries hurling ice, rain, dust and wind at anyone unlucky to be caught in their path, but we had no way of understanding how their powers worked. Storm hunters tried to find them, but failed. The Stormkind couldn't be found or studied. Though it was pretty clear that the Guardians were responsible for keeping them out of the public eye.

With the Internet and news stations were still down, I didn't know which city had been struck by a thunder-Stormkind, though I imagined the damage would have been catastrophic.

"Do Stormkind usually work together?" I asked hesitantly.

Hadrian shook his head. "Not usually. When they're released, they choose a spot away from their siblings. They like to have an area all their own to desecrate."

"Where do you keep them?"

"We have been able to conceal them in caves on the mountains. Along with longevity, the Primordials gifted us with a form of teleportation. The Stormkind are able to move at the speed of one of your fighter jets, which is why they look like comets when they find a target they want and choose to fall."

"Whoa," I said. "Am I going to be able to do that?"

His smile was lopsided and perfect. "I have no idea, Ava. Though I would guess the answer is no. You are only half of a Stormkind, remember?"

"So what you're saying is I could *potentially* move at supersonic speeds?" I teased.

Poor Hadrian, fighting that smile so hard and losing so effortlessly. "Potentially. But I would not recommend you try it. You may find yourself immensely disappointed."

I crossed my arms. "You're no fun."

He shrugged.

"Here's another question."

Hadrian smirked. "Of course there is."

I cocked a hip, trying to look tough. I don't think it worked the way I planned, since he was looking at me like I was being overly ridiculous, but at least I was getting that darkness out of his mind.

"How do you lock the Stormkind up?"

His grin faltered, though he answered honestly. "We use our tempest-blades. They are the only things strong enough to match and absorb the power of a Stormkind. We create a circle of them, caging the Stormkind inside. It is effective, but the issue is that for every bit of power that the tempest-blades consume, it is delivered back into the Stormkind. There is a push and pull of energy between the Stormkind and their cages, which sets them into a frenzy and makes them strong enough to eventually break through the gaps of their cages."

"And you feel it right when it happens?"

Hadrian nodded.

"How many charges do you have?"

His eyes darkened. "Over the years, I have had many. Right now, I only have one."

"Do others have more?"

"Some. Vitae and Zephys have already obtained theirs and put them back in the cages."

"What about yours?" I said after he remained silent.

The silence stretched. Hadrian became a statue, and I slowly started to guess the answer to my question.

"One of two things happens when we find our charges," he told me in a low voice. "First, we confront them, subdue them, and return them to their cage."

"And the second thing?"

"We find them, and they have absorbed too many life forces, or have utilized too much of their powers and burned themselves out completely."

I gasped. "That can happen?"

Hadrian nodded sadly. "More than I care to admit. We call it enervation. You experienced it before I brought you here."

I winced, remembering how I'd passed out in Hadrian's arms from sheer exhaustion. After sounding like a drunken idiot, of course.

He lowered his face and hid his eyes from me. "We are trained by our fathers and mothers. In that hundred year gap between the Centennials, we continue to train. But sometimes… Sometimes it is simply not enough. No matter how strong you are, no matter how fast, it is not possible to rescue them."

Heartache was raw in his voice. I wondered if he remembered that he was talking to me, or if he was just thinking aloud. I was hesitant to break him out of his spell, but I didn't want him to think he was alone.

I shuffled closer and gently clasped his hand. I felt his arm go rigid and his eyes cut to me, but I didn't draw back.

"I know it doesn't mean a whole lot," I whispered, "but I am sorry for whoever was taken from you."

Hadrian's eyes searched mine. For what, I wasn't sure. I could only imagine what it was like to be thousands, maybe even millions of years old, to have a family that stayed with you through dangerous missions and an even more dangerous world. The amount of love you would need to have to survive a century of tension, waiting for the deadliest beings on the planet to inevitably break free of the prisons you worked so hard to build. Perhaps even becoming attached to them, somehow. The ache of the loss when you knew they were gone.

He must have seen the pity on my face, because Hadrian withdrew his hand from mine and stepped back.

"We are not here to speak about me, Ava. We are here because you need to learn."

I pouted. "I'm trying. Why do you think I'm asking so many questions?"

He arched one of his eyebrows in a dangerously sexy way. "I am not sure I have a polite response to that particular question."

I folded my arms across my chest. "Jerk."

Hadrian's mouth was its usual stern line, but his eyes sparkled. "May I begin?"

I unfolded one of my arms to wave him on, then crossed it again.

"As Vitae told you yesterday, my particular talent involves ice. While I can occasionally handle a water-based Stormkind, I am adept with ice and cold."

"How do you determine what kind of Stormkind you're good with?"

"Ava."

"Fine, fine, keep explaining."

His lips quirked, probably against his will. He was very good at regaining his control.

"You have shown that you are capable of channeling some of your abilities on a wide scale. They have likely adapted to your body without you realizing it, similar to the scar that changed, oblivious to you."

I grimaced, but Hadrian didn't miss a beat.

"Stormkind do not do anything in small measures. They attack easily on an expansive scale because it is natural to them. They do not reel back like Guardians can. We know about control, because it is not possible for us to create storms. We merely manipulate elements of them. The key will have to be that you are consciously aware of what you are doing. Making more with less, a phrase I am sure you have heard."

"It's actually less is more, but I get the idea."

Hadrian nodded. A delicious shiver went down my spine. I remembered how he did that at my work, how it seemed like a gesture meant for me and me alone, though he likely did it to everyone he met.

"Ice is a challenge for Precips. Our instinct calls us to water, and freezing it to snow or ice takes considerable concentration. It took me thirty years to master the art and turn it into a reflex."

"Geez. No pressure, or anything."

Hadrian's eyes softened. "You will be able to do this, Ava. First, I want you to feel the world around you, similar to how you did when you sensed the thunder-Stormkind. Relax your body and mind, absorb the feel of the air surrounding you. Touch the air, but do not attempt to grab it."

I nodded. "Like the cookies on the baking sheet."

He blinked and cocked his head. "What?"

"Touch them to make sure they're fully baked, but don't eat them before dinner."

Hadrian stared at me like I was a fish that just learned now to speak. He quickly masked his confusion and said, "If that helps you."

Well, I think it will. Hadrian raised one of his slick black eyebrows in challenge. I ignored how astonishingly sexy that simple motion was, and did as he asked. I could feel the Stormkind in the air, but I figured it wouldn't mind sharing. It's not like there wasn't enough air to go around.

The air settled like a cool blanket over my shoulders, a gentle wind wrapping around my body. I inhaled the fresh air and tasted the dryness on my tongue when I breathed through my mouth. I wondered how close the thunder-Stormkind was that I could taste its energy, but I forced the thought from my mind. I didn't want to lose control at the beginning of my lesson. Hadrian would probably get pissy. So I concentrated on breathing, and kept my traitorous hands at my side.

"Good," Hadrian said calmly. He came around my back, hovering close. I struggled to keep my relaxed state of mind. "Do you know what snow feels like?"

I cracked my eyes open. "I live in Florida," I said bluntly.

"And yet you caused a hail storm yesterday, then froze the floor of the prison a few hours later."

I grimaced. "I didn't know what I was doing. It was an instinct."

"Which is what Stormkind have, and what you must learn to control. We need to find a way for you to harness your powers, without relying on the energy straight from the earth and air. Otherwise, it will be too easy for you to lose control."

"I did fine before," I pointed out.

"Because you kept your distance and were not consistently fighting. Human nature slipped through when you were scared and confused." I must have looked ready to protest, because he held up a hand defensively. "I am not trying to belittle you. I've never encountered this before, and am simply talking aloud to understand it." He lowered his hand. "There are two sides to you now, Ava. A human, and a Stormkind. When you access your Stormkind self, you will be able to harness stronger energies just as they can. As a human, you will be able to recall moral sensibilities. The trick is to find a way to balance the two."

He studied me with an intensity that almost made me uncomfortable, yet I didn't want him to look away. I knew he was only looking at me like that because he was trying to think about what to do with me, but I let myself wonder what it would be like to have that vivid blue gaze locked on me in another situation. If he would look at someone this way before he kissed her.

Not wanting him to catch onto that thought– or fully understanding where it came from– I was relieved when Hadrian found his line of thought.

"You are tethered to me," he said. "Guardians draw power from the natural word to charge the tethers. Perhaps you can draw on that."

I glanced at him over my shoulder, having to tilt my head back because he was so tall. "How?"

He drifted a little closer, until his chest was hovering around my shoulder. "I'm going to touch you and let you feel the tether. You will recognize the sensation, and you can draw remembrance from it."

I hesitated. "Aren't you worried that I'll suck the life out of you or something?"

Hadrian didn't even blink. "Not at all. You are in control of your impulses right now. You will not harm me."

"You seem pretty sure," I remarked cautiously.

"I am."

Damned if I didn't believe his confidence. I was still hesitant, but Hadrian didn't wait for permission. He slipped his hand into mine and squeezed my fingers. I felt the warmth from him for a minute, until a sudden chill replaced it. I gasped at the sensation, but it didn't really hurt. A cool feeling slipped into my chest, like a thread was floating to my heart and wrapped around it, spinning like a cool breeze until it solidified.

Hadrian's tether really did feel like some kind of rope, but it wasn't a noose. It wasn't tight or constricting. It was just there. Cool, relaxed, and strong, as he was. A steady stream of energy that worked away tensions I didn't know I had. A smooth caress that ran next to my very bones and veins.

"Was it the tether I felt when we first touched at the restaurant?" I asked, a little breathless.

"Yes," he answered. He sounded a little husky himself. "That was the tether initiating between us. Tethers are indicative of our particular gifts. Mine is ice, so mine is cold."

Cold is *not* what this was. Hadrian's tether was a gentle fall breeze, or a glass of water on a hot day.

"What does mine feel like?" I asked, curious.

Hadrian paused, brilliant blue eyes looking nowhere but mine. It was beyond intimate, but I wasn't going to ask him to stop. I liked the way he was looking at me. There didn't need to be a reason for it.

"Like every element. The flow of water, the coolness of ice, the strength of wind, the warmth of sand." He tilted down, getting even closer to me. "You are like nothing I have ever felt before, Ava."

My pulse raced under my skin. I watched him, waiting and wondering if he would get closer. My eyes dropped to his lips, and I suddenly wondered what they would taste like.

That was when he stopped. He drew back and released my hand. I still felt the cool caress of the tether around my heart, but the intensity was a fraction of what it used to be. Saying I missed it was an understatement.

"Now you know what my tether is like," he said. "If you find yourself in need of energy, reach for it. My power will give you strength."

"And vice versa?"

"Yes." Hadrian smiled roguishly. "But it is very unlikely that I will find myself helpless."

I snorted. "Good to know your ego will always be intact."

"Confidence and egoism can be separate."

I wouldn't know. "Okay. Next lesson."

"Imagine the feel of the tether outside of your body. We'll find a way to interweave the energy in the air with the tether's power so you can use it. Your range may not be as substantial, but we can work on it once we have a trick figured out."

Something told me that would take a *very* long time. "Is there no way I can draw it straight from the air?"

Hadrian frowned. "Not unless you are distanced from everyone. Otherwise, you could give into temptation and seek to strip anyone close to you of their life-force. Which is why we must do it the long and hard way. Stormkind react on impulse. You must rely on conscious control. Giving up too much of that will make you lose control, much as your friend Declan did."

I tensed at his name. "Declan is not my friend. I want nothing to do with him. Ever."

Hadrian paused for a beat. "Then do it the hard way. Exercise control."

Sure, that sounded easy enough. Imagine the tether inside my body, *outside* of my body instead. Shouldn't have been very hard.

Shouldn't have been, but was.

It was like standing in a dark basement and trying to feel the heat of the sun. Yeah, I *knew* what the sun felt like, my brain would recognize the sensation, but if I were standing in a dark basement, my body couldn't react to something it couldn't feel, let alone see.

I imagined everything from ice on my skin to jumping in a cold pool. I thought about the tether, felt it inside, tried to push it out.

All I did was give myself a headache.

"You are trying too hard."

I snapped my eyes open and glared at him. "Sorry I can't master it after the first try. How many tries did it take you?"

Hadrian crossed his arms. "One."

I rolled my eyes. "Of course it did," I mumbled.

From my peripherals, I could have sworn Hadrian grinned, but I avoided it so I wouldn't be distracted. For what seemed like the next forever, I tried to imagine the sturdy chill of the tether mixing with the lazy chill of the air around me. The textures were similar, but different enough that I wasn't sure what they would feel like together.

I did everything I could think of, except touching the air. The last thing I wanted to do right now was give in to some kind of impulse I didn't understand and manipulate the air around me.

I thought about different temperatures I'd felt over the years, how different the coolness in October was compared to the chill in January. I imagined fall breezes and cool nights, but I didn't recognize the tether's solid texture in the air around me. The tether seemed determined to stay inside my body rather than sneak out of my skin and help me create some snow.

My life was getting *insane*.

I finally gave up and sighed, opening my eyes and turning to Hadrian.

"This isn't working," I complained, drifting off when I saw that his militant stare was fixed on the clouds. I looked up. They were much darker than they had been earlier, becoming thick rolls of smoke that turned the sky from a pale grey to an ominous gunmetal shade.

"Hadrian?"

"The storm is getting closer," he stated, eyes still bolted to the sky. "The Stormkind will likely attack soon."

Fear punched into my heart. "But– how? The Centennial already happened! How could there be another storm so soon?"

"The thunder-Stormkind is probably weaker than it was, but it has probably not been gathered and placed back in its cage." His eyes were almost as dark as the clouds when he turned them to me. "This could be Mortis's design."

Hadrian headed for the exit of the prison. Thunder rumbled over my head. I flinched at the crushing roar and hurried to catch up with him.

"What are you going to do?" I asked, worried about the answer.

"Gather the Precips. Track the Stormkind. Capture it. Kill Mortis."

The last goal was spoken with pleasure. It was something Hadrian wanted to do.

That was when I heard it. The sound of thunder rolling backward, quiet at first, and growing louder with each passing second.

The same sound I'd heard before the Stormkind attacked in the Centennial.

Real thunder smashed the clouds. Sharp white flashes of lighting dashed the ground. I gasped and spun around, bumping into Hadrian. The lightning continued to flash wildly, slashing like serrated knives that stabbed into the ground beyond the wire fence.

A blazing streak of white light cut through the sky like a comet. It descended less than a hundred feet from where we stood. I could almost feel the static in the air.

Rain poured from the sky in buckets. Lightning sparked wildly, each strike getting closer to us.

Hadrian's arm wrapped around my stomach. He pulled me back into the prison, then set me behind him and looked at the blinding white flashes beyond the door.

"I truly loathe thunder-Stormkind," he grumbled. He turned to me. "You need to stay here until we come back."

"I thought I was supposed to stay with you," I said. At least it didn't make me sound like I was afraid of being alone, which was the actual, undisputable truth.

"You will be safe," he stated. "The tether will let me know if you are in danger, and I will return to protect you."

I glanced out the window. Lightning slammed into the middle of the yard. The roar of thunder sent a shiver through my bones. Hadrian gripped my arms and squeezed.

"Go ahead of me, Ava. I'll be right behind you."

Terror still had me in its unforgiving claws, but I nodded and started to jog down the hallway toward the core of the prison.

We didn't get more than ten steps before the lightning struck again– directly onto the roof.

I screamed at the sound of disintegrating concrete and groaning metal. A funnel of air slammed into my back and pushed me forward. I landed face-first on the cold floor, air heaving out of my lungs. I groaned and clutched my stomach, trying to regain my breath. Thunder snapped and crashed over my head, cold rain hammering against my back.

I really need to take a vacation in a desert, I thought.

Dragging to my hands and knees, I looked for Hadrian. He was on the ground a couple feet behind me, and he wasn't moving.

Panic choked me. I crawled over to him. I clutched his shoulders and turned him over. He flopped onto his back, revealing his closed eyes and the bloody gash on his forehead.

My heart lurched. I touched his neck, whimpering with relief when I felt his pulse. I brushed his hair away from his forehead and looked at the wound. It was a nasty tear, but as I prodded his skull, I realized it wasn't fatal. There were no dents in his head or strange decompressions. He had just been knocked out.

I looked down the hall we'd run from. Or what remained of it. The walls had been sheared, like hooks had embedded in the doorway and pulled it clean off to leave only crumbling remains. The entire space was open, the metal door lying dented and useless on the destroyed concrete. Beyond the rubble, I spotted the fence. It too had been bent and warped in the storm, curled over so that if I climbed it, I wouldn't gut myself on the razor wire.

It was a perfect escape route.

I knew the right course of action. That I should stay here until Vitae and Zephys could come look after Hadrian.

But I also watched the blinking flashes of lightning. I saw how they were moving in a pattern– one close to the prison yard, another down the street, another further than that. Almost like the lightning was stabbing down in a path I was supposed to take.

I thought about the direction of that path in relation to the prison.

How it wasn't far from the school where my family was hiding.

I should have been rational. I knew that whatever powers I might have, I wasn't a warrior like the Precips. I knew the lightning path– if that's what it even was– could lead me into some kind of trap.

I also knew my family was in danger, and even untrained, I might be able to help them.

My eyes went to Hadrian, unconscious and unmoving. I set his head down as gently as I could. My fingers cupped his cheeks, smooth and strong. My thumb brushed his lips, full and soft.

"I'm sorry," I whispered.

I got to my feet and ran for the newly created exit. I would find a way back to my family and protect them. That was the only thing I could think about right now.

The consequences would have to wait until after I survived.

If I did.

CHAPTER 8

Rain pounded down on me as I sprinted. Lightning flashes lit my way through the streets. I wasn't familiar with the area– I wasn't someone who hung around prisons for fun– so I relied on the storm to guide me. A naïve part of me hoped I was wrong, that the thunder-Stormkind wouldn't be near my family.

Honestly, I had no idea why I thought I would ever be lucky.

I don't know how long it took me to find Park Vista. But when I did, it was half buried.

I skidded to a stop, my heels slipping on the slick concrete. I clamped my hands over my mouth to keep from screaming. The high school I'd once spent so much time in was caught in a whirlpool, the heaviest of the rainfall smashing into the roof and the front lawn. The water and pressure was so thick that it was creating a sinkhole. Slick mud gulped at the brick, fuelled by relentless water. Lightning danced around the edges of the lawn, tormenting the petrified survivors inside. The windows on the first floor were half submerged, which had to mean that the rest of the floor was filling with rainwater and mud. When the lightning flashed, I could see human shaped-shadows flickering behind the windows.

Standing across the street, the rainwater barely touching it, was the thunder-Stormkind.

It looked similar to the one I'd faced a couple weeks ago, but the differences were apparent. They both had the same humanoid shape and glowing skeleton, and both seemed to have flesh made of water, but the resemblances ended there.

The watery exterior of the Stormkind was jagged and rough, like it was being chipped off with a pickaxe. Violent sparks of lightning spat from the fingers, joints, and face of the Stormkind. It paced back and forth quickly, like a man-eating tiger watching the humans behind the glass.

My stomach twisted. That was probably more accurate than I intended it to be.

Especially when I saw the man on the roof of the school.

He was too far away for me to see who he was. I didn't know if he was a survivor or an SPU guard... Or my father.

The Stormkind didn't care. It lashed its hands out, a bolt of lightning ripping from the sky and hammering into the roof. The flash was so bright I lost sight of the man. White spots still danced in my eyes when the darkness of the storm crept back into the world.

I blinked rapidly to refocus, long enough to see the man on the roof wasn't incinerated on the spot. He was lying in the mud in front of the Stormkind.

I didn't know if he was awake or even alive. A twisted part of me hoped he wasn't. Having your life force drained by a Stormkind wasn't a fate I would wish on anyone.

The Stormkind picked the charred man up by his throat. He didn't stir as it dangled him. Light glowed from its mouth. While all of this was happening, one question rolled through my mind:

How was I going to get to my family?

I was no match for a Stormkind's power. I had piece of it, but that piece wasn't enough. Unless I was smart about how I used it.

Fighting the Stormkind one on one wasn't an option. Using the storm to get into the school?

Much more viable.

I didn't use Hadrian's theory. I couldn't waste time on figuring out how to weave the tether into the air. Instead, I felt the rain flaring around me, and thought about how I wanted it to be snow instead. I imagined every drop crystallizing into a small white flake, creating an effective white shadow that would cover me until I was in the school.

Closing my eyes, I opened myself up to the cool air around me. I let it dance across my face and fingertips. I reveled in the rain pattering and weaving through my hair. The thundering roars from the air filled me with excitement. I could feel the very life of the storm, and knew it would be mine to manipulate.

I opened my eyes again, and changed the storm.

The rain turned into a white curtain of snow. Soon it was so thick that all I could see was white. I shivered, the chill of the thunderstorm's wind blasting the snow against me.

The downpour hadn't stopped, and white blasts of light continuing to flash as thunder erupted through the smoky clouds.

And now the Stormkind had noticed.

It dropped the burned man into the mud and slush, its sparking white eyes searching the blizzard for its brethren. Hadrian mentioned that Stormkind were mostly solitary, so it probably wasn't happy someone was encroaching on its territory.

I bet its mood would swing to joy if it found out I was human.

Before its gaze could lock on me, I thought about concealing myself in swirling snow. It wouldn't make me completely safe, of course, but it was better than the damn thing knowing I was carting around a scrumptious life force.

I swung my arms around myself, as though I was throwing a double roundhouse punch. The thick snow responded, spiraling around my body until it was so thick I could hardly see through it myself. It would have to do. I squinted and started running as fast as I could.

My boots splashed through the slush, spraying my calves with cold muck. My legs were stiff with the chill from the rain and my clothes were plastered to me, but adrenaline and utter terror were good at boosting my speed.

The Stormkind throwing lighting at me kind of helped, too.

Blasts of light exploded into the ground mere feet away from me. The world would go totally white, then snap back into a pale version of itself, like someone was flashing a camera in front of my face.

I ran ungracefully, the slippery mud, sleet, and wet road threatening to send me flying. Every breath was icy and charged with static, as if I would inhale the next lightning strike. Through the sporadic lightning flashing and flurry of snow protecting me, I managed to see the school. I was close, and one of the windows looked cracked, so I could–

The ground disappeared beneath me. I screamed when I lost my balance. I tumbled down a slope, thick mud sticking to me with every turn. I lost my hold on the whirlwind of snow acting as my shield and came to a stop on my stomach, my side bumping against hard brick.

Well, at least I reached my destination.

Shaking the dizziness from my head, I looked up at the slope I'd fallen down. The Stormkind stood at the top of it, against a background of cycling snow, torrential rain, wild lightning and death-black clouds. Its skeleton and eyes were beacons in the dark, bolts of lightning spitting from its eyes, joints, and hands in angry pulses.

It could see me. It knew what I was.

It raised its hand and slammed it down like a hammer. The sky exploded overhead, the shaft of lightning mirroring its movement. I shoved to my feet before the blast hit. My back crashed into the brick wall as the bolt pounded into the space where I'd stood. Static made even my drenched hair stand on end. Painful needles danced along my skin.

The flash darkened and I threw out my hand, remembering the way Hadrian fought. The spiked walls of ice he'd used against the Mistrals. A sharp chill covered my bones and pushed out of my skin. White frost wrapped around my hand. My palm prickled as shards of ice blasted from it. The ice moved like fire over oil, blurring up the incline and exploding into a jagged wall in front of the Stormkind.

Holding the wall in place, I looked over my shoulder and tilted my head up. The window ledge was within jumping distance, even for a short girl like me. I planted my other hand on the wall and sent frost up its length. I pictured the frost hardening the glass until it fully shattered. I wrapped my arms around my head so my face was protected from the falling glass.

Once I thought it was safe, I lowered my arm and jumped for the window ledge. My fingers curled around it while my feet scrabbled for a hold. I used all the muscles in my skinny arms to drag myself to the top of the ledge and hauled my body inside. Light ignited behind me the moment I hit the floor. Brick and pieces of wall blasted inward and coated the floor at my feet.

I scrambled up and backed away from the window.

That was when I watched the world tilt. I threw my hand out to the wall and grabbed an open locker. I nearly fell into the thing, but maintained my footing. I panted, each breath sawing in and out of my lungs. Tremors wracked my body, each one sharper than the last. The spinning in my head wouldn't slow down.

I breathed through the pain as best as I could. I'd made it into the building. That was half the battle. I mean, I had no idea how I was going to get anyone out safely while the school was sinking with a thunder-Stormkind raging outside, but I would cross those bridges when I came to them. For now, I would rely on adrenaline. It was supposed to numb pain, right?

I found my footing and dashed through the bleak, empty hallway.

"Mom! Dad! James!"

As I ran, I could hear voices carrying through the hallway below me. I followed its direction, swinging around the corner to the other end of the hall. A crowd of people were huddled in the corridor, some of them backing against the walls while others shoved each other in search of an exit. A spike of fear went through me when I saw there weren't anywhere near the three thousand people who had been staying here before I disappeared the second time. A fear that heightened when I glanced in the classrooms and saw they were packed with desperate people trying to punch and push open the windows to escape. SPU soldiers dressed in black uniforms shouted for order, but no one appeared to be listening to them. Their commands couldn't even be heard amidst all the screams and shouts.

Though the number was still far smaller than it had been. If I had to guess, I would say two hundred people stood in front of me. A pathetic fraction of the three thousand I'd seen before.

I didn't see my parents anywhere, so I started calling for them again.

"Dad! Mom! James!"

From within the crowd up ahead, a familiar face turned at the sound of my voice. My father was a tall man, and it was easy for him to see me over the crush of panicking people.

My heart lurched. I'd been worried they might not have been here, they could have left sometime after I disappeared– again– or worse, they had been trapped in the sinking lower level.

"*Ava!*" he shouted, pushing people aside to run for me with wide eyes.

Sobs choked me when he crushed me into my arms. My mother called my name, rushing up with James in her arms. We embraced, none of my family caring about the mud I was plastering them with.

Subtly, I could feel the warm pulse of their life forces inside them, but the sensation was small enough that

I could ignore it. I was determined to ignore it as long as I could.

My family pulled back and looked at me.

"Ava, where have you been?!" my father asked in a choked voice. "You went missing again."

I nodded vigorously. "I know, but I'm safe. I'm okay." I winced, knowing the last part was a lie. If I was half-Stormkind, I was *far* from okay. "I can't explain right now. We need to get out of here."

"How?" whimpered Mom. "One of those... those *things* is out there."

Her eyes were filled with fear. So were my little brother's. James had grabbed my hand sometime during our embrace, and now he refused to let go.

If they felt half as terrified as they looked, how would they react when they found out I was one of those *things* myself?

I didn't linger on the thought. I had to trust that they were my family, and they would still love me. After all, I was the same daughter and sister I had been a month ago. Except now I was a little more... complicated.

"I can help you," I said. "But you need to trust me. Can you do that?"

James was nodding, agreeing and believing in his big sister as only a child could, but my parents were older and wiser. They knew there was a reason I was asking, and they weren't going to like it.

Forcing myself not to linger about the consequences, I focused on the issue at hand. "The Stormkind out there is one that can make thunderstorms. It's using the rainwater to sink the school, then electrocuting anyone who tries to escape."

That was enough to scare them. They didn't need to know the truth– that the electrocution wouldn't kill them. The Stormkind would rather suck out their life force than burn them to a crisp.

"I can distract it and lead you to a window, but as soon as you hit the ground, you have to run as fast and far away as you can."

"How are you going to distract it?" Dad asked, at the same time Mom gasped and exclaimed, "You can't risk yourself!"

I hesitated, then smiled weakly. "This is where the trust part comes in."

They didn't want to simply accept that response, but a sudden vibration shuddering through the building quickly forced their hand. The Stormkind must have used the power of the storm to strike the school. We couldn't stay here any longer.

The tremble caused every person in the hallway to burst into a cacophony of screams and shouts. The SPU soldiers were overwhelmed, trying to hold back the frenzied masses. Their commands were lost in the chaos.

I tried to shout over the crowd to get their attention, but the panic and fear in the air was infectious. I shouldn't have been surprised. I'd been transformed– I didn't even know if I counted as human at this point– but on the outside, I still looked like a skinny, forgettable red-haired girl. Not exactly the figure of an inspiring leader.

My eyes scanned the open classrooms, fixing on a toppled metal chair on the floor. I darted inside the room and picked it up from the floor. Waving my parents and brother aside, I gripped the chair with both hands, then hurled it into the ceiling. The chair screeched when it smashed into the roof and clattered loudly onto the floor. The crowd jumped violently, but the noise had gotten enough attention that I could do something.

"I know a way out!" I called to the survivors looking at me. "Everyone who wants to come, follow me!"

Like I'd predicted, not everyone followed me. Some sought their own escapes. I couldn't do anything about that. I wasn't a leader and would never have the presence of Wonder Woman or Supergirl. But I was doing *something*. I had a way to fight the Stormkind. Bullets were less than useless, and it wasn't as though the SPU could get a hold of a tempest-blade.

My thoughts strayed to Hadrian. I hoped his head was okay. I also hoped he wouldn't be too mad when he found out I took off. Hesitantly, I reached for the tether. It was smooth and cool around my heart, resting as though it had always been there.

Deciding it couldn't hurt, I reached for the connection in our minds.

Hadrian, I know you're probably pissed, but I could use your help at Park Vista high school right now. That thunder-Stormkind is trying to kill a bunch of people, including my family. I might be able to hold it off, but not for long. As a desperate afterthought, I added, *Please help me.*

I snapped the thought off as soon as my family corralled everyone they could from the hallway and classrooms. Satisfied that anyone else would follow when they saw us running or find their own way out, I turned and ran back down the hallway from where I'd come.

Nervous comments and demanding questions echoed through the hall, but I didn't stop to answer them. I slowed down near the window I'd shattered. Beyond it, a chunk of the school walls and roof had been blown away, exposing the storm raging outside. Rain pounded the tile floor and the shattered rubble piled on top of it. Cold air pushed against my frigid body. I couldn't remember what it was like to be warm, and constantly moving would only keep my body temperature raised for so long.

I looked at the crowd of huddled survivors.

"Stay here for two minutes after I get down, then–"

Light flashed behind me. Then the survivors began to scream. I whirled around. The Stormkind had appeared on the edges of the wall it had ruined. Lightning dashed the sky, illuminating the slashes of rain and its disturbing, translucent body.

It could see all of us, a smorgasbord of life force.

I faced it fully. It was already running. I thought about creating a thick wall of ice between the survivors and the Stormkind. I felt a familiar chill wrap around my bones and lifted my hands, pushing them at the rushing Stormkind. Frost circled my wrists and burst from my palms, rapidly interweaving and lacing together until a solid wall was formed. I could see the shape of the Stormkind beyond it, the brightness of its skeleton. Gritting my teeth, I made the wall deadlier. I thought of icicles like spikes stabbing out toward the Stormkind. Frost snaked through the ice wall and obeyed my command, jabbing outward like a spiked booby trap.

The Stormkind backed away, but I knew it wasn't going to leave. I was really going to have to fight it. I turned to look at the survivors.

If they didn't go slack-jawed, they gasped. If they didn't shriek, they screamed. Everyone was terrified of me.

Even my family backed away. Mom hid James behind her for protection.

Protection from me.

A lance of heartache struck my chest.

All the while, I felt trickles of warmth sliding through my skin. The enticing lure of hundreds of life forces, each one more tantalizing than the last.

And close. So close…

"Ava…" My dad tried. "How… Your eyes…"

He looked like he didn't know me. He stepped back like he was afraid of me. It was then that I knew my eyes were likely bleached of color, and glowing. The same way Declan's had.

The same way a Stormkind's did.

I should have looked away, kept them from seeing me as I was. But it was like looking at the faces of survivors dragging their broken bodies from a car crash. I couldn't look away, not even when I knew I wanted to. This was the last time I would ever see them.

Shame slid its ropes around my heart, cinching tight and squeezing my chest until I couldn't breathe. This was how they would remember me. Not as the klutzy, curious girl they'd raised, not as the daughter who bought them time to hide in the Centennial, not as the big sister who held her little brother when he was scared.

They would remember my glowing eyes. The hunger growing inside me.

They would remember the monster that wore their daughter's face. Just as I would remember the confusion and horror carved into their faces now.

The lance plunged deeper into my constricted heart, and split it in two.

"Get them out." were the only words I could shout. My voice was ragged and desperate. Shaking. "Please."

I pointed to the window then turned around and raced away from the crowd. I couldn't be around them while I was fighting the Stormkind. I had no idea how much control I did– or didn't– have right now. I dragged more power from the storm raging above me. It filled me like a knife filled its sheath. It was simple and right. Nothing else in the world made more sense to me now.

I couldn't see if the survivors were running from or listening to me, but I felt the heat of their life forces sliding across my back like a rippling heat wave. Gritting my teeth, I pushed against the wall or thorny ice, shoving it toward the Stormkind. It leaped away and raised its arm. I staggered back and shielded my face as its arm slashed down. A bolt of lighting smashed into the ice wall, shattering it with a single loud crack. Chunks of heavy ice battered my body like baseballs. I yelped and lowered my arm, seeing the Stormkind rushing at me.

I pushed out my hands, my fingers capturing the cold wind and blasting it at the Stormkind. Flakes of snow were swept up with it. The Stormkind didn't move in either direction. It just stood there and stared at me.

Then its head snapped left. To where the survivors were piling out of the broken window. Not all of them were taking the route I offered, and I couldn't really fault them for that. All I could do was hold the Stormkind off, and pray to God that Hadrian and the other Precips were on their way. They were the professionals in this situation. I was the idiot who couldn't think more than one step ahead.

And that was the last thing I needed to think right then.

Maybe my confidence was what made my power slip. Maybe it was exhaustion. It didn't matter in the end. The Stormkind still found its shot at me and took it.

Electricity danced between its fingers, then fired it straight at me.

The attack happened too fast. Even if I could have prepared, there was nothing I could do. The blast hit me square in the chest. The bolts of lightning were smaller than the ones tearing from the sky, but no less agonizing.

I was the wick on a Roman candle. Every cell in my body exploded with a snap, every nerve burning to a cinder. Invisible hornets stabbed my flesh. Each beat of my heart was a fist that threatened to shatter like glass. I knew I was screaming, but I couldn't hear myself past the pain. Couldn't think through it. Could only absorb it, and hope I wouldn't die.

When it ended, I was on the floor. I don't remember falling or hitting the wet, freezing tile. The electrocution was over and I was able to see again, yet I could still feel the tremors wracking my body. Even my eyes throbbed when I cracked them open.

The Stormkind towered over me, as if debating on finishing me off. It had no face, aside from its glowing eyes. No emotions or intent that I could read. There was no reasoning with something like this. It was so far beyond human, so intense in its power, that it could be considered a god.

Which was why I was so stunned when it didn't kill me. It turned and stalked away.

Relief flooded my sore body, but it was short-lived, because the Stormkind didn't abandon me out of mercy. It was going after the larger targets that escaped through the window. The herd of humans it could devour, one after the other.

It was going after my family.

I rolled onto my stomach, dragging myself to the window. The Stormkind leaped through it and disappeared from my sight. The fear I felt right then was as strong and as sharp as any ounce of pain I'd felt tonight. I had tried to do the right thing, a simple thing, and all I had done was make it worse.

That seemed to be a trend, as of late.

Ignoring the cynic shouting in my head, I clutched the edges of the window ledge and pulled myself to my knees. Wind and rain slapped my face and threw my drenched hair away from my shoulders. Glass scraped my knees and dug into my palms.

Lightning sparked through the sky, illuminating the slush and mud below. The survivors were screaming, each of them running in a different direction from the Stormkind that landed behind them.

The entity reacted quickly, without deterrence. Bolts pounded into the ground at seemingly wild directions. Each strike blocked the direction of a survivor, forcing them to find another route.

But there wasn't one, because the strikes weren't random.

The Stormkind was corralling them like sheep to slaughter.

And it *would* be a slaughter, unless I could stop it.

I was feeling the effects of using my powers. My energy was all but gone, and my head was a nail being steadily smashed with a hammer. My adrenaline had gone as far as it could go. Desperation and survival instinct were going to have to be my secret weapons now.

I wasn't sure how much I could concentrate to stop the Stormkind, so I didn't try to. I felt the air around me, imagined it cooling until I could feel it in my bones. The rain changed into snow. White flakes twisted through the air, and as the temperature dropped, the slush hardened into ice.

The Stormkind reached up to grab lightning from the clouds, but it was too cold. I glanced up, and saw that I had altered not only the temperature or the rain, but the very clouds.

My storm had taken over.

The survivors were confused at the sudden change, but they didn't stand still long enough to see what had caused it. All but three of them scattered.

Three familiar faces looked up into mine. Three people I loved enough to do a reckless stunt like this.

Three people I was about to lose.

There was no way I could make it down before the Stormkind attacked them, or me. If they were going to get away, it had to be now.

And it had to be without me.

I smiled weakly and waved at them, hoping they would know it was safe to leave me and run, but my eyes never left the Stormkind as it turned to face me.

I pictured the snow getting thicker, turning a snowstorm into a whiteout. I had to trust that my family would make it through the blizzard. I'd done all I could for them. Now I had to take care of myself.

I pushed back from the window ledge and staggered to my feet. I raced to the broken wall and peered over the ledge. It wasn't a far drop, but I was worried about the ice forming at the bottom. If I slipped when I landed, I could break my ankle or worse.

So I crouched low, gripped the ledge, and dropped off. The tips of my boots skidded until they found purchase in the cracks of the outer wall, and I was able to climb down without any trouble.

Ironic, considering that I was running directly into new trouble.

I pressed against the wall and eased around the corner to where I would see the Stormkind, wondering if it figured out what I had been doing–

A blast of wind slammed into me and knocked me onto the ice. I yelped at my hard crash and the cold. When I looked up again, the Stormkind was looming over me, electricity sparking from its fingertips.

If I had to guess what it was feeling now, it was probably rage.

I raised my hands, even though I knew I wouldn't be able to defend myself, unable to see anything but the entity that would rip my life force out of my throat—

A shadow and a blur of silver moved behind the Stormkind. I saw the motion *through* its jagged, flickering body. Then I watched the tip of a sword punch through the skeleton of the Stormkind, out of the front of its chest.

I jumped as much as the Stormkind did, clamping a hand over my mouth to stifle my scream while its back arched. The motion was oddly human, and for a moment my heart broke for it. When the pale silver blade left the Stormkind, a gaping hole remained in its skeleton. The light within it began to blink on and off, quickly at first then slower and slower. Then too slow. Then not at all.

As soon as the light diminished, the Stormkind's body dissolved into a puddle of water. The thunderstorm stopped instantly, the clouds lightening and the rumble of thunder disappearing.

It was dead. I could barely wrap my mind around the concept. A Stormkind was dead at my feet, killed by a sword.

No, I realized. *Not just any sword. A tempest-blade.*

I looked up, fear crushing my chest as my mind registered Turve towering over me. He grinned cruelly, dark blue eyes shimmering with malice.

"There you are. We were not sure you would come. Thank the Primes that your Guardian is lax with your safety."

I was too stunned to move, so it was easy for him to roughly grab my arm and haul me to my feet. I slipped across the ice, but Turve didn't slow down. He kept pulling me up the hill, where the rest of the Mistrals were waiting.

My heart as pounding as I saw Ferno standing vigilantly near the top, his sandy eyes riveted to me even as Turve dragged me past him. To my left, I spotted Declan and a girl on her knees. He looked paler than usual, but he grinned and wiggled his fingers at me, the harmless gesture making me shudder. His other hand was firmly clamped on the girl's shoulder, his fingers drifting far too low along her chest.

Her head was tilted forward, her matted, dark hair hiding her face, but there was something about her that seemed familiar–

Turve yanked me in front of him and stopped us both. I staggered and turned my head to see the man in front of me. My legs trembled.

I knew him immediately. His steely hair, hard face, and dead black eyes were forever etched in my memory, just as the feel of his fist was when it slammed into my chest, along with a crystal blade.

Mortis looked me up and down quickly. He smiled.

"You have been coming along nicely," he remarked. His grin widened. "I am proud."

CHAPTER 9

Proud. Mortis, leader of the Mistrals and the man who'd stabbed and tortured me, was proud of my progress. I had no reasonable reaction to that. So I ended up doing the stupidest thing imaginable.

I laughed.

It was more of an awkward, skittering sound in my throat, but it was the only noise I could make.

Mortis blinked slowly, no emotion crossing his face.

Turve shook me violently. "Show respect," he growled.

"Peace, Turve," Mortis said.

The shaking stopped. I was still dizzy. Mortis took a step closer to me, placing his hand on Turve's arm. The stocky warrior released me, but I didn't try to run. No way I would get more than a step before Mortis or Turve caught me. Even if luck were on my side for once, Ferno and Declan would mow down any other escape attempt.

Maybe escape would have been possible if I hadn't already been in a fight. As it was, I was weaker than a pane of glass against a wrecking ball.

Mortis tucked his fingers under my chin and tilted my head back. I flinched, my fingers curling reflexively. Jet black eyes scoured me, predatory and precise.

"I am told you are tethered to Hadrian, and the evidence of that is clear around me," he nodded at the ice covering the mud and the snow sweeping around us. "Has he begun to train you?"

I didn't think about an answer for his question. I was fixed on the two more important words. *Tether* and *Hadrian*.

I had no way of knowing if my message got through to Hadrian or the Precips. I didn't know if they were coming to help me, and I couldn't keep waiting. I didn't want to gather energy from the air again, to give into my Stormkind half, but I knew I couldn't hold back against people like Declan and the Mistrals. They wouldn't hold back with me. Maybe Hadrian was wrong, and I could control my powers without letting myself become consumed by the energy in the air.

Might as well try. Wasn't like I had anything to lose.

Except my life.

"Answer him girl," growled Turve.

I still hesitated, then said, "Nothing. We didn't have time."

It was mostly true. I learned more about Hadrian and the Guardians than I did about any kind of control or finesse with these so-called gifts.

The reply seemed to satisfy Mortis. He released my chin. "A pity for him. He had no idea what he had."

"What does that mean? What did you do to me?"

The questions were more like demands, and probably the reason Turve stomped toward me again. Mortis held up his hand, not sparing him a glance. Once Turve halted, he lowered his hand.

"I have given you a gift, but I did not know how it would respond to you. So many other experiments have failed, yet you are my first success. A vast improvement from others like them."

He jutted his chin behind me, in the direction of Declan and the girl. I turned. Declan was scowling, but the girl was still weak. She lolled her head to the side, dark hair swaying off her tanned face–

My heart jumped. "Piper!"

Hearing her name, my best friend tilted her head to follow my voice. More of her hair fell away, showing me the dark bruise on her left cheek and the blood running from her split lip. A haze covered her eyes, but Piper still recognized me.

"Ava?"

Her horrified expression mirrored my own.

I balled my fists and whirled on Mortis. *"Bastard,"* I seethed. "What did you do her?!"

Mortis didn't blink or show any emotion he might have felt at my outburst. He reached for his belt and plucked out a knife.

The same crystal one that scarred me.

"The same thing I did to you." He put the knife back in his belt. My eyes were glued to it until he spoke again. "Only she has not yet found her tether. We have tried to assign her one, but she proved difficult, and needed to be taught obedience."

I shuddered, knowing exactly what kind of "lessons" Mortis was capable of.

"It was a shame your body had not recovered before the Precips launched an attack upon us. I was forced to leave you on that rooftop. I fully intended to return to you and make you my charge, but it seems a lesser warrior has taken that honor."

Mortis's eyes darkened to voids as he referred to Hadrian, but the flicker of emotion disappeared as quickly as it came.

"And so I was forced to tether myself to a weaker experiment."

There was a yelp of pain behind me. I spun, seeing that Declan had thrown Piper onto the ground and was marching toward me with clenched fists.

"I've done everything you asked!" Declan bellowed. "I found Piper, I told you which safe house Ava would run to, I lured that Stormkind here so you could see what she could do–"

"And she has done far more than you ever could." Mortis extended his arm and swept it across the expanse of snow continuing to cover the ice.

"All of this, drawn from a single tether." Mortis lowered his hand and looked at Declan. "How do you intend to impress me?"

Declan snarled, "By eliminating competition."

His cold dark eyes flashed and he swung his fist at my chest. The punch didn't connect with me, but the wind he gathered did. It hit with wrecking ball force, literally picking me off the ground and hurling me past Mortis and Turve. I barked out a cry of pain when I struck the rough, icy mud.

"A trick we have seen before," Ferno rasped. His arms were folded across his chest, and he looked even less impressed than Mortis.

Declan shot him a murderous glare. "Fine. How about this?"

I tensed, seeing an unnatural glow begin in the whites of his eyes, blotting out the vengeful blue. Whatever he was going to do to me would be worse than the supercharged shoving he seemed to prefer. I moved to get up as he drew back his arms, but I was too slow–

A slender form knocked into Declan's legs and caught him off balance. Piper.

They landed in a heap and she scrambled to get on top of him. Turve barked a laugh. Ferno shook his head. Mortis just watched.

Piper managed to straddle Declan. She'd taken a self-defense course over the summer, and she knew how to protect herself.

It just wasn't enough.

Piper struck Declan twice before he grabbed her wrist and punched back. His fist collided with Piper's chin, knocking her off him. Declan rolled and pinned her onto the ground. He slammed another punch into her face to daze her, then stood up. Drawing his hands back again, Declan threw whatever he'd intended for me at my best friend.

Even from where I lay, I could feel the pressure in the air as it was crushed onto Piper's injured form. Eighty mile per hour winds could break her bones. When she started to scream, I knew that's what was starting to happen.

Forgetting all my aches and exhaustion, I rolled onto my knees. Since the wind Declan was using was so strong, I was able to target it and use it for my own powers. I pulled it away from Piper and shoved it at Declan. He launched back, carried by snowy, blizzard strength winds. He landed hard, but quickly rolled to his feet and fixed me with a look that promised pain and death. It took the last of my energy, until I felt a cool tug at my heart.

The tether's pull seemed like a sign for me to use it. I just wished I knew how. It wasn't like I could use the tether alone...

Unless I could.

Hadrian's power relied only on the tether. I might not be able to combine it with the energy in the air and create a massive blizzard, but I knew exactly what it felt like inside of me. Maybe I could use it as a smaller way of attacking, like Hadrian had. No harm in trying. Hopefully Hadrian wouldn't mind, and if he did... Oh well.

Declan shot his fist out, but not at me. His knuckles pointed at the building behind me. The massive brick structure that wasn't ready for the ruthless amount of wind that ripped off pieces of the desecrated roof.

Dozens of bricks the size of my torso shot down at me. I grabbed the tether and pulled as much strength from it as I could. It felt like a muscle being stretched taut, strained to the point of tearing. Yet I knew it was strong. I knew it would hold.

The tether's sudden charge was an electric shot straight to my heart, a welcome pulse that cooled the burning pains under my skin. It filled me in an instant, and then I dropped to one knee and slammed my hands against the frozen mud. The ice lurched as power rippled past my palms toward my boots. I felt its chill and heard it creak when it curled over me. The ice shielded me, a trick I stole from Hadrian. But this was on a much, *much* larger scale.

The bricks torn from the school pounded against the shield, each strike causing the ice to crack. I focused on the tether, drawing more power from it. I had no idea how much I could take until it was useless or I passed out, so I resolved not to think about it right now. I thickened the ice wall, stretched it taller and wider. Finally, I heard the last of the pounding.

From the corner of my eye, I watched the ice curve like a wave fifteen feet on either side of me. The tips of the wave jutted out in hundreds of sharp spikes, a fierce warning to Declan. I turned my head toward him.

Declan's jaw was slack, shock on his face as the white glow in his eyes faded. Beyond him, Ferno and Turve watched me with wide eyes, their expressions only a little less restrained than Declan's.

Mortis didn't react the same way they did. Instead, he smiled.

"It appears you have been bested, Declan," Mortis goaded. He glanced at the bully he was tethered to. "Again."

Declan snapped, but not at Mortis. He charged straight for me.

I could feel my energy draining. Either the power from the tether didn't last very long, or I was more exhausted than I thought. I worked to draw more ice around me, to block me from Declan completely. It wasn't a great plan, but it was all I could think of.

And it didn't work at all.

Declan shoved his fists toward the ice wall. A torrent of powerful hurricane winds slammed against my shelter, shattering it under his knuckles. I shrieked and covered my face from the shards. Declan grabbed one of my outstretched arms and pulled me out from under the protective wave. He swung me around and buried his fist in my stomach. Air flew out of my lungs in a painful rush. I barely managed a gasp before he hit me again. Declan roared like a beast and pushed me onto the ground.

Stars exploded when my head struck the hardened muck. I couldn't see clearly, but my body was completely awake to the pain. To the fingers that snared my throat and squeezed, the palms the pushed my trachea toward the back of my throat.

I could taste the air. Recognize the taste on my tongue. But it didn't go any further. It didn't sate the fire burning in my lungs. It didn't stop the pounding in my head. I slapped at Declan's face, but it only made him squeeze harder.

Not knowing what else to do, I dug my fingers into his wrists until my nails broke his skin. He didn't register the pain. The tether shuddered against my heart, the last vestiges of power shooting through my veins and out of my hands. Frost covered my fingertips and sank into his skin–

Energy whipped into me, as if a torrent of wind had crushed through my skin. I lost the cold sensation of the ice. It was smothered by a new, wild sensation that rushed up and down my veins like a Ferrari on the Autobahn. It was like physical adrenaline, yet more. It was chaos beneath my flesh.

An agonized croak drifted past my lips, and I wanted all the sensations to stop, I just wanted it *out*–

Declan was thrown from me. An unseen force swooped under his chest and picked him up like a ragdoll. I didn't know where he went, or how he'd been thrown– if *I* had thrown him– and I didn't care. I rolled onto my side, coughed, groaned, gasped, whimpered. I couldn't fight anymore. I wasn't sure I wanted to.

"Impressive," I heard Mortis say. "It seems you don't need to absorb a Guardian's power to wield it–"

A clash of steel cut him off. Surprised shouts and furious cries rang through the air. Wind whipped violently. Mud shifted and rose from the ground. Rain poured from the clouds. Ice creaked nearby.

I groaned. "No more rain. No more cold."

I felt someone kneel down beside me. I curled into myself, jumping when a hand found my shoulder and carefully rolled me onto my back. I opened my eyes, meeting the most beautiful blue eyes I'd ever seen.

"Took you long enough," I mumbled.

Hadrian set his lips in a firm line and slipped his hands under my shoulders and the back of my knees. He lifted me as gently as he could, but the motion still caused my head to loll to the side and see what was happening.

Vitae and Zephys were in front of us, fighting the Mistrals wildly. Zephys had both blades in his hands, slashing them at Ferno and Turve. His torso snapped back and forth as he kept them both at bay, knocking swords away from his chest, stomach, and head. The Mistral warriors were enraged, and kicked him when their sword-strikes failed. Zephys jerked from each hit, but never slowed down and never stopped fighting. I didn't know if he was a better fighter than Hadrian, but he was still damn good.

Behind him, Vitae battled Mortis. He'd grabbed Declan from where he lay and clamped his hand on the back of his neck. Declan was slumped, possibly unconscious, yet Mortis was still holding him with one hand and using his gifts with the other.

Rapid, pummeling winds billowed toward Vitae. She raised her hands and pushed back, bending the water and hardening it midair, freezing the rain until it resembled broken glass. Mortis gripped Declan's neck tighter and swung his hand up, hurtling the ice shards away. With a flick of his wrist, mud broke out of the ice and split into tiny particles. The mud launched at Vitae and she cried out in pain as the hardened mud struck her like a flurry of wasps.

Panic filled my chest as I watched them both fight. Hadrian kept carrying me, and then I saw another slumped form in danger.

I grabbed his arm and pulled. "Piper! Take me to her!"

"It is too dangerous out in the—"

I looked at him desperately. "Take me!"

Hadrian hesitated, then changed his direction from the school to my best friend. He carefully set me down so I could crawl next to her. I put my hands against her neck, grateful for the pulse I felt under her skin.

I felt the heat of her life force teasing my fingertips, but shoved the desire away. This was Piper. My best friend. I would never hurt her. I *wouldn't.*

"Ava, you must get to safety."

"Not without her."

"Ava—"

"She's like me, Hadrian!"

That gave him pause. He glanced at Piper, then at me. Hadrian cupped the back of my neck and brought his face dangerously close to mine. My breath hitched, and I was suddenly consumed by the intensity of his eyes and his cool, saltwater scent.

The heat of his life force was even more tempting than Piper's, and much harder to ignore.

"You must keep away from the fight," he instructed. "We don't know how to combine your tether with your Stormkind senses yet. I felt you pull on the tether. It told me where you were, but it weakened me. It is a shared bond, Ava. That is why it took me so long to find you."

Melancholy slashed through his eyes and into my chest. "I didn't—"

His hurt disappeared. "I will send Zephys to guard you."

He got to his feet and sprinted to the fight without another word. I watched him, fear coiling around my heart. How much strength had I taken from Hadrian? He didn't look weak, certainly wasn't running like he was tired, but what about his abilities? Would he be able to use them if he needed to?

Was it even worth using the tether if I weakened us both each time?

I had to trust that Hadrian could take care of himself. Besides, he was right. I couldn't trust myself to fight with all the energy roaring through the air, and inside of me. I could still feel the coolness of Hadrian's tether, but the pulsing energy I'd felt when I touched Declan was still there. I had no idea what it was or what it could do, and I couldn't find out unless I wanted to risk going Stormkind on everyone I saw.

Hadrian raced for Zephys, Ferno, and Turve, but I was horrified that he wouldn't make it in time. Zephys was still matching strike for strike, but even I could see he was growing tired. He kicked Ferno in the stomach and brought both his swords around his body to stop Turve from slicing his head off. Metal shrieked as they split off. Turve started moving fast, the tempest-blades becoming blurs of liquid silver. Zephys could only block.

He had no idea Ferno was still behind him, both swords poised directly at the Precips spine and throat.

But Hadrian did.

His swords were still tucked in their scabbards, and instead of drawing them, he held out his hands. Frost consumed them, the rain condensing and hardening into a thick spear of ice. Hadrian spun his wrist, and the massive icicle responded. It pitched end over end, crashing into Ferno and splintering into a million pieces. Ferno staggered and turned, Hadrian's boot catching him in the chest.

Never missing a beat, Hadrian drew one of his tempest-blades, slid beside Zephys, and caught one of Turve's swords, the one that had been about to chop at his friend's throat. Hadrian knocked the blade aside and slammed a kick into Turve's ribs. The stocky Guardian jerked, unprepared when Hadrian leaped forward and smashed his elbow into Turve's head.

With both opponents stunned, Hadrian quickly whirled to face Zephys. He shouted briefly, the only words I could make out being "protect her."

Zephys hesitated, but Hadrian didn't give him any space. His sword collided with Turve's, his free hand swinging vicious punches into any space he could find. Ribs, stomach, chest, face, Hadrian had no preference. I wanted to warn him that Ferno was still there, but I didn't have to. As he spun around Turve, he swung up his free hand. Slivers of ice rose from the ground and punched into Ferno, halting his charge and drawing an outraged scream from him.

I didn't know Zephys had arrived until he knelt down next to us. He didn't act like he was in a lot of pain, but I knew he was hurting. I also knew from the grim shade of his hazel-blue eyes that he didn't want to be here playing bodyguard. He wanted to be back in the fight.

I wanted the same thing.

"What happened to her?" Zephys asked, glancing at Piper and reaching to touch her face.

"I'm not really sure," I said through the tightness in my chest. "Mortis said she was like me, but she doesn't have a Guardian–"

Zephys's fingertips brushed Piper's cheek for an instant. Then he gasped and drew them back, staring at her with wide-eyes. Piper hissed in pain and groaned, though her eyes remained shut. My heart squeezed and I clutched her hand.

"She does now," Zephys remarked, though his eyes didn't move from my best friend's face. I looked at him, unease and relief sliding together. I was glad that Piper's Guardian was a Precip, and I trusted Zephys, but I didn't want her to be like me. It meant nothing but danger for her.

A yelp of pain captured my attention. I raised my head and watched Vitae crashed into the ground. Mortis encircled her in a tornado of mud, so thick I could hardly see her. Bits of debris or rock flew inward and struck her. She tried to dispel it with rain, but the muck was too thick. She couldn't see anything, and the tornado was closing in.

So was Mortis.

He released Declan and drew one tempest-blade over his shoulder. Declan collapsed, but Mortis gave him a second glance. He walked straight toward the tornado, ready to drive the blade through it– and her.

"Vitae!" I shouted.

She couldn't hear me. But someone else did.

Hadrian risked a glance at his leader. He saw what was going to happen, and he erupted into action.

Moving faster than ever, my Guardian swung a wide roundhouse kick into Turve's temple, snapped another kick into Ferno's chin, and sheathed his swords. Hadrian's hand frosted over and he curved it like he was holding a whip. As his arm moved, the rain around him crystallized into ice. By the time his arm was in front of his chest, the rain was sharpened darts of ice. A dozen of them shot directly at Mortis's throat and face.

The attack drew attention away from Vitae, but not one of the darts found a home in Mortis's face. Instead, the leader of the Mistrals pivoted on his heel and slammed out his hand. The ice-darts exploded into a billion shards. They'd never even gotten close to him.

It didn't stop Hadrian. While the darts flew, he'd been running full tilt toward Mortis. He drew both tempest-blades from over his shoulders. His face was terrifying. I had never seen someone so hell-bent on destruction. Hadrian looked like a monster, a scowling demon finally freed from the pits of Hell, hungry for flesh and thirsty for blood.

Mortis let his hands fall to his side. Other than that, he didn't move.

Hadrian shouted a war-cry and hurled one of his tempest-blades at Mortis. Quicker than I could register, Mortis twisted and avoided the blade.

Mortis kept turning, swinging his blade at Hadrian. My Guardian pulled to a stop just in time to block the sword aimed at his throat. Mortis took the offensive, slashing and swinging without pause. Hadrian matched him strike for strike, but that was all he could do. He was so intent on cutting Mortis he didn't notice the way his opponent's free hand drifted over the bottom of the ground. The way the mud shifted and steadily rose.

He was drawing Hadrian into a trap.

One that Ferno and Turve were waiting to jump into.

"Zephys–" I said.

"I see them." But he didn't move. He was taking his oath to protect us seriously.

Screw it, I thought. *I'm not bound to any oath. I can control the weather, and I'll watch how much energy I use so I don't devour any life force. I can do this.*

With a grunt, I pushed to my feet. It was way harder than it should have been.

"Distract Ferno and Turve. Get Vitae. I'll take care of the rest."

He looked at me. "Ava, you do not know your limits, and I promised Hadrian–"

"Just do it, Zephys!" I hissed. It covered up the strain in my voice.

He hesitated, but nodded. Time wasn't a luxury we had right now. Declan was lying incapacitated on the ground, just as Piper was, but I was still awake. If luck took my side for once, I could end this here and now.

Zephys stormed toward Vitae's crumpled form. Ferno and Turve noticed him and worked together, with Ferno dragging mud up from the road and Turve pushing a wall of it toward Zephys. The Precip made it to his leader, roughly grabbing her shoulders and pulling her up. Vitae looked weak, her entire body slathered with mud.

But she didn't stay that way for long. As soon as she was roused, Zephys was on his feet and drawing on the rain. Vitae scrambled up, planted her feet, and waited until Zephys's attack launched past her to block the two Mistrals. The funnel of rain that Zephys threw crashed into the mud wall. Vitae drew her hands together. The rain that hit the wall hardened the mud, freezing it in its tracks. She pushed again, and the whole frozen-mud wall skidded back into Ferno and Turve. Zephys wrapped his arm around Vitae and started to haul her back. Now that she was turned to me, I could see the blood staining her face and body, like a thousand blisters had erupted on her skin.

Zephys shouted for Hadrian, but his friend didn't listen. He was still locked in deadly combat with Mortis. The fight was more violent than before.

Hadrian pushed on relentlessly, catching Mortis' tempest-blade and swinging his arm around to fling it from his grasp. It worked, but Mortis wasn't fazed. He kicked Hadrian hard in the stomach, bending him double. As Hadrian recovered, Mortis unsheathed his other blade from the scabbard on his back and slammed it down at Hadrian's head.

Hadrian moved quickly, bringing his sword up and stopping the attack. Metal screamed against metal, and I had never been so relieved that tempest-blades couldn't be broken.

Though that didn't mean bodies were safe.

Mortis kicked Hadrian in the ribs. The impact jarred my Guardian and his resistance against the blade slipped. Mortis drove his knee into Hadrian's stomach, then pounded both his elbows into his back. He twisted and slammed his boot against the right side of Hadrian's ribcage. He lost his footing and landed on the ground on his back.

Hadrian swung his sword at Mortis in an effort to wound his leg. The Mistral leader kicked it down and pinned his arm. Hadrian tried to rise again, but soon a boot was on his throat, and he was trapped.

As I watched with horror, I felt the energy around me— from the struggle Vitae and Zephys were enduring against Ferno and Turve, to the crumpled forms of Declan and Piper, to the restrained control of Mortis, to the fragile tether with Hadrian.

I could feel it all now, and I knew the only way to help my Guardians was to unleash it.

While I centered myself and prepared to grab the energy swirling around me, I heard Mortis's voice carry over the sounds of battle.

"Impatient and inferior. Just as Sonus was. I always knew you would take after him. You are not even half the Guardian he was." Mortis pressed harder on Hadrian's neck. "At least he could keep his charges alive."

I felt the weather and the air sweeping over me, and the rough energy coating my tether. I gripped them both, and then I let go.

I screamed and felt my body rip apart. The pressure in my body erupted like a volcano, fierce and merciless. A huge gale crested behind me. The energy was everywhere, snared by the power I was wielding. The pain was unrelenting, but the feeling of complete control and undiluted power was even stronger. And far more welcome. I felt that if I pushed hard enough, I could take it all.

Winds the speed of rockets detonated toward the Guardians. I saw them look at me, shock widening their eyes. A tiny pulse beat at my brain, as if telling me not to do anything to the Guardians dressed in shades of blue. It was like I was supposed to recognize them. But I couldn't remember why.

It was probably better that way. The Guardians were not my friends. They were my keepers. They would lock me away as soon as they could. They had told me as much.

I did not want to be controlled. I did not want to be stopped. I would take what I could for as long as I could.

Loose snow, shattered ice, and thick mud burst from the ground, scattering across the horizon. The wind pushed on, barreling into the Guardians. Three of them— the ones dressed in black and silver— were hurtled through the air and out of sight. The wind pushed on, smashing into half-constructed buildings and knocking them over. Debris thrashed wildly— metal beams, furniture, the leaves of palm trees, anything not bolted down was thrown twenty feet from where it originally lay.

I grinned and breathed deep. Felt the cold chill in the air and the wildness of the wind rushing past me.

Sensed the energy of a life force behind me.

I turned around, then looked at the body of a human girl on the ground. She was unconscious, but alive.

She was mine.

I knelt down, drawn by the heat of life under her skin. The pulse in the back of my head tapped my brain again, as if something was trying to make itself known to me, and stop me from taking what I wanted.

Yet as soon as my knees hit the cold, snowy earth, the power shut off like a switch. Where the wind had been roaring inside me minutes ago, now there was a stillness so sudden it made my head spin. Something wet and thick dripped from my nose and my ringing ears. I couldn't see straight. I felt my legs shiver and become liquid.

Then I couldn't see at all.

Chapter 10

Tender warmth glided down my face. I didn't know what it was, but I could happily get used to it.

Yet the moment I started feeling the gentle sensation across my cheek, other feelings made themselves known. The elevated arch of my back as it rested on a sturdy mattress. The thick blanket tucked under my arms and around my chest. The warm cloth rubbing my cheek. The slow, steady fingers moving through my hair. The smell of cool water and musk.

My breath hitched. *Oh man. This better be a dream.*

The circles on my cheek stopped. The fingers unthreaded from my hair.

No! Come back!

"I know you're awake, Ava."

I really needed to figure out how to control my thoughts.

I was tempted to ignore Hadrian, but he wasn't easy to fool, and there was an exhausted weight to his voice I couldn't disregard. So I slowly blinked my eyes open and found him.

He was a mess. Mud was splattered on his armor and clumped in his hair. Light bruises covered his face, ghosts of what they must have been. Blood had caked on his forehead, though I couldn't spot the cut that spawned it.

The worst was the bruise ringing his neck. An awful, dirty print with angry red dots lining the design. I squinted at the dots, trying to figure out what they were, why they looked like...

I noticed the dried blood spots on them, and an image of the boots ice-climbers used flashed through my mind. I inhaled sharply and reached for Hadrian's neck before I knew what I was doing.

He gently clasped my wrist before I could touch him. "I'm all right. The worst wounds have healed."

Hadrian held my wrist for another long moment, then set it back onto the bed. I took a minute to take in my surroundings. The walls were a familiar bland pale grey that told me were back in **Loxahatchee** prison. This room– which I quickly discovered was the prison infirmary– was bigger, with hospital beds covered in an ugly aquamarine fabric, like they were on loan from a dentist's office. The curtains were drawn back to let in dreary grey sunlight, which spilled over the desks covered in paper and blank screened computers, and into the cabinets filled with unused medical supplies. It was a wonder this place hadn't been raided yet. The SPU and volunteering doctors could use this stuff, and the gangs would literally kill for it.

Then again, the Precips weren't about to let anyone steal anything from them.

Thinking about them– and how I'd forgotten them when my Stormkind-half took over– I turned to Hadrian. His indigo-azure eyes didn't leave my face. He looked intense, as if a million accusations were on his tongue and it was taking an effort for him to hold them all back.

I was in major trouble, but first things first.

"What happened? Is Piper okay?"

Hadrian nodded once. "Zephys is explaining things to her. She's been tended to. Her injuries were far less severe than yours."

I winced at the bite in his words. Avoiding it, I said, "I want to see her."

"No. You need to rest."

"I'm fine," I half lied. Sure, I was talking, but now that I was fully awake, I was starting to feel the effects of my little adventure.

My body felt like a wet towel, twisted and wrung and squeezed too tight against my bones. There was an unrelenting pulse behind my eyes, as if boots were in my skull and trying to kick my eyeballs out. All of my limbs seemed to be encased in concrete, heavy and sluggish whenever I moved. Every bruise I took throbbed angrily, a silent reminder that I'd done something really, really stupid.

But I didn't want to stay in this bed any longer. I wanted to see my friend. I wanted to find out if my family was all right. I wanted to figure out what the hell I was, and how I could make it stop.

"I'm fine," I insisted again. I reached for the blanket to pull it away. "Just let me–"

Hadrian's hand clamped over my arm and pinned it to the bed. Doing so caused him to lean over me. His impossibly handsome face was inches from mine, his body slightly pressed against mine. I could feel the heat of him sinking into me, a delicious, welcome burn that I didn't think was coming from his life force.

"You almost died!" he snapped. His eyes seemed bluer than ever, deep and tormented. He relaxed his temper, but didn't move. "You almost died."

It was a whisper this time, a broken sound that both caressed my skin and struck my heart.

Hadrian's chest brushed mine when he breathed. I could almost feel the race of his heart, as wild as the pain in his eyes. I wondered what happened to Guardians when they lost their charges.

Then I remembered Mortis's last taunt to Hadrian, and suspected he knew all too well.

Believing I could touch him without hurting his life force, I used my free hand to cup his cheek. I smiled at him, hoping it would draw away the darkness swimming in his eyes.

"But I didn't. I got lucky for a change."

Hadrian closed his eyes and sighed, as if breathing was an effort for him right now.

"Do not joke about this, Ava. Do not."

Fair enough. Hadrian was on an emotional tripwire. I had to be very careful, because I had no idea what he would do if I set him off. I hadn't known him long, but I'd sensed early on that Hadrian was all about control. He was good at keeping a lid on any anguish he felt, preferring to go the broody, mysterious route.

But the problem with control like that was it never lasted. Everyone snapped, sooner or later.

"The lightning was a beacon for me," I said quietly. "It was heading straight for my family. I couldn't let anything happen to them."

Their faces flashed through my mind again. The way Mom shielded James. The terrified whisper in Dad's voice. I closed my eyes and swallowed the sobs lodging in my throat, forcing them to lump in my chest, grateful that Hadrian couldn't see how heartbroken I'd become. I didn't want his sympathy, only his understanding. That wasn't too much to ask for, was it?

"So you knowingly walked into a trap." Hadrian's eyes were still closed, but I heard the anger simmering underneath.

Apparently it was.

"It wasn't when I got there," I protested. Then I thought about it. "Okay, so maybe I didn't realize it was *then*, but I was able to find a way to get my family and the survivors free. It didn't really hurt me–"

Hadrian's jaw tightened. So did his grip on my arm. "You knowingly took on a thunder-Stormkind alone, having no concept of your gifts or how the damage they could inflict on you."

My lips quirked and I opened my big, stupid mouth. "Not really the best gifts, are they?"

Hadrian opened his eyes and glared at me. My smile faltered. I didn't think Hadrian would hurt me, but there was no mistaking the warning in his eyes.

Before I could explain any further, Hadrian continued. "Then you fought another like you. That man.

Declan. In front of the Mistrals. Using the energy from the air rather than the tether. Something I instructed you not to do."

Now I was starting to lose my patience.

"I didn't know they were there. What was I supposed to do? Stand there and let them kick the crap out of me?" I took a deep breath to calm myself. "I had no choice, Hadrian. We haven't even started to work on your method yet. I've used the air's energy before. I used it, and I didn't hurt anyone."

"But you could have," he argued, the intensity of his anger creeping into his eyes. "You were supposed to hang on until I got to you. You were not supposed to use your powers. You were not supposed to fight."

I dropped my hand from his face and pushed his chest. Hadrian moved back, but he still felt too close.

"My friend was in trouble! They could have killed her! I never asked for these *gifts*, but if I'm stuck with them, I'm going to use them to keep the people I love safe–"

"Even when they make you bleed?" Hadrian bit out, his voice starting to rise. "Before I brought you back here, your nose and ears were bleeding. You have no idea what your limits are, but you exceeded them. You nearly snapped the tether, draining both of us of power. How do you expect me to do my duty if you steal my tools for it–"

"You weren't there!"

"Because you left!"

His shout froze me. I couldn't think of any kind of argument, but even if I had one, Hadrian would have overridden me. I'd stepped on the tripwire, and set off the explosion.

"If you had just stayed in place, done what I asked you to do, none of this would have happened," he exclaimed, eyes fevered and wild. "That Stormkind would have been contained. We would have subtly tracked the Mistrals. Mortis would not have escaped again." The venom in his voice startled me with that last condemnation, but he still wasn't done. He lowered his voice, but his neck and face were still burning with anger.

"You tell me that you do not want these powers, yet everything you do suggests otherwise. Tell me what I am supposed to make of that, Ava? Tell me how I am supposed to protect you from Mortis when you play right into his hands? When you ignore my warnings and let your Stormkind half overcome your control, leading you to nearly attack your friend and become no better than the monsters we've spent centuries trying to contain?"

Hadrian took another breath, then stopped. An uncomfortable, stricken look crossed his face. That was when I felt the tears lining my cheeks.

I wiped them away. "Are you done yelling at me?" I asked.

"I... " Hadrian stopped. He wouldn't apologize to me, because he wasn't sorry, though his eyes still seemed to plead with me. "Ava, I didn't mean–"

"You should probably go," I whispered. "Being around me is only going to piss you off more. And if you can't see the reason I did what I did, or why I don't regret it, then I don't want to be around you, either."

Every word I spoke felt like a hook being embedded in my heart. The pained expression in Hadrian's perfect blue eyes made every barb tighten. But I wouldn't take a single word back. I couldn't.

He saw that in my eyes. Felt it in the tether around my heart. Whatever pain he felt didn't last as long as mine did. His face became stony, all emotion locked away from me. I looked the blanket covering my body, and tried not to wonder if Hadrian was the one who tucked me in. I tried not to remember the gentle way he'd cleaned my face and stroked my hair.

As if I were precious to him, and not just a charge.

Hadrian's heavy footsteps strode toward the door. The door creaked open, and all I could think was *Don't go. Not yet–*

The door closed with a heavy, silent click. The hooks ripped open my heart violently. A sob racked through my chest and spilled out of my throat. I clamped my hand over my mouth and squeezed my eyes shut.

That was when the tears really began to pour.

***

I couldn't remember falling asleep. I was still in the infirmary when I woke up, but it wasn't Hadrian in the room with me.

Vitae had settled in the chair he'd sat in earlier, her sharp, intelligent blue eyes boring into mine. She was dressed in a simple black sweater and jeans, her well toned arms folded over her chest. Her hair was tied back in a tight braid, wet from being washed. If she bore any bruises or wounds from her fight, I couldn't see them. Vitae was as unreadable as Hadrian had been before he left.

My chest pinched at the fight we'd had. It was crazy to miss someone who was in the same building as you, wasn't it?

"You've been recovering rapidly," announced Vitae blandly.

I couldn't really argue that. I still felt like emotional crap, but my body was stronger. I felt normal. Maybe that tear-induced rest did me some good.

"Your body must have absorbed some of the tether's self-healing capabilities."

Or not.

Trusting Vitae but choosing to confirm with my own eyes, I lifted the blanket and peeked underneath.

Someone had stripped me of my dirty clothes and replaced them with clean ones. Even my underwear was fresh. There had only been two people to come in my room that I knew about, and I had been too busy arguing and defending my actions to Hadrian to know if my clothes were different. I didn't want to think he would be that pervy, but...

Heat flushed my cheeks when I looked at Vitae. Her expression remained blank, but I swore there was a twinkle in her eyes.

"The garments you wore were beyond saving. I took the liberty of discarding them and redressing you shortly after Hadrian departed. They are more of my own. Please try not to ravage them."

Vitae, badass warrior and leader of the Precips, was a clothing freak. Who knew?

"No promises," I muttered.

Vitae's lips quirked as I looked down. I pulled up the bottom of the dark grey sweater and looked at my stomach. Nothing. I prodded my ribs. Nope. Poked at my face. Nada.

Lucky me.

"How did I heal?" I asked.

"Once the tether is activated, it remains that way. It never fades unless both a Stormkind and Guardian perish. Usually it is the Guardian that perseveres long enough to pass the tether down to their sons or daughters. Stormkind simply die."

"They don't have little Stormkind babies running around setting off random thunderstorms and tornadoes?"

I spoke bitterly, but the antagonism died when I saw the grim look on Vitae's face.

"No, Ava. They do not. They were not created to breed. Even if they had the capacity for it, they are too volatile. Too single-minded in their purpose for consumption and destruction."

I gulped, hesitating to ask my next question, but needing to know more about the Stormkind. About what I was potentially going to become.

"Then... How do they multiply?"

Vitae's stare unnerved me. "They do not. The Stormkind you see here are the last of the Stormkind to exist. They are nearly extinct."

My jaw dropped. I had no love for the Stormkind, but I had to admit they were kind of like wild tigers. Extraordinary to look at and worthy of respect, but not exactly the kind of creatures you keep as pets.

"You must remember that the Stormkind were created as experiments by the Primordials. They were made due to boredom, and for millennia, we have suffered the consequences of their creation. But they are part of the old world, the world that we know. It is important to preserve them for as long as we can."

I hesitated before I asked my next question. "What happens to the Guardians if all the Stormkind die?"

Vitae hesitated, and I could have sworn a glint of fear passed through her eyes. It was gone before I could be sure.

"I do not know," she admitted. "Without a tether, it is likely our extended lifespans will dwindle at human rates. The tether is a shared bond of energy. It strengthens the Stormkind and the Guardian it is connected to."

I blinked. "What kind of energy?"

Vitae smiled, but there wasn't a lot of warmth in it. "The kind the Stormkind crave."

"Wait," I said, "Are you telling me that when I use the tether, I'm using Hadrian's life force?!"

Vitae didn't seem surprised by my outburst. "As he will do to you whenever he needs extra power. Remember that we were created to siphon Stormkind gifts. It is the only way we can contain them."

"But the whole point of using the tether is to keep me from draining his life force!"

Vitae held up a hand to stop my rant. "You are not absorbing it, Ava. Merely *using* it. Think of the tether between you as a battery. Both of you can use it, and it will recharge over time. When Stormkind reach the end of their lifespan, Guardians quickly find a new one to tether to so we do not age and eventually die. Using the tether will exhaust Hadrian, but not hurt him."

I looked down. "So... If I lose control again and try to hurt someone... Will he take all the energy from the tether so I can't use it?"

It was a stupid question. Of course he would. He'd been here chewing me out about how I was too uncontrollable. Maybe he was right to do just that. Hadrian was a Guardian first, my ally second, maybe my friend third. Definitely nothing else, and even the second and third options were pushing the limits–

"It is the wisest course of action for him, the one he knows is right, yet I do not think it would be what he will choose in the end."

I glanced up. Vitae's smile was soft. "I was a friend of Hadrian's father. I've known Hadrian since he was a child. Though he has been unlucky with the stability of his charges, he remains one of the best Guardians I've ever known. Yet I have never seen any charge get under his skin the way you have."

I had no idea if that was a compliment or an insult, so I decided not to answer. I picked the edges of the blanket. "What do you mean by stability?"

Please don't tell me I really am as crazy as a Stormkind.

Vitae sighed. "Hadrian has always gotten the wildest charges. Even when they were in their cages. Stormkind that fought him savagely at every turn, nearly escaped, proved too uncontrollable. More than once, he has been forced to eliminate them himself."

I winced. "Is... Is that why he didn't want me as his charge?"

Vitae held my eyes sadly. "I cannot speak for Hadrian's heart. He is dedicated to his task, yet I sense he longs for something else in his life. It was the most significant way he and Sonus were different."

The name rang a bell. "Mortis mentioned that name. Sonus. Who is he?"

Vitae's blue gaze darkened, a violent combination of grief and rage.

"Sonus was Hadrian's father."

"Was…" I whispered the word.

She nodded. "Mortis killed him."

Things began to click into place. Hadrian's tension when he mentioned Mortis to me when I was in solitary. The way he fought Mortis as soon as he had the chance. How effectively Mortis's taunts worked on him.

Despite the hundreds of questions that popped into my mind, only one stood out above the rest.

"Why?"

Vitae sighed. She reclined in her chair, more a slump of exhaustion than relaxed seating. For a moment, she looked her age, as if centuries of hardship and bitter memories were resurfacing and shadowing her face. "I wish I knew. Though my assumption is that it had something to do with power and position." Seeing the confusion on my face, Vitae launched into a story.

"There have always been two factions to the Guardians, but we were once united as one. It was necessary, given how many Stormkind were spread across the world. Someone had to bring us together and co-ordinate us. That person was Sonus. He was the strongest of us, the wisest." Vitae smiled, a small, sad expression. "I suppose you could say he was our king. But that wasn't enough for him. He wanted to be more than the leader of one faction of the world. He wanted to be a Guardian, a father, a peacekeeper, a sympathizer, a historian. In the end, Sonus simply wanted too much."

"What happened?" I asked, enraptured.

"Sonus and Mortis had always been rivals. They could never agree on the Primordials or their choice to leave the world in the hands of humanity. Mortis believed that if humans were more like the Stormkind, humans would not be killing the Primordials in their sleep. Mortis was known for… experimenting with the Stormkind. Using the tempest-blades to draw on their powers, eager to study charges that were not his own. One day his experiments went too far, and he killed one of Hadrian's charges. Hadrian was younger then, younger than you in human years. He was filled with arrogance and immaturity, and he confronted Mortis about it.

"Mortis was in the middle of a project, something he did not want anyone to know about. He saw Hadrian and beat him within an inch of his life. Sonus loved Hadrian, and when he realized what Mortis had done, he repaid him tenfold. He destroyed everything Mortis had worked for, and cast him out of the Guardians. For three hundred years, Mortis walked the earth alone. We never knew what happened to him in those centuries, and we had no desire to care."

Vitae's eyes became cast in shadow. "Until he returned. To this day, we do not know how he managed it. He attacked all of Sonus's supporters, caught him unaware. He gathered his own followers and turned them on Sonus. It was a bloody day for all of us, and a stalemate was reached. Mortis wounded Sonus, and disappeared with his followers before retribution could be exacted. That was how the Mistrals formed. I was Hadrian's mentor, Sonus's trusted friend. When we returned and saw what had been done, the task of leading the remainder of the Guardians– the Precips– passed to me. It was Sonus's final wish."

Vitae looked down, whether to hide her shame or her tears, I didn't know.

"To this day, I wish he had not given it to me. Protecting Hadrian is one thing, but I was not ready to take over for his father. I am a soldier. Not a leader. It is no wonder so many Precips have died under my command."

"It's not your fault–" I tried.

"Do not speak to me about faults or failings," Vitae snapped. "You have no concept of how much has been lost because of me."

I was about to lose her, the same way I'd lost Hadrian. I needed one ally if I was going to find out what Mortis did to me, and how I could reverse it. Vitae didn't strike me as the kind of person who needed a kind, loving hand to guide her out of her turmoil. She needed the truth, simple and absolute.

"I know you're doing the best with what you have. I know Hadrian and Zephys are loyal to you. I know it takes balls to stand up to Mortis. I know that's what you need to beat him."

Vitae stared at me for a long, almost awkward time before she spoke again. Then she smirked.

"No wonder Hadrian is so flustered by you."

I snorted. "Not the word I would use."

"You do not know him the way I do."

I didn't want to think about what she meant by that, so I decided to switch tracks.

"Can you find out what Mortis did to me?"

Vitae took a deep breath. "I can speculate. Tell me again what the dagger looked like."

I explained it. By the time I was done, Vitae was frowning. "It sounds like a modification to a tempest-blade. The swords we use are meant to be longer. We use two not only for greater skill in combat, but because the power of one blade can be overwhelming. Condensing that power into one small, single dagger is... insane."

"Because it's what all super villains have in common, right? Insanity?" I really wished the tremor hadn't been in my voice.

Vitae stared at me with confusion. "I suppose. But perhaps the more pertinent question should be what the consequences of such a weapon will be. If he managed to alter the energy of a tempest-blade into a single dagger, using it could mean that you are now infused with whatever gifts he filled it with. Ice, wind, rain, dust, any of these could have been forced into you. We should be lucky you were channeled with ice and able to gain a tether to Hadrian."

"Umm..." I bit my lower lip. "Uh, about that... I think he did something else to me."

"What do you mean?"

"After Mortis attacked me, I had this dream– or maybe it was a memory, I'm not sure– but I was with Mortis and Ferno, and I kept having these painful sensations. One minute I was freezing, then I felt like I was drowning, then I was drying up, and then I..."

Fear had been creeping into my voice as I relived the horror of the torture I'd endured. I was shaking like I was about to shudder out of my skin.

Vitae shifted uncomfortably on her chair. Pity filled her eyes. I turned my head away, shame flooding hot in my cheeks. I wished I were stronger. Tough enough to handle this. To at least stand up for myself and tell Vitae I didn't want any pity.

But that would make me a liar. I had already lost my family. I didn't know what Hadrian would think of me now. I could only guess at how Piper had been changed. The last thing I wanted right now was to feel alone.

"You believe you have more than one gift?" Vitae asked tentatively.

I nodded without looking up, still trying to catch my breath and steady my racing heart.

I closed my eyes and sighed. I didn't want it to be true. I wanted to tell her that I only had one "gift," and it was the one that tethered me to Hadrian.

But not wanting to admit the extent of my damage would only make it worse.

So I nodded. "When I touched Declan, I felt something in him push into me. It was like I was taking the wind into my body."

Vitae's eyes sharpened. She leaned forward. "You felt his power go into you? The same way you felt Hadrian's?"

I took a breath to tell her it was different than that, except it wasn't. The more I thought about the jolt that connected me to Hadrian, the more it reminded me of the powerful shock Declan shoved into me.

"It wasn't cold but," I nodded. "Yeah. It was kind of like that."

Vitae continued staring at me, her jaw clenched. Her fingers gripped her knees tightly. Now I was the one who felt awkward. It seemed like she was restraining something. Part of me didn't want to know what she was thinking, but if she was looking at me like a secret was about to burst past her lips, I felt I had a right to know what it was. It was *my* life that was being turned on its head, after all.

Just as I started to ask her what she thought had happened to me, a drop of wetness splatted onto my head. Confused, I looked up. Water began to steadily drip from the ceiling.

Vitae's eyebrows creased and her lips were pulled down in a frown. "Strange. The water has never leaked before."

Said leakage was continuing to dribble on me. Because of course it was. I had been clean and comfortable. My recent adventures had been getting in the way of maintaining that status.

When I heard the pipes groan beyond the ceiling, I knew it was time to move. I tossed the blankets aside and swept off the bed. Not a moment too soon, either. There was a crack of metal, a crunch from the roof, and the hiss of water spitting from the destroyed fire sprinklers.

I was a bit unsteady on my legs because I'd been laying down too long, but Vitae was on her feet and running out of the door. I followed her as quickly as I could, more water spraying wildly from the busted sprinklers. I clung to the walls and shuffled my feet so I wouldn't trip.

It wasn't long until I started hearing the screams.

My heart stuttered at the sound of them, convinced that there was some kind of attack and we were caught in the middle of it again. But as I entered the main cell block, I realized the screams weren't cries of pain or fear.

They were screams of anger.

"I said get away from me!"

I turned around the corner and watched Piper shove her hands against Zephys's chest. He held out his palms, showing that he was unarmed, though I spotted coiled tension in his hazel-blue eyes.

"You must relax–" he called through the rain.

"Relax? Did you just tell me to *relax*? How am I supposed to *relax* when I can do this?"

Piper lifted one of her hands toward the sprinklers. Water pooled and collected into a swirling ball in her hand, a sphere of water that looked more like cracked glass. She shouted wordlessly and dropped her wrist. The ball of water crashed into the floor and splashed Zephys. He pushed his hands down, keeping the water from spraying him in the face.

"Normal people aren't supposed to do that kind of thing!"

Zephys was trying to do his job, act as Piper's Guardian and tell her the truth, but he knew nothing about my best friend. She was strong, but she wasn't like Vitae. She listened to gentle truths better than harsh ones.

Which is why Zephys said the worst possible thing he could say when he responded with, "You are not normal any longer."

Damn damn damn!

I scurried into the prison block as horror swam across Piper's drenched face. She screamed again and charged Zephys. She needed something tangible that she could rail against, and he wasn't going to hurt her.

The moment she touched him, her eyes started to glow.

Oh no.

I ran faster than ever, my heels threatening to give way under me. Piper's eyes were wide and wild as she grabbed Zephys's forearms and lunged in like she was going for the world's boldest kiss.

That was when Hadrian appeared, slipping up from the sidelines and standing in front of me like a brick wall. I hadn't even known he was there. His hands found my shoulders and held me in place. He made it more than clear that I wasn't getting past him without a fight.

"You must stay back, Ava," he said, void of all the emotion I'd seen from him earlier. He was almost robotic now. "It is not safe."

I glared and balled my fists. I was really not in the mood for this, or him. "I must not do a damn thing you say," I mocked. "Move."

Hadrian stood in place.

"Move or I'll make you move. I think we both know I can do it now."

Empowering blue eyes burned dual holes in me as I waited for him to call my bluff. Angry as I was for how he'd yelled at me, for calling me a damn monster, I wouldn't hurt Hadrian. I didn't know what we were to each other, but I wanted to move past our spat. If only to believe that I wasn't exactly what he thought I was.

Water soaked his hair and snaked down his face. He was as striking as ever, but I was becoming better at resisting him. I gripped his wrists and pulled his hands from my shoulders, then hurried around him. Zephys was keeping Piper away from him, but she wasn't giving up. She attacked him wildly, hunger in her glowing eyes. Water hammered down in thick drops from the broken pipes. We were all soaked.

Again.

I was totally spending some time in the desert after this.

In the background, I watched Vitae inch closer, a silent hunter approaching her cornered prey. I waved my hands at her, telling her not to attack Piper. I could handle this. Piper couldn't see me yet.

Darting forward, I nudged Zephys away and grabbed Piper's wrists–

A wave crashed into my chest, nearly knocking me from my feet. Cold water flooded my veins, filling them like engorged tubes. It swelled in my lungs and slipped into my skull, making my brain feel like it was floating on a gently moving river.

I gasped and pushed Piper away. I couldn't be around her, or anyone else right now. I felt the hunger gnawing at my insides. The desire to devour anything tangible. I recognized this sensation. The way it consumed me when I tried to devour Hadrian, and when I nearly went for Piper.

I closed my eyes and bent double, my stomach swimming with nausea. I wrapped a hand around my middle and groaned. The floor wasn't supposed to be spinning, was it?

When I opened my eyes, I could see Hadrian moving toward my side. I held out my hand to halt him.

"I'm okay," I mumbled. "Just stay back."

I don't want to hurt you.

Pain cramped my stomach and I winced.

"Ava?"

"One second, Piper."

Silence fell over the cell block, disrupted only by the sprinklers overhead. I couldn't feel the energy in the air the way I could when I was inside, but I could feel the hot, inviting pulses of life from the people surrounding me. So much, so close, all I had to do was trick them, get them closer…

Hadrian, get everyone to back up to the walls.

"All of you, back up," Hadrian growled.

The heat became distant, stretching farther away. A portion of my mind roared in protest. I pinched my eyes shut and tried to block out the pain.

I am here, Ava. Hadrian's voice was a soothing balm to the ache in my head. *No matter what happens or what we say, I will be here.*

Something like regret filled his voice. Was it for the things he'd said to me, the things I'd said to him, or was I indulging in another wishful fantasy?

Doesn't matter, I told myself. *Block it out. Nobody can stop this but you.*

I concentrated on regulating my breathing, just as I had done in yoga with Piper or when James had an asthma attack and we couldn't reach his inhaler yet. In, hold, out. In, hold, out. After a few seconds, the pain began to subside, and I could no longer feel the heat pulling me toward my best friend and the Guardians.

The flow of water fizzled out, probably shut off by one of the Guardians. As soon as the water was gone, the ache in my belly started to ease. There was no aggression or elements I could misuse. The water on the floor was still there, but it was thin. I couldn't do much with it, even if I wanted to.

And even if I could, I didn't want to think about the damage I could cause.

I straightened up slowly, fighting the vertigo that sloshed through my head. Hadrian started toward me, then pulled back at the last minute. Things hadn't diffused between us, and probably wouldn't for a while. He didn't seem to know if he should touch me. That shouldn't have stung as much as it did.

Piper didn't have any such reservations. My best friend barreled into me, crushing me into her arms. She trembled and sobbed.

"Oh my God, Ava, what happened to us?"

I curled my arms around her back, for her comfort as much as mine. "Did Zephys explain it to you?"

"Yeah," she whimpered. "But I don't understand it. How do we get rid of it?"

"I don't know. But you can trust these people. They'll keep us safe. I know they will."

She whimpered again, then composed herself and let me go.

My eyes slid in Hadrian's direction, though I stopped them before they reached his face. I was still weak from the transfer when I'd touched Piper. I was glad I had been able to do it without going crazy and trying to eat her.

Becoming a soul-sucking cannibal was a good way to ruin a friendship.

"Ava," Vitae's voice finally cut through the silence. "Did you absorb your friend's power?"

I turned my head to the leader of the Precips. Her eyes were wide, her expression torn between awe and horror.

"Um," I started guiltily. "I think so. It wasn't as strong, but… it felt the same."

Vitae's mouth closed firmly, but the shock in her eyes remained.

"It is clear to me that your training must continue. Piper's must begin. She must learn to control her gift, but Ava, you must learn your limits. Until we understand how you can draw and contain our gifts, you must know how far we can push them."

"Vitae–" Hadrian started.

His leader held up her hand. "It is not negotiable, Hadrian. You have managed to rid us of two Mistral guards, but the three that remain are the most dangerous."

I glanced at my Guardian, and could practically see his molars grinding together. Nevertheless, he nodded briskly.

"It is best that we take our rest now. I will begin first watch. Zephys, ensure the comfort of your charge. Hadrian, do the same for yours."

Zephys moved past me toward Piper. He reached for her arm, but she recoiled like he was a snake. Hurt crossed the Guardian's eyes. I swear he even pouted a little. Piper glanced at me. I nodded once, a silent confirmation that she could trust him.

Piper relaxed enough to let Zephys escort her out of the cell block. I would try to find her later and catch her up on everything.

Swift movement passed behind me as my best friend disappeared down the hall. I spun around to see Hadrian confronting Vitae. He was taller than her by almost a foot, but she didn't look weak or small when she gazed up at him.

"I want to know everything," he whispered, thinking I couldn't hear him.

Vitae didn't blink. "Then do not ask me."

Casting me a final glance, Vitae nodded respectfully and walked down the opposite end of the hall, heading for the front door.

Leaving me alone with Hadrian.

The cell block didn't seem so big anymore.

He took a hesitant step toward me, confidence growing every time his foot touched solid ground. He stopped just a foot away, gazing down at me. I curled my arms around myself. It was a reaction that must have made me appear weak in his eyes, but I couldn't control it. I was scared, not just of the things that were happening around me, the confusion and chaos.

I was afraid of what I was starting to become.

"Will you tell me what you and Vitae discussed?" he asked tightly.

I wanted to. I really did. I wanted to tell him that I knew more about the Guardians, the coming extinction of the Stormkind, the exile of Mortis, and his part in Sonus's murder. I wanted to tell him that I was capable of containing multiple powers within myself, and that I was terrified of what I could do with them.

My heart slumped against my ribs. I sighed and shook my head. "Not now."

Hadrian didn't push me. He moved closer, sliding his hand to my lower back and gently nudging me in the direction of one of the cells. I jumped away from his touch and quickly shuffled inside, flopping on the cot. Water from my soaked clothes instantly dampened the blanket. I sighed.

"I will bring you new clothes and another blanket," Hadrian said from above me. I closed my eyes and nodded. I hated being this tired.

Fabric rustled. I opened my eyes and looked over my shoulder. Hadrian was kneeling by my head, as close as he'd been in the infirmary. His eyes danced over my face, alight and concentrated on me.

"Are you all right?" he asked, almost hesitant.

"Yeah," I snapped. "The monster is going to be fine in her cage."

Hadrian's jaw tightened. "I did not mean to call you a monster."

"So all those accusations just slipped out?"

"Your lack of control is not an accusation," he attempted to reason. "It is the truth, and you will have to accept it." A pained look crossed his face, and he quickly looked down. "But what I said about you being like the other Stormkind… That was a mistake, and I am truly, deeply sorry for it. I was not thinking. That is no excuse, but it is the truth." His eyes lifted, finding me. "I do not know exactly what you are, Ava. You are unlike anyone I have ever known," he told me softly. "I am sorry all of this has happened to you. If it is possible, I will return you to your family."

Heartache swelled in my chest at the thought of them. Not knowing where they were or if they were okay. If Dad was finding supplies or if Mom was offering her skills as a nurse. I didn't know if James had gotten more inhalers or if his face was now on the Missing Boards, one of a million ghosts trapped in a photo on a wall.

If they even saw me as their daughter after what I'd done in front of them. Knowing they probably would never want me back.

"Promises, promises," I muttered, rolling onto my side and turning my back on him.

Hadrian sighed. "I have had thousands of charges in my life. You are the first one who has ever talked back to me."

I fought the comeback pressing against my lips, if only because I swore I heard a smile in Hadrian's voice. I didn't want to see it. He might have apologized for calling me a monster and made a promise to try and return me to my family, but that didn't mean he thought I was someone who could adapt to these powers.

It certainly doesn't mean that he trusts me.

"I am trying," he said, letting me know he'd read my thoughts, "but I am a Guardian. I am meant to–"

I flipped over on my side to face him again. I propped myself on an elbow so I could be level with his indigo-azure gaze.

"Don't lie to me."

Hadrian's jaw tensed, a conflict of the wounded look in his eyes. "I'm not–"

"You don't think I can handle myself. You think these powers will consume me."

His eyes narrowed. "Did I not listen to you when you advised me to draw the others back?"

I raised an eyebrow at him. "You're telling me you wouldn't have done that anyway?"

He didn't reply. Smart man.

"Don't go inside my head anymore, Hadrian. I don't want to know what you think of me."

I turned quickly, not wanting to see the expression on his face. The anger or hurt or whatever it would be. I closed my eyes, wishing I could fall asleep without him watching me.

He stayed in the cell for a long time, as though he thought I would turn around and apologize the way he had to me. I didn't. I had no reason to. His words about my lack of control echoed through me. Apologizing meant admitting I could have done terrible damage to people I cared about. I wasn't ready to face that reality just yet. I had to believe that whatever I was now, I could overcome it. Or at least find a way to make peace with it.

I wasn't sure I could trust Hadrian to help me with that anymore.

Finally, he stood up. I listened to the heavy stomp of his boots as he walked out of the cell.

I closed my eyes to fight the tears burning in my eyes.

Trusting Hadrian was proving to be one of the most dangerous things I had ever done.

CHAPTER 11

I wasn't sure who would kill the other first– Piper or Zephys.

"After seven tries," he droned with his arms folded over his chest, "I would have assumed your aim would have improved. Is seven not the lucky number you humans favor?"

Piper balled her fists. I could all but see the steam coming from her ears.

"Sorry, *old man*, I don't have your thousands of years of practice."

"Millennia," he corrected. "And even when I was considered young, I exhibited more control than you have."

Piper scowled. I held my breath and waited for the inevitable slap.

Only to watch my best friend huff, swing her braid over her shoulder, and aim at the target again.

We were back in the prison yard in the dead of night. I'd protested, but according to the Guardians, it was safer to practice out here since storm clouds were harder to spot and neither one of us knew how to conjure lightning yet. Since Zephys's power was based on rain and thunderstorms, Piper was supposed to have that ability, but as he repeatedly told her, it was something that came with immense practice and careful precision. He made it his mission to point out how little she had of both.

We'd been standing in the cool night for almost two hours, using the backboard of the basketball nets as targets. While Piper was focusing on drawing rain-based energy from her tether with Zephys–when she wasn't trying to murder him with glares and bitter comebacks– I was back to using my ice-based powers from Hadrian's tether. I was curious to see what I could do with the powers I'd taken from Piper and Declan, but that seemed like a temptation too reckless to indulge in. As morbidly curious as I was to see what kind of limits Mortis had created me with, I wanted brain damage even less. Using too much power and pushing past my boundaries had given me a bloody nose and bleeding eardrums. I was lucky to be alive.

"You are not focusing, Ava."

I blinked and turned my head to look at Hadrian. He was standing five feet away from me, his strong arms crossed over his muscular chest. I could see those muscles beneath the tight black shirt he wore. Hard muscles my fingers ached to trace–

I shut down the thought and whirled around before he could see my blush. We were still angry and bitter with one another, and our tempers remained at a simmer. Though he'd kept his word and brought a blanket, towels, and fresh clothes to the cell while I was sleeping, he refused to speak to me casually.

Which was fine. I didn't want to talk to him anyway.

Though I don't know why I thought today would be different. That maybe he would man up and admit he was wrong.

I could have laughed at that. When did a man ever admit he was wrong about something?

"Ava."

I threw a glare over my shoulder. And saw Hadrian through a mist of snow. I glanced up at the light clouds drifting over the midnight sky. Snowflakes flitted lazily through the air, a complete contrast to Hadrian's disgruntled demeanor.

I shrugged at him. "Oops."

A muscle in his jaw twitched. I wondered if he were halfway between rolling his eyes, or crying out to the heavens that I was hopeless.

Leaving him to whatever thoughts were coursing through his head, I gathered my focus. Now that snow was falling, I had something more tangible to draw on. The temperature out here was similar to the tether, so I was able to adjust what I sensed inside me to what I felt out here. I could feel the snow on my face, as gentle and sweet as a first kiss.

Then I felt it, the tether uncurl from my heart and press lightly against the underside of my skin. It was creepy and weird, but I concentrated on that gentle pull, feeling it rise out of my body. My skin tingled at the cold sensation, though I knew the moment the tether was out of my body. I could feel it settle around me like an aura, ready and secure.

I did it!

I turned around, smiling at Hadrian, wondering if he'd sensed my thoughts.

He stared at me without emotion, no indication that he knew what I'd done.

Oh. Right. I'd told him to stay out of my head.

"I brought the tether out," I stated.

He plastered a fake smile onto his face and inclined his head. "Excellent. Now use it to strike the target. Add in some of the energy from the air if you wish, but do not push yourself as you do so. The tether will need to return to your body before it is completely used."

Losing some of my enthusiasm, I turned and narrowed my eyes on the target standing twenty feet away from me. Then I unfocused my eyes to gaze at the snow. I found the tether hovering around me and concentrated hard, but the flakes wouldn't move in the direction I wanted. I swiveled my wrist, but gravity did more work than I did.

I reached out with my fingers, directing my attention to the way each flake felt against my skin the instant before it melted. I could feel the tether, but it wasn't as strong as the power in vast expanse of air circling me. Maybe I would be able to use a little bit of that instead of the tether, get a feel for it and remember the feel so I could use it with the tether later. After all, I couldn't weave them both together if I didn't know what they both felt like, and this was as close as I had been to combining natural energy with the tether so far. I would just have to be careful.

Besides, this was training, not a fight for my life.

Ignoring the tension in Hadrian's voice when he called my name again, I raised my hands and twisted them like I was forming a snowball. The energy in the air came alive. Snowflakes spun together and clumped into a ball the size of my palm. Since it was loose snow, I couldn't hold it. But I did imagine it flying across the basketball court and hitting the backboard.

The snowball careened forward and smacked into the board. Not the center like I'd been aiming for, but that didn't keep the smile from my face. I turned on my heel and beamed at Hadrian. I didn't feel the heat of his life force, which elated my spirits even more. I put my hands on my hips and cocked an eyebrow, a gesture that screamed, *I told you so.*

He stared at me, then dropped his eyes and shook his head. Laughing a little, I turned and went back to creating the snowballs. I took pieces of natural energy as well as bits of the tether, being careful about how much I used. I made single snowballs, some big but most small, and aimed them at the basketball board. My aim was still off, but I wasn't up for improving it yet. I chose to focus on the limits of energy I could take, and made multiple snowballs.

I started with two. Then I moved onto three. Then four. Then six. Then ten. Then sixteen. Pretty soon I was hurtling dozens of snowballs at the board, making each one splat against the metal. I was always conscious of the tether and the natural energy around me, making sure I didn't steal too much from either. I needed to make snowballs, not a blizzard. By the time I decided I was done, the basketball hoop was covered and surrounded in snow, as if a bucket had been dumped over its top. All that could be seen clearly now was the red hoop and the frayed netting.

"Impressive."

I almost jumped at Hadrian's voice so close to my back. He didn't look at me, staring over my head at the board. "Imagine what you could do if that were ice instead of snow."

My smile tripped across my lips. If I turned that snow into ice, I wouldn't be temporarily blinding my enemies. I would potentially be cracking open their skulls.

Wind gusted on my left, tossing my hair into my face. I spat it out of my mouth and drew it away from my face. Piper was flinging her hands wildly, an uneven pattern as she attempted to control the wind. Zephys hadn't moved an inch, and looked even less pleased than before.

"The wind is your ally. You must not punch your allies."

"Shame," she spat. "Because I'm seriously considering punching you."

Zephys grinned. "It would be a pity for you to damage such a handsome figure, don't you think?"

Piper scoffed. "You're not that handsome."

"Ah, but I am handsome enough that you noticed it."

Piper didn't say anything. She went back to slapping the air uselessly.

I took a step closer to my friend. "Are you using the tether?" I asked.

"Of course," she replied, exasperated. "Pretty boy back there won't let me use the energy in the air." She dropped her hands and tilted her head back, breathing deep and closing her eyes. "I can feel it, Ava. I can even *taste* it."

I bit my lower lip. "Maybe you should channel it for a little while."

"No. You should not."

I glanced at Hadrian. His eyes were as dark and cold as the ocean when they flicked to me. "For now, you must learn to rely on the tether, and nothing else. Otherwise you will lose yourself as every Stormkind has done."

"I used some natural energy a minute ago," I said, shooting him a pointed glare. "Do I look out of control to you?"

He blinked. "I am not sure there is a safe way to answer that question."

I snapped my arms over my chest. The snowfall was heavier than before. "Did you miss what Piper said? We don't have eons of experience to work with. We never asked for this. We're working with what we have. Besides, doesn't it make sense to learn how to control the tether and natural energy, so we don't let it overtake us?"

"In practice, that theory is sound. In combat, it cannot be your weapon. Adrenaline will overwhelm you, and you will lose control the same way Stormkind do."

"That hasn't happened to me yet," I seethed.

He didn't react to my anger. "*Yet* is merely another word for *soon*."

I wanted to narrow my eyes, twist my lips into a scowl, and ball my fists so he wouldn't know how much his words stung me. Why did I expect any different? Hadrian had never believed in me. All he cared about was getting his revenge on Mortis. I was a tool to him. That was why he was so tender around me. He wanted to make sure his insurance policy was intact. If, for some reason, he wasn't able to take Mortis down himself, or if he needed a distraction, I was the perfect substitute. I wasn't like Piper or Declan. I was able to control different types of storms. The only ones I was missing were dust and rain. I had a pretty good handle on ice and snow. I was more than enough to give Mortis and the Mistrals some problems.

Why Hadrian was even bothering to teach me about drawing power from the tether was beyond me. Probably just a way to appease Vitae in case she came by.

Fine. If that's what he wanted, that's what I would do.

I spun so my back was to him and felt for the tether, which had sunk back into my skin while I was talking to Piper. It was cool and relaxed in my chest. I didn't want to be rough with it, but I was angry. Nobody did anything rational when they were angry.

Piper was arguing something beside me, but I blocked out her and everything else. I pulled energy from the tether until it was taut as a whip, like a cool piece of string had been stretched inside me. Hadrian said something sharp, but I ignored it. I concentrated on the whip, and thought about what I wanted. Something detailed. Something small and precise.

Didn't take me long to figure out what I could do to prove Hadrian wrong.

I exhaled, relying on steady, even breathing, and held out my hands. Cool tingles danced along my wrists, poked my palms, and prodded my fingertips. Settled into the sensation, I stared directly at the net of the basketball hoop. I coaxed a whisper of ice from my veins and pushed it toward my target.

Snowflakes parted as the frosty breeze moved through the air. I nearly lost a few times when the stronger, natural breeze gusted around me, but I didn't lose my concentration.

Beads of sweat started to form around my hairline when the breeze passed the halfway point. The tether vibrated as I dragged energy from it, but I figured this was like working out a muscle I hadn't used before. All I had to do was push harder and keep it from tearing.

Finally, the breeze met the netting. Now came the tricky part.

I pictured the frost wrapping around the netting, but only the netting. I had to avoid the metal ring above the netting as well as the board. Freezing the snow didn't matter, I figured. I was making this hard enough already.

The frosty breeze drifted over the net. It hardened the rope in a cool blue case. I almost went cross-eyed from staring so hard, but at least I could see it happening.

Took me two more exhausting minutes, but I did it. The visible parts of the net were frozen in ice, the board hardly touched. I relaxed my hold on the tether, and felt the bones in my legs disappear.

My head spun like it was caught in the tango with an overzealous partner, and my knees buckled. Firm hands clutched my shoulder and pressed against my back to steady me. I sighed and relaxed into them. Then I smelled seawater and musk behind me, and pulled away. Hadrian's hand disappeared from my back, but the touch on my shoulder lingered until I turned around and plucked it off.

"I'm fine," I said, planting my hands on my hips and trying to focus on his swaying face. I blinked quickly. "Don't need your help, don't need to learn control."

Hadrian stared at me with sharp, blue eyes. He looked ready to lay into me, but all that came out was, "You are infuriating."

Maybe I should have been a little more insulted, but honestly, no one had ever called me infuriating before. Driving Hadrian crazy was so far the highlight of my day.

I smiled wickedly. "Looks like I'm going to have to find another word to describe you, then."

Hadrian's lips twitched, like he was fighting a smile. His eyes betrayed him, and my heart did that little skip it did whenever he was around.

"Look, if you're not going to help me, get back. Ava can teach me instead."

Oh, boy.

I tore my eyes from Hadrian and looked at Piper and Zephys. He was closer to her than before, his hands slightly outstretched like he wanted to touch her. My best friend's fists were balled at her side, like she would punch him if he tried.

"Ava is still learning her abilities. Her tether could be stronger than usual, given that she does not contain one power."

I grimaced, sort of wishing that Vitae hadn't dropped that little snippet of information on our trainers before we came out here while she went hunting for supplies. I was barely comfortable with the knowledge myself.

"She'd still be more help than you!" Piper shouted. "All you do is berate and insult me! You haven't even shown me how to use your little magic tricks. For all I know, you don't have any power at all!"

I glanced up. Against the dark night sky, I could see rolling thunderheads closing in above us. I heard the warning rumbles, but the people causing them didn't.

"Um, Piper, Zephys–"

They ignored me. Pride was getting the better of them.

Zephys took a step to the right, standing between Piper and me. The thunderclouds landed directly over our heads. He snapped up his wrist. Rain began to pour and thunder began to rumble.

Goddamn it.

Zephys snapped his fingers. A streak of lightning erupted from out of the storm cloud and slammed into the basketball hoop. The flash of light vanished, and nothing but a warped, charred square of metal remained.

"Whoa, Zephys, what are you doing?!" I blurted.

The Guardian's eyes were fixed on Piper, though I think his words were meant for me. "I am demonstrating the control I have over my gifts, as my student has doubted me."

Piper's arms were rigid at her sides. The clouds grew thicker above them.

"Look, I know she accidentally tried to kill you, but you need to get over that. Throwing lightning left and right is only going to draw attention to us."

"I agree," Hadrian said from close to my back. "Unwarranted impatience will earn us nothing."

"That's all I have to do?" Piper snapped. "Fine. Easy."

"Piper–"

She ignored me, too, whirling on her heel and slapping her hands down. Twin bolts of lightning crashed into the prison yard, kicking up snow and singeing the ground. Thunder exploded over our heads. I have no idea what she was trying to hit, if anything, but I don't think she cared. Piper's anger had bested her.

Hadrian wrapped his arms around me and drew me back. I let him, grateful for the protection from my crazed friend as she hurled lightning at a rapid pace. It sliced into the ground like a knife in the hands of a maniac. I dug my fingers into Hadrian's arm as the rain showered us both, hoping to God that Zephys would realize how badly he'd crossed the line and fix it.

Thankfully, he managed the first part. Wide-eyed and slack-jawed, he watched my best friend in her rage for two seconds before he understood that she was out of control, and it was his fault. Then the mask of a seasoned warrior covered the shock, and he drew one of his tempest-blades over his shoulder.

I pulled on Hadrian's arm, trying to rip it away from my body so I could stop Zephys.

He tightened his grip and drew me into his hard chest. "Be still, Ava," he said through the storm. "He will not hurt her. He will use the tempest-blade to lure her away, the same as we do with Stormkind. She will be safe."

I believed that. I knew the Precips weren't the kind of Guardians that would kill their charges. The Mistrals were the ones that killed the Stormkind, for whatever sick reasons they decided on.

But it was almost impossible for me to watch an experienced soldier approach my best friend with a ready blade.

I saw the instant Piper felt the power in the tempest-blade. She whirled around to face Zephys. I cringed when I saw the white flash in her eyes. The thunderstorm pounded us with rain and wild flashes of lightning shuddered through the sky. I shook violently, even as Hadrian wrapped his arms around me and whispered that it would be all right.

Piper stalked toward Zephys with a feral snarl. My friend was beautiful, even when she was angry. But what I was seeing now wasn't just anger. It was ferocity. Animalistic fury, untamable, and unnatural. I never thought I would be afraid of Piper. Piper, who was strong, beautiful, independent, generous, unbiased, the best friend any girl could ask for.

But I never imagined that either of us would be stuck with Stormkind powers, either.

Zephys remained calm, backing up as she approached him. One hand was raised in complacency. The other held the tempest-blade at his side. I was so tense I could have snapped. She stormed forward, and I instinctively reached out to stop her.

Big mistake.

She suddenly stopped and whipped her head in my direction. I recognized the look in her eyes as the same one I'd seen in the Stormkind when they were starved.

Oh, no.

Piper abandoned Zephys and went straight for me.

Hadrian let go of my arms and jumped in front of me. His hands went up and filled with ice. A frosted barrier formed between him and Piper. She bounced off it and landed on her back. While I didn't want her to so much as crack a fingernail, I also grimly hoped she would get some sense knocked into her. Even if it had to be literally.

Zephys rushed her while she was on the ground. Lightning slammed into the yard a foot away, and he was thrown onto his back.

So much for grim hope.

Hadrian slowly curved his hands inward, turning the wall into a cage. Lightning crashed down around him, each strike closer than the last. He didn't notice, but I jumped at every strike. Piper might not be able to see him– the wall was taller than her at this point– but that didn't mean she wouldn't get a lucky strike. I remembered the man on the roof of the school. How the thunder-Stormkind had struck him with a bolt of lightning that threw him off the building. The horrid, scorched lump he'd become when he landed at the Stormkind's feet. How the Stormkind lifted him up to be devoured without a second thought.

I might butt heads with Hadrian, might know that he saw me as just another insufferable charge, but I didn't see him as my broody teacher. He was more than my Guardian. He was my friend, a friend I was hoping might see me as something more one day.

It was his job to protect me. It was my choice to protect him.

Gritting my teeth, I closed my eyes and reached for the natural energy around me. I didn't risk the tether, since Hadrian was busy containing Piper in an icy cage. Snow began to fall heavily around us, and I imagined a blast of cold wind curving into the open end of the cage. Maybe a serious chill would stop Piper's rampage.

She screamed, a sound of rage or pain or both, I didn't know. But it struck me as sharply as any lightning bolt I'd seen tonight.

I raced around Hadrian, charging for the back of the cage even as he shouted for me to stop. The cage was about three quarters done, only the back open for Piper to escape if she chose. I swerved around the icy block and came face to face with my friend.

The warm brown eyes I was so familiar with were replaced by a bleach-white glow. Even without her natural eyes, I knew Piper could see me. I dragged on the natural energy again, trying to push her back in the cage. The blast hit her in the chest and she was shoved against the frosty wall. She thrashed and screamed, trying to fight the invisible force holding her back.

A man shouted. I didn't hear what he said. I saw Zephys running toward me from the corner of my eye. He grabbed my arm, making my control falter. Piper took a shaking step forward.

"We must move!" Zephys shouted at me. "Hadrian will lock her inside until she weakens, then release her. She will be weak, but not hurt. You must stand aside, Ava!"

He was right. I knew he was right. He and Hadrian knew all about subduing Stormkind, and like it or not, that's what Piper and I were halfway to becoming.

But all I could see was my best friend. Someone I loved, who'd stood up for me when I was bullied, who'd invited me to her big house for hide-and-seek and sleepovers filled with popcorn and terrible romantic comedies. I didn't want that girl to get hurt. I wanted her back.

My hesitation cost us.

Lightning shattered the ground three feet away from me. The sharp white light seared my eyes and blinded me. I screamed and Zephys shouted. I knew I lost my hold on the cold breeze. I still couldn't see when a force slammed into me and knocked me onto the ground. It kept me pinned. Hard knees crushed out the air in my lungs. My vision was fading back to color when I felt her lean forward to my mouth.

I covered it with one hand and lashed upward with the other. My palm slapped against her face–

And fire exploded through my chest. I screamed at the shocks thumping my nerves like fists. Searing pain ripped through me like fabric pulled by cruel hands. My heart danced under the touch of a livewire. My lungs and brain swelled until I thought they would burst.

Pressure shot through my chest. Desperate, terrified voices called my name. Another jolt of pain wracked me, and I rolled onto my side. My stomach cramped until I thought it would snap in half. Blasts of white light tore the world around me and the ground shuddered.

I peeled my eyes open and saw three pairs of feet hovering around me. Three warm pulses of energy teasing my senses. All so close. All within my reach. I just had to extend my arms and take them.

I rolled my head and looked up. Two men and a woman stared down at me. The men were tense and gripping swords. The woman covered her mouth with her hands and started to weep.

Two strong pulses, filled with emotion and energy. Pure and undiluted life.

I dragged to my knees and found my footing. They all backed up. The two men reached for their swords. The blue-eyed one drew his with a tortured expression. The woman screamed. I think she shouted for them to stop. She might have yelled *what the fuck are you doing*? I didn't know. I didn't care.

I wanted the life. The light and warmth hiding under their skin beckoned me. I would take it. By any means necessary.

The blue-eyed man barked an order at the dark-skinned man. He hesitated, then grabbed the woman by her arm and dragged her back. I snarled and rushed for them. The blue-eyed man stepped between them and me. I drew to a stop, narrowing my eyes at him. He spoke, and he was close enough that I could hear his words this time.

"Ava, please do not make me do this." Pain flickered in his beautiful, life-filled eyes. "Please do not make me control you."

Cold rage rolled in the pit of my stomach, twisting into my chest. I was nothing he could control. And once I had the heat of his life buried in me, I would become even stronger. Then I would take the other two.

The dark-skinned man was restraining the woman. She was shouting at me, but her words were lost in the wind.

Wind. Yes. That was exactly what I needed.

From the corner of my eye, I saw horror sweep the blue-eyed man's face. I felt the air around me and swept out my arm, pushing him aside. I curved my arm and pulled it toward my chest. The dark-skinned man and the woman launched toward me. They landed in a heap at my feet. The heat rolling from their lives was liquid pleasure. So much brighter than before.

It was about to become mine.

They scrambled to get away from me, the dark-skinned man reaching for his sword. I snarled and shoved out my hand, drawing on the static in the air. It snapped around my hand and struck him in the chest. He fell back and screamed. The woman's scream was louder. I riveted my eyes to her. Wasting no more time, I dove–

Thick arms wrapped around my stomach and yanked me back. We both stumbled and fell onto the ground. I landed hard, crushing the body beneath me. I thrashed and screamed, unable to see where he was. Yet I could feel him, he was so close, his sweet, warm life mere inches from me. But I couldn't *see* it. If there was a more cruel torture, I didn't know what it was.

I slammed my elbows back into his stomach, kicked his legs, dashed my skull against his head, clawed his arms until they bled. I wanted the life from his very veins, but I couldn't take it by making him bleed. I had to drink it. All I had to do was turn and take it–

Cold steel pressed flat against my skull. A sharp bite of pain sliced my skin. I yelped and felt a vicious, cold yank in my chest.

The tether.

Hadrian's tether.

I went still. Rain doused me and my head throbbed. The world was spinning again. Hadrian's breathing was rapid beneath me. Something warm trickled down my temples. Tears pricked my eyes.

Zephys and Piper rushed toward us. My best friend choked on a scream, covering her mouth with her hands to keep it at bay. Zephys set his jaw and extended his hand.

I cringed at the sight of it.

"No," I whimpered. "No... can't hurt you."

His hand remained extended. "That will not happen, Ava. Stand if you can."

Hadrian's arm loosened from my stomach. "It is all right, Ava. You cannot hurt us. It is over."

I shivered. A sob strangled me. Zephys knelt down and pushed his hand closer to me. Hadrian's hands were on my shoulders to either comfort me or push me off.

My arm was heavy as lead when I set it in Zephys's hand. His grip was sturdy and he had no problem standing and pulling me to my feet. The horizon tilted, but Hadrian had risen with me. His hands never left my shoulders. I looked back at him.

Hadrian had a bloody– but intact– nose. I felt woozy, but I lifted my hand and let my fingers wipe the blood away from the space between his nose and upper lip.

"Red's not your color," I mumbled. "You're definitely a winter."

Hadrian's jaw tightened until I thought it would shatter. One of his arms slipped around my back to hold me upright. His other hand swiped under my nose.

It came away bloody. The horizon tilted again.

"Oh boy," I murmured. "Looks like we're a pair of winters."

The sentence was barely past my lips before my legs gave out and I collapsed into blackness.

CHAPTER 12

"I leave for three hours. *Three hours*. And your training exercises nearly kill one of your charges."

Yikes. Vitae did *not* sound pleased. Though she was right.

I was lying in a familiar bed. Probably the infirmary bed again. My clothes were dry– so either Vitae or Piper had changed me as I slept– and a blanket was pulled up to my chest. A bandage was taped to my head. It stung, but no worse than a paper cut.

Not that I was going to let anyone know I was awake just yet. I wanted to hear what was going on without being fussed over.

Though I wasn't going to let go of the strong hand holding mine any time soon.

"I am to blame," Zephys said with a heavy voice. "I aggravated Piper instead of training her. I thought a strong arm would curb her anxiety. But I was wrong. I am so sorry."

"It's not only your fault," Piper added. She sounded far away, like she was hiding in a corner. "I shouldn't have let him get to me. I just... I lost control. I had no idea what would happen. I didn't want Ava to get hurt."

Piper's voice broke on the last word, thick sobs dragging out of her throat. I couldn't bear the sound of it. I cracked my eyes open and followed the sound of her voice.

"No worries, Pipe. It could have been worse."

Like I'd guessed, she was in the corner across from my bed, hiding her head in her hands. The sound of my voice caused her to look up and unthread her hands from her hair. Piper's eyes widened and another sob choked her.

She sprinted out of her corner and rushed to the bed in a flash. She threw her arms around my neck and hugged me tight.

"Oh, thank God, Ava, I'm so sorry, I'm so, so sorry."

I laughed a little, silently glad she wasn't afraid of me after the way I'd looked at her when I was under that weird trance. Thinking about it took away the joy I felt, so I closed the memories away and focused on my friend.

"Piper, you're choking me."

She dropped me like I was on fire. "Shit, I'm sorry."

I waved my free hand through the air. "It's okay. I'm not mad. Sore, but not pissed off." My humor thinned. "Are you okay?"

Piper nodded. "Yeah. I... I never expected that to happen. I wasn't able to control it. I saw you and you were giving off this energy..."

She wrapped her arms around her body. Zephys took a step closer to her and placed his hand on her shoulder. Amazingly, she didn't push him away. Progress was being made.

I looked down. "Yeah. I know what you mean."

Finally, I slid my eyes to Hadrian. Brooding blue eyes pierced me. A few days ago, I would have shied away from them. But I slowly understood what was behind them. I could see the anxiety he was trying to hide. The guilt over hurting me, and the fear that he would have to do it again.

I could feel it in the way he gripped my hand, like it would take the Jaws of Life to pry him away from me.

"How is your head?" he asked. The words were strained.

I prodded the bandage. It was about half the size of my palm, but still didn't hurt more than a sting.

"Fine," I admitted. "What did you do?"

Hadrian's jaw clenched. His free hand gripped my wrist and pulled it down from my forehead.

"I used one of the tempest-blades. We gain control of Stormkind by..." he looked at my hands, so small and pale in his, "by cutting them. If they are our charge, they will feel the tether and become subdued. In truth, they have the same vulnerable areas as a human. Though cuts to the head are often the most efficient." Hadrian squeezed my hands. "It was the only thing I could think of."

Pain and regret laced his deep, gorgeous voice. I sat up– which took way more grunting and effort than I want to willingly admit– and tilted my head until I could see the hints of blue that always sent welcome shivers through me.

"You didn't scar me, did you?"

His head snapped up, hurt I would even suggest it.

"No, of course not. I would never forgive myself if I saw the mark every time I looked at you."

I smiled, and for a minute, I could imagine his concern for me was actually about *me*, not about my capabilities as his student. For now, I was willing to look past our fights and imagine that we could get back to at least a comfortable understanding or a level truce. I could pretend it was just the two of us alone in this room, and maybe I could guilt him into kissing me.

But I knew better. Guilty kissing was the worst kind. It only left a trail of regret and pain behind. I curled my fingers around his wrist as he squeezed my hand. I smiled, though my chest was tight with longing.

"Then you can forgive yourself. I'm okay."

Hadrian acted like he'd lost control of his arms. I had to set his wrist down on the bed next to my hip– maybe not the best idea, in hindsight, because he was oh so tempting– and he still wouldn't let go of my hand.

I didn't mind. He drove me crazy, but the simple truth was that I enjoyed the comfort of his hand in mine. The warmth of his skin, the calluses that spoke of strength, the gentle security when he tightened his grip.

Turning away from Hadrian before the fantasies could start, I looked at Vitae, Zephys, and Piper. "What kind of damage did we do to the building?" I asked.

Vitae stared me down with her arms folded over her chest. "None. At least not to the main prison complex. The prison yard has been entirely obliterated."

I cringed. Obliteration was now one of my least favorite words.

"Both Hadrian and Zephys have told me what happened. I believe that your desire for life force will only come to light when you are lost in the rush of your powers."

I shifted awkwardly. "Can you not make me sound like a bloodthirsty vampire, please?"

Vitae's lips quirked, but her smile was sad. "I apologize, Ava. But it is the most obvious answer, is it not?"

I nodded grudgingly.

"Then you will also need to forgive me for this next statement, but I believe that Mortis designed you– all of these false Stormkind– to be his weapons against us."

My stomach dropped. Hadrian's hand tightened over mine.

"But... But why would he choose humans?" Piper whispered. Zephys remained behind her, his hand still secure around her shoulder. "Doesn't he have his own soldiers and Stormkind?"

"He does. But they are hardly an army. If he wishes to avenge the Primordials, he will require a much more potent weapon." Vitae's eyes lingered on me for a beat too long. "Which leads me to our next challenges. First, we must determine if Piper has only one gift, or if she is like you, and capable of holding more."

Piper sputtered. "What? How are you going to determine that?"

"By turning his weapons against him."

Zephys stiffened. Hadrian squeezed my hand a little too hard.

"What do you mean?" my Guardian asked. Nobody could miss the subtle danger in his voice.

"While I was obtaining supplies, I overheard rumors of dust storms on the island of Cayo Costa. Apparently, they can be seen from the mainland, and wisely, no one is attempting to see what is causing them. They have no desire to encounter another Stormkind."

"Sounds like Ferno could be maintaining his practice," Zephys said bitterly. I wiggled in the bed so my shiver wouldn't be so noticeable. In my head, all I could hear was Ferno's disregard for me as Mortis filled me with power that made me feel like I was disintegrating cell by cell.

"That is my assumption, yes," she agreed. "If more of Mortis's false Stormkind exist, it is best we engage them. If we cannot convince them to abandon the Mistrals, the least we can do is subdue them."

I blinked at her. "What do you mean by subdue?" I asked cautiously.

Vitae's eyes were colder than any ice I could ever control. "I mean subdue. By any means necessary."

Anger boiled through my blood. "It's not our fault that we're like this," I barked. "Mortis did this to us. We didn't ask for it."

"Yet it does not change the fact that you are equally as dangerous and more unpredictable than any Stormkind we have faced before," she countered. "You are beyond our control, and so we must—"

"We're not slaves," I shouted. "We're human beings!"

Vitae's eyes flared. "Do not rail against me, Ava. Not when you sought to devour two of my friends, your own best friend, and drained your body to the point of exhaustion."

Her words were a kick to the chest after a punch in the gut and a shot to the face. I searched for air to refute her, but my lungs were breathless. She was right, but so was I. The things I had done—and nearly done—were terrible beyond words.

But it *wasn't my fault.*

"When will we leave, Vitae?" Hadrian rumbled.

I snapped my head at him, shock rushing through me. Hadrian didn't meet my eyes. He simply gazed at his leader.

"At dawn," she informed. "The false Stormkind will need to recuperate."

"Whoa, I'm not going anywhere," Piper said. "Not unless you're taking me and Ava home."

Vitae looked at her. "That is not an option. Mortis remains at large. While he is loose, none of your loved ones are safe. Alone, we are not enough to stop him. If he obtains either of you, the world you know and love will be destroyed forever."

Piper's eyes welled with tears. "I can't– I can't use these gifts. If I get another one, I don't know what I'll do."

"We will protect you," Zephys soothed, squeezing her shoulder. "We are your Guardians, and it is our duty to–"

She threw his hand off her shoulder and whirled on him. "I don't care about that," she yelled. She spun again and pointed her finger at Vitae's chest. "You have no right to keep us here."

Vitae was unmoved. "Perhaps not. But if you leave, I guarantee that your life is forfeit. Mortis cares little for experiments that do not serve him well."

Piper's breath hitched. She was a tumult of rage and fear.

"We will be prepared by dawn," Hadrian confirmed. I looked at him again. This time I needed to get his attention.

"What if this is a trap? The exact thing that Mortis wants?"

Hadrian's beautiful eyes were blank. I couldn't read him when he didn't want me to. "If it is, it will not be strong enough."

His gall astounded me. So much so, that I yanked my hand from his. He didn't look away, but he didn't react either.

This was when I realized I needed to stop thinking he would.

Over and over, I had to remind myself that Hadrian didn't care about me half as much as he cared about getting revenge on Mortis, something he had wanted for centuries. The concept might be the only thing he *could* care about.

And I had been a fool to think any different.

Hadrian's stony expression cracked a little. He took a breath, as if he was going to say something, but I turned away. I had no desire to hear it. I was tired of making myself hurt over him.

"So we're going to run around an abandoned island and hope we don't get swallowed in either a dust storm or a sociopath's trap?" I asked bitterly.

Vitae didn't flinch at the barb. "Essentially."

"Ava," Piper pleaded. "You can't agree with this."

My eyes rose to hers, heavily. "Of course not. But they will keep their word about protecting us, just like they'll keep their word about holding us here until Mortis is stopped. This is one of those 'it's for the greater good' scenarios, Pipe."

Her shoulders slumped. I felt like slapping myself, or at least someone.

Hadrian was still sitting close, so the thought seriously crossed my mind.

But like whatever romantic fantasies and hopes I had about him, it wasn't meant to be. Vitae told us all to rest for the next six hours. Traveling the way Guardians traveled was going to be an experience, she said ominously.

Whoopie. I looked forward to it like I looked forward to a needle in the eye.

Zephys helped a stunned Piper leave the room. I imagined he was going to have his hands full when everything that just happened sank into her.

Which left me alone with my Guardian. The man I couldn't stand to look at right now, because I wouldn't be able to look away when I did.

"Ava, this is important not just for us, but for your whole world," he tried. "I know you are upset, but you have to–"

"Get some sleep." I interrupted. "That's what Vitae said, right? Get six hours? She would know, Queen of Forward Thinking, and all."

I turned my back to him and rested on my side. I grunted and shuffled, trying to get comfortable. The mattress was too hard, but it was better than the mattress in the cell.

I could feel Hadrian's eyes on me. I pulled the blanket up to my neck so he would get the message. I could still feel him.

"Do you want me to stay with you?" he asked, as if uncertain of himself.

"No point. All I'm going to do is sleep. No thrilling magic shows or near-death experiences. I'll save those for tomorrow."

Inside my chest, the tether constricted, like cold fingers clenching on reflex. I closed my eyes and bit my lip. I didn't want to feel him in there. He was already in my head. Wasn't that enough?

It was a long time before he spoke again.

"It has never been my intention to hurt you, Ava."

The softness, the sincerity, the pain in his voice... It almost broke me. It sounded like he was pleading, begging for me to listen to him and forgive him.

Except there was no point. He was already breaking my heart, and he probably didn't even know he was doing it.

Maybe it was time to return the favor.

"Then go."

It was a whisper, two words that barely made it past my lips thanks to my heart's ache and demand to let him stay, but I got them out.

It was the right thing to do. It had to be. Otherwise, I wouldn't have felt like shit.

Hadrian remained seated for a long time while I pretended to sleep. Maybe fifteen minutes passed before I heard him rise from his chair and walk around the bed. I concentrated on yoga-breaths so he would truly think I was asleep. That whatever I felt for him was nothing more than respect and a grudging allegiance.

Then he lowered his hand. I felt it hover above my face, like he was going to brush away some of my hair or stroke my cheek. The thought of him doing that made my heart pinch. If he touched me, I might be able to at least partially forgive him. I would know that he cared.

But then the presence of his hand disappeared. His footsteps started again. The door opened. It closed. The room fell silent.

And the hole in my chest grew wider.

Chapter 13

Mornings without coffee are not mornings. They're a sign that the end is on its way, and we should all be running for the nearest shelter.

Getting up at the crack of dawn after a measly four hours of rest was pure torture. I made a mental note never to brood before bed again.

At least the bandage was gone from my head, so it no longer looked like I'd had a brain operation that took away my reason and stuck me with a bunch of superhuman warriors that spent all their time hunting beings that could create and control storms that sucked out human life-force like energy drinks.

Nope. That was just my reality.

Piper trudged out of the cell block to meet me. Her eyes were half opened and her hair was messy from tossing and turning, and she *still* looked like a super model. I don't know how she did it, and she would never tell me her secret.

Standing in front of us like drill sergeants were the Guardians. Each one was dressed in their midnight blue leather and pale blue iron armor and wore their tempest-blades crossed over their backs. Vitae looked wide awake and ready to take over the country. Zephys looked grumpy, possibly not being a morning person himself. Hadrian looked...

I don't know how Hadrian looked. As soon as my eyes drifted toward him, I pushed them to the ground.

"We travel by storm-sight," Vitae explained, not caring about the gloom hanging over our heads. "With a hold on our tethers, we can concentrate on any storm going on around us. Knowing what kind of storm to look for makes things easier. While dust-Stormkind are not our specialty, we are trained to confront and engage them. From there, the storm-sight projects an image of the location into our minds, and we travel through our tempest-blades."

That brought my head up. "Wait, we're traveling *through* a sword? How?"

Vitae smirked. "By now, you should realize that tempest-blades are nothing like regular swords. They were created by the Primordials to be our weapons, our justice, our transport, our tethers. Blades that will never break must serve more than one purpose."

I looked at the swords crossed behind her back. Of all the crazy things I anticipated I would do today, traveling through an unbreakable sword was the last one.

"Is it going to hurt?" Piper asked, trying to hide the nervousness from her voice.

Zephys smiled, bright and charming, all traces of his morning grumpiness seeming to have disappeared.

"Not at all," he promised. "Though you will feel some uncomfortable tingling sensations."

She grimaced. "Great. Don't make it sound awkward and creepy or anything."

Zephys smiled a genuine smile, then held out his hand for Piper. She hesitated, glancing at me. I smiled and gave her hand a reassuring squeeze. It did wonders for her confidence. She walked with her head high to Zephys, taking his hand and letting him wrap his arm around her shoulder to pull her close.

That made sense. The Guardians would have to hold onto us tightly if we were going to travel through the tempest-blades...

Oh, great.

Holding my breath, I trudged toward Hadrian. I stood close to him, but didn't let him touch me. I wouldn't do that until I needed to.

He looked at me, but said nothing. A quiet yet heavy sigh escaped his lips.

Vitae withdrew the tempest-blades from her back. Zephys followed suit, his arms curving around Piper to keep her close.

"Hold onto me," he instructed.

She did so, closing her arms around his back and resting her head against his chest. Once she did, she looked way more relaxed.

Hadrian's swords were still on his back. He was waiting for me.

Taking another breath, I edged closer to him and wrapped my arms around him. The leather and metal armor was rough and cold against my cheek, but he felt solid and real. I tried to resist the impulse, but I couldn't. I nestled my head on his chest and sighed. Every breath smelled like warm seawater. He was too damn comfortable.

I felt his muscles shift and flex as he reached back and drew his tempest-blades over his shoulders. He brought his arms around and secured me to his chest. I should have felt constricted, but I didn't. I felt safe. No matter what I thought about Hadrian and his lack of concern for me, I had no doubt he would protect me.

"I shall depart first and ensure the security of the island," Vitae said. "I shall then unleash a small rainstorm to alert you to my location."

"Ferno might sense that you created the storm," Zephys said.

"Perhaps," she agreed. "But rainstorms have become quite common, and if we are about to enter a trap, I am willing to fall into it first." Vitae looked at me. "I am prepared to endure the consequences of any choice I make."

Well, that's something, I thought.

Still, I nodded to her. Vitae turned her head and straightened her back, lifting both swords and placing them on top of each other, the tip of one blade pressing against the pommel of the other. Standing on top of each other, the swords were close to ten feet tall. I had no idea how she was able to balance both– or how she wasn't cutting open both her hands right now, holding both weapons by their blades– but then I guessed living for thousands of years made you good at certain things.

She sighed deeply and exhaled. As she breathed, a pale blue light began to glow from the sigil printed on the pommels, the sword-in-the-rain mark of the Precips. The light trickled down the hilt, past the cross guard, and into the silver blade. Then it burst into a haze of azure, illuminating the cell block. My eyes widened as the light grew brighter, shimmering down the second blade until I couldn't see Vitae anymore. The light began to pulse, increasing in speed until it was like a strobe light, and then exploded into a single blazing flash. I shut my eyes and turned my face into Hadrian's armor, seeing the red flesh of my eyelids instead of the regular black.

After a minute, the brightness faded, and all I could see was blackness.

Between this and the lightning, I think I'm going to go blind.

"You won't," Hadrian murmured. I felt the words rumble through his chest and into my face. I shouldn't have liked the feeling but... Oh, God, did I like the feeling.

Stupid hormones.

Hadrian's muscles relaxed. I tried not to wonder if he peeked into my thoughts, and relaxed because of me.

"How do we know if she makes it?" Piper asked.

I turned my head, still keeping my cheek pressed to Hadrian's chest.

"Patience," Zephys said, his eyes focused on something distant. "Patience... Patience... Pa– there she is."

Hadrian must have sensed the same thing Zephys did, because they stacked their tempest-blades at the same time. Piper buried her face into Zephys, and he didn't seem to mind at all. Pale blue light shimmered and blinked rapidly. I crushed my face against Hadrian and tightened my grip.

"There is nothing to fear, Ava," I heard him say.

I tightened my arms even more, not wanting to tell him this wasn't the part of our journey that was scaring me. No, thoughts of what we would find at the destination were doing all that work.

Pale blue light flooded my vision. I couldn't see anything else, but the other sensations were crystal clear. I felt Hadrian's arms press against my back, the flats of the blades sliding against me. I tensed and took a deep breath, inhaling his scent. I drew comfort from that. Hadrian wouldn't do anything to hurt me. I knew he wouldn't.

"Don't let go," he told me.

I almost scoffed. *As if I ever would.*

Then I felt him tip forward, like he was about to step off the edge of a cliff.

It sure felt like that, because the next thing I felt was falling.

I let out a stupid, girly shriek into Hadrian's chest when the tingling started. Well, *tingling* was Zephys's word. He could have just told the truth, that it felt like a thousand elastic bands snapping against me by the world's most insatiable bully.

I didn't know what we were traveling through or how. All I knew was that my hair was whipping so wildly it was probably blinding and muffling Hadrian, and if I held onto him any tighter, I was going to crack his ribs.

Then the world pitched again, throwing me upright. I gasped and staggered, still gripping Hadrian like my life depended on it, even though my hair had settled against my back, I could feel a softer ground, and color was filling my vision again.

Hadrian's arms unwound from me and jerked to the side. I heard metal sinking into sand. One of his hands rested on the small of my back, the other sliding between his chest and my chin. He leaned back and tilted my head up. I blinked the white spots from my vision.

My breath caught when I saw him. The strong lines and angles of his face, the silky black hair that swayed over his shoulders, the sensual line of his lips, and the depth of his navy blue-azure eyes. For a moment, I forgot where I was and what I came to do.

Hadrian's hand slipped through my hair, pushing it behind my ears. He looked at me with tender eyes and a gentler smile, tracing his eyes over my face.

"That was not so terrible, was it?" he asked.

I stifled a laugh. "I wouldn't recommend it as a travel service, but I'm alive. That counts as a success, right?"

Hadrian grinned, sending a warm jolt through my heart. His eyes dropped from mine, resting on my lips. Another welcome jolt struck me. Was he really looking at my lips, or was I dreaming it? Had I even forgiven him? Did it matter when every moment I spent with him made me feel alive and electric?

I got my answer as Hadrian leaned close, slowly parting his lips and holding his breath–

"It seems we have a larger problem than anticipated."

Hadrian dropped his hands from my body and swept around me, ripping his blades from the sand. I stood in place, still reeling from my latest hormonal daze. I blinked and shook my head, turning to see what Vitae thought justified what could have been one hell of a kiss.

Turned out she was justified.

I hadn't spent much time on Cayo Costa, but I knew it was a secluded island known for isolated beaches and small cabins for honeymooners looking for a private getaway. It was supposed to have pine trees, camping grounds, hiking trails, and information centers.

It was *not* supposed to be an island completely covered in sand.

Everywhere I looked, the white-gold sand from the beach had been dredged up and hurled onto the island. Uneven lumps of it were piled near the middle, covering up the forests and campgrounds that were supposed to be visible. The trees had likely snapped under the pressure of the sand, since I couldn't see them at all. The entire island looked like a giant blanket draped over a broken Lego fortress.

"Do you think this island was empty?"

Though Piper whispered to me, I jumped at the sound of her voice suddenly at my side. I glanced anxiously at the clumps of sand, slightly damp from the brief rainstorm Vitae must have caused to get here. I wondered at the piles near the bottom, the ones that looked to be around six feet long. I bit my lip and grabbed her hand, squeezing tightly. Selfish as it might be, I thought it was better not to know what lay under that sand. There was nothing we could do for them now.

The Precips walked along the beach ahead of us. Lazy ocean water slithered up and down the sand. The sun had just crested over the horizon, spilling orange and gold light onto the island and breaking out of the dark blue sky. I walked with Piper across the haunting island, feeling like I was about to walk off the final edge of the world. Piper's stride was cool and calm, but she didn't let go of my hand.

The island was nine miles long and while we weren't directly ambushed, we couldn't see across the island because of the craggy dune on our right. I wasn't sure how we were going to find Ferno or any other Mistrals if they were on the island… until I saw the thin wall rising about a hundred feet away obscuring the sun.

A wall made of fine sand.

The Precips drew to a halt, each one of them reaching for the swords on their backs. Piper and I edged closer to each other.

"Sandstorm," Zephys muttered. "Definitely Ferno."

"Wait," Hadrian said.

The five of us watched the wall of sand split in two. The left half hovered in the air lazily. The second half twisted inward, spinning faster and faster until it was a solid yellow tornado.

"Ferno must have been tethered," deduced Hadrian.

"It cannot be a Stormkind," Zephys said. "The storm is not violent enough."

A collective thought seemed to pass through the Precips, because they all turned to look at me. I hesitated, then said, "Mortis said there might be... others."

"Primes," Hadrian cursed, gripping his tempest-blades tightly as he spun around again. He looked ready to march headfirst into the storm and hack Ferno to pieces. I had no doubt he would do it if he were pushed. Moments ago he had been tender and careful with me, but I could never forget how different he was when Mortis was brought up.

"We will flank them," Vitae said. "I will lead the attack up the dunes," she said. "Zephys, take Piper and follow behind me. Hadrian, continue straight ahead. Draw their attention. You may engage, but remember that without Ferno, we will not be able to locate Mortis."

"Ferno is loyal to the Mistrals," Hadrian grumbled, never moving his eyes from the sandstorms ahead. "He will never betray Mortis."

"We shall see," Vitae said with a hint of danger. She beckoned Zephys and began jogging for the closest hill. He hurried over to take Piper's hand and led her after Vitae. My best friend threw a nervous glance over her shoulder, and I smiled weakly. If I kept telling myself she would be okay and nothing would happen to her or the other two Precips, maybe it would be true.

"Okay, so–"

When I turned my head to talk to Hadrian, I saw that he was already running ahead. Of course he was. He pounced on any chance for revenge like a starving wolf pouncing on a fresh steak.

Cursing under my breath and gathering my courage, I sprinted across the sand to catch up with my much more athletic Guardian. It was supposed to be *his* job to keep *me* out of trouble, not the other way around.

Though the more I ran, the more I started to recall that Ferno had been present at my torture. He might know exactly what was done to me, and how to reverse it.

The idea of getting rid of these damn gifts made me run a little bit faster.

As we drew closer, I watched the wall of sand rise in height. The tornado grew with it. I could almost taste it in the air. The sun was a faded circle behind the wall of grit.

Just before we reached the tip of the island, Hadrian veered to the right. He knelt down beside the rising dune. I followed and huddled close to him. Carefully, we looked around the corner of the dune.

Standing on a flat clearing of sand, feet away from the tornado, was Ferno. He wore his black and silver armor, the firm breeze pushing his blood-red hair around his face. His arms were folded over his chest, his body language screaming boredom.

Standing next to him, containing a wall of sand at least twenty feet high and just as broad, wasn't a Stormkind, but a man. His stood with his feet shoulder-width apart, his hands spread wide, as if he were going to embrace the wall. It didn't take me long to see the way his arms trembled. He was using a lot of energy, and it was taking its toll.

Exhaustion overcame him, and he gasped and dropped his arms. The wall of sand collapsed, half of it falling in front of him and the other half splashing into the ocean.

"I can't," he panted. His voice was almost as deep as Hadrian's, making me think he was about the same age or older. "I can't, it's too much–"

While the man gasped for breath, Ferno released the tornado. It collapsed inward and slumped onto the beach with a heavy *whump*. Ferno didn't even notice. He simply marched toward the tired, gasping man, and punched him in the jaw. The man yelped and toppled onto the sand. Ferno loomed over him with balled fists and a cruel scowl.

"You dare complain about what you have been given?" Ferno kicked the man in the stomach. "You were nothing, Austin Chambers!" Another hard kick. "Less than nothing!" Kick. "You will embrace what was bestowed on you, or it will be ripped from your very bones!"

This kick was harder than the rest. The man, Austin, hacked and gagged against the sand. I cringed and looked away. Hadrian's eyes were fixed ahead. There was a darkness to his face, a cold calculation that almost made me shiver. He turned to me.

"You must use the wind to bring the ocean deeper inland."

"I… Why? How?"

"If the sand is dry, it will blind us easily and smother us. Wet sand will still pose a problem, but it will not smother us asphyxiate us as quickly."

I narrowed my eyes. "You're really not selling this plan to me, Hadrian."

He continued as if I hadn't voiced any concerns. "Rely on the gifts you stole from Declan, but use the tether if you can." A sense of urgency fell over his eyes. "I cannot use my powers on the ocean, Ava. The water must be on land if I am to freeze it."

The importance of that was not lost on me. I wasn't the fighter here. Hadrian was. I nodded. "Okay."

He set down one of his swords and quickly cupped the back of my neck. "Do not approach Ferno. Restrain the false Stormkind. I will protect you when I can."

Oh God, he expected me to fight? Didn't he know how bad I was at that? Everything I had done so far was survival and desperation and terrible ideas that made me pass out. My stomach heaved at the thought of deliberately marching into a fight.

Hadrian pulled me closer, pressing his forehead against mine. "I will not let anything happen to you, Ava. I swear it."

I believed him. God help me, but I believed him. I closed my eyes and nodded again. Hadrian pulled away and recollected his sword. I glanced over his head and watched Vitae, Zephys, and Piper creep across the top of the dune. It didn't seem like they had been noticed so far, but I couldn't be sure. I could see Zephys talking to Piper with his hand on her shoulder. I also noticed the clouds forming overhead.

Clouds that could bring us the rain we actually wanted this time.

I set my eyes on the ocean and breathed deeply. The tether moved fluidly against my heart, a feeling I welcomed. I stared at the waves, imaging a subtle wind caressing them, pushing them deeper up the beach. A cool breeze drifted over my head, past Ferno shouting abuse at Austin, and hovered over the water. I reached out and turned my hand, picturing the wind dipping low and reversing to return to me. I tugged my hand back, dragging the breeze against the waves.

They rolled up the beach, moving ten feet further than the shoreline. I stopped before they could reach Ferno, who was stalking away and letting Austin pick himself up. Neither of them seemed to notice the change in the water, the chill in the air, or the clouds forming over their heads.

Hadrian shifted beside me, holding out his hand and letting his four extended fingers frost over while gripping the sword with his thumb. The water soaking into the sand began to harden, a shimmer of ice layering over it and steadily moving toward Ferno. The ice formed faster, streaking toward him–

That was when Austin stood up, and noticed.

"Ferno!"

The Mistral Guardian whirled around, his eyes dropping. Hadrian clenched his fist. Spikes of ice burst from the sand and plunged through Ferno's leg. He screamed and clutched his shin, dropping to one knee.

Hadrian jumped from his hiding spot and charged the clearing on the beach. Austin whirled to face him, and I saw just how big he was. Broad-shouldered with a thick middle, he looked like a retired linebacker. His jaw was wide and strong, his nose flat and his eyes small. Streaks of grey combed through his thin, unruly hair. He raised his fists and threw a punch as soon as my Guardian was in range.

Hadrian ducked and spun around him, stopping to launch a kick into Austin's back. The false Stormkind sprawled face first into the sand.

Ferno tore his leg free of the ice, scowling and withdrawing one of his swords. His other hand slammed into the sand. He yanked it up, tiny particles dripping from his fingers. Particles that soon spiraled together, twisting into a small tornado.

Dark clouds thickened overhead, and soon the rain began to pour. I glanced at the top of the dune to check on Piper. Her beautiful face was a mask of concentration, and I was glad Zephys was there to support her. Vitae stood like an assassin in the dark, her tempest-blade at her side and one hand shoving down the dune.

The wind hit Ferno and sent him sprawling. Hadrian was on him in an instant, pressing the blade to the Mistral's throat.

"Move, and your blood will be spilled," Hadrian threatened.

Ferno lay still on the ground, but even from where I was, I could see the smile on his face. I cut a glance to Austin. He was on his knees, his back to me, and his fists clenching again.

"There will be no blood, Hadrian," taunted Ferno in his awful, rasping voice. "Not when I can bury you."

Austin reacted instantly, punching his fists into the wet sand around him. The beach heaved and rocketed thirty

feet into the air behind him. Wet, clumpy sand rose over
Austin and curved toward Hadrian. It fell on him in one
massive crush.

I thought I saw white frost fly up in front of my
Guardian, but I couldn't be sure. The sand was too thick for
me to see clearly. But I knew that sand ate through ice like
acid, and the torrent being dumped on him wasn't slowing
down. It was cycling, churning down onto Hadrian over
and over.

If Hadrian spent too much time concentrating on a
shield to protect himself, he wouldn't be able to fight Ferno
if he attacked with a sword. And I was willing to bet that
was exactly Ferno's plan.

I was on my feet and running into the clearing even
as the horrible scenario crossed my mind. I skidded to a
stop at the back of Austin's sand wall. I focused my
breathing, centered myself, and gained energy from the
tether. It tightened, a sign that Hadrian must still be using
his ice powers as I used mine. I drew up my arms, slowly
gathering strength from the tether, then slashed my arms to
the side.

The burst of wind struck the side of the sandy wall,
shoving it away from Austin. He stood up and whirled
around, eyes glowing white even though he was no longer
controlling the wall. I glanced past him.

Sure enough, Hadrian had used his abilities to build
an ice shield taller than he was. It had been gouged by the
dark sand, and he could no longer hold it. Ferno was on his
feet, swinging his tempest-blade at Hadrian's neck.

The strike never connected, and not only because
Hadrian leaned back.

Vitae, who'd charged down the hill while the fight
began, hooked her arm through the bend in Ferno's arm and
dragged his arm back. He whipped his head around, and she
slammed the pommel of her sword into his face.

Motion in front of me captured my attention.
Austin, white-eyed and wild, was running straight for me.
A moment of panic snared my heart, but I pushed it away. I

gathered the rain Piper was dousing over the beach and flipped it in my hands. The rain tilted horizontally and slammed into Austin's face. He roared and staggered back, momentarily blind. I hesitated, not sure what to do next and knowing I couldn't fight him physically.

Zephys was barreling down the hill with Piper close behind. Instead of running to Ferno, they ran for me.

Austin didn't notice them yet. He swung his hands up across his chest. Sand pitched up from my left side and shot toward me. I twisted and used the tether to get some energy, pushing out my hands and freezing the water in the sand. It slowed the oncoming wall, but didn't halt it. At least I was able to stagger back and escape being pummeled.

By sand, anyway.

Austin slammed into me like a truck. We hit the sand, his heavy weight pushing all the air from my lungs. I scrambled and slapped at him, but his hand quickly found my throat and squeezed. The white glow from his eyes and the snarl on his lips made him look like a man possessed by a demon. Terror ripped through me at his strength. If he squeezed any harder, he could break my neck.

But he never got the chance. Ice thudded around his neck and enclosed it. Austin was viciously torn from my body. I coughed and clutched my throat. Everything seemed to be in place. I rolled off the drenched sand and looked across the beach.

Hadrian held out his frosted hand, his illuminated blue eyes meeting mine. The look only lasted a moment before he dropped his hand and went back to fighting Ferno, who was not making it easy for the Precips to capture him.

The Mistral tossed sand left and right, hurling it into Vitae and Hadrian's bodies to disorient them. When their vision was clouded, he used his swords to try and stab them. He would have succeeded, if Zephys hadn't gathered lightning and slashed it at him. Ferno would avoid the worst strikes, stepping to the side or backing away. He was frighteningly quick.

Piper continued to make her way toward me, grabbing my arm and helping me to my feet. We both glanced at Austin. The icy noose around his neck wasn't killing him, but it had enraged him. He roared and flipped onto his back, gripping the sand next to him. The dune on our right exploded, thick chunks of soaked sand flying outward like it was being vacuumed away from the island.

Piper yelped and I held out my hands, pushing a cool breeze into it to keep it from shredding into me. Even as I kept the worst of it back, I could feel hard flakes of grit stinging my face and fingers. It tangled in my hair and swept past me in a blur, threatening my vision. Piper stood behind me and shouted in my ear.

"What do I do?!"

I glanced at her. "See if you can absorb his power!"

She hesitated, and I didn't blame her. After seeing how I reacted after touching her and taking her gift, it didn't exactly seem like a thrilling prospect. But we needed to know if it was possible.

Piper nodded and ran to Austin's side. The ice around his neck kept him in place, but the sand was melting it at a rapid pace. She had to hurry.

I turned my head, glancing through the thick, sandstorm sweeping over the beach. Ferno was using the storm to his advantage, seeming to be unaffected. He swung one of his tempest-blades at Vitae's throat. She jumped back from it and snapped a kick into Ferno's face. He staggered back as Hadrian pounced, shooting a blast of ice at his chest. Ice collided with sand, the grit fighting against the chill that battled to freeze it.

Hadrian lunged with his sword. Ferno saw him coming and blocked the strike. I watched the rage seep over him, spreading like a cancer about to claim its victim.

Ferno snapped his elbow back, catching Vitae in the head. He ducked under Hadrian's punch, slamming a fist into his stomach. He swung his hand, commanding the sand beneath him to rise and hurl the wet granules into his eyes. Hadrian grimaced and staggered back, Ferno lunging for him with the sword outstretched while Vitae and Zephys tried to stop him.

"I can't do it!"

Piper's scream tore me from the awful sight ahead. I cut my eyes to her, telling myself that Hadrian would live. I couldn't believe anything else.

Piper's hands were pressed to Austin's chest, her thumbs holding down his neck. She was straddling him, using her self-defense training to adjust her weight so he couldn't move. He snarled and swung his fists at her, the blows grazing her chin and stomach.

Dread realization filled me. Piper couldn't absorb Austin's gift.

But I could.

My stomach tightened and rolled, like a rag being wrung out. I didn't want to take Austin's powers. Of all the sensations that tore through me when Mortis tortured me, dust had been one of the worst.

But we were out of options. Ferno was on a rampage, and if I didn't do something soon, he could hurt one of the Guardians.

Or worse.

I risked a glance at the battle across from me. The Precips were still alive, but Ferno was locked in frenzy. He was a wild animal pushed into a corner. He sliced the air with his swords, keeping the Precips back. When he had the distance he wanted, he punched down at the earth and used his tether to unleash chaos on them.

The sand collapsed under Vitae's feet, becoming quicksand that pulled her deeper into the earth. Zephys ran to help her when the ground bucked under him and threw him into the dune. Some of the sand had sloughed off the hidden debris, revealing broken trees. Zephys slammed into them, landing in a heap on his side. Hadrian rushed forward and sliced his sword across Ferno's ribs. The Mistral roared and slashed back. Hadrian ducked and stayed close, smashing his knee into Ferno's stomach. He bellowed again, drawing on his tether to command the sand. It wrapped around Hadrian's back like thick, muddy tentacles and dragged him back onto the earth. My Guardian kicked and fought, but the sand constricted around his chest and limbs and held him on the ground. Hadrian released his grip on the tempest-blades to better control his ice gift, but the sand crawled up his neck and covered his face.

Smothering him.

Ferno grinned and spun the sword in his hand.

I dropped down beside Austin and looked at Piper. She was about to lose her hold on the false Stormkind.

"Keep the rain going," I said, "and run."

My best friend hesitated, then nodded. She launched off of Austin and sprinted away from me. Austin lurched up with a savage howl. The sound was so barbaric that Ferno stopped his final approach to Hadrian and looked at me. The whiteness still consumed his vision. Austin's eyes locked on me and he lunged for my neck. Ferno screamed for him to stop and Vitae yelled my name, but neither call made a difference.

Austin's hands clamped around my throat and pushed me into the thick sand. Tendrils of it curved over my cheeks and crawled toward my mouth. Grit stuck between my teeth and clumped on my tongue. I clapped my hands on Austin's face–

And felt every particle in my body evaporate.

Rain poured onto my face, but it didn't absorb into my skin. Blood turned to ash in my veins, clogging my arteries and forcing my heart to beat at a rapid pace. My lungs burned as I drew breath from my ragged throat. My eyes burned and my skin prickled as it lost all moisture.

I blinked as the man in front of me wailed and collapsed off of me. I flipped onto my hands and knees, pain dashing through my skull and slicing into my stomach. I grimaced and gripped the thick sand between my fingers.

I could feel the moisture, knew it was there, but I couldn't get it.

But I *could* get the life force in the man's body. That would be good enough.

His eyes widened when he looked at me. I don't know what he saw. I didn't care. I snarled and rushed him. He yelled and slammed his boot into my shoulder. Pain spiked through my chest, but I didn't stop moving. I pounced on him like an animal, digging my nails into his face and pinning his head to the ground.

I stared at his mouth, feeling that warm, sweet energy whispering across my face like a promise. I had never tasted that kind of power before. This would be my first time. Not ideal conditions, but what did I care? He was nothing to me.

I crunched forward, diving at his mouth for a venomous kiss. My lips pressed over his mouth, and the first taste of that light flicked against my tongue, a soft, melting sweetness that tasted like milk and honey—

Something heavy smashed into my skull, knocking me away from the man's lips. I groaned, white spots dancing in my vision.

"Worthless," a man rasped.

I blinked and shook my head, gazing up and meeting the dusty stare of Ferno.

My limbs froze. I glanced away to see where Piper and my friends were. Behind Ferno was a massive wall of sand, blocking them from me, likely drawn up by him while I was busy trying to devour Austin. The horror of what I'd nearly done hit me like a sledgehammer. Austin stared at me like he didn't know what I was.

Like I wasn't a human, but a monster.

"You were a waste of our time," Ferno grated out. He gripped his sword tight in his hand, and I knew this was it. This was the moment I died.

Shudders wracked my body and tears burned my dried eyes.

I don't want to die I don't want to die I don't want to—

Ferno lunged with the sword. It plunged through flesh.

Flesh that wasn't mine.

Austin gaped at the tempest-blade in his chest, as though he couldn't understand why it was there. He understood what happened when I screamed. The tether in my chest snapped taut, and I thought I heard Hadrian's voice in my head.

Ferno pulled the blade free and looked at me with shadowed eyes. He drew the second tempest-blade over his back and set it overtop of the bloody one.

"You live because you are not yet complete," he told me. "Once you are, you will not escape your purpose."

Light blinded me as he drew on his storm-sight. He became an illuminated pillar, and then he was gone.

White stars swirled through my vision. Darkness closed in, and kept closing until I passed out on the sand.

CHAPTER 14

"We cannot continue this."

Hadrian sounded like he was on the edge of homicidal fury. I wouldn't have wanted to be on the receiving end of it. I was perfectly content to lie on the infirmary bed. It was a sad sign that I had been here so many times I could recognize it by touch without even opening my eyes.

"Ferno killed his charge," Vitae's voice carried through the room. I figured she would be the one Hadrian was fighting with. "He left Ava alive when he could have taken her. We must find out why."

"If that mistake on Cayo Costa taught us anything, it's that she cannot contain her abilities like this. She is human, and every gift she absorbs is killing her."

My heart plummeted. I was dying? I didn't *feel* dead. Weak, yeah, definitely. I couldn't even open my eyes yet. But *dying*? That couldn't be right.

Until I remembered Hadrian telling me that I had bled from my nose and ears when I Enervated, exerting too much power and took it from another false Stormkind. Bleeds like that meant there was cranial damage. A warning that said if I pushed myself too far, a part of my brain could burst and instantly kill me.

My hands tightened on the bed sheets. I didn't want to die.

A smooth, warm hand slipped over mine. Piper. She knew I was awake, and she was here for me.

I wished it were enough.

"I do not wish any harm to come to Ava either, Hadrian," Vitae continued with restrained calm. "But we must look at the larger issue. Ferno had the opportunity to capture Ava, yet he did not. Are you not curious about why that is?"

"No. Not anymore."

Hadrian didn't even hesitate with his answer. He said it like it was the simplest thing in the world. I knew the truth wasn't quite so black and white.

Vitae pressed on. "Unless we discover what the Mistrals intend to do with Ava, we must continue to lure them out."

"We are not using her as bait," he snapped.

"We have no choice—"

"I have already put her in too much danger," Hadrian bellowed. The sudden silence clashed with his seething breath. It was a long, quiet minute before he calmed down enough to speak again. When he did, his voice was solemn and gravely serious.

"She is my charge, and I have failed her over and over again. Now that I can see clearly, you want me to put her in the path of those who would break everything she is. I will not allow you to do that. I will protect her the way she deserves to be protected, from *anyone* who means her harm."

This time I opened my eyes. There was no mistaking the implication in that threat. I turned my head to see Hadrian standing in the infirmary, towering over Vitae, his leader and friend of his father. I'd never seen anyone so enraged. His knuckles were white, his eyes wide and burning, his shoulders rigid with tension. He was one word away from punching something. Or some*one.*

Which is probably why Zephys was standing so close to Vitae, ready to fight his friend if he attacked their leader.

"The only other option we have is the one we discussed, and you refused even more vehemently—"

"Because Ava is not a tool for us to use," Hadrian fumed. "She is a human girl who should never have been given these powers. She does not want them. If we had any care for disrupting Mortis's plans, we would be looking for a way to free her and the other false Stormkind from them."

"You are the *last* person to speak of what Ava needs, considering you were going to use her for the same thing."

Vitae could not have picked a worse thing to say.

Hadrian lunged at Vitae, but Zephys grabbed him, shoving him back before he could touch her.

But Hadrian didn't snap out of it. He rushed again, hands curled into fists.

I bolted upright. "Hadrian!"

My voice sounded horrible, like sandpaper dragged over concrete. Felt about as pleasant, too. Still, it was enough to halt Hadrian in his tracks. His head snapped in my direction, eyes churning like whirlpools. He relaxed when he saw me, the anger fading like shadows burned under daylight.

"Stop."

This time I did whisper to spare whatever remained of my voice. It was still enough.

Hadrian's eyes traced over mine, and I watched the realization dawn on his face. He knew I'd heard basically everything. His guilt for pushing me into combat that I couldn't handle, the self-loathing he'd turned on his oldest friends and allies. Like so many times before, he knew he couldn't take his words or actions back. Now he had to pay the price for them.

That price was seeing the disappointment in my eyes. His assumption that he'd failed me.

Hadrian's arms dropped to his side, his head lowering soon after. He didn't say another word. I didn't need to touch the tether to know how deep the humiliation and remorse ran into him then. It was a rock heaped onto his back, crushing down on his shoulders and breaking his control. When he turned and walked out of the infirmary, no one followed him.

I sighed and fell back against the pillows. I clapped one hand onto my forehead and wondered if I could ever go back to being a regular waitress whose only major concern would be what I would do with my weekend.

The odds weren't looking great.

"How are you feeling, Ava?" Vitae asked, sounding genuinely concerned about my welfare.

Maybe I was being cruel in thinking that wasn't the case. I mean, yes, her first interest was stopping the Mistrals and protecting humans from the Stormkind, but she didn't have any open hostility toward me. I wasn't sure that we were friends, but I hoped we were more than allies.

"I kind of wish I'd woken up under better circumstances, but I feel okay."

"Yes. I am sorry you had to witness that. Hadrian has been in quite an agitated state since you fell unconscious on the beach."

I shrugged, trying to act casual. "Don't apologize. I saved you from being punched in the face."

Vitae's smile was so weak, she shouldn't have bothered at all. "You should be proud, Ava. You've done what no other Stormkind has ever done. You've driven Hadrian into madness." Under different circumstances, I might have awkwardly laughed at her weak, terrible joke. I probably would have genuinely laughed if Hadrian had been in the room to glare daggers at his friend.

But the mark had hit too close to the target, and Hadrian was nowhere to be seen. He was probably hidden so we wouldn't be able to find him until he wanted to be found. Zephys sighed and scrubbed a hand across his face, appearing just as rueful as Hadrian had before he took off. He wasn't alone in that dejected little rodeo.

After all, it was hard to stay upbeat with the elephant in the room.

I looked at my hands as they knotted in the blanket. Then I took a breath, and asked the question I didn't really want an answer to.

"Am I really dying?"

The shuddering whisper in my voice was embarrassing, a pathetic hoarse sound that I would probably make when I really did die.

Each breath was jagged in my throat. Piper clutched my hand tightly to secure me to reality.

"Hadrian brought it to our attention," Vitae admitted quietly. "Guardians can feel when their charges weaken or pass on. Because you are human, he did not realize what it was at first. Now that he has, he made sure to tell us." She paused, then added. "I am sure you can see how greatly it has upset him."

Talk about an understatement.

"And you still want me to go with you on these missions? You want me to be bait to track down the Mistrals?"

Vitae exhaled sadly. Her shoulders drooped. "Please believe me when I say it is not a fate I wish for you, Ava. Risking the lives of our charges is never something we do lightly. Already, I fear Hadrian is considering mutiny. The only way to find out Mortis's goal is for him to have the key to it. That key unfortunately, is you."

My heart pounded as that sank in. Piper couldn't absorb any other gifts. Declan hadn't taken mine. Austin was dead. I didn't know if there were any other false Stormkind like me, but if the warnings that Ferno and Mortis left me were anything to go by, I was betting the answer was no.

"You are a conduit, Ava," continued Vitae. "You have taken almost every kind of Stormkind gift available."

"Except for Turve's," I muttered.

Vitae nodded solemnly. The ache built in my chest. I closed my eyes.

"What do you want me to do, Vitae?"

She answered honestly. "The same thing we originally planned. I want to use you against Mortis. I want you to become our weapon rather than his."

I opened my eyes and looked at her. "I'm one superpower short. We don't know where Turve is."

"We do," Zephys said. He didn't sound or look any more pleased than Vitae did. "Tornadoes have been forming in Sanford. Your government has evacuated as many human survivors as possible from the area, but I fear it will not hold them back for long. Turve enjoys destruction."

I looked at my hands again. My knuckles were as white as Hadrian's had been when he was arguing with Vitae.

"It's going to be a trap," I stated.

"More than likely." Vitae didn't mince words.

I nearly choked on my next words. "How will you get me out of it?"

"By any means necessary," Vitae announced at the same time Piper burst with, "What? Ava, you can't consider this."

I dragged my eyes to my friend. "Mortis won't stop coming for me. He'll use his cronies to attack innocent people until the Precips have to go hunting for him. If they're killed, I won't have any Guardians to keep him from taking me." My breath shook in my throat. Tears burned my eyes. "My family is still out there, Piper. If I don't help stop the Mistrals, I won't even have time to check the Missing Boards."

The tears spilled free. Piper scooted closer and wrapped her arms around me. I was so used to her being the strong one. I didn't know when things had changed.

"You can't do this, Ava," she begged. "It could kill you. This isn't worth your life. It's not."

Except it was.

Don't get me wrong– the last thing I wanted to do was die, but dying to save thousands of already shattered lives would be a pretty noble way to go.

Right?

I didn't want to know the answer.

I pulled back from Piper and wiped my eyes with my palm. Keeping my best friend's hand in mine, I looked at Vitae. The Precips leader had her chin held high, but her cool blue eyes were tortured. She looked like a woman desperate for another option, but knowing there was no time for one.

"How–" I lost my voice, and struggled to find it again. "How certain are you that I'll... die if I take Turve's power?"

Vitae spoke quietly. "It is not the collection of powers that worries me. I worry about what will happen when you are forced to use all those powers simultaneously."

My stomach pinched. "I... I don't think I can."

"I know that. We all do. Mortis likely does as well. The difference is that he will not care."

I wrapped my hands around my stomach. My head was feathery and all but out of my body. I couldn't help but play through the scenarios that could lead to my death.

Would I be frozen from the inside out? Would I drown in a flood I created? Disintegrate to ash? Blow myself to pieces?

Or... Would Mortis see me as a failed experiment? Would he choose to kill me if I didn't form to his design?

Or would Hadrian be forced to put a tempest-blade through my heart when I became too wild to control?

Thoughts of knives and blistering pain consumed my thoughts. The flash of a crystal blade stabbing into my chest with a vicious punch, ripping a scream from my throat and pouring violent energy into me–

I looked at Vitae. "Could a tempest-blade reverse it?"

She hesitated before giving her answer. "I fear I do not understand."

"You said that Mortis used a special blade on me. When I was stabbed, all that energy went into me. If that blade was used on me again, would it take the powers away?"

She rolled the thought through her brain. "It is possible. But there is no way to be certain. It could simply be a dead blade."

"When Hadrian cut me," I pointed to the faded red line on my forehead, which was now a mere scratch that didn't even sting, "I felt myself come back. It could work the opposite way if it touched me, couldn't it?"

I was grasping at straws. It was obvious in my voice and probably in my eyes. But I wanted to get rid of whatever magic or spells had been put inside me. I hated the things it made me do, the things I *wanted* to do when I lost control. I had to believe I could back to the normality I'd taken for granted, even if I knew it was a lie.

That was the only way I would be able to keep going without screaming.

"Perhaps," Vitae said, though I knew she was merely humoring me. "If it is indeed possible, Mortis will still have the crystal blade with him, and he will not part with it. We must take it from him."

"I recommend removing his hand," Zephys offered with a teasing grin. "It will be the most efficient method."

I grinned sourly. Hadrian would jump at the chance to chop a limb off Mortis.

Oh, crap. Hadrian. I had to talk to him about this. Find a way for him to agree to it. Pulling teeth with a pair of dull pliers would be easier.

Sighing with no small amount of dread, I pushed the blanket off my chest and sat up. Moving was a little dizzying at first, but once I started the motion, I felt much stronger. Piper kept her grip on my hand as I moved.

"I'll go talk to him," I mumbled.

Piper squeezed my palm and gripped my shoulder, trying to push me back onto the bed.

"You need to stay here and rest," she insisted. "You can't push yourself."

I gripped her wrist and drew it away from my shoulder. "I feel better when I move. I'm okay."

I scooted up the bed and dumped myself off. I used the edge of the bed to steady myself, but my legs were able to support me. I was dressed in fresh, clean clothes again– another one of Vitae's tactical black outfits– just as everyone else. I knew would have to get some food before the next mission for energy to recover and to keep moving forward, yet I didn't feel hungry. I couldn't help but wonder if that was because I was dreading the conversation I was about to have.

Vitae looked at me as I walked past. She nodded and stepped aside. Zephys whispered, "Good luck," to me as I walked out of the room.

Luck. Yeah. Because that had served me so well in the past.

***

If I were a brooding warrior that just had a temper tantrum in front of my commander and best friend, where would I be? What would I be doing?

I'd be finding something to punch away the rest of the rage.

There weren't many places in the prison where Hadrian could train. My first instinct was to go outside. That was really the only place he could go for relative quiet. Where he could slip away if he decided not to be on the compound at all.

Hadrian, you better be here. I am not in the mood to track you all over Florida.

Silence met me. I wondered what the range on this weird mental connection was as I walked to the shattered hallway that would lead to the prison yard, of if he was just ignoring me.

I reached the collapsed hallway that led to the yard, carefully stepping over broken slabs of wall and other detritus the Precips hadn't bothered to move. Cool night wind slid through my hair and gathered around my head. Once I stood on solid ground outdoors again, I looked up and scanned the yard for Hadrian.

He wasn't there.

"Hadrian?"

I called his name again and again, sometimes with my voice, sometimes with the tether. Each call was louder and more panicked than the last.

I raced for the crumbled fence and crawled over it, scanning the streets for any sign of my Guardian.

"Hadrian!"

I yelled again, even though I knew the truth was staring me in the face.

Hadrian was gone.

CHAPTER 15

There was one consolation to Hadrian's disappearance:

We knew exactly where to find him.

I was forced to travel with Vitae, and the journey was far less comfortable than it had been with my Guardian. Vitae had a harsher grip and was much less concerned with my comfort than Hadrian was. Probably because she was *furious* with him.

That, at least, I understood.

Vitae let go of me as soon as we touched ground. I nearly pitched into the middle of the road, but managed to find my footing. Someone bumped into me from behind and threw me off balance again. I spun around to glare at the person who hit me, but then I finally registered the screaming.

We were standing on the middle of a highway. I couldn't tell which one because all the signs and markers had been ripped from the ground and flipped on their backs. Uprooted trees lay haphazardly on the cracked road, broken branches, shattered limbs, and lost leaves pressed onto the tops of smashed and overturned cars. Terrified survivors barreled through the ruins, tripping over the debris and each other as they stampeded toward safety.

I turned around, and saw their desperate escape was totally justified.

Two tornadoes swayed along the ground across from us, tearing up the ground near another highway road. The funnels twisted out of the hazy grey sky like pythons, kicking up dirt and fractured trees, dragging them into a tumultuous dance.

The twisters moved close together, but had different targets. One skidded a path across the road across from us, while the second moved further north, heading toward a crumbling housing development. I had to squint, but I could see the metal skeletons of new structures being erected. Fresh homes for new lives. The first trace of hope that some of them had seen in over a month, and it was about to be torn to pieces by rogue tornadoes.

My eyes lowered from the thin funnels and started searching for Hadrian. I crouched beside a dented sedan to stay clear of the crowd, which continued to squeeze through the crevices of trees and vehicles blocking them from safety. Even then, I was still shoved away from the Precips. I had lost sight of Vitae, and had no idea where Piper or Zephys were. Not that I was too concerned about them getting hurt right now. Zephys would never let anything happen to Piper, and Vitae was more than capable of taking care of herself.

I didn't really think they would ditch me, but it would be hard to find each other with the screaming masses surrounding us. They were too scared of the ravenous tornadoes shredding the ground a few yards behind them, they didn't seem to notice or care that four people had just appeared out of thin air in front of them. Panic always gave way to survival instinct, and they would think about anything strange they saw when they believed they were safe again.

I grunted as a shrieking woman knocked into my shoulder. True, I was feeling better than I had when we left, but I wasn't exactly in tip-top shape. I rolled my shoulder and stood on the tips of my toes. I was too short to see over anyone's heads. I needed to get higher.

Turning around the side of the car, I jogged to the hood. Carefully gripping the torn, scrunched metal of the sedan's hood, I crawled onto its surface and scrambled for the roof. Now that I could see over everyone's heads, I saw the situation was way worse than I originally thought.

The tornado lingering on the road wasn't just blocking the road. It was *growing*. The base spread like a gaping mouth, widening around the middle like a snake devouring an animal twice its size. The clouds darkened from grey to black, suffocating all traces of blue from the sky.

And it was moving closer to our highway. It was an attack being set against the innocent people running for their lives.

For a single, dreadful second, I worried that a Stormkind was controlling both the thin tornado making its way to the developing houses, and the thick twister churning toward the scattering survivors. All these life forces would have been a feast for them.

But as I digested that stomach-churning thought, I knew they weren't here. I would have seen their bright, liquid form. If I hadn't, I would have noticed the bright flashes of light as they guzzled fresh human life. Yet I didn't see either.

And I still couldn't find Hadrian.

Fear was contagious, rising up from the road beneath me.

"Keep running! Don't stop!"

"David! David, where are you?"

"Help me, please, someone help!"

I squeezed my eyes closed and tried to breathe. I balled my fists to stop them from shaking. I reached for the tether, feeling its smooth, cool strength caress my heart.

Hadrian, please, show me where you are. You can't fight them alone.

There was no reply. I pinched my eyes shut and gripped the tether as hard as I could.

I'm here. Show me where you are—

The tether shuddered violently. I gasped and snapped my eyes open. Ahead of me, in front of the thick tornado, there was a flash. It was so small that it could have been mistaken for the glimmer of the sun on a car mirror, but the longer I looked, the more flashes I saw.

Two men fighting with two swords between them, mindless of the huge tornado converging on them.

Hadrian.

"Vitae!" I screamed. "Vitae, I found him!"

I didn't know how close she was until she climbed onto the hood of the car and nudged me to the side.

"Primes," she cursed. Fury and fear mingled in her crystal blue eyes. "The fool is going to get himself killed, unless you talk him out of it." She glanced at me. "You must be ready to fight."

If she'd said that to me a month ago, I would have choked. Me? Fight? Sure. As soon as I had a helmet and suit of indestructible armor and a jetpack that would carry me to safety when I panicked and needed to run.

But I wasn't the same girl I'd been a month ago. Not one person could say the Centennial hadn't changed them, but not many could say they'd been changed the way I had been.

I was still terrified of what I was about to face, but my friend was out there. A man who'd saved my life and was making me fall for him. I wouldn't abandon him again.

I nodded to Vitae. Whatever she saw in my eyes satisfied her. She nodded and sheathed the tempest-blades onto her back. "Keep up."

She bolted before I could tell her I would try. Vitae's long, graceful legs hammered into the trunk as she slid down it and leaped to the next vehicle.

So we were car-jumping now. Never thought I'd be grateful for a major car pileup on a highway.

Vitae outran me, but I followed her path easily enough. There were times when I slipped or had to run over a stretch of road to get to the next forgotten car, but with adrenaline fuelling my veins and the unshakeable desire to get Hadrian to safety so I could slap him for being so damn stupid, I felt like I could overtake anything in my way.

Zephys and Piper were running on another row of empty vehicles on my right. He was ahead of her, but Piper was athletic enough to keep up. She probably wasn't as out of breath as I was.

Then again, she had no reason to lose her calm. I did. My Guardian's life was on the line. He was out here fighting for a reason I couldn't understand. Didn't *want* to understand.

Please, please, don't do anything stupid Hadrian. Well, stupider. If you're hurt or dead when I find you...

The thought of him in any kind of pain sent a fresh jolt of adrenaline through me. There was no response from the tether. I had to believe Hadrian was still alive and intent on staying that way. I refused to accept anything else.

Soon enough, the crowds thinned out. Anyone who would make it out alive was already gone. The only people I could no see were two men standing in front of a massive cyclone, slashing and kicking each other without restraint.

Turve's attacks were barbaric. He put as much force as he could muster behind them and struck with the intent to cleave off an arm if he couldn't take a head.

Hadrian focused on being faster. He swept under Turve's arm and snapped a kick into his kidneys. Turve absorbed the blow while Hadrian sliced for his neck. Turve used one sword to block the strike to his throat and shoving the other toward Hadrian's stomach. My Guardian knocked the second sword away before it could skewer him. Turve roared and kicked Hadrian in the chest. He staggered back and raised his swords, never missing a beat as he fended off Turve's latest whirlwind of strikes.

I wanted to scream to Hadrian that we were here to help him. That he could stop. That he was an idiot for running off in the first place. But if Hadrian became distracted, Turve wouldn't hesitate to run him through.

I didn't come here to watch Hadrian die. I came here to slap some sense into him so he could see the bigger picture.

That was when I saw her. A tall girl with wild black hair and sightless white eyes standing between the tornadoes, her arms outstretched to welcome the destruction.

Turve's charge, and another false Stormkind.

"Ava, Piper, take care of her," Vitae ordered. She reached over her back and drew her tempest-blades. "We will handle Turve."

I hesitated, not even sure where to start with a girl who could control not one but *two* tornadoes, not wanting to think about what would happen to me if I touched her, and knowing that just seconds ago, I was ready to berate Hadrian for not seeing the bigger picture.

I looked at Piper. She nodded. She was ready.

I wished I felt as confident.

Vitae and Zephys were already leaping from the cars and bounding across the road toward Hadrian and Turve. I jumped off the hood and sprinted toward the false Stormkind with Piper following behind me.

She turned her head in our direction, white eyes searing her face like a fresh brand. She twisted at the waist, both of her hands coming up to face us. The sky rotated like a drain, a spiral of water, dust, and debris churning into the ground. We stopped as it touched ground, greedy winds yanking at our hair and clothes. I dug my heels into the ground to keep from flying into the twister.

I looked at my friend. "Can you push her back?" I shouted over the wind.

Piper nodded, but she couldn't keep the worry from her eyes. Worry that didn't seem to be for herself.

She reached up and pinched her hand together like she was plucking an apple from a tree. When she drew her hand back down, a corkscrew of rainwater came with it. Heavier rains poured around us, but Piper directed the funnel directly at the false Stormkind.

She sneered and wrenched her hand. The twister all but snapped in half at her command, gathering the rain into its winding path.

That was what I waited for.

Gripping the tether and pulling strength from it, I shoved out my hand. The rain turned to ice as it became caught in the tornado's spiral. Chunks of ice spat wildly around us, though I captured most of the stray pieces in another wind and pelted them at the girl.

Not very nice of me, but I figured we were past niceties. She was trying to kill people who didn't deserve to die, and the only way I knew how to fight was to take dirty cheap shots.

From the look of pure rage she gave me through the ice, she didn't appreciate it a single bit.

The false-Stormkind spread her arms and split the tornado wide in front of her. One more push sent it toward us. Piper gritted her teeth and pushed back, but she was holding back. The girl wasn't. The wide tornado spun wildly, dragging up cracked pieces of road and clumps of grass and hurling them at us. Piper swung wildly, pushing monsoon winds at the false-Stormkind.

Turve's charge smiled like a demon possessed.

The winds of the tornado hooked me like claws, dragging me forward. Piper stumbled forward before planting her feet again. I staggered back and grabbed Piper's arm. I dragged her back onto the highway, which wasn't easy as she kept shoving rain and wind at the false-Stormkind. I finally reached cover behind a car and yanked Piper down. I was surprised at the sharpness of the stare she gave me.

"What are you doing?" she demanded.

"We can't fight her on open ground like that," I shouted back. Before she could argue, I continued. "You keep pushing her back. I'll go around her."

It didn't take Piper long to see the logic in my plan. She straightened and grabbed at the sheets of rain tumbling from the clouds. The rain was like a sheet, nearly impossible to see through. I could hardly see the tornado or the girl controlling it beyond the downpour. Though I knew they were close. I could feel some of the rain whipping back into my face, stinging my cheeks.

I was terrified at the idea of running blind, but I didn't have a choice. There was a tornado snaking toward the houses behind me, dozens of innocent people about to lose what little remained of their lives. Another massive twister was feet away from me, where Hadrian, Vitae, and Zephys were fighting Turve. My stomach turned at the thought of them fighting against the winds of such a massive force of destruction– a problem Turve wouldn't have since he was helping to control it– but I consoled myself in knowing the numbers were in their favor. That counted for something, right?

Trying not to think on it more than I had to, I ran toward my own goal, trying not to think about how Dorothy felt when she was yanked out of Kansas and thrown into Oz.

I passed by the curtain of rain Piper poured onto the road, ducking behind another car and glancing over its hood. The false-Stormkind was still trying to push her tornado forward, but its gait was slow. She must have exhausted most of her energy earlier, not that you could tell from the unfiltered rage on her face.

I gripped the tether and felt my body cool. My hands frosted and I stood a little higher to get better aim–

A painful shout came from behind me. I lost focus and glanced back, and saw why Turve was winning.

He drew his hands toward himself, pulling more strength into the tornado. The Precips were gripping onto the edges of cars fiercely, but their grip was slipping. Turve lunged forward, running for Zephys. He slashed at the Precip, catching him in the arm. Zephys yelled and flinched, losing his grip on the edge of the car. He slipped, and the force of the wind dragged him across the road. Turve laughed and kicked him back toward the car he'd slipped from.

Turve turned and locked eyes with Hadrian. My Guardian was bleeding from a scrape on his cheek and was missing one of his swords, but there was no masking the conviction on his face. He let go of the car and charged toward the Mistral. Turve laughed again and beckoned with his hand. The tornado shifted in Hadrian's direction, the intense pull dragging him closer. Hadrian skidded to a stop, trying to fight the tornado. He rooted his feet in place, but couldn't move forward or back. If he couldn't shift his feet, he wouldn't be able to fight. Turve had no problem running for him with a sword aimed at his chest.

I had no problem gathering energy from the tether and slapping my hand on the ground. I watched frost creep from my hand and cover the road, a line of white gloss streaking toward Turve. My heart squeezed, not knowing if it would move fast enough–

The line of ice glided under Turve's boots. He didn't know what hit him until he slipped, his legs flying out from under him. He slammed onto his back, cracking his head against the road. I winced, hoping I hadn't just killed a man.

The winds before me dwindled, the thick tornado slowing down and breaking up now that the man on the ground was out cold. I looked up and cast a quick glance at Hadrian, who met my eyes at the same moment. Dozens of emotions rushed through his eyes, most of them moving too fast for me to fully comprehend. I caught glimpses of shock, confusion, annoyance, gratitude... And something so heated that it sent a warm shiver through me.

All I did was smile and shrug.

His sparkling eyes moved past my shoulder, and every emotion melted into horror.

"Ava!"

I whirled around, and watched the false-Stormkind racing toward me, her white eyes scorching into mine. The snarl on her face was inhuman. The tornado she controlled was gliding past her, toward where Piper was trying to hold it back.

I got to my feet and backed up, letting frost cover my hands. The false-Stormkind jumped onto the hood of the car I'd used as cover. She swung her hands like she was gripping a bat. Wind slammed into my ribs and hurled me across the road. The world became a blur until I slammed into the side of a car.

Then the world became pain.

I shook my head and got to my knees, searching for my vision–

A crush of pressure snared my ankles and yanked. I landed hard on my stomach, air knocking out of my lungs. My hands scraped along the rough, broken road, tearing as I was pulled back and leaving lines of blood on the pavement.

All I had was the frost. It would have to be enough.

The dragging stopped. I heard names shouted over the highway. Piper's. Hadrian's. Mine. Voices too far away to help me.

I flipped onto my back. The false-Stormkind leaped from the hood. I snapped up my hands and made a shield of ice. It pieced together lightning fast, covering my torso. The false-Stormkind slammed face-first into the icy shield, eliciting a yelp from her. The weight of her body shattered the ice– and almost my entire arm. She tumbled off me and landed in a heap on my side. I rolled away from her, watching her eyes. They were closed, so I had no idea if she was still possessed by the tether and the lure of life force.

Not wanting to take any chances, I got to my knees and crawled away. I gripped the side of the car closest to me and stood up. I peered over the hood and searched for Piper.

She was shaken, but standing. Her big dark eyes found me, relief sweeping across her face. I followed her gaze to the housing district. Stress left my shoulders like a weight when I saw the tornado hadn't made it within their boundaries. Hopefully, by the time the Mistrals arrived, we would have Turve tied up or thrown in a trunk or something. I didn't know what the Precips would do with the girl, who groaned and clutched her head we she rolled on the ground, but as long as they didn't torture her or kill her, I was happy.

I turned one more time to see if I would be able to track Hadrian down, only to find that he was right in front of me.

"Holy hell!" I gasped as my heart skipped. "Don't do that!"

His face was tight and stony, but his eyes were blazing with surprise and concern. "What are you doing here?"

Straight to the point, for a change. Now that my minor cardiac episode was over, I could get back to the major issue:

Being mad at him.

"That's my question, you jerk! What was the goal here? Take out whatever anger you have at Mortis and his goons by running at them headfirst without a plan?"

"I had a plan," he grumbled.

"Oh, good," I put my hands on my hips. "Explain it. Please. I would love to hear it."

Hadrian glared. He didn't say a word.

"That's what I thought," I stated, proving my point.

His eyes narrowed to slits. He still didn't have an argument. As we stared at each other in the ruined, empty highway, I could see there were words on the tip of his tongue. His lips were pressed together too firmly for him to simply be angry. Something was hidden behind his rage, something he didn't want me to see.

I wasn't afraid of it, though. Not like he was. I didn't think there was anything he could hide from me that would cause me pain. Hadrian was difficult and aggressive, but he wasn't unreachable. When I had been lying in the infirmary after passing out from Ferno's attack, something inside him snapped. I heard it in his voice, watched it unravel when he nearly punched Vitae.

Hadrian was breaking.

I took a careful step toward him and slid my hand into his. He stiffened, but didn't pull away. That counted as progress, right?

"Tell me what you were trying to achieve," I whispered. "Tell me what you're looking for."

The rage shielding his eyes began to waver. He quickly dropped his gaze to the ground. His fingers curled gently around my hand. "It was my intent to retrieve answers from Turve."

At the sound of his name, I glanced past Hadrian to see what our recently defeated Mistral was up to. He was frowning as Vitae stood next to him with a sword pressed to his neck. She was asking him questions I couldn't hear, and he was replying with one or two word answers. He looked bored, and I couldn't shake the wrong feeling to the casual way he sat on the ground, like he was still waiting for something.

Dismissing it, I retuned my attention to Hadrian. "And how did that work out before you started punching him?"

Instead of answering, he tightened his jaw.

Exasperation made me lose my patience. "God, Hadrian, did you even ask him *anything*?"

"He would have answered me once I subdued him and his charge–"

"Did it ever occur to you they might not tell you where Mortis was, or what his next step was–"

His hands were cupping my face and drawing me closer before I could blink. His scent was cool and familiar, yet his hands were all but burning.

"You think I tracked Turve because I care about Mortis?"

I was about to say yes, because that was what mattered to him. He wanted retribution for his father, and punching answers out of Turve would have been a good way to do it.

But then I looked into his eyes– *really* looked– and saw the desperation, the hurt, the fear.

Emotions I wouldn't see if he were thinking about Mortis.

But if he were thinking about *me*...

"That would have been true once," he whispered, his shields completely stripped now. "But now every time I think of him, I worry about you instead. I know what he is capable of, what he has already done to you, and it terrifies me that I will not be able to protect you from it again." He dipped his forehead, pressing it against mine. I didn't know if he were shaking, or if it was me.

"I tracked Turve because I cannot bear the idea of losing you, Ava. I do not know how you are undoing me, but I do not want you to stop."

I could see everything he'd tried to hide from me. The contrition, confusion, loneliness, desire... It was open to me now.

Only to me.

I fought to regain my thoughts as Hadrian struggled to regain his control. I wanted to keep berating him for scaring me, but after what he'd said, the way he was holding me—

A crush of wind knocked into us and stole the ground from under me. Hadrian's arms came around me as the wind whipped us violently. His back became a shield as we were thrown against the side of a car. I wasn't hurt, but I felt the breath punch from Hadrian's lungs as he was crushed. He grunted, still holding me as we toppled forward. He twisted at the last possible second, landing on his back again and keeping me from smashing face-first into the pavement.

I wriggled out of Hadrian's arms and turned to check on him. My Guardian was already on his feet, grabbing his last tempest-blade from his back and shifting his feet into a fighter's stance. I got to my feet and stood behind him.

The false-Stormkind was on her feet, the color back in her dark eyes. Her lips were peeled back into a savage snarl. She pushed her hands out to Hadrian, but he was stronger than her. He flipped the sword in his right hand so the blade was extended horizontally. Gripping it carefully between his thumb and index finger, Hadrian pushed out his hand. A gust of cold wind cut a path straight to the false-Stormkind. It struck her in the chest and shoved her toward a car. I jumped at the screeching sound I heard when she hit it.

But Hadrian hadn't pushed her hard enough for the car to make that kind of noise. Which was coming from the left.

I turned my head, breath catching in my throat.

The abandoned cars were skidding along the highway like toys being pushed by an invisible bulldozer. They spun off the side of the road and flipped over, parted forcibly as the wind picked up around us. My hair whipped across my face, coming from both sides. I huddled closer to Hadrian as he pushed the false-Stormkind back again.

"Hadrian," I whispered, tugging his arm to get his attention.

"I know. I hear it. Stay close to me."

His voice was calm, easy, and confident, all the things I wasn't. I glanced around, searching for Piper. I quickly found her with Zephys. He stood in front of her with one arm stretched across her middle, pushing her away from the cars being knocked aside by an unseen force.

I turned around and caught sight of Vitae. She was still holding Turve in place, but her eyes were locked on the cars. Turve was watching with a satisfied smile on his face.

That was when I knew Turve had been the bait in a trap all along.

It just hadn't snapped shut until now.

I took a breath to warn Hadrian, but everything happened so fast.

The false-Stormkind snapped out her hands and pushed a fierce blast of wind at Hadrian. Brutal wind smashed into us. Cars were pitched into the sky. Vitae shifted her balance and Turve stood up. Dirt clogged the sky, spreading and thickening around us like a dark fog. Hadrian was pushed back, and I was yanked away.

My shoulder hit a car. I winced at the smack of pain, my eyes searching for Hadrian as the hurricane winds thrashed around me. I could see shadows of movement. Nothing was clear. I couldn't be far from Hadrian, but with the wind pinning me where I was, I couldn't move quickly.

I turned so my back was pressed to the car and held out my hands. I knew I ought to use the tether, but I'd taken too much from it already. Hadrian would need it to fight now that Mortis, Ferno and Declan were here.

And I knew it was them. My gut told me this was the moment Turve had been waiting for. He wouldn't have looked so damn smug if he hadn't known they were coming.

Drawing power from the air around me was easy. There was just so much of it. I inhaled sharply when the flood of power shoved through my veins, like it was trying to push my blood aside. I let it glide through me, spreading my hands and forcing the air to split open ahead of me.

The dirt parted like a ripped seam, opening the world around me. Hadrian had been forced back, still holding the false-Stormkind at bay. Beyond him, I could see Piper and Zephys crouched and running through the dirty wind, scurrying to the open space I was creating.

I glanced back, seeing Vitae had gotten into a fresh fight with Turve. He no longer had his swords, but he was sheltered in a column of wind. The dirt wasn't hindering his vision, and the particles striking the tornado bounced back into Vitae's eyes. She gritted her teeth and fought with her swords, unable to use any gifts because the second she lowered her guard that way, Turve would pummel her.

She didn't even see the shadowy figure creeping up to her back. The sight of Ferno's crimson hair made my blood turn cold.

I gathered more power from the air and the dust that clogged it, taking a little more energy from the tether to harden the clumps of dirt.

Vitae slashed down at his neck, but he caught her wrist. The stab she aimed at his ribs was caught as well. Turve yanked her forward and drove his knee into her stomach. He did it again, tearing one of the tempest-blades from her grip. Turve's hand flew back, slamming into the side of her temple. Vitae staggered from the blow, blood streaming down her temple from where the pommel struck her. She lost her footing and collapsed onto the road. Ferno pulled his tempest-blades from their scabbards and aimed them at Vitae's back.

I pushed the hardened dirt at the Mistrals with the speed of a hurricane.

The grit collided with Ferno or Turve like hail. They yelled and cursed as I battered them. Vitae remained motionless.

Panicked, I whirled to find Zephys and Piper. Thankfully, they had made it to me.

"Vitae!" I shouted over the howling winds and pointed to her.

Zephys glanced at where she lay, anger lashing through his hazel-blue eyes when he saw Turve and Ferno. He nodded, took Piper's hand, and dragged her with him. She glanced at me, but I waved her on. Ferno and Turve were tricky Guardians. Zephys would need backup if he were going to help Vitae.

Besides, I had my own Guardian to protect.

I spun around, pushing apart the clumpy dirt to find Hadrian. He'd been forced further away from me, still holding the false-Stormkind back. A wall of ice had gone up between them, but she refused to relent. She grabbed a torrent of wind and hurled it at him. I watched the tornado wind twist horizontally and funnel at the wall that was only big enough to protect Hadrian's body. The salt in the dirt would eat through it in seconds.

Another shadow crept on top of the car beside Hadrian. He reached back and drew a blade over his shoulder. My eyes widened, dirt stinging my eyes.

"*Hadrian!*" I screamed.

He snapped his head at me, gripping both his swords. He saw the horror in my eyes and dove into a somersault that carried him toward me.

Mortis slammed down into the ground bare inches behind him, the tempest-blades hammering into the road with a terrifying shriek. Hadrian found his footing and swung around. Mortis dragged his arm up and lunged to drive both swords into Hadrian's stomach. My Guardian stepped back and knocked both blades to the right. Mortis lunged forward and pounded a kick into Hadrian's face.

I pushed away from the car, scrambling for a way to help him when a sudden impact sent me into the ground. I landed on my side rather than my head, though the person on top of me was doing their best to crack open my head.

Fingers twisted in my hair and pulled it by the roots. I winced at the sharp pain in my scalp and threw my elbow back. It crashed into a hard jawbone, drawing a yelp of pain from the false-Stormkind.

I rolled onto hands and knees, wishing the girl would just stay down. I didn't want to touch her, not knowing if dragging her power into me would finally kill me, but not wanting her to beat me to death either.

I backed up and turned my palms upward, waiting for her to run at me. Meaty hands slapped onto my back and shoved me forward. I didn't have time to see who was responsible. The false-Stormkind wrapped her hands around my throat and started to squeeze.

I balled my fist and punched her in the belly. Her grip loosened and I yanked free. The damn meat-hands found me again, this time grabbing my elbows and controlling my arms.

"You never used to be so difficult," Declan growled in my ear.

I thrashed and tried to rip free of his grip, but he pinched the nerves at my elbow and shoved my arms at the girl. She had no idea what she was running toward.

"No!" I cried.

It was too late. As soon as she was in arm's length, Declan slapped my hands onto her face. She skidded to a halt and screamed almost as loud as I did.

I didn't know what it felt like to have all my internal organs rearranged, but I imagine it felt something like what happened to me then in those crushing seconds of agony.

My insides became passengers on a roller coaster. They flipped up and down, looped and circled wildly, straining so hard in my body I thought they would snap from their valves and arteries. The whole churning sensation sent spikes of nausea into my head and searing lights into my eyes. I wanted to throw up, but I couldn't remember where my stomach was.

No wonder the girl in front of me had gone crazy. All the other pains I'd felt when I stole a gift were agonizing, but none of them felt as out of control as this.

I don't know when I let go, or if Declan finally forced me to release the girl. When my vision returned to color– the horizon still wobbled violently– the girl had backed away from me, her eyes wide with horror and confusion. Declan's crushing grip was gone from me.

I couldn't stop screaming.

I pitched forward, clutching my middle when it squeezed. I had to get rid of this power, do something with it, anything to stop the blender whipping up my insides.

Voices carried through the wind. Familiar ones. I didn't know who they belonged to, and I didn't care. Pain snapped through me again and I landed on my knees. I lifted my head and looked at the cars surrounding me. It was too much. Too much clutter, too much restriction. I needed space. I closed my eyes and dragged on the energy spiking through the air.

Wind thrashed over my head, spinning my hair in chaotic directions. The voices faded, drowned by the screaming winds. The scent of dry earth carried over the gusts. Rubber tires skidded along the road. Metal groaned and glass crunched. I opened my eyes.

A thin twister danced in front of me. Dirt swirled around it like a protective shield, the abandoned cars creeping toward it like possessed beings.

The pain in my body was a dull throb now. I pushed outward, testing the limits of this new ability. The tornado slithered forward on my command, drawing the cars forward with sharp squeaks. The pain lessened again. That seemed to be the key. I could get the pain away if I used the new gift I had been given.

The tornado whipped faster and faster, thickening and gaining speed. The cars tilted backward, showing their bellies. The winds from the tornado dragged them around its base in a screeching circle. I was able to breathe again.

A terrified yelp dragged my eyes from the twister. I saw the girl I'd stolen the gift from. She was scrabbling to hang onto the back of a truck, terror turning her words into incomprehensible noise. Her eyes caught mine, desperate and pleading. I thought about the hunger replacing the pain in my stomach. The warmth I could take from her to replace the chill inside me.

There was a tug on my heart. A final plea.

The tether.

Delirious, I turned my eyes away from the girl and sought out Hadrian. He was on the ground, blood pouring from the slices on his chest. It streamed down the sides of his face from where he'd been pummeled. He dragged his abused body toward his tempest-blades, using the tether to slick the road with ice so movement was easier. I was horrified at the pain he was in, but he wouldn't stop fighting.

Mortis didn't seem to care that Hadrian was returning to his weapons. He was watching me, appearing impressed.

Smiling, even.

Anger crushed the pain. *Let's see how impressed you are with this.*

I looked at the girl, still terrified and clinging to the truck.

"*Run!*" I shouted.

She didn't need to be told twice. Hoping she would get far enough away, I snapped out my arm and made a fist, like I was gripping an invisible rope.

I grabbed the tornado instead.

With a shout, I threw it in Mortis's direction. His grin faltered as the twister carved a violent path toward him. Cars smashed into each other as the spiraling grey and brown storm barreled toward the leader of the Mistrals. Clouds rolled over each other viciously, repelled by the tornado collecting them.

While he was distracted, I looked at Hadrian. He watched me with wide eyes, black hair snapping in front of his face, a terrified expression that made my heart pinch. I didn't know if the fear in his eyes was for the danger our enemies were bringing toward me, or simply for what I was doing.

What I was becoming.

My eyes burned when they met his. *Get the others to safety. Don't forget the girl.*

A rough arm wrapped around my throat and squeezed. My scream was an awful choked sound, but I didn't give in to the strike of fear. I stomped on my attacker's foot. He stumbled and I slammed my elbow into his ribs as hard as I could. He grunted and released my neck. I spun and plowed my elbow into the side of his head.

Shock reverberated up my elbow, but Declan was disoriented. I had a minute. Less than that, maybe.

By now, the tornado was in front of Mortis. I thought it would batter or sweep him down. That would have solved a lot of my problems.

I didn't expect he would shove out both his hands, and send out a hurricane wind unlike anything I'd ever felt before. It ripped through the tornado like a knife through butter, sending grey and brown dust flying in opposite directions. Cars lifted from the ground beside him, hurtling through the air like kicked toys. I was lifted with them.

My arms flailed uselessly, grabbing for something to grip and stop the motion, but finding only dirt and air.

Then it all stopped in an explosion of pain. My back hit unforgiving metal like a baseball meeting a bat. Glass cracked and gave way. I toppled forward onto my stomach, feeling broken pieces of glass and rock dig into my belly. My head pounded and swelled, growing until I thought it would burst. A copper-smelling wetness coated my nose and dripped into my mouth.

All my remaining strength went into lifting my head. Two blurred shapes stood over me. I could make out the furious scowl of Declan, and the disappointed glare of Mortis.

"This is troubling," Mortis declared. "We cannot eliminate the Precips now that she is about to die. We must leave. Take her."

Declan's scowl was the last thing I saw.

CHAPTER 16

Whatever room I was in, it needed a heater. Goosebumps riddled my body, and every breath I took was frigid and dry.

At least I was breathing. That was something, right?

The aching pulses strumming through my body begged to differ. My body felt like it had gone through a meat grinder. It was my head that felt the worst. A headache pounded against my skull, and there was a goose egg growing on my right temple.

Though it went against every rational thought in my mind, I opened my eyes.

And found myself staring at rocks.

I blinked slowly, letting the focus come back into my eyes. There was little light in the room, but enough for me to see the craggy roof over my head. I pushed myself up– very, very slowly– and followed the curve of the roof downward until I spotted the floor. It was a mismatched puzzle of rumpled bed sheets and blankets layered over dirt. The light was coming from a kerosene lantern glowing in the left corner of the cave.

Where in the world was I that I was in a cave? Was I even in Florida anymore?

The thought that I might be out of the city– out of the *country*– filled me with sickening dread.

I flipped over and crawled for the lamp. I didn't trust myself to stand just yet, though I knew I would have to get on my feet and run if I were going to get out of here and back to my friends.

Thinking about them made me halt. The last I saw, Vitae was unconscious, Zephys and Piper were running to help her, and Hadrian...

My chest tightened. It hurt to breathe. I closed my eyes and fought the tears burning them.

He's alive. He has to be alive. He's strong. He's okay.

Oh God, Hadrian, tell me you're okay.

There was no reply.

I pushed the horrible thoughts away before they could take me over. First step was getting out of here. There was a tunnel straight ahead. I could try going through it and hope I wouldn't be caught by one of the Mistrals.

Yeah. And maybe a white unicorn would appear and let me ride it to safety.

I gripped the lantern and pushed to my feet. My legs burned like I'd done five hundred squats before running ten miles. Not very pleasant at all.

Vertigo made my head swim, but I kept my footing. I glanced around the cave, which was only about eight feet across and just as deep. There was no exit that way, and there was nothing on the floor that I could use as a weapon. Not unless I wanted to wave one of the blankets like a beacon of surrender.

I trudged toward the mouth of the tunnel. I frowned as the lantern's light dispersed through the hollowed walkway, pushing the shadows deep into the gouged walls. I put the lantern behind my back, darkening the tunnel again. I knew it was risky to have any kind of light with me when I was making what I hoped was a sufficient escape attempt, but I wanted to be able to see where I was going, since I didn't know where I was, or how long I would be able to stay away from the Mistrals before they realized I was missing.

I got my answers far sooner than I wanted to.

The smell of smoke and cooking meat was my first warning. I paused, my stomach rumbling. When was the last time I had eaten?

It didn't matter. I had to get out of here first. Then I could find some kind of ration station. I couldn't be far from civilization, and enough time had passed that more effective food supplies would be put up. Production was probably starting as I walked.

Dear God, why did they have to be cooking bacon?

Struggling to ignore the hunger cramping my belly, I shuffled around a curve in the tunnel. I slowed down when an orange glow flickered along the wall. The light from my lantern wasn't strong enough to emit that kind of glow, so I set it down behind me and edged around the curve of the wall.

Sitting in a wide cavern around a fire were the Mistrals. Camping gear was tossed around them, everything from jugs of filtered water to sleeping bags to coolers of food. Ferno was contently moving a frying pan over a grill set on top of the crackling fire, the culprit for the delicious scent of cooked meat. Mortis sat beside him with a tempest-blade stretched across his lap, slowly rubbing a cloth along the bare steel.

Their actions seemed so normal, I could almost forget they were killers that didn't have any problems torturing others for their personal gain. Seeing them like this might have made me think they were normal men enjoying silence and simplicity.

If I hadn't been one of the victims of their torture, maybe I might have.

I glanced across the cavern searching for Turve and Declan. I couldn't see them, and had no idea how to get past the two Guardians without making myself known–

"You do not need to stand in silence, Ava. You are welcome to join us."

Damn Guardians and their enhanced senses.

I glanced back, wondering if I could use the lantern to crash against Mortis's head, and if I could conjure up some wind to whip the fire into Ferno's face–

A shadow fell over me. I turned around and stared up at Mortis. He was taller than I remembered, and the tempest-blade in his hand greedily sucked up the light of the fire.

"Allow me to make the choice simple for you," he said. His face was barely visible among the shadows. "There is one exit in this network of tunnels. You are not strong enough to run past us, and even if you had your strength and were capable of using your gifts, both Turve and Declan are outside, and they will surely re-capture you with far less kindness than I would."

He tilted forward. All I could see with clarity were the whites of his eyes and the glow of the fire behind him. Everything else was shadow, and it made my skin crawl.

"And suppose you did succeed in passing them. You are in the middle of a forest, miles away from any residence or aid station. You will be exhausted and alone in the dark, easy prey for the wolves and other beasts that still roam freely. You strike me as an intelligent young woman, Ava. Do not prove me wrong."

I figured my situation would be bad, but obviously didn't think about every possible worst case scenario. I wanted to lift my chin and tell Mortis that he was wrong, that I was strong enough to face all of those obstacles and find my way back to the people who cared about me.

But I wasn't a liar, and my luck had never been that good.

Seeming to sense my defeat, Mortis stretched his back and peered down at me. "You must be hungry."

He stepped to the side and extended his arm, like a gracious host welcoming me to his home. I didn't want to move an inch, but his gaze was turning into a sharp glare. Ferno watched me from across the flames, blindly taking a paper plate and filling it with fried meat. My stomach groaned and I wrapped my arms around my middle to hide the sound.

I raced through the reality of my situation again. I could defy the Mistrals to show them that I wouldn't give into any demands and that I trusted them about as far as I could throw them… Or I could swallow my pride, regain my strength, and think of a way to sabotage them so I could escape, or at least send a signal to the Precips.

Dropping my chin, I trudged into the clearing and sat on the dirt floor. I drew my knees into my chest but didn't take the plate when Ferno handed it to me. He grunted with impatience and set it on the floor, returning to the fire to dish out more food for him and his leader.

I pulled the plate toward me and looked at it. Four thick strips of bacon sat next to roughly chopped potatoes and fried corn that probably came from a can. Ferno didn't look like much of a cook, and I didn't want to think about where the "fresh" bacon actually came from, so I cast all doubts and unease aside and dug into the food.

It was blazingly hot and seared my tongue, and it wasn't really classy to eat with my bare hands, but I didn't care. It was fuel, and I knew that the Mistrals could care less about my manners. I was their weapon. The toy they created to wind up and set loose on a path of destruction.

Eating became difficult with that thought racking through my brain and Mortis slowly sitting next to me.

His eyes never left my face as I nibbled my food.

"Do you feel well?" he asked.

"Do you care?" I shot back before I could think.

He paused for a beat, then said, "This statement may come as a surprise to you, Ava, but yes, I have great concern for your well-being. You displayed an impressive amount of power out there on the highway. That kind of power comes with a cost."

Didn't I know it.

"I'm breathing. That's all you need, right?"

"True," he admitted. "Though your compliance would make this much easier."

I stopped eating and looked at Mortis. He wasn't eating, the tempest-blade resting on his lap like a warning.

"For what?" I asked. "What are you going to do to me now that I'm... wherever we are."

Mortis smiled thinly. "You are in the Florida Caverns, three hundred and fifty miles from Sanford."

I froze, the gravity of that sinking into my brain like a shard of glass pushed into putty. The Florida Caverns. Three hundred and fifty miles. I might as well have been in the tunnels under Hong Kong.

"As for what we intend to do to you," Mortis said, dragging me into reality with the cold promise in his voice. "I offer my word that you will be part of something great."

"I'll pass," I whispered.

Mortis smiled at me like I was an impatient child he had to scold. "Even if it means you will be at the forefront of a renewed dynasty? A veritable goddess?"

Only Mortis could make becoming a goddess sound like something terrifying. "Still gonna pass. You can take these powers back. I don't want them." How many times was I going to have to say that until someone got the picture?

Mortis's fake smile slipped. He slowly reached for his belt and withdrew a knife with a quick, violent tug. I jumped and shuffled back. Ferno's rough hand clamped on the back of my neck and clenched, making it clear that I wasn't going anywhere.

Mortis flipped the knife in his hand. I stared at the crystal blade of the dagger, my chest burning as the ghostly memories of a violent, bloody punch and scorching agony swam through my mind. My body went stiff, on the precipice of trembling.

He twisted the knife between his fingers, letting the smooth crystal absorb the light from the fire and shining it in my eyes.

"Has Vitae told you my story?" he asked, never moving his eyes from mine.

I nodded, unable to look at anything except the dagger that had been the cause of my agony. The dagger that could also mean the end of it.

Though I wasn't holding my breath.

"She did not see how we were being dishonored. That the Primordials we loved were allowing their torture at the hands of your kind. Sonus was even less open-minded than his protégé. They could not see that change was needed to save the world that belongs to us. And make no mistake, Ava. It *is* ours. We existed before the human race was even a thought. We fight to keep the earth whole beneath our feet, to ensure that natural order is respected and preserved. We lingered in the shadows and in the clouds, keeping you alive century after century."

He lowered the dagger, but his knuckles were white where they wrapped around the hilt.

"And we are repaid by watching your kind poison the clouds. Ripping trees from their roots. Defiling the soil. Treating the oceans like your garbage dumps." Cold, black eyes drilled into me, betraying the calm in his voice. "Tell me how we are supposed to condone that, Ava. Tell me why we should."

I didn't, because I couldn't. I knew humans were corrupting the earth. *Everyone* knew it. But the problem was there was only so much to be done. I couldn't speak for the major corporations who cut down trees to help build my house. I couldn't stop oil companies from drilling for gasoline that would help mothers and fathers drive to work to support their families. I couldn't stop the use of pesticides on farms. It wasn't my fault when a heavy wind blew a candy wrapper from my hand and into the ocean, dragging it miles out to sea where I couldn't reach it.

Thousands of generations and billions of people were the cause of earth's decay. That was the simple– and complex– truth of the matter. We endured by using what was around us. It was how we knew to survive. Maybe it was the wrong way of looking at the world, but it wouldn't change the facts.

Facts that Mortis would never listen to, no matter how calm he appeared to be.

"Then why did you make me? What am I supposed to be?" The questions came out as whispers, nearly drowned by the fire spitting at my right.

He was quiet for a very, very long time. Then he said, "As I told you once before, you are the first of many. A new generation of beings. We cannot remake the Stormkind. Only the Primordials have that capability, and they sacrificed themselves to feed the earth you violate." He made no effort to hide his contempt for the human race, and I was too scared to stop him.

"In my exile, I was forced to contemplate the nature of our predicament. It was clear that the Stormkind are the most effective weapon against your kind, but left unchecked and untamed, they are too wild for even Guardians to control. As powerful as we are on our own, we cannot commit the sort of cleansing required to eliminate humanity from the equation."

Mortis lifted the crystal dagger in his hands. "But if one were able to gather energy from tether and tempest-blades, and lock them into a concealable weapon, to release them all into a human body, there would be no need for the dying breed. The Stormkind are becoming obsolete. Humans on the other hand," the coldness of his grin made me shudder, "well, you produce an extraordinary number of offspring. I knew that with a little effort, and a reasonable amount of theft, it would be possible for my experiment to work.

"At first, there were failures. The bodies I chose could not withstand the immersion process. They Enervated too quickly, or died from the pain. I thought I was choosing insufficient specimens, but it was simply a matter of luck. Then it became a matter of control. Am I safe to assume that you have found yourself consumed at times? You have been using your gifts in the presence of another being, and have suddenly been compelled to devour them at any cost?"

I shuddered without warning, recalling the way I attacked Hadrian, Piper and Austin, the rush of desire, the desperation. I dragged my knees to my chest and wrapped my arms around them.

"As I thought," Mortis continued smugly. "Yet another symptom of the process, I fear. Each successful specimen displayed more traits of a Stormkind the more life force they absorbed. I worry that Declan will enter the final stage of his alteration soon."

My head snapped up. "Declan's been *eating* people's life forces?! He's becoming a *Stormkind*?"

"Yes," Mortis said with that smug, patient smile. "A vexing one, if I may be blunt. He is consumed by proving his worth, to be accepted now that he has lost his human family."

I cringed a little. I had no idea Declan had lost his family in the Centennial. It didn't excuse his actions, but it made me feel a little sorrier for him. I wondered if there was a way to appeal to his humanity– if he had any left– and let him know he could rebuild, the way we were all supposed to.

Then I thought about his hands abusing my body, and decided that reasoning wasn't a very good idea as far as Declan was concerned.

"If I am continuing to be honest, I do not know why I chose you. Perhaps it was because you were there. Perhaps I saw your endurance in the hurricane and the flood. Perhaps I just wanted to see what would happen. In any case, I am grateful that we crossed paths, Ava. With you, I will achieve more than I ever dreamed. You have saved your kind from certain extinction–"

Every word coming from his mouth poisoned me. They made my body quake, my blood boil, and my eyes see red. As he spoke, I thought about the pain I had suffered. My missing family, the screams of my best friend and the girl I could have killed. I thought about the burdens and struggles of the Precips, the heartache in Hadrian's eyes when I realized how much I meant to him.

The nightmares, the pain, the confusion, the burden, the fear, the lack of control...

All of it welled together into a savage void inside me as this man– no, this heartless *monster*– told me he was *grateful* for everything he put me through. Like I had earned it.

Like I should be thanking him.

That was the last straw. The last goddamn *fucking* straw.

I launched up from where I sat on the ground and slammed into Mortis. I didn't even think about the blades he was holding. I didn't stop to care. All that mattered were my hands around his throat, the pressure I applied to his neck, the power I could draw out to *crush* him–

A heavy thud smashed into the back of my skull. Stars erupted in my vision. The world pitched as I collapsed. I blinked my blurred eyes, straining to figure out what the swirling shapes above me were supposed to be.

Dirt skidded up the sides of my chin and tunneled into my mouth. I thrashed and reached to dislodge them, then felt clumps of dirt wrap around my arms, legs, hips and chest. They tightened into rough ropes, pinning me into the ground. I closed my eyes and twisted my aching head from side to side, but the dirt kept filling my mouth. Smothering me.

It stuck in between my teeth and coated my gums, clustered around my tongue, clogged my throat. The dirt swelled in there, becoming a painful lump that I couldn't swallow. My lungs burned and my heart thumped wildly, snared by panic. I couldn't die this way. I couldn't, I *couldn't*–

"Release her, Ferno."

With agonizing slowness, the dirt bonds unwound from me and the dirt was pulled from my mouth. I rolled onto my side and gagged, dry heaving to choke the wretched taste from my mouth. I hacked until my lungs and throat burned, though I could still taste the rough, salty dirt on my tongue.

"Are you finished with your little rebellion?" Mortis asked blandly.

I wanted to growl. I wanted to cry. I wanted Piper to stand up for me, for Hadrian to hold me and tell me he would keep me safe.

I wanted things I couldn't do and wouldn't have, because no one was coming to save me. If they were, they would be coming far too late.

So I said nothing.

"I will take that as a yes."

Rough fingers scraped along my scalp and clutched my hair. I gasped and swallowed lingering dirt as Mortis dragged me to my feet. He whirled me around and jerked my hair back. I winced at the spike of pain.

"I have been kind to you, Ava. Hospitable. I am offering you a chance at glory and honor. I do not appreciate my gift being thrown back in my face."

"Then take them back yourself," I hissed. "Take that damn knife and reverse what you did."

Mortis tilted his head. His smile was wicked and sharp, like a knife glinting before it split open tender skin. "Is that what you were hoping for? Another little cut to recall the powers of a Stormkind?"

Mortis released my hair and shoved me hard. I lost my footing and would have landed on my ass if Ferno hadn't grabbed my arms in his thick, vice-like hands.

The leader of the Mistrals plucked the crystal dagger from the ground and approached me, spinning the weapon in quick, flashing circles. I twisted and struggled in Ferno's grasp, but I couldn't move. Unlike Declan, I doubted I would be able to tear free of him with cheap shots and dirty defense tricks.

"Tell me, Wild One. Why would I want to take back the powers of my greatest creation? Why would I want a failsafe that left her alive in case she thought to resist me?"

He reached for the collar of my shirt and tugged it down far enough to reveal my scar. The white skin forever marked with the twisted sigils of the Mistrals and the Precips. Mortis pressed the tip of the dagger to the ruined flesh. I swear he could feel my pulse hammering through the blade.

"I suppose I could try again," Mortis offered icily. "After all, you are my anomaly. I could attempt taking your gifts back by slicing into you again, and then dispose of you in a permanent fashion."

He pressed the knife deeper into my skin. I gasped at the hot sting that burst from my chest. I glanced down, watching a small stream of blood oozing around the crystal blade.

"Hmm," grunted Mortis. "It does not appear to be working. Should I try harder?"

The dagger sank deeper. The pain swept across my chest like wildfire, though the burn wasn't the same, crushing agony I'd felt when he stabbed me the first time.

But that wasn't a comfort. Because if Mortis pushed the blade any deeper, he was going to kill me.

"You cannot erase what you have become, Ava. You are no longer human. You will be a revitalized Stormkind until the day you die. And as troubling as you have become, I will not kill you."

Mortis withdrew the crystal dagger from my chest. My legs wobbled and nearly gave way. Ferno jerked me upright. His leader drew closer.

"Make no mistake, Wild One. You will do as I command you. The consequences of failure will be worse than death."

I didn't see how. He'd already tortured me into creation. Unless Hadrian could feel the tether from three hundred and fifty miles away, no one was coming for me. At this point, there was nothing I could use.

I felt no shame when I looked into his eyes, scowled, and gave him a bitter, "Fuck you."

Mortis stared at me, blinking only once. I could sense the barely controlled rage beyond his eyes. See it in the way he clenched the hilt of the dagger. He wanted to hurt me. He wanted me to be his perfect little monster, capable of genocide so he could take revenge for the Primordials he worshipped.

Guess he didn't think his little pet project would be so insufferably human.

"Perhaps we should allow her to see the incentive," rasped Ferno.

The way he said *incentive* made my stomach roll.

"Perhaps you are correct, Ferno."

"*Perhaps* you should stop saying *perhaps*," I snapped, still feeling my confidence on the rise. "It's getting really annoying. Besides, there's nothing you can do to me to make me help you."

"Oh, I beg to differ," Mortis countered. "You see, Declan knows what you value. He may have failed me as a new Stormkind, but he has his uses. He and Turve have likely returned with their prizes. I believe it is time for you to see them."

Mortis stalked past me and walked out of the cavern. Ferno released one of my arms and whirled me around, dragging me behind him. I had to all but run to keep pace with him. I glanced left and right as we stormed down the corridor, but didn't spot any exits or turn-offs. If there was a way to escape, I couldn't see it.

That being said, it didn't take us long to reach the end of the tunnel. Cool night air washed over my face. The smell of pine swirled around me. I glanced up and saw scattered stars gathering near a full moon split in half by slashes of clouds. I would have found it to be hauntingly beautiful, if not for the terror and confusion warring inside my head.

Ferno stopped abruptly and grabbed both of my arms again. He practically lifted me off the ground when he whirled me in front of him. Planted on my feet again, he crushed my biceps and forced me to look ahead.

As soon as I saw what was before me, I knew Mortis was right. There was no chance I would defy him. Not with this kind of weapon.

My family on their knees, with terror in their eyes and blades to their throats.

I sagged in Ferno's grip. Even he couldn't hold me up this time. Tears welled in my eyes and spilled down my cheeks as I looked at their faces in turn.

I'd allowed myself to fantasize about what would happen if I ever saw them again. Of feeling my father's strong arms when he hugged me. My mother stroking my hair and telling me how proud she was. James tugging my hand and smiling when he wanted to show me something.

I hadn't imagined the bruises on my father's face, the cut on my mother's lip, or the tears lining James's cheeks.

Mortis stood behind my little brother with the crystal dagger. Declan had wrapped one of his fists in my mother's hair, a short knife to her throat. Turve had his hand clamped over my father's forehead, drawing it back and exposing his neck to a tempest-blade.

"How…" It was the only word I could get out.

"It seems they frequent the Missing Boards," Mortis announced. "Declan knew where to find them. He recalled where you lived and where the local resource stations were."

"Wasn't hard, Ginger," the bully announced with pride.

My eyes turned to him, finally seeing how awful he looked. I'd noticed the paleness before, but when I was captured on the road in Sanford, he was either behind me or I was too delirious with pain to notice his physical changes. Now I could see the utter transparency of his flesh, so thin I could see his blue veins beneath. The texture of his skin was uneven and almost wrinkled, like a burn victim.

Or the texture of a hurricane-Stormkind.

I wished I could feel the anger I was supposed to feel. That I wasn't so overridden with terror I couldn't even straight.

"Allow me to make this perfectly clear, Ava," Mortis said. It was a monumental effort to drag my eyes from my kidnapped family to him. His expression was stony and empty. As if holding a dagger to a little boy was commonplace for him.

"You will strengthen your abilities. You will become our weapon. You will increase your strengths until I am prepared to unleash you. I will create more new Stormkind like you. If you do not agree to my terms, or if you attempt to contact the Precips, I will kill your family in front of you."

He put his hand on James's shoulder and squeezed. My baby brother winced.

"Starting with this one. If you do not agree, he will die now."

My parents screamed. Declan and Turve shouted at them to be silent. James started to cry. Mortis stared at me. I felt my world begin to collapse.

"See what will become of them if you refuse. Ava? You will lose more than a brother. Your parents will be ruined. You will see it all, and suffer from a pain greater than any physical torture I could ever inflict."

He paused, letting me listen to my parents' tortured sobs.

"Or, you can swear here and now to obey me. To be exactly what I made you to be. You can say goodbye, and embrace your new life."

I knew then that there was no painless choice for me. Either I would watch my little brother die and see my parents succumb to grief before they were killed, or I would agree and be forced to leave them forever. No matter what, Mortis would have what he wanted. I was his weapon. His experiment.

"Decide, Ava."

James's sobs caught in his throat. The tears I'd been trying to hold back spilled down my face.

"Please," I cried, "please, he has asthma—"

"Decide."

He wasn't offering me a choice. He was giving me a command. The worst part was, I knew what my answer would be. I only had one. There would be consequences for it, and I would suffer regardless. Me and countless others.

"I'll do it," I whispered. Gathering my voice and letting go of my pride, I wearily met Mortis's eyes. "I'll do it. Just please, please let them go."

Mortis stared at me for a long time, searching for some kind of deception or trick. I let him stare, because I had no tricks. I had no way of defeating the Mistrals.

Not yet, anyway.

Mortis released my brother, then looked at Turve and Declan. They let go of my parents and backed away a couple steps. My parents huddled together, keeping James between them and soothing him so his breathing relaxed.

"Release her, Ferno. Let her remember what she stands to lose if she fails us."

The grip on my arms disappeared. I tore across the dirt and skidded to a stop in front of my parents and brother. I was amazed when they didn't recoil from me, and even more stunned when they wrapped their arms around me and held me close. None of us could stop crying.

"Don't do this," my father pleaded. "Don't give in."

"I don't have a choice," I sobbed. "You don't know what they're capable of. If I don't do what he says…" Tears choked my throat.

"We can't leave you here," my mother begged. James clutched my stomach like he would never let go.

I wanted them to stay with me. I dreaded the thought of being alone with these psychopaths. But I couldn't risk my family again. I couldn't lose control around them. Not when I'd witnessed the depths of their terror when I got that damn glow in my eyes.

So I lied.

"I'll come home," I whispered. "I'll find my way back to the old house. I don't know when or how, but I'll be there. I promise."

The words gagged me. My cheeks flared with heat and my eyes burned with tears.

My family believed me.

"You're a strong, brave girl, Ava," my mother told me, her blue eyes shining. "We're so proud of you."

The three of us embraced again. James's words were muffled in my shirt, but I heard him loud and clear.

"Come home soon."

I wondered if my tears were ever going to stop.

"The goodbyes have been said," Mortis announced blandly.

Ferno's rough hands grabbed my shoulders and yanked me back. My family wailed as I was torn from them. My father shot to his feet with his fists balled. I shook my head frantically, begging him not to risk his life and help me.

Defeated, my father turned to Mortis.

"March west. If you do not find a resource station, you will find the coast. Follow it south from there."

That was it. No other advice, no supplies, nothing. If what Mortis told me about the forest was true, it was all but a death sentence, and it was the only thing he was going to give.

My father realized this. He slowly helped James and my mother to their feet. Wrapping his arms around their shoulders, he looked back at me.

I don't think I had ever seen my father cry before.

"We love you, Ava. We love you so much."

Then my father shuffled away with my family. I could feel my heart leaving with him, abandoning me to nothing but grief and dread.

CHAPTER 17

"You are about to witness something that no human has ever seen before."

I stared at the ground, not caring one single bit about Mortis's grand proclamation. I was exhausted even before we started the long walk across the forest. I hadn't slept a wink last night, too busy crying and wondering if my family would make it would out of the forest alive. I had to believe they'd be okay. Even though I would never know, because I was never going to see them again.

Don't think like that, I scolded myself. *Figure out what the Mistrals want to do with you, turn it against them, then run.*

That was the extent of my master plan. How I was going to accomplish it was a mystery, but I figured I would jump that hurdle when I came to it. Right now, I had to pretend I was curious about what the Mistrals wanted to show me.

It was cold here, and the spare sweater they gave me wasn't doing much to keep the chill away. Wind whipped my hair, and I finally looked up. Half bent trees surrounded us, their splintered branches dangling over our heads like shattered bones. Toppled branches and twigs dug into the middle of my boots, and the smell of pine and cedar filled the night. The full moon's light poured over us, a ghostly glow that sank into the ground and illuminated the tragedy of the ruined forest around me.

I hadn't asked any questions since I said goodbye to my family. I hadn't even tried to contact the Precips to ask for help. I could barely feel the cool thread from the tether in my chest. It was like it had been unplugged, separating me from Hadrian and any possible chance of rescue. I had no idea if I would still be able to use it in a fight, but if it came down to it, I would try. No matter how hopeless I felt right now, I refused to go down without a fight.

After what seemed like hours, Mortis came to a stop. Turve and Ferno stood on either side of him. Declan shoved his palm into the middle of my back and urged me forward. Not because I had slowed down– just because he was an asshole.

I turned to glare at him, maybe even give him a piece of my mind, when a flash of light shone across his scowling, transparent face. I turned and watched the flash again, like someone was wielding strobe light at the bottom of the hill.

I stalked away from Declan and stood on the top of the hill next to Mortis. I peered down the hill, seeing instead that it was a crater. It looked like some giant god had taken a massive spoon and scooped out a chunk of the earth. The curves of the walls were perfect and smooth, drawing my attention to the dozen cages clustered in the middle. One of them contained the harsh, blinking light, but there were other lights in the cages. Thinner lights, each one spread into five lengths that connected together like a...

My eyes widened. I whirled my head to look at Mortis. His smirk was smug. He nodded.

"Behold the last of the Stormkind, Ava."

Even though I knew that's what I'd seen, hearing it made it real. Real and terrifying. I turned to look down the hill again, looking at each cage and its imprisoned Stormkind. My mind screamed at me to figure out what we were doing here, but I shied away from the answer. Whatever the reason was, it couldn't be good.

"How can these be the last ones?" I asked, desperate for answers to all but the most obvious question. "What about the Stormkind around the world?"

"Fellow Guardians did as they were ordered. They brought the Stormkind to the mountains. They would have returned to their posts, training and waiting for the next Centennial. Though their positions have become useless, I knew they would be reluctant to release their charges to us. It was their choice to make the situation complicated."

I stared at him. "You killed them?"

No, he couldn't have, that kind of betrayal would lead too deep, the burden of duty unable to pass onto new generations of Guardians...

Mortis met my gaze without a flicker of remorse. "They made their choice to stand against us. To stand in the way of progress. I did what needed to be done."

My stomach sank. Just when I thought he had some kind of code, a single line that he wouldn't cross no matter what, he did something like this. I was too horrified to move when Mortis leaned down and pressed a hand on my shoulder. It felt like a lead weight about to crush me into the earth.

"Sacrifices must be made when you reshape the world, Ava," he told me with absolute certainty. "You sacrificed a future with your family. I was forced to sacrifice the lives of seven brothers and sisters."

"Like you sacrificed Sonus?"

Mortis didn't flinch outright, though his fingers pinched my shoulder harder than before. "Sonus was blind to the future. He was too weak to embrace change. Too stubborn to bring the Guardians the glory we deserve." A bitter light gleamed in his eyes. "Weakness and stubbornness that passed onto his son, it appears."

My fists balled. "Hadrian is stronger than you think he is."

Mortis paused as if to consider this. Then he nodded slowly. "Perhaps." His steely eyes sent shivers down my spine. "But he is not strong enough."

I took a breath to defend my Guardian, but Mortis soldiered on.

"I will atone for the deaths I have caused, I am certain. But until the new Stormkind have taken their place in the world, I will not look back. The future is here. It is time we embrace it."

Without another word, Mortis began climbing down the hill. Ferno and Turve followed him diligently. I trudged after them, not wanting Declan to push me again and send me falling head over heels into the dirt.

The slope wasn't actually that bad, but every step I took felt like the beginning of the end. The closer I got to the Stormkind, the higher the hairs on the back of my neck rose. The stiffer I became. The heavier the unease became in my stomach.

By the time I was on the flat part of the crater, just fifty feet from the nearest cage, I could hardly move. I could see the Stormkind in crystal clarity under the moonlight now.

The cages were exactly the way Vitae had described them to me. The bars were made of tall tempest-blades. The sides of the cage were made of standing swords, the tips driving deep into the earth. The sides of the hilts touched along the edge, and on the top of the cage, the swords were laid flat like they were on display. I could feel the steady pulse of power coming from each cage, like the heavy bass beat of a nightclub sinking through my skin.

Behind each cage was a Stormkind. I recognized a couple of them– the hurricane-Stormkind with its rippling exterior, and a sparking thunder-Stormkind, but there were others I hadn't seen before.

A Stormkind covered in ice and capped with shimmering snow. Another with water melting down its body and dripping from its fingers. A Stormkind whose skin spiraled in circles like a top out of control. A fourth with dirt-covered flesh that rolled and crunched together when it moved its joints.

Two of each Stormkind paced in their six-by-six cages, their glowing white eyes fixed on us as we approached. Without pupils, it was impossible to tell who they were really looking at, but I felt like I was the center of their attention. I didn't know exactly how sentient the

Stormkind were, but I was willing to bet they had enough instinct to know the Guardians were harder prey to devour. As far as the Stormkind were concerned, I was a simple human. Fresh and mere feet away.

The two thunder-Stormkind pulsed with light, bursts of energy throbbing under their lightning skin. The others increased the speed of their pacing, until they were all but running from one side of the cage to the other. Their silence gave me chills.

"Don't be shy," Declan taunted in my ear, his clammy hand sliding down my spine to the bottom of my belt. I shivered and pulled away. "We're not the ones who are going to get hurt."

I glanced over my shoulder. Declan was smiling and looking over my head, an awful excitement filling his eyes. I turned again, watching Mortis, Turve, and Ferno spread out. Each one of them drew a crystal dagger.

I watched with horror, now realizing that Mortis must have perfected the design of his dagger and given it to his most trusted generals. During the Centennial, they could have run through the chaos, choosing victims to stab and inject with unwanted powers.

The Mistrals didn't choose cages reflective of their abilities. Ferno stood in front of a thunder-Stormkind. Turve was before a dust-Stormkind. Mortis chose one made of ice. They didn't flinch as they looked at their prey. The Stormkind went wild, throwing their bodies against the tempest-blade bars. The moment they struck, they bounced back as if the bars had electrocuted them. They rushed forward again, absorbed the pain as they flew back, then ran forward again.

I cringed. The Stormkind must have been desperately hungry. Their century long starvation was beginning. Having felt that pain, I knew how it would drive them mad. Seeing the Mistrals standing there, taunting them and provoking that hunger... It was simply cruel.

"Strike on my command," Mortis said, never looking away from the Stormkind frozen in place in front of him.

"Wait," I said, taking a step forward. Declan gripped my shoulder and yanked me back. My heart hammered against my ribs, each pulse becoming a knot of dread.

"Strike."

When the Stormkind launched into the bars again, the Mistrals moved with blinding, accurate precision. The crystal daggers flashed and punched through electricity, dust, and icy flesh. The density didn't matter. Nothing could shatter a tempest-blade, no matter how small it was.

The Stormkind stood frozen place, unable to back away. I watched in horror as the light from their skeletons retreated to the core of their being, then funneled into the blade. The crystal glowed to life, so bright it seemed to scorch my eyes.

I didn't know if the tears lining my face were caused by the searing light from the daggers, or the crushing pain in my chest.

It wasn't that I adored the Stormkind. I would never forget waking up on that rooftop and seeing the endless horizon of disaster and destruction. I would always remember the sight of my ravaged house and the broken furniture on the lawn. I would have nightmares about the Stormkind that devoured life forces in front of me, the electric light in their eyes when I knew I was next.

But they couldn't be blamed for what they'd done any more than a starving hawk could be blamed for eating a field mouse. They were predators simply doing what nature intended them to do. Not even the Primordials could be faulted for this. If the legend Vitae told me was true, then the Primordials knew what they had created was beyond their control. That's why they created the Guardians and gave half their powers to them. It was all nature, action and reaction. Despite the horror it endured in the Centennial Storm, I knew the human race would survive. It was what we were best at, and if Vitae was right, the Stormkind would eventually go extinct.

The world wasn't supposed to be unbalanced this way, through intended violence and slaughter. Every time someone tried to change the world to match their own twisted ideals, it ended in disaster and needless death.

That's what would happen here, even though Mortis was convinced otherwise.

The final light from the Stormkind faded. One by one, their bodies collapsed in heaps of sparks, dust, and melted ice. Mortis stepped back, examining his dagger pensively.

"These blades are not as strong as the previous ones we used. We will likely have room for one additional absorption. After we use them on our chosen targets, they will need to be disposed of."

"Are we going to try again?" Ferno asked. "If the daggers cannot hold another power, they could be rendered useless. There is no guarantee that our targets will survive the same way Hadrian's charge has."

The crystal daggers could only be used once? That explained why there weren't more freaks like me running around. I imagined it took time to create each dagger, and there was no guarantee the person the Mistrals targeted would be able to hold more than one power. Maybe that was why Ferno killed Austin– he saw him as a failure as well as a means of escaping the Precips.

There was nothing I could say that would make the Mistrals stop killing the Stormkind. I knew that. They completely believed what they were doing was the right thing.

If I couldn't get through to them, I had one more person to try with. While the Mistrals approached a new set of Stormkind, I turned and looked at Declan.

"We have to stop this," I told him.

He blinked and looked at me. "Why?"

"The Stormkind are just acting on instinct," I explained, hoping to make this conversation as quick and simple as I could. "They're starved for a hundred years. You must have felt that pain. I have."

He kept staring. "Yeah. I've felt it." Declan pointed to his face. "How do you think I got like this?"

Any words I'd thought to speak died on my lips when I looked at him. Declan's features were still familiar enough for me to recognize, but I took in the thinness of his body. The transparency of his skin and paleness of his hair. The unstable glow building around his irises.

"Have you ever fed like a Stormkind, Ava?"

I cowered into myself and shook my head. Declan didn't blink.

"It's an adrenaline rush like nothing you can imagine. It's like swallowing a star. It burns through you, filling your body until you think you're going to explode. When you absorb the last of it, your whole body becomes a pulse of light. You can feel it sinking into your very bones, making you stronger. Making you *better*." Hunger filled his eyes, and I felt my confidence shrink. "It's a drug. The longer you go without it, the more fucked up you become."

I hesitated, realizing I wouldn't get through to Declan, either. It wouldn't be long before he became a Stormkind. His humanity was skin deep. Behind his flesh was something I was too terrified to think about.

It was the same thing hiding beside my bones, the monstrosity that would be unleashed if I ever gave in and devoured a life force.

Light sparked behind me. I jumped and spun around. Three more Stormkind had fallen prey to the crystal daggers, their skeletons shrinking and dissolving into the blades. I almost wished the Stormkind had been able to scream. Maybe then, the horror of this extermination would reach Declan, and make him think twice about what he wanted to become.

I looked at him again. "Declan, please, this is only going to make things worse. The Stormkind need to be dealt with by Guardians who respect them. They can't be slaughtered like this."

"Why the hell do you care?" he snapped. "The only reason you're not in those cages is because Mortis's plan worked with you." He shook his head. "You have no idea how fucking lucky you are."

I gawked. I was many things, but lucky had *never* been one of them.

"The person you were tethered to gave a shit about you. You didn't have to struggle and beg to please him or make him see that you were worth something. This little experiment worked with you. It didn't work for me, and now I'm being cast aside like I'm goddamn worthless."

Declan's hands suddenly clamped onto my arms. "Maybe I should just absorb you. Then I would have it all. I would be able to give Mortis the power he wants, and show him how loyal I am. I've earned that much. You've earned nothing."

Declan's eyes ignited like flares and fixated on my mouth. His head snapped down toward mine. I leaned away and raised my arms. I turned my head and slapped at his chest, trying to get him away. All I did was agitate him. He shoved me away and drew back his hand to slap me.

I moved first, kicking him hard between the legs.

Declan yelped and stumbled, nearly losing his balance. I scrambled to run, only to find myself face to face with Mortis. I skidded to a stop when I saw the sharp frown on his face, and the glowing dagger in his hands. Ferno and Turve stood behind him, each one gripping their dagger tight.

Beyond them were three more empty cages.

"What is the meaning of this?" Mortis demanded coldly, flicking his eyes between Declan and me.

"The fucking bitch doesn't deserve to be here," Declan hollered. "*I* fought for you. *I* killed for you." His control dissolved, erasing into oblivion and replaced by something cold, lifeless, and dreadful. "All you've done is

cast me down. Make it sound like I'm goddamn worthless."
Declan eyed the dagger in Mortis's hand enough, and
stabbed a finger at it. "Give me that. Make me into what
she is. I've got the stomach for killing. She doesn't. She'll
never do what you ask her to. She'll never follow your
orders."

"Her family–"

"*That won't matter*," his roar echoed through the
crater. "She's weak! Always been a fucking coward," he
cast me a gaze poisoned with contempt. "You just got lucky
with her. You don't need her. I'm stronger and better than
her. You tell her to unleash all those powers at once, and
it'll goddamn kill her."

A jolt of fear shuddered through me. I whirled and
looked at Mortis. He stared blankly at Declan, then looked
down at me.

"I fear the surprise has been spoiled, Wild One," he
stated.

"You… You want me to use all my powers? At the
same time?"

Mortis nodded. "You have no concept of how much
energy resides in you. How rigid your control is. You did
not just absorb power, Ava. You absorbed *tethers*."

I gaped, every question catching in my throat before
I could speak it.

"What I placed inside you were the tethers of every
variation of Stormkind. You reacted strongly to the one of
your Guardian, but the others are there, dormant until you
choose to wield them. It takes a toll on you, but the strength
and distance at which you can send those storms is
unparalleled. They will move across the globe, instigating a
second Centennial."

My mind throbbed at the insanity of his words. A
second Centennial Storm? When barely a month had passed
since the first one? The world wouldn't be able to take it.

And neither would I.

"It won't work," I said. My voice was hoarse, even though I hadn't been screaming. "I pass out when I use too much power. I start bleeding."

No readable emotion passed through Mortis's eyes. "Because you have not been absorbing life-force. Although your resistance is impressive, it is unwise in your condition. You must feed, or you will die before you have served your purpose."

"I... I can't!"

He reached out and clasped my elbow, digging his fingers into hidden nerves and sending fireworks of pain up my arm.

"You can, and you will." He dipped his head, casting shadows over his face. "Why do you think I brought him here?"

My head whipped to Declan. He understood the implications as well as I did.

"Wait, what? You want me to be her appetizer? No, Fuck that! *No!*"

Faster than any of us could react, Declan raised his hands and shoved them forward. A massive gale force slammed into us, as strong and as sudden as a speeding train. My body was out of my control, forced down like a felled tree. Even the Mistrals had difficulty keeping their footing. Declan charged forward.

A wall of dirt kicked up in front of him, blocking his path. The wind pushing against my chest was lifted, but I didn't give away my freedom yet. Until I figured it was a better idea to look helpless while I formed a plan of attack.

Ferno stomped ahead of me, holding up his hands and directing the dirt wall with one hand. The crumbling, dark curtain obscured Declan from view. Turve sprinted around to flank the crazed man.

Declan shouted, his war-cry carrying through the walls of the crater. The wall exploded outward, dirt flying in a thousand directions as he broke it down. Declan saw Turve aiming to sideswipe him. He ducked and caught the

Guardian around the middle, tackling him into the ground. Turve struggled and punched Declan in the jaw. He took the blow like it was nothing. He didn't care about the punches. He went straight for the dagger.

"*No!*" Mortis bellowed.

It was too late.

Ferno sprinted toward the fight, but Declan whipped up his hand. Wind curved and struck Ferno in the middle. He bent in half so sharply I thought his spine had snapped in two. Mortis gathered his own wind and shoved it toward Declan, but he only gripped Turve tighter.

He punched the Guardian in the face and ripped the dagger from his hands. He turned it until it was pointing at his heart. Without hesitation, he drove it through his chest.

Then Declan screamed.

He collapsed off of Turve, clutching his heart as the crystal blade pumped stolen energy into him. I wanted to scream, but I could scarcely breathe. I watched Declan writhe in agony on the ground, his fingers clawing at his chest and sweat beading down his face.

Turve rose to his feet and reached for the tempest-blades on his back. Ferno joined him, drawing one of his own swords over his shoulder.

"Wait!" Mortis yelled.

Both warriors looked at him.

"Let us observe what happens to him. He boasted that he could take it. Let us see if he can."

Ferno and Turve hesitated, but faced Declan in compliance. They laid the tips of their swords against the earth, though their muscles didn't relax. Mortis stalked past me, his footsteps cautious and curious.

I waited until he was past me before I sat up. I turned around and gathered my feet, rising and backing away.

Declan's screams gripped my heart, but I couldn't help him. He'd done this to himself. Even if I could have done something, there was no way Mortis would let me get close to him now. If this insane experiment worked, Mortis would no longer have a use for me. If not... I would die when Mortis forced me to create another Centennial Storm.

This was my chance to escape. The only one I would ever get.

I was so focused on backing away, I didn't know something was behind me until I bumped into it.

I jumped and opened my mouth to scream. A hand clapped over my mouth and silenced me. I pressed my lips together to bite him, then stopped when the tether vibrated to life.

Peace, Ava. You are safe now.

That was the biggest lie I'd ever heard, but I was so happy to hear Hadrian's voice that I didn't even care.

How did you find me? And what the hell took you so long?

Turve's charge was here. She told us where to find you. We came as fast as we could with our injuries. Traveling with storm-sight was difficult, since we did not know which storms to follow. He tightened his grip around me. *I am so sorry, Ava. You should never have been with them for longer than a minute.*

I heard the regret in his voice, felt the weight of it in my mind, but I knew they'd played it smart. If they'd come in guns blazing, they could have died. There was nothing I wanted less.

Make it up to me now, I thought. *Help me stop them.*

I felt his hesitation. *Promise me you will not use anything but the tether.*

As if I would use anything that would kill me. *I promise.*

Hadrian released me and took my hand. I turned to see him, drinking in the sight of his pale face, midnight black hair, and luminous blue eyes. I wanted to hug him. Kiss him. Tell him that I was pretty sure I was in love with him.

But until I was out of here, all those things were on the back burner for now. We had to stop the Mistrals while they were distracted by Declan's transformation. Or death. Whatever was causing him to scream so much.

Over Hadrian's shoulder, I spotted Vitae, Zephys, and Piper sneaking down the hill into the crater. Piper smiled with relief when she saw me. Vitae looked at the captured Stormkind, an angry scowl twisting her lips when she saw the empty cages. She put her hand on Zephys's shoulder and pointed to the cages that still contained Stormkind. He looked nervous, but nodded at whatever command she gave him,

Hadrian continued pulling me across the clearing. We were almost there when Declan's screaming stopped.

Someone else started in his place.

Hadrian whirled around and pressed his back to my chest, shielding me from whatever was about to happen.

I peeked around him, watching Declan rise from the ground and pounce on Turve. Ferno shouted and rushed for his friend, but Mortis held him back. He watched as Declan smashed his head down onto Turve's. He did nothing as Declan widened his jaw and absorbed his life force.

I don't know why I still saw him as Declan. The jerk from my college football team was long gone. His clothes were shredded from his violent struggle, his skin had been replaced by a shimmering exterior of water over an illuminated skeleton. A skeleton that grew brighter and brighter the more power he absorbed from Turve. The Guardian kicked and thrashed uselessly. Then his motions stopped, the light between their mouths steadily fading.

Turve's body became limp. Declan rose, no longer a human, but a complete Stormkind. His human skin was gone, replaced by a shuddering, clear texture. Through it, I could see the bright pulsing light of his skeleton, the essence of the lives he'd devoured to become a monster.

His blazing white eyes locked on us.

On me.

Mortis and Ferno turned and frowned. The pain on Ferno's face was replaced by hate. Mortis looked annoyed at first.

Then he smiled.

"Hadrian," he said in a slithering voice. "You have arrived just in time. I believe my latest specimen is still hungry."

Mortis had barely finished speaking before the Stormkind that used to be Declan barreled past them and came straight for us.

CHAPTER 18

Hadrian moved like lightning. His turned his hands upward. Frost coated his hands and funneled out of his palms. A flurry of icy darts rocketed toward Declan. Mortis swatted his hand through the air, blasting the darts aside. Hadrian was already drawing his tempest-blades, and I was beside him gripping the tether I shared with him.

Thick grey clouds rolled across the sky, clashing together and dragging cold winds beneath them. This time, the rain was welcome. It poured in buckets around us, and I instantly used the tether to turn the raindrops into sharp pieces of hail.

Declan didn't seem to notice the hail, any more than he noticed the dagger still embedded in his chest. His only goal was rushing Hadrian. My Guardian pointed both blades at the new Stormkind, drawing him to a halt. I watched Hadrian's back, seeing Mortis and Ferno running toward his sides. I slashed my hand through the air and pelted hail down on Mortis. I couldn't do anything about Ferno, but Hadrian must have seen him because he didn't stand in one place to be cut down.

He shoved one of the tempest-blades into Declan's chest, just above the dagger. The Stormkind halted and fell back. I didn't know if he was still alive or not. Hadrian ducked under the sweep of Ferno's swords, drawing his last blade up and blocking it. He hammered a kick into Ferno's kidneys and twisted to punch him in the face.

Mortis shouted and my eyes cut to him. The hail ricocheted away from him, spinning wildly as he pushed it back. He raced toward Declan. I lifted my hands and pushed an icy wind toward him. He glared in my direction and threw his hand upward. Thick mud splashed in my direction until a torrent of rain pounded it back into the earth.

Vitae was suddenly at my side, slinging rain into Mortis's face and holding him back. She spared a glance at me.

"Take care of the Stormkind," she ordered.

"How? The dagger gave him extra power, and both Mortis and Ferno have spare ones."

Vitae frowned, clearly unhappy about that extra information. "Hadrian's sword will kill it."

That was all she told me before she took off to meet Mortis in combat. Both leaders gave up on their powers and went straight for their swords. They met in a clash of rain and steel, moving too fast for me to comprehend.

Piper rushed to my side, her dark hair slicking the side of her face. Her eyes widened at the sight of Declan, who was beginning to sit up despite the two blades in his chest.

"Is that…"

"It *was* Declan," I told her. "It isn't him anymore." I would have to remember that if I was supposed to kill him. Willing that thought away until I needed it, I looked at my best friend. "He has more than one power now. We have to stop him."

Piper understood my meaning the moment she looked into my eyes. She didn't try to talk me out of it or offer me another option. All she did was nod, and assure me she was by my side.

I glanced at Zephys to make sure he was all right. He was standing in front of one of the cages, holding his swords on top of one another and touching the blades barring a dust-Stormkind in. In a flash of light, he, the cage, and the Stormkind vanished.

I had no idea where he was taking them, but as long as it was somewhere far away, I didn't care.

Piper grabbed my arm and dragged me toward the fight. As we raced to Declan, who was now on his feet, I glanced at the sword battles on either side of the crater.

Vitae whirled her tempest-blades with ruthless force, using one to block a strike aimed for her legs while the other hacked down for Mortis's neck. It didn't look like either had taken a strike yet, but it would happen sooner rather than later.

On my other side, Hadrian was gaining power over Ferno. He kicked him in the stomach and waited for the rushed attack. When it came, Hadrian turned on his heel and let both blades slide past him. He swung his elbow, the hard joint crashing into Ferno's face and knocking him on his ass.

"Get the dagger!" I shouted at Hadrian.

I don't know if he heard me– I hoped he did– because Declan raised his watery palms and blasted wind at us. I used the tether to draw up an icy wall that protected us from the initial blast. Piper whirled her body around the side of the wall, snapping her arm down at a sharp angle. Light exploded across the sky, a bolt of lightning slicing through the night and into the spot where Declan was standing. After the blinding flash, I swiveled around to see if he was still standing–

Declan's shivering, transparent body slammed into the ice wall, carrying the force of a cyclone. The wall instantly shattered and threw both Piper and me into the mud. I wiped it from my eyes and looked for my friend. The second I found her was the same second Declan leaped onto her.

Piper screamed as the hilts of a sword and a knife crushed her chest. She pushed against Declan, but her hands slipped across his watery skin. He snapped his head down and aimed for her mouth. I shoved my hand through the muck, coating it in ice. A sharp spike of it jumped from the ground next to Piper, sliding clean through Declan's face.

The Stormkind lurched off my best friend. Piper coughed and clutched her bruised chest, heaving and gasping as she crawled away. I jumped to my feet and rushed around the ice, standing in front of her and lifting my hands.

Declan stood up, his clear Stormkind face unmarked by the icicle. His body shifted, sparks zipping and skittering across his flesh. Thunder cracked through clouds, a sound like the breaking bones of a god. Lightning jumped down from the clouds and struck the ground in front of me. I covered my face with my arms, gripping the tether and tearing power from it to protect myself. I used the same clouds to force hail down onto Declan, hoping it would hinder him–

Mud shot up from the ground and wrapped around me. I yelped as the mucky ropes tightened around my body and dragged me toward Declan. Lightning flashed around him, keeping any hope of rescue at bay. My arms were pinned to my sides, the tips of my boots dragging through the soaked earth. I twisted and writhed, desperate to free just one of my arms, that was all I needed–

Declan reached for my head. Sparks spat from his fingertips. I wrenched my body as I entered his embrace.

One of my arms slipped free. I reached for Hadrian's sword. Static touched the edges of my hair, short shocks bouncing over my face.

I gripped the hilt of the sword and leaned forward, using my shoulder to drive the tempest-blade deeper into Declan's chest.

There was no real resistance. The blade trembled against the torrent that was Declan's Stormkind skin, but pushed straight through and out his back nonetheless. It sliced through his light-skeleton, making him stiffen and drop his arms. The shocks near my face stopped. The muddy hands slithered away from me. I staggered on my feet and looked down as he fell onto his back. His body evaporated against the dirt, pushing it away in a splattered

Rorschach. All that remained of the Declan I knew were tattered clothes and a grimy outline.

I stared, dazed at what I had done. Still wondering if it was the right choice. Knowing I deserved the hollow feeling in my chest.

A feral roar cut through the air. I pivoted and looked at Mortis. He must have seen what happened, because he stared at me like he wanted to tear my head from my shoulders.

His hand snapped outward, a huge blast of wind shooting past me like a rocket. I staggered and struggled to keep my balance, my body turning against its will. Metal screeched together, and I looked up...

To see the remaining cages had been torn open. The Stormkind Zephys hadn't managed to transport away were now freed.

Zephys stumbled away, running from the Stormkind that were snapping their heads left and right, their eerie white eyes taking us in, as though deciding who they would devour first.

Zephys shot out his hands, duals blasts of lightning striking the ground and circling around the freed Stormkind in a deadly ring. Keeping one hand raised to hold the ring in place, he backed toward us. I knew we had a little more time now, but I also doubted it would be enough.

Desperate to find out if Vitae had the advantage against Mortis, I turned around.

Vitae rushed him when she thought he was vulnerable, both of her tempest-blades aimed at his neck. For a second, I thought she had him. I truly believed Vitae was going to take Mortis down.

Then he pivoted, and rammed his tempest-blade straight through her stomach.

Vitae jerked to a halt on the blade, her own swords falling from her hands.

I think Hadrian screamed, but I couldn't know for sure, because I was screaming too.

Mortis snarled and poised his second blade at her throat. I swung my hand, commanding the wind to slam into Mortis. He flew back, the sword ripping free of Vitae's stomach.

Her hands covered the wound. She dropped to her knees, then onto her side. She didn't move again.

I was already running for her, not sure what I would do but knowing I had to help her. There was a sharp shout of pain from behind me, but I didn't stop to see what caused it, or who was injured. I gathered strength from the tether and pictured the hail connecting together until they were icicles. Jagged daggers descended on Mortis. He growled and lashed his hand through the air, a gust of wind knocking them all aside. He swept his arm in a wide arch, then slammed his upturned hand toward me.

The air was punched from my lungs as I flew back through the air. Hitting the ground was going to hurt–

Arms wrapped around me, catching me just before I struck the ground. Hadrian grunted when he landed in the mud, then gently rolled me onto my side. His eyes darted over my face, looking for injuries.

"Stay here," he said before leaping to his feet. He spun and charged at Mortis, drawing out both his tempest-blades, which I was grateful to see he'd recovered.

I glanced over my shoulder. Fenro was lying motionless on the ground, though I couldn't see any blood around him. I hoped Hadrian had gotten the dagger–

My thoughts slammed together again, and I whipped around as metal collided with metal. Mortis and Hadrian struck high and low at each other, each blow meant to kill. I sat up and raced toward Vitae.

Zephys barreled past me, dropping to his knees by his leader. He rested his hand on her shoulder and stiffened. Piper caught up to us, gasping and putting her hand over her mouth.

Zephys turned to look at us, his expression grim. "I need protection while I help her," he said. "A barrier, anything that will help focus my concentration."

Piper looked at me. I nodded to her. I was the stronger one here. I could wield my abilities better than her. I could help defeat Mortis.

"You can do this," I promised her. I put my hand on her shoulder and squeezed, then turned and ran from my friend. All I could hope was that between Hadrian and me, we could buy enough time to stop Mortis and the Stormkind.

I watched the rainwater bend on my left as I ran. I whipped my head to where the Stormkind loomed and shoved out my hand. The rain pelting me hardened into chunks of ice. I pushed again, the chunks of newly formed ice rocketing back at the Stormkind. I looked back, seeing two of the Stormkind rushing toward Piper, who'd created a rippling shield of rainwater. I could see her outline as she snapped her hands, throwing down lightning to the dust and tornado-Stormkind hurling dirt and small twisters at her defense. Beyond her, Zephys was holding his tempest-blade up to a Stormkind using pulverizing winds to keep him on his knees.

The three remaining Stormkind– thunder, ice, and hurricane– circled my back. I turned to face them, lashing at the ground and sending three rows of icy spikes toward them. The Stormkind wove around the spikes easily. I cursed, knowing the only way they would submit was to a tempest-blade.

I needed to get Hadrian to fight with me.

I dragged my hands down, pulling a curtain of heavy hail from the clouds. It pounded into the icy ground like a boulder thrown from a cliff. I forced the torrent to descend faster and harder, until it formed a thick wall between the Stormkind and us.

Piper, seeing what I was doing, sent a horizontal wave of water toward my wall of hail. I gathered a freezing wind in my hands, so cold it numbed my fingertips, and pushed it at the wave. The frigid air smacked into the wave, freezing it in place, and blocking the Stormkind.

For now.

I nodded to Piper as I stepped back, feeling my head throb and the tether tighten painfully. I spun around, finally reaching Hadrian and Mortis.

Hadrian had lost one of his swords again. His movements were slower, the attacks from Mortis coming far too close. I hoped he was feinting, but I couldn't be sure. Hadrian was a fierce, passionate fighter, and Mortis was too clever to fall for any tricks when he could simply crush his enemies.

Hadrian swung his pale tempest-blade at Mortis's throat. The Mistral leader blocked it with his sword and plowed his free fist into Hadrian's cheek. Blood sprayed from Hadrian's mouth, but he didn't stop fighting. He kicked Mortis's knee to make him buckle, then spun his sword to drive it down into Mortis's neck.

Mortis knocked Hadrian's sword back, striking his wrist. He must have also struck a nerve because Hadrian dropped his last tempest-blade. Mortis lunged with his sword. Hadrian let it glide past him, locking Mortis's sword-arm to his side. He smashed his elbow into Mortis's face, then snapped his knee into the other Guardian's chin. He dragged Mortis's blade out of his grip as he collapsed, standing over the older man with heaving shoulders.

Mortis lay on his back, and began to laugh.

"You fight like your father," he remarked cruelly.

Hadrian's fist clenched around the sword. "Do not speak of him. You have not earned that honor."

"Honor. Yes. That is what matters to you. I nearly forgot. Such a shame that honor will not save you."

Mortis moved too fast. I hadn't noticed his far hand dragging toward his belt until it was too late.

He pushed himself forward and kicked out Hadrian's legs. My Guardian slipped and landed on his back, the sword jarred from his grip when his elbow smacked into the cold, grimy ground. Mortis scrambled to his feet and jumped on top of Hadrian, arching his arm back and driving it down toward his throat.

I screamed and pushed out my hands. I didn't think about using the tether or the hurt I would cause myself. I grabbed the air around me, and pushed it at Mortis with all my strength. The wild gust of wind collided with Mortis at the same moment his blade descended. Fear wrapped a noose around my heart. I didn't know if I'd been fast enough.

I hadn't been, but instead of punching straight into him, the tip of the dagger sliced through Hadrian's armor, catching the edge of his collarbone and cutting a bloody path down his chest to the top of his ribs. I didn't know the wound was deep until Hadrian cried out in pain. The sound ripped at my heart, freezing me into the mud.

Mortis rolled to his feet, dagger in hand and eyes locked on me. His hatred was a visible, terrifying thing. But I wasn't afraid. He'd given me these powers, and assumed I would be under his control. That I wouldn't dream of fighting back.

He was wrong.

"Give up, Mortis," I called. "Your plan isn't going to work." *And I don't have time to argue with you. The Stormkind are going to get through my wall of hail soon.*

Hadrian lurched to his feet, wincing and clutching his bleeding chest. It took all of my control not to run over to him and try to help.

Mortis glanced past me, the dagger tight in his grip. Then he looked at me again. "Yes. It seems my original plan has failed."

Hadrian gathered his sword from the ground and stood beside me. It was agonizing not to look over my shoulder and see how close the Stormkind had gotten.

Mortis straightened his back and held my eyes with an eerie sense of calm. "It seems I will be forced to take a more drastic course of action."

With no hesitation, he flipped the dagger in his grip, pointed it at his chest, and stabbed himself through the heart. It all happened to fast for me to stop. Mortis dropped to his knees and bellowed in agony.

Hadrian took a step to run for him when the hairs on the back of my neck stood up. I spun around and saw the Stormkind staggering through the wall of hail and ice. The thunder-Stormkind held its hands open to the sky, calling down shafts of lightning that smashed against the drenched soil. A streak of lightning snaked over the earth and aimed toward us. Hadrian and I stepped back from one another. The bolt leaped from the ground and flared to life between us. I could feel the searing heat and the piercing shocks that stung my skin. I screamed and stumbled away, not sure if I'd been struck by the bolt or not. I couldn't see Hadrian, not even when the light died.

I swayed drunkenly, blinking against the sudden darkness. A gleam of skeletal light and a cyclone of snow rushed toward me. The tornado-Stormkind, with its swirling grey skin, sent a twister directly at me. Hadrian skidded in front of me, swinging his hand up. The ground beneath us froze over just before a tower of ice jutted upward and captured the tornado. It didn't stop the Stormkind, but Hadrian was shifting his attention.

He twisted at the waist, punching his fist forward. A ball of ice shot from his fist, slamming into the ice-Stormkind charging our right. The Stormkind held up its clear, icy hand. It punched the sphere of ice, shattering it in one strike. It swiveled its wrist, capturing the shards of ice as they fell. Then it launched them back at us.

This time I stepped forward, sweeping my arm and sending a powerful wind to brush the shards away. As I turned, a bolt of lightning shot past me like a burning arrow. A piece of it grazed my arm, pain bursting in a white-hot explosion over my bicep. I screamed and backed into Hadrian. His hand found mine and he squeezed tightly. I felt him shift, and looked up to see the rain freezing around him. I glanced back and watched him sweep the tempest-blade around him like a lasso. The pieces of hail followed him.

In one wide, twisting move, Hadrian whipped the shards of hail at the Stormkind. As each piece shot through the air, they connected to other shards of hail until spears as long as my arms formed. The spears struck the ground in front of the Stormkind and exploded into clusters of deadly spikes that pierced the beings through their arms and legs. I didn't know if that would be enough to stop them, but I took a second to breathe.

Hadrian looked at me. His free hand cupped my face, his eyes riveting me to the ground.

"What happened?"

I glanced at my seared arm. The burn was blistering red and pulsed in sharp stings, but it would heal. Hadrian frowned when he looked at the wound, his concerned blue eyes rising to mine. He was about to speak when something captured his attention behind me. Hadrian's eyes widened just before a violent swirl of wind snapped around me and ripped me from his grasp.

I screamed as I flew through the air. Clumps of dirt and dust snared my wrists and ankles, then yanked me back onto the earth. I screamed again when I struck it, pain exploding up my back and through my head. One more smash like that, and I would break at least one of my bones. If I were lucky.

Groaning against the pain swelling in my head, I cracked my eyes open and stared at the swaying image of Mortis looming over me. Unlike Declan, he had kept most of his human form. Only his eyes were different. Gone were the creepy black irises, replaced by unfiltered, shocking white.

Mortis smirked. "This appears to have been a success," he remarked. His voice still retained its familiar depth, but there was a strange echo to it now. A haunting, hollow noise that sent shivers through the pain in my body.

"*Mortis!*" screamed Hadrian. I lolled my head to look at him, watched him run as fast as he could, forgetting about the Stormkind sliding off the icy spikes that had punctured their bodies. Saw that while he'd called Mortis's name, his eyes were only for me.

The Mistral-turned Stormkind, or whatever he was now, shifted the angle of his head. He turned his hand upward, his fingers becoming vicious claws. Thin whips of lightning shuddered down from the black clouds, and struck the cold ground around Hadrian. Caging him in a circle of blinding light.

I rolled onto my side, aching from the pain cutting through my back, my heart breaking with every desperate pulse.

Following the turn of Mortis's wrist, the lightning split off again, flipping up and coiling around Hadrian's limbs. They tightened and pushed him onto the ground. His screams of pain ripped the rest of my heart to pieces.

Knowing I had to save him, that I had to save *all* of us, I crawled across the ground to Mortis's feet and pulled cool strength from the tether. My hands frosted over, a dagger of ice filling my palm. I gripped it tightly and stabbed it into Mortis's ankle. He barked in pain and lost his hold on the lightning. I stabbed again, aiming higher on his leg. The ice-dagger punched through the skin at the bottom of his knee–

Mortis's heavy boot slammed into my shoulder. Searing pain burst across my chest and upper arm. I had no idea if it was because he'd kicked my burned arm, or because my shoulder was now dislocated, but it felt like my entire left arm was now useless.

Good thing I was right-handed.

Mortis roared and reached for my neck. I shoved my right hand up and threw a gust of wind at him like a punch. It struck his chest and knocked him away from me.

I rolled onto my side, my eyes finding Hadrian across from me. The lightning had disappeared from his body, but I could see the agony etched into his face. Behind him, I saw the Stormkind rush for him.

The choice was in front of me. Help Hadrian and let Mortis destroy us while we fought together, or put every ounce of strength into stopping Mortis alone.

To use these so-called gifts, and find out exactly what I was capable of. No matter what the cost would be.

Faces flashed like lightning through my mind. Mom and Dad's loving smiles. James's big, excited eyes. Piper's laugh. Zephys's smirk and Vitae's sad eyes.

Hadrian's slow smile and polite nod. The glimmer in his sapphire eyes when he looked at me.

It wasn't much of a choice at all.

Hadrian, get up. Keep the Stormkind away from me.

He moved slowly– too slowly– pushing onto his hands and knees. I cringed at the sight of his charred wrists and bruised face.

What are you doing, Ava?

My heart twisted. He would never agree to my plan if he knew the whole truth about it.

Buying time so we don't have to take on so many enemies. I hesitated, then added, *Let me protect you for once.*

That should have been his first sign something was wrong. Maybe deep down, he knew there was. But he couldn't do anything about it, because the Stormkind were closing in and surrounding him. Hadrian gathered his strength, fought his pain, and came up swinging.

It was time for me to do the same thing.

I slapped my hands against the sleety, slimy ground and grabbed the energy in the air in front of me. I pushed down, letting power ripple underneath me. The ground bucked under my feet, throwing up a wave of mud high enough to knock anyone off balance. Rolling to my feet, I watched Mortis push himself from the muck. His white eyes burned like the deepest fires of Hell, bright promises of a slow, torturous death.

I refused to endure the first two parts. I didn't let myself think about the third.

Sweeping and twisting my hands in the air, I felt a surge of power rising in my chest. I gathered a tornado of thick mire and pushed it at Mortis. Frost covered his palms as a huge rush of freezing, snowy air curled out of the oily clouds. The snow from the blizzard surrounded the tornado, dropping the temperature and causing it to slow. The flakes of snow became shards of ice, and soon my muddy twister was a crystal block of dirt.

Light snapped through the sky, my only warning that Mortis was calling down lightning. I jumped to the side as my thin, muddy twister exploded into chunky clumps of dirt. The bolt of lightning ripped through the space where it had been, a spear striking the ground I'd been standing on. I grabbed the rain pouring from the clouds and combined it with the water soaking the earth. It became a monstrous wave cresting and splitting behind me. It poured across the space between us, crashing into Mortis. The water smothered him, completely taking him from my view.

Now that I had trapped him, I started to feel the throb in my head. I was soaked to the skin, but a thicker liquid was sliding over my upper lip. It tasted sharp, hot, and metallic.

I knew what it meant for me, but I couldn't stop. Not yet. Not until I knew we were safe from Mortis.

My stomach turned at the thought of drowning a man, no matter how much misery he'd put me and my loved ones through. I started to draw back. Could I live with myself after I did this? Would I see blood on my hands, even though his wouldn't be spilled?

The wave lifted, and not because I commanded it to. It was pushed up by another force, one stronger than mine.

In a single massive push, the wave leaped through the air and descended back onto me. I grabbed the water at my feet and dragged it over me, freezing the liquid until I was shielded. The cocoon was barely formed in time when the wave smashed into me. I screamed at the thunderous crash and continual roar of the water battering my safety. The murky ice groaned and cracked, half of it snapping under the pressure.

Water spewed into the broken ice structure, and I scrambled to fix it. My hands were shaking and blood coated my tongue. My brain swelled against my skull and pressed into my eyes.

An explosion of light dashed through the water, striking the ruins of my ice shield. Shards of ice shattered around me, the water punching at me.

Water that was electrified.

The charged water stabbed into my skin, lighting every nerve as it scorched me. Fire streamed through my blood like it was made of gasoline. It swelled in my lungs and seeped into my heart valves, punching my heart until I couldn't breathe. My brain felt squeezed, as if trying to retreat into itself.

I'd never wished for death until that moment. I wanted the blackness to consume me again, just to take me away from the agony. I couldn't bear it.

I don't know how much time passed until it was over. The searing hooks of pain that had dug into me had been torn out, leaving a pounding stab in their wake. The ice-shield and electric wave had split around me, soaking deep into the earth. I collapsed with them.

I could hear Hadrian in the distance, but his voice was too far away for me to make out what he was saying. Or maybe he wasn't too far, and I just couldn't bear to hear the pain in his voice.

Mortis loomed above me, melting out of the shadows and blocking the moon behind him. The only light I could see came from his lifeless, bleached eyes.

"So much potential," he told me with a slow shake of his head. "So much wasted."

Mortis bent at the waist, stopping when his face was inches away from mine.

"Let me show you what you what you were meant to become."

Mortis stood up and held out his hands. Then the world exploded.

Dirt launched into the air. Rainwater poured in buckets and pooled onto the ground. Lightning skidded across the sky. Ice hardened along the edges of the crater and crept up the sides. Felled trees lifted and spun around twisters dropping from the sky. Hurricane winds swelled and pushed more trees further inland.

I could feel every speck of energy fuelling the storms, the unfathomable power of it all. The destruction so immense and widespread that it demanded respect and attention.

The power to end hundreds, if not thousands of lives.

Power *I* was supposed to have.

I shut my eyes. At least I didn't have to scramble for a plan. The answer was in front of me. I just had to face it, and hope it would be over quickly.

I closed every distraction out. I didn't think about Zephys and if he contained the other Stormkind. I locked away Piper as she guarded Vitae. I hid Hadrian behind my heart though the winds carried his voice. I kept my family in the back of my mind, where I wouldn't miss them so badly.

I took a deep breath, felt the very earth shiver with energy and let it consume me from head to toe. It all became part of me– the ice under my skin, the mud squishing between my fingers, wind sweeping my hair over my face, the rain dancing on my skin...

I remembered the one day I left the restaurant and walked in the rain, how calm it had made me. How I was able to take a step back from the broken world and smile at the simplicity of it all.

Then I opened my eyes, and took it all for myself.

The hurricane winds rolling toward innocent lives suddenly lurched and tumbled backward, returning to me. Tornadoes spun too fast, obliterating and losing shape until they disappeared. Flying clumps of mud splattered onto the ground. Ice cracked and melted, slipping down the walls of the crater. The rain no longer slammed into the earth, light and tapping.

I imagined it all. The winds pulling back, the tornadoes being wiped away, the mud pushed down, the ice losing its chill, the rain exhausting and relaxing. The smell of copper filled my nose and my head throbbed violently, but I didn't let go. Not even when my sight grew fuzzy.

Above me, Mortis whirled in a circle, confusion mixing with rage as his ambition retreated. He pushed back, loosing all his energy to force the storms back inland. I was calmer than him, more embracing. My body was too weak to move, so I couldn't seek his life force for energy. My stomach cramped at the thought of it, but I didn't dare release myself from my trance. I had to make sure the storms faded, that the danger passed.

Blood streamed from Mortis's nose. Veins bulged in his neck and temple. A sharp, shuddering breath escaped his lips. His body relaxed involuntarily. He panted and gasped, dropping his bloodshot eyes to me. Rage crept back into his face, a snarl splitting open his lips.

"You... What do you think you are doing?"

I heard him, yet I didn't allow his words to register. I kept my breathing slow and even, imagined smoothing out the winds, felt the cool water from the melted ice drift under my body, let the rain whisper against my cheeks. It was almost over. The pain in my head was becoming a vicious distraction, but I knew I wouldn't have to worry about that for much longer, either. It was almost over.

"What are you doing!"

I didn't move when he lunged down, reaching for my neck. Hardly flinched when a silver tempest-blade pierced the air between us, lodging deep in Mortis's belly. Drops of blood splattered against my stomach, but they would be washed away in the rain and rising water beneath me. Mortis looked at the blade stupidly, like he couldn't figure out how it got there.

"She is doing what you were too cowardly to do."

My lips twitched, in what I hope was a smile. It would be nice to hear Hadrian's voice one more time. Even though the circumstances were disturbing, since he was literally killing someone over top of me.

Hadrian pulled back the sword. Mortis staggered out of my line of sight. The storms stopped. Even the rain was gone now. I was cold, drenched, and dirty. Not the best way to go. But when Hadrian dropped down beside me and lifted me into his arms, I figured the circumstances had improved.

I released a shaking breath, the last bursts of energy drifting from me. I was numb everywhere. I could see Hadrian touching me, his hands skimming the surface of my face, but I couldn't feel him. My senses were failing me. His face, tormented and broken, was burning into my memory. I didn't mind that he would be my last thought. I just wish he didn't look so heartbroken.

"Ava!" he shouted, shaking me gently. "Ava, stay awake."

"Can't," I mumbled. "Did it to myself."

He shivered, drawing me closer to his face. "Ava, please, stay awake."

I was too close to his lips. I could feel the warm of his breath, the temptation of his life. I turned my head and edged away.

"Don't," I whispered. "Don't let me hurt you."

Hadrian watched my expression uncertainly. Then it hit him.

"My life force," he breathed. "You can feel it?"

I nodded. My eyelids began to droop, the world became hazy and dark around the edges.

"Can't hurt you," I muttered. "Can't... Can't..."

I could hardly see, though I felt his arms heft me higher. I was too weak to speak, to tell him it was too late for me to be saved. To tell him it wasn't his fault.

To tell him I loved him.

"You won't hurt me." Hadrian's voice was agonizingly close. I smelled seawater and musk, the most comforting smell I'd ever known. "I know you won't."

Soft, firm lips pressed against mine. Hadrian was kissing me, knowing what I was, what I was capable of doing. What I had *tried* to do to him before. I wanted to resist, to tell him to stop before I killed him...

But then I felt the heat. The luscious warmth spilling from him to me. It slid down my throat like melted chocolate, sweet and welcome and satisfying. I drank it in, letting it pool in my belly and spread to up to my chest. It brushed along the tether, sending a delightful shiver through my body. Sensations returned to my limbs, the tips of my fingers tingling as they returned to life. The pain in my head dulled.

I reached up and traced my fingers through his thick, rain-soaked hair. I cupped the back of his neck and pressed my lips harder to his, taking another breath and gathering more strength. Each drop was overwhelming, and yet it wasn't enough.

The tether vibrated against my heart like a plucked guitar string. I ignored it once, twice...

Not the third time.

My hand slipped from the back of his neck, my body sliding back into the water. A shudder went through the arms holding me. I closed my eyes and felt the world tilt once before my sight went dim.

Chapter 19

There were three things I was sick of: being wet, being dirty, and blacking out. I vowed to never do any of those again for a long time.

So far, the only goal I accomplished was waking up moments after I passed out. I blinked my eyes open and stared at the night sky over my head, watching the clouds drift apart to reveal the full moon once more. It bathed me in a spread of pale blue, as though it were a beacon of peace.

Voices shouted my name... and Hadrian's name.

The minute before my latest unconscious episode shot through my mind. The certainty in his voice when he said I wouldn't hurt him, the moment before he kissed me and pushed his lips against mine.

The taste of his life force sinking into me.

Hadrian.

I sat up too quickly, vertigo snapping through my head like an elastic band. I swayed and slapped my hand against the mud, feeling it squish between my fingers. I breathed through the swirling in my skull, then dragged my eyes across the muck to find Hadrian.

He was lying right beside me, his eyes closed as if he were asleep. Except he was too pale to be asleep, and he wasn't moving.

My heart sliced open. I crawled toward him, picking him up and holding him the way he'd held me.

Tears burned my eyes as I shook him. "Hadrian! Hadrian, wake up!"

"Ava!"

I glanced away, looking for Piper as she called my name. She was across the crater and walking closer. Zephys was with her, and they were both supporting Vitae as she shuffled toward us. I glanced at her stomach, seeing a patch of ice acting as a bandage to the stab wound in her stomach. I cringed at the sight of it, and the paleness of Vitae's face.

"I assure you I will survive," panted Vitae. "The wound will heal beneath the ice. As Hadrian said, our wounds heal quickly."

A sob lodged in my throat. I clutched Hadrian tighter. "What about life force? You can't heal that."

Vitae and Zephys hesitated, glancing down to where Hadrian lay. Vitae slumped, but Zephys managed a small smile. "I'm sure he will endure," he said. "Perhaps you need to initiate some more incentive."

I gawked at him. "You want me to kiss–" I caught myself, "er, breathe into him again? I was the one who stole his life force in the first place."

"You did not steal it," a familiar voice rumbled. "I offered it."

I glanced down at Hadrian. His eyes were sleepy and a little delirious, but they were open. Alive.

It should have relieved me, but I was still scared I would hurt him somehow. Hadrian didn't seem concerned, smiling that gorgeous half-smile at me. "And I would prefer a kiss."

So would I, my mind betrayed. Hadrian's smile widened. His hand reached up and cupped my face. I stiffened and clutched his wrist. The steady beat of his pulse reassured me, but I was scared I would do something to make it disappear.

"I… Are you okay?"

He nodded. "A little weaker than usual, but in no pain."

I swallowed the lump building in my throat. "How did you know I wouldn't hurt you?"

Hadrian pushed himself out of my lap gracefully. His hand never left my face, and I swore his eyes were bluer in the pale moonlight above me.

"You exercised the most amazing control I have ever seen, Ava. You brought the storms back and did not attack us when the power overwhelmed you. You were calm, at peace. I knew you would not bring harm to anyone. I knew I could help you." His thumb skimmed along my cheekbone, sending a warm shiver through me.

"You are not the kind of person to want to cause others harm. You are too strong for that." He pulled me closer. "Too perfect."

It felt like Hadrian and me were the only people in the crater, and I wanted it to stay that way. But I couldn't forget what had happened here, and that the others were watching us anxiously.

I dipped my chin and let his forehead bump against mine. Hadrian stayed there for a moment, then leaned away and let go of my neck. He slipped his hand into mine and helped me to my feet. I glanced past Vitae, Zephys, and Piper to take in the battleground.

Murky rainwater filled the massive crater, ankle-deep mud lining its grimy surface. Hundreds of discarded tempest-blades glimmered under the water. Declan's clothes drifted through the mire. Ferno, Turve, and Mortis's bodies floated on top of the muck. My stomach tightened at the sight of the corpses. It was clear they were dead, so I quickly averted my gaze. My eyes found Hadrian.

My Guardian's eyes were fixed on Mortis's body. I don't know what I expected to see on his face; maybe relief or peace or something darker. Instead, all I saw was grim acceptance, as if he was feeling indifferent or empty toward the man who had his father from him.

Taking my eyes away from Hadrian before I stared too long, I looked at Zephys. "What happened to the Stormkind?"

The Guardian's hazel-blue eyes rose to meet mine. His shoulders slumped. "Most of them escaped in a weakened state. They will recover their strength to hunt again, and we must stop them before they regain power." He glanced at the tempest-blades shining under the water. "It seems we will need to make plenty of return trips to gather their cages."

"You do enjoy boasting about your strength, Zephys," teased Hadrian.

His friend shot him a pointed look. "I was considering electing you to carry them all, seeing as you have a disturbing fondness for swords and all other weapons."

Hadrian just smiled. I was thinking about the first half of their conversation.

"You're leaving?"

I hated how small my voice sounded, and how the Guardians looked at me with pity. Vitae unwound herself from Zephys and Piper and took careful steps toward me. I wanted to tell her not to, to conserve her strength, but she wasn't weak. She carried herself with pride and confidence.

"Once the Stormkind are contained, there will be no need for us to remain here. The human race must endure on its own, as it has for thousands of years. We are to carry on as we always have, ensuring the safety and well-being of the Stormkind until they free themselves again."

"So nothing's changed," Piper said bitterly. "The Stormkind are going to keep coming."

Vitae looked at her. "Yes, but you are wrong about change, Piper. Many circumstances have been altered. The number of Stormkind has decreased, the Mistrals are no longer a threat, and we must be able to care for their new generation." Vitae's gaze returned to me. "The girl from the highway, the one who directed us here– Corrina– has agreed to return home with us. She chose to be trained, to learn the secrets of being a Stormkind. Perhaps she simply wants to find herself. Regardless, we will monitor her."

"What about us?" I asked warily, feeling the weight of Hadrian's eyes on me.

Vitae closed her emotions. I couldn't read what she was thinking or feeling, but it didn't seem like a good sign.

"The choice is yours, Ava, as well as yours, Piper. Our home is in a veil of the world, invisible to human eyes but connected to earth all the same. We will welcome you to our care should you decide to return with us. Or, you can remain here with your human families."

Vitae paused a beat to look at both of us, though her eyes lingered on me when she continued.

"You are not a threat to the world or your loved ones. We have seen your restraint, your control, your strength. If I had any doubt regarding you or what you were capable of, it has long since disappeared."

I hesitated to ask my next question, especially with Hadrian's weighted blue eyes on me, but I had to know.

"If we choose to stay... We won't see you again, will we?"

Sorrow filled Vitae's pale blue eyes. "No. Returning with us is a commitment. Time passes differently for us in our realm. What is an hour for us is a month for you. Zephys and Hadrian may watch you from the distance, but they must remember their duties as Guardians before anything else."

She looked at Hadrian when she said this. My heart sank to the mud beneath me, which was now thick enough to swallow me whole. I was ready to let it.

I knew what Hadrian would choose. He might have cared about me, but he'd been a Guardian well before I was even a smidgen of thought. I couldn't expect a happy future with him. Only a handful of people would know the truth of the Stormkind, the Precips, and the Mistrals. By the time the next Centennial came around, most of us would be dead. Sure, we could write records of what happened, but I didn't want to put danger or pressure on the Guardians when they returned. Watching over humanoid storms was difficult enough. Being chased by shameless paparazzi and hounded by nosy reporters would seriously hinder their jobs. It was better if the truth stayed between a handful of people.

To know Hadrian would be watching me from a distance didn't alleviate the pressure growing in my chest. He would be looking out for me, doing his job, but I would never see him. He was a good soldier, and I was one of the least subtle people I knew. I wasn't going to do anything to get him in any kind of trouble, not when he was so recognizable.

So I had to say goodbye. Let him go.

No matter how much it hurt me.

"I'm staying here," I whispered quietly. I dropped my eyes and pushed mud around with the tip of my shoe. "I need to know if my family is okay. I need to find them and... explain things."

Even if they're afraid of me now. My father's words before the Mistrals released them echoed around my skull.

We love you, Ava. We love you so much.

It was the right choice. After all of this, skipping in and out of their lives with no explanation, it was wrong to make them think I was dead. They were like me. They wouldn't give up hope. They would be looking for me at every SPU station, scanning the Missing Boards for a photo of me smiling, listening to any word of my location. If I went with the Guardians, I would never see them again, and that wasn't a choice I could live with.

Piper shuffled to stand by my side. She put her arm around my shoulder and tugged me closer. Probably for her comfort as much as mine.

"I'm staying, too." She looked at Zephys sadly. "I'm sorry, but I can't leave my parents."

Zephys hid his disappointment with a smile. "Perhaps it is just as well. I am sure we would be at each other's throats before the end of day one."

Piper laughed, probably for Zephys's sake rather than her own.

We all stepped forward and hugged goodbye. True, we hadn't known each other for very long, but I felt closer to these strangers than I had to most of my friends in college. Nothing brought people together quite like devastation did.

When Zephys pulled back from me, he turned his eyes to the right for a moment. Then he looked at Vitae. "I shall begin recovering the tempest-blades. Piper, would you mind watching over Vitae?"

My best friend squeezed my arm. There was only one more person I had to say goodbye to.

Wonder if there's a way to delay this.

Perhaps it is best not to.

Damn mind reading.

With the others gone to give us space, I turned to face Hadrian. He'd moved closer to me during the goodbyes, and I didn't find the lack of distance bothersome. In fact, I was wondering if I could convince him to come closer.

"So," I mumbled.

When I didn't add anything, he repeated, "So."

"Are you upset that I'm not going with you?"

"No," Hadrian replied quietly. I couldn't find that spark I'd seen in his eyes when his internal walls collapsed. "I know how much your family means to you. The moment Vitae offered the choice, I knew what your answer would be. I would never have pushed you for another one."

I looked up. "You didn't want me to come with you?"

Hadrian's somber eyes and tragic smile tugged at my heartstrings. "What I want is irrelevant in this situation, Ava. My care has always been for your contentment and safety."

I should have left it at that. I shouldn't have pushed deeper, searching for the truth about what I meant to him. But this would be the last time I saw him. I had to know.

"Why?"

Hadrian's smile fell.

"Why did you care about keeping me safe? I keep thinking about what you said to me on the road, but what was I to you, really? Another charge, a friend, or…"

I trailed off. I hadn't been accusing him of anything, keeping my tone level and calm. But when the silence grew in the seconds that passed, a hole grew in the pit of my stomach. I let my heart shine through my eyes, let him see I'd fallen for him. Showed him he was more than my protector and ally. He was more than just a friend. He was the person I'd fallen in love with.

And now he was leaving.

"Never mind," I said, fighting tears and squeezing out a smile. "Stupid questions." I held out my hand. "Thank you for everything, Hadrian. I owe you my life, and… I'm going to miss you."

My voice nearly cracked on those last words, but I held it together. I didn't want him to see me cry. I dropped my head and clutched his hand. Let my palm linger there long enough to memorize the texture of his calluses, the heat of his skin. Remembered how softly those fingers had brushed through my hair, and how I would have given almost anything to feel them again, when I didn't need to be saved.

I shook his hand stupidly, thinking it would be better to let him see this like the end of a business arrangement or something.

"Take care of yourself, Hadrian."

I loosened my fingers, but Hadrian didn't let go. When I looked up, he had a stunned expression on his face, like an epiphany had occurred to him.

Uh oh.

Hadrian's voice was almost too quiet for me to hear, but he might as well have shouted the words.

"Are you in love with me?"

I'll never claim to be the fastest thinker on my feet. I could have done all kinds of things to make him think otherwise. I could have let go of his hand, looked confused, shaken my head, told him no. All of those possibilities, and I chose to stand there and stare at him like he was a light about to be snuffed out of my life.

Understanding hit his face, and I knew I'd screwed up.

I pulled my hand out of his and shoved it through my hair. A terrible idea, because I could still feel the warmth of his skin on mine. Images of him touching my face with perfect tenderness as I recovered in the infirmary slammed though my head, the memory of each gentle caress sending a splinter into my heart. The way he'd clung to me on the road, when he broke in a way that only I could see.

Hadrian's hand hovered in the air like he didn't know what to do with it. I might have laughed at his expression if I didn't think I would burst into tears.

"I should get going," I mumbled, wiping my hands on my jeans in an effort to clean them. All I was doing was smearing the mud to new places.

"I will take you home," Hadrian said quietly.

"It's okay," I rushed out. "I think I can figure out my way back."

But my Guardian was already in front of me, looping his arms around my back.

"I would prefer that you did not attempt to cross a wasteland in the middle of the night with no orientation and a variety of starved animals hungering for your flesh."

I couldn't help but fall into his chest when he closed his arms around me. "You make it sound like there are zombies out there instead of wolves and cougars."

He chuckled. I pressed my cheek to his chest and let the warmth of him wrap around me. He only let go to take the swords from his back.

Pale light burned behind me. I pressed into Hadrian's chest like I would melt into it. I closed my eyes as he leaned forward.

Falling through storm-sight wasn't comfortable, but it didn't last long. I thought it was a little creepy that Hadrian knew where I used to live, but I guess he had to know where his charges stayed when he was watching them from afar to make sure they didn't have a mental collapse that caused them to destroy entire cities.

In seconds, it was over. Hadrian's arms uncurled from me and I was able to back away. I missed his warmth as soon as it was gone, though turning around and seeing the remnants of my house took Hadrian from my mind.

The debris was cleared off, presumably taken and dumped in one of the man-made landfills. The lawn was clear of furniture. New frames were erected to give the house a set of bones with fuzzy pink insulation between them. Corrugated metal lay flat on the top to act as a makeshift roof. Ahead of me was a missing piece of insulation with a small yellow light glowing behind it.

A new house with a wide open door leading to my family. I almost cried at the sight of it.

And it wasn't just our house that was being rebuilt. Next door and across the street, dozens of newly framed homes stood in various states of repair. Almost every one had a glowing yellow light inside it. Dozens of beacons of hope.

This was when I knew we would endure. No matter what the Stormkind threw at us, no matter what trials and obstacles, we would find a way to survive. We would learn from our mistakes, adapt from them, prepare for our children's children. We were too strong to accept anything else.

"They will be so happy to see you again," Hadrian said.

I turned and met his eyes. He was smiling that slow, mysterious smile that never failed to make my heart melt.

"I know," I agreed. "I wish you could meet them. My brother would love you."

Hadrian grinned, then swept a hand down the bloody, grimy, tattered and dented armor covering his body. "Perhaps when I am more presentable."

He was doing everything I wanted him to. Everything that made my heart sing and adore him. It hurt too much to bear.

"Please don't say those kinds of things."

His grin faded. "Ava–"

"I made a mistake. I don't know what I did to make you think that I..." I lowered my eyes. "I guess I hoped..."

"Hoped for what?" he asked when I didn't answer.

My eyes burned. I couldn't stop them from filling.

"That I wouldn't just be a person you had to protect."

I was going to break. I knew it. I had to get away from him before he saw it, or lied to make me feel better.

Hauling my head straight, I looked at Hadrian for one last time. It was hard to see him through the watery fog of my vision. I smiled as best as I could.

"Thank you again, Hadrian. Goodbye."

I spun on my heel and all but ran into the house. Maybe I should have knocked, but I needed something I could trust. Something I understood, that would never hurt me.

Dad was the first to see me. He always was. He jumped to his feet, staring at me like I was a ghost.

That kind of made sense, since I had literally appeared out of nowhere.

James and my mother rose to their feet, their familiar faces basked in the welcoming yellow light of some kerosene lanterns. I took a breath to greet them, but I couldn't even get a weak "Hi" out past my lips. I swallowed my hello and ran straight for them.

I crashed into my parents, a mess of tears and joy. They wrapped their arms around me, the same way they'd done when I returned from my lost week, the same way they had when I rescued them from the school.

But this time was different. This time, they knew I would stay. They knew I'd come home, and would never leave them again.

It was our unspoken, answered prayer.

It was over. Finally, we could rebuild.

EPILOGUE

One year later...

"Order up, Ava!"

I loved my job. I really did. But if I heard that command one more time, I was pretty sure I would scream.

Now that Papaya Cantina was completely refurbished and open, it was a madhouse. Since Mikey had been so popular with the construction crews (and had possibly bribed them with the possibility of future discounts), we had one of the first fully renovated restaurants in all of West Palm. I had to admit, the place looked fantastic. Sky blue wallpaper soaked in the sunlight when the curtains were drawn back and the windows were opened, bright circular light bulbs threaded over the roof and hooked into the generator in the kitchen, smooth beige tile beneath seashell white tables and chairs, and new dishware imported from Mexico. The North and South Americas really came together after the Centennial, knowing we had to help each other if our continent was going to recover. I was happy to hear how the coalition was still going strong over a year later.

As much as I liked working and keeping busy—trade was still the prominent form of payment, but banks were starting to recover financial data as well as structures—it was still strange to believe Papaya Cantina was the epicenter of hope in the remains of West Palm. In a way, it made sense. Normalcy was becoming commonplace again, with homes and apartments being rebuilt now that the last of the ruins had been carried away. The ration stations, medi-centers, and SPU stations were still standing and remained busy, but the need for them had lessened now that farmers were producing crops and trade could be made with other countries.

Electricity was spotty at the best of times and the Internet was still an uncatchable ghost (the people who'd been trapped underground until eleven months ago had a meltdown when they couldn't access their Twitter accounts), but things were getting back on track.

It helped that the storms had stopped seven months ago.

For a little while, strange, scattered storms ranged over the country. Rumors of tornadoes in Nevada, dust storms in California, blizzards in New York, thunderstorms in Texas, and a few abrupt hurricanes in the Florida Keys kept us all on our toes. But the storms didn't last for long. Nobody questioned why. Nobody knew but me, Piper, and my family. Maybe it hadn't been a good idea to tell them the truth about what had happened to me, but since Mortis used them as a bargaining chip against me, how could I lie?

Truthfully, it was good to get the truth off my chest. I couldn't keep it locked inside where it could destroy me. Not if I wanted to face the trauma and nightmares about what had happened to me. It became easier to be around people again. For the first while, it was hard. I didn't want to have a panic attack and lose control. My gifts were dormant. I hadn't had the urge to use them since that night in the crater, but I knew they were still there.

That's why I worked with Piper. She volunteered as a yoga instructor, and I helped teach her classes when I wasn't working as a waitress. I think the reason we had so many people attend our classes was because yoga was almost better than therapy. We could open our eyes, see the devastation around us, accept it, and breathe. What had happened, happened. There was nothing we could do about it. This was a time to heal, to help, and to move on.

Okay, so I stole Piper's words from the speech she gives at the beginning of every class, but she was more eloquent than I was.

But her words were important, and some days, I needed them more than I cared to admit.

As I wove through the packed tables to set down plates, refill water glasses, and take new orders, snippets of conversation cut into my thoughts.

"I'm telling you, I saw one! A Stormkind controlled the lightning!"

"Of course it was a Stormkind. How the hell do you think we got snow in *Florida*?"

"Honest, the guy was some kind of medieval soldier. Fancy armor, two swords, everything. He took on the Stormkind like it was nothing!"

I cringed a little at the last statement, pretending it meant nothing to me, and that I wasn't wondering which Guardian he was referring to.

Since only Piper and I knew the truth about the Stormkind and where they came from (we agreed not to mention this to our parents, since trusting them with the truth about the Guardians was risky enough), conspiracy theories became widespread. You name it, someone had an "answer" for it. Everything from aliens to angry spirits, witches, angels, demons, the Horsemen in the Apocalypse, fairies, and a screwed up government science experiment to control global warming were the most popular explanations for the Stormkind. Some of them made me laugh, others made me roll my eyes, and some of them made me want to scream. I could only imagine what the textbooks would say when history was written about the Stormkind to prepare our great grandchildren.

But I kept my mouth shut, did my yoga practices, worked at my job, helped my neighborhood rebuild, and thought about what I would do when the beach was open to swimmers again.

Despite the promising outlook to the future, there were still problems we needed to overcome, not just supply shortages and grief. The gangs still posed major threats to the vulnerable and the desperate. Lootings, robberies, and small riots were prominent at night, forcing the newly elected Governor of Florida to enact a statewide curfew that forbade anyone from being on the streets after dark. Those who were caught by police and riot patrols were arrested and thrown into one of the cleaned up prisons, no questions asked. It was harsh, but it was necessary. Murdering liars could wear a disarming and cheerful smile right until they stabbed you in the belly and stole everything but the clothes on your back.

And sometimes even those.

Tension was thick whenever a new law was passed, but I knew we would get back on track. Knowing the entire world had been on the precipice of total destruction, having *felt* the intensity of it as it spread, I knew we'd all get past whatever drama unfolded around us. Even if no one else knew it yet.

Moving on was part of human nature, the same as breathing. It took a while to do, but once we wrapped our heads around it, the concept was easier to accept.

Shame there was one thing my mind refused to wrap around.

I tried not to see Hadrian every time someone with long black hair walked in, or when I looked at a customer with sharp blue eyes. I tried not to imagine his arms wrapping around me when I was cold, or wonder if he was watching me when I walked home alone from work.

I really did try to forget him… But I couldn't. Love wasn't a switch that could be flipped on and off when we wanted or didn't want to feel it. Love was a constant, powerful force that existed whether you chose to believe in it or not. It would take me a long time to grow out of my love for Hadrian, especially when I wasn't sure I wanted to.

"Ava, honey, you okay?"

I blinked out of my thoughts and looked over my shoulder at Maci. I smiled. "Yeah, I'm good. Just got lost in thought."

Maci returned my smile sagely. "It should be slowing down now. You can go clean up the tables, if you like and then go home."

I nodded. It was almost closing time before the curfew, and I was looking forward to helping mom cook tonight. She needed a break from the relentless nursing shifts, so she was making cookies for the SPU volunteers now that she had too many bags of sugar and flour. No way was I going to complain about that.

I walked out into the emptied restaurant, amazed it had cleared out so quickly after we were swarmed earlier on. Just went to show how busy everyone was. They barely had time to sit down and enjoy a fresh meal before scurrying off to their next volunteer project or getting home to hold their families close.

I was ready to do the same thing.

Though by the sound of heavy footsteps stalking across the tile behind me, not everyone was ready to settle in for the night.

Without turning, I said, "We're closing up soon so you might have to be quick with your order."

"I know what I want."

I jumped near out of my skin when I heard his voice. At first I stood there, telling myself it wasn't him. Just someone else who sounded like him and could move with that same, freakishly quiet grace.

Though I wouldn't be sure unless I turned around.

The footsteps approached slowly, and I finally turned. My butt hit the table, but I hardly felt it. I could only see him, standing in front of me the way he had over a year ago.

A brown leather jacket hung over his shoulders, covering the tight navy blue shirt and stopping at the belt of his dark jeans. His hair was neatly combed against his shoulders. Azure-navy eyes watched me with certainty, a small smirk tugging his lips.

I tried to tell myself I was hallucinating or fantasizing– again– but he was too real to be a dream or a hope.

I would recognize Hadrian anywhere.

"Hadrian... what... um... Hi?"

He made it very hard to concentrate when he was standing that close, and only moving closer.

"Hello," he replied.

His eyes traced over my face, taking in every detail. It had been a year since I'd seen him, but it couldn't have been that long for him. Time moved differently in the realm of the Stormkind and the Guardians. I didn't know why he was looking at me like I was the one who'd disappeared.

"You have no idea how good it is to see you again, Ava," he told me.

That one sentence sent my heart into overdrive. I could feel my pulse jackhammer through my veins while my brain scrambled to think of something to say that wouldn't come out as a stutter. Something suave that would keep him here for just a little bit longer.

Once I opened my mouth, the words tumbled out.

"Why– Why are you here? I mean, it's good to see you. You look great. Not that you don't always look great, but I mean, you look cleaner and…" I grimaced.

Suave, I snickered internally. *Yeah. That was a great plan.*

While I mentally stumbled, Hadrian leaned closer. He smiled, but didn't touch me. I wasn't sure I wanted him to yet.

"My duty is over. The remaining Stormkind have been returned to their cages until the next Centennial Storm. Corrina is being monitored, and she is a sufficient Guardian in my place."

"In your place," I repeated.

Hadrian nodded. "You might say that I have temporarily retired."

I couldn't stop my jaw from dropping. I had a hard time even thinking that he was telling me the truth. Being a

Guardian was Hadrian's life. Centuries of dedication and training had ensured he was one of the last ones alive. He lived for the action and excitement of his position. It was his everything. I couldn't believe he'd given that up, just as I couldn't believe he was standing in front of me.

"What about the others? Zephys, Vitae–"

"There was little they could do to stop me," he smirked. "And when I explained my need for being here, they understood."

Hadrian stopped mere inches from me. I curled my fingers around the edge of the table, my pulse drumming through my veins.

"I told them that because of your combination of gifts, it was important to stand by your side and support you." He leaned down. "While that is true, I still lied."

"Why would you do that?" I breathed.

He didn't answer right away. Instead, he lifted his hand and let his fingers skim across my scalp, gently tugging my ponytail free. He curled my hair behind my ear, smoothing it with his hand.

Hadrian's smile was soft, warm, and only for me.

"You didn't let me finish that day," he said. "When I learned that you loved me."

"Because... Because I didn't think you wanted me for... me."

His thumb traced gentle circles behind my ear. "On that road, you undid me Ava. You broke through my defenses and saw me for who I truly am. And you did not run." His thumb slid back to the side of my face. A welcome shiver surged through me. "I have much to atone for. You thought I would only care about you because you were a Stormkind, and I was honor-bound to protect you as such. You thought that was all I would see, and that I would not be able to look past the Stormkind to see the woman beneath."

Heat flushed my cheeks. I shrugged and smiled sheepishly.

Hadrian leaned down and kissed me.

I was so caught off guard that I didn't react at first. Then I took a breath and fell into his familiar, salty musk. I unclenched my hands from the table and ran them up Hadrian's arms, telling myself that he– that *this*– was real.

The ends of his hair tickled the back of my hand. The pads of his thumbs ghosted across my throat and stroked my cheekbones. When he drew back, I almost whimpered.

Hadrian's face was pressed close to mine, his lips tantalizingly close. His long eyelashes brushed against my face when he looked at me again.

"But I did not fall in love with a storm or her power, or the tether that bound her to me. I fell in love with a woman who showed me kindness and honesty. I fell in love with a woman who gave my knife back to me because she was strong enough without it. I fell in love with a woman who stood in the rain and smiled."

I melted, my whole body becoming a mess of heat and hope. I smiled until my cheeks hurt.

"Good to know we're on the same page."

Hadrian was halfway through his laugh when I kissed him. I wasn't afraid of what he would or wouldn't accept from me. I didn't doubt any longer. Hadrian had seen me as I was, and decided that I was worth a century long retirement.

Since I had no intention to use my gifts ever again, I didn't know how long I would live, if Stormkind could last as long as their Guardians. Certainly, Hadrian would live longer than I did.

And I was okay with that. I would have maybe sixty, seventy years with him. More, if I turned out to be more Stormkind than human. I would have to stay with him, and see what happened.

It would be worth it.

Though I did have a question…

"What are you going to do now?"

Hadrian nudged my forehead with his. "I have yet to consider all my options, but I suppose I ought to work with the Storm Protection Union, maybe even become a more formal storm hunter."

I laughed and looped my arms around his neck. "I'm sure they would love to hear about your work experiences and references."

Hadrian kissed me slowly, gently. Long enough for me to stroke the sturdy muscles of his arms and shoulders, to feel the heat of his body pressed against mine, to taste the salty sweetness of his lips.

Too soon, he drew back and held my arms. "I am sure I will find a way to earn their trust," he said wickedly. "For now, let me escort you home. You mentioned you have a younger brother that will like me?"

I beamed, happily taking his arm when he extended it to me. We walked out of the restaurant together, the sun beginning to set across the growing structures and homes of West Palm Beach.

There wasn't a cloud in the sky.

THE END

Acknowledgments

The first round of thank-you's go to my family. You've all been amazing with your interest and excitement (especially you, Mom), which pushes me to work harder and continue to surprise and impress you. I can't thank you enough for all the love and support you give me, inside and outside of my writing life.

To Kim and the fantastic team at Deranged Doctor Design, bravo yet again. Every person that's seen this cover or the other promotional materials have told me how much they adore it, and you already know that I love it with all my heart.

Thank you to my editor Eden Royce for her hard work. *Storm Born* was unlike any story I've written so far, but you helped me polish it to the story it is and helped give it the strength it needed to be published.

Thanks to Kathy and Amanda of WritingGIAM Pro, Christina and the indie authors from Weekend Writing Warriors, and my inner circle of Kaitlyn, Kristi, and Beth. You've all been so wonderful and helpful with your encouragement and advice.

Big, big thank you to all the reviewers who made time to read this little novel, especially Ivana and Nell of One Book Two and Cassandra of The Bookish Crypt. I honestly can't accurately express how much it means to me knowing that I have readers excited and eager to receive my books to review them. You all rock!

Lastly, I bow to you, dear reader, for giving this novel a chance. I was honestly nervous. The idea's pretty bold and I would be lying if I said I wasn't crazy nervous about it. But if you've gotten to this page, hopefully that means you've enjoyed Ava's adventures and experiences with Hadrian and the Precips, and that you might come along with me on another adventure sometime soon. Until then, thank you.

About The Author

Amy is a Canadian urban fantasy and horror author. Her work revolves around monsters, magic, mythology, and mayhem. She started writing in her early teens, and never stopped. She loves building unique worlds filled with fun characters and intense action. She is the recipient of April Moon Books Editor Award for "author voice, world-building and general bad-assery," and the One Book Two Standout Award in 2015 for her *Cursed* trilogy. She has been featured on various author blogs and publishing websites, and is an active member of the Writing GIAM and Weekend Writing Warrior communities. When she isn't writing, she's reading, watching movies, taking photos, gaming, and struggling with chocoholism and ice cream addiction.

Website: literarybraun.blogspot.ca
Twitter: @amybraunauthor
Facebook: www.facebook.com/amybraunauthor

More From Amy Braun

CURSED

DEMON'S DAUGHTER

DARK DIVINITY

DAMNATION'S DOOR

DARK SKY

CRIMSON SKY

STANDALONE NOVELS AND NOVELLAS

PATH OF THE HORSEMAN

NEEDFIRE

ANTHOLOGIES AND COLLECTIONS

THE MAKER OF MONSTERS in SPAWN OF THE RIPPER from April Moon Books.

HELL TO PAY in LEGENDS OF SLEEPY HOLLOW: ORIGINAL TALES OF TERROR FROM AMERICA'S SPOOKIEST VILLAGE.

SURVIVALISM in THE DEAD WALK: VOLUME 2 from FOF Publishing.

DISMANTLE in THE STEAM CHRONICLES from Zimbell House Publishing.

LOST SKY in AVAST, YE AIRSHIPS! from Mocha Memoirs Press.

SECRET SUICIDE in THAT HOODOO, VOODOO, THAT YOU DO from Lincoln Crisler and Ragnarok Publications.

BRING BACK THE HOUND in STOMPING GROUNDS from April Moon Books.

HOTEL HELL in DEATH'S CAFE from Mocha Memoirs Press.

CALL FROM THE GRAVE in TOIL, TROUBLE, AND TEMPTATION from Mocha Memoirs Press.

CHARLATAN CHARADE in LOST IN THE WITCHING HOUR from Breaking Fate Publishing.

DARK INTENTIONS AND BLOOD in AMOK! from April Moon Books.

www.ingramcontent.com/pod-product-compliance
Lightning Source LLC
Chambersburg PA
CBHW051329250626
47155CB00007B/2511